by

Kahlen Aymes

**TELEMACHUS PRESS**

Cover designed by Telemachus Press, LLC

Cover art:
Cover design : Kristen Karwan
Cover Model: Colby Lefebvre
Cover Photograph by Martin Ryter
iStock Photo 000005616986
Depositphotos 14627719

Published by Telemachus Press, LLC
http://www.telemachuspress.com

Visit the author website:
http://www.kahlen-amyes.blogspot.com

ISBN: 978-1-940745-08-4 (eBook)
ISBN: 978-1-940745-32-9 (Paperback)

Version 2013.12.17

Printed in the United States of America

10  9  8  7  6  5  4  3  2  1

# Acknowledgements

Special thanks to my mother, who took a chance on my "steamy" books, and to my father for his continued reminders to keep my hands and head firmly around this little venture. Your love and support mean so much to me. OXOX

To Olivia, I'm so proud of the young woman you're becoming. Keep chasing your dreams and don't forget to feed Riley and Sophie. ☺ ~I love you!

My street team, the many, MANY bloggers and readers who believe in my characters and my words; you are my inspiration and you are invaluable to me! I couldn't do this without you! I wish I could name you all, but there aren't enough pages in this book.

The WFD author group, thank you for all your snarky, fun, and laugh-filled support! You bitches rock! That is all.

Raine Miller, Kailin Gow, Kelly Elliott, Madeline Sheehan, Gail McHugh, Kendal Ryan, Kim Karr, Rebecca Shea, Lissa Bryan, Melissa Brown, S.L. Jennings, E.L. Montes, Sydney Logan, Tiffany Carmouche, Debra Anastasia, Karina Halle, J.L. Brooks, Karen Avivi, Kimberly Knight, Liv Morris, L.V. Lewis, Sophie Davis, J.M. O'Bryant, and Lauren Blakely... I'm so grateful for your kind words, high standards, unending advice and support! I'm humbled to know you and proud to count you among my friends.

Tons of gratitude goes out to my agent, Elizabeth Winick Rubinstein, and my foreign rights agent, Shira Hoffman, of McIntosh & Otis Literary. Thanks for helping me navigate the quagmire. XOXO

Chasity Jenkins-Patrick and Donna Soluri of Rockstar PR—Thank you for your wisdom and unending enthusiasm. ~Hugs

Thank you to Colby Lefebvre for becoming the gorgeous face of Alex Avery! Perfect!

Thank you to Kristen Karwan, for your hard work on this amazing cover! XO

As always, my editing team, Liz, Sally and Kathryn... I truly appreciate every green, purple, blue and yellow mark-up. XOXO

Life is short... live it to the fullest.

Love,
Kahlen

# Table of Contents

# Prologue

MARK SWANSON WAS a repulsive worm of the lowest form. Angeline Hemming felt it in her gut. It was one of those instinctive things that grabs hold and festers down deep, eating away at your insides, bringing the sour bile up into your throat and keeping you awake at night. Unfortunately, looking at the bastard, there wasn't much about him that screamed 'pedophile' or 'criminal' but, wasn't that true of the sickest fuckers in history? Jeffrey Dahmer, Denis Rader, Ted Bundy; they all looked like they wouldn't hurt a fly, and this bastard was no different. Maybe he was a tad smarmy, but nothing more.

Her job as a criminal profiler had thrown Dr. Angeline Hemming in the paths of more than her share of shady characters, but Mark Swanson made her skin crawl. After interviewing his stepdaughter and hearing the girl's terrifying stories of how she'd been repeatedly assaulted and raped for the past 3 years—nothing, not even inconclusive tests—were going to convince Angel he wasn't guilty as hell. Too bad the test results would be the only thing she could base her opinion on. Creepers like Swanson had a way of slithering out of the grasp of justice and nothing infuriated her more. *Freaking deviant!*

Angel shivered as she entered the Home Depot store near Lincoln Park. Despite the warm Spring weather, her thoughts left her shaking and she wasn't sure if it was out of anger or fear. Her head never shut off and it was driving her crazy and giving her a headache. Sunday afternoon stretched out in front of her and she needed something to take her mind off of her troubled thoughts for a few hours. It seemed as good a time as any to redecorate the spare bedroom of her apartment, or at least begin making preparations. Her best friend, Becca, and her baby daughter, Jillian, stayed over quite often and Angel thought she might brighten the room up by painting and ordering new curtains and bedding. Maybe she'd even use some of that chalkboard paint on one wall. Jillian would certainly love that. With a sigh, she realized Becca might protest Angel teaching the little girl how to draw on the walls, but she looked forward to picking out the colors, at least.

The new project might be a nice way to spend the evening, and it would give her plenty of time to revisit the plaguing case she was working on. Her life was full, but sometimes the loneliness got the better of her. She considered getting a pet, though she wasn't lonely in the true sense of the word. She was too busy for that, but it might be nice to have something to take care of and to love.

She chose a soft teal and a cool cream, planning on painting two of the walls teal and the others plus the ceiling the contrasting cream. The en suite bathroom would be mostly cream with brown and teal accents in the accessories and towels. After deciding to purchase Jillian an easel instead of opting for the on-wall chalkboard, she took her choices to the counter. The man mixing her paint gave her a thorough once over. He was tall and skinny with thinning greyish hair and a thick iron-colored mustache that grew grotesquely over the top of his upper lip. *Ugh!* Angel's stomach turned. *Dirty old man*, she thought in disgust.

Admittedly, her job made her jaded. More and more, she concluded men were just a necessary appliance, that to her chagrin, were needed every once in a while. It had been three years since she'd been in a relationship that went beyond sex. Not since Kyle. He was the last man she'd had any sort of real feelings for, but he had turned into a major disappointment. Now she was colder and harder. If she was honest, it was much easier, and certainly less hurtful, to keep her guard up. It kept her in control of her life and emotions. Men were messy, self-obsessed creatures, most of them needing mommies to tell them what to do, and Angel found that trait annoyingly unattractive. Whoever said women were fucked up and ruled by their emotions never considered it was better than being led around by a swollen appendage. It seemed, at least to Angel, that when their dicks inflated, men's brains lost all conscious thought. Most turned into rutting dogs, their minds flopping around like a proverbial fish out of water, completely helpless to the outcome of their actions.

She huffed loudly enough for the woman a few feet further down the aisle to glance in her direction and Angel flushed.

It was their excuses that Angel couldn't tolerate. It often seemed they were 5 and didn't have any self-control. Even Kyle. How depressing it became when someone you thought was so strong, took the lamest, most cliché way out. Angel had no time for that bullshit, anymore.

She paced back and forth in front of the counter, and the man looked over his shoulder more than once, finally blatant about his staring.

He disconnected the cans one by one from the paint-mixer and handed them to her, and, as he did so, his fingers brushed against hers.

"Have a nice day," he murmured, still holding on to the last can of paint. He leered down, obviously straining to get a look down her blouse, his eyes roaming over the soft swells beneath the purple cotton and to the creamy skin and sumptuous curves showing where the top three buttons were left undone.

Angel paused and threw him a scathing look, her eyebrow shooting up. She cleared her throat to get his eyes to snap up to her face. "If you're done pissing yourself—can I please have my paint?"

Instantly, his face infused red, and he hastily handed it over, clearly embarrassed at being caught looking. "Ugh, yes, ma'am," he stammered. "Sorry."

Angel put the paint in her cart, turning away without speaking, while the clerk turned and darted from behind the counter then down an aisle. She wasn't even dressed up. She had on a casual five-dollar top from Wet Seal, old cut-off Levi's and two-dollar flip-flops. Her face was devoid of makeup save for moisturizer and light eyeliner, and her hair was tied up in a messy bun. She stopped to look through the brushes and rollers, wondering what she'd need for her little fix-it project.

"What else does she want to do?"

Angel glanced up at the sound of the deep male voice coming from a couple aisles over.

"She wants the sunroom painted and to re-do part of the patio around the pool. The concrete is cracking. She wants one of those stone things." Another man's voice answered. It had the same deepness, but sounded older and very dignified.

"Not that I mind helping, Dad. But just hire someone to do it."

Three men turned the corner, all of them tall, close to the same height, two with dark, almost black hair, and the third salted with grey. Angel's hand reached out to choose a paint roller and a few brushes, adding them to her cart before she moved around the other side of the waist-high shelving.

"It wouldn't hurt you to help your mother, Cole," the older voice said.

Angel sensed movement across from her and found herself staring into a pair of beautiful, deep green eyes, and the most stunning face she'd ever seen on a man. Strong features, beautiful; but still very masculine. The dark, almost black hair that fell thickly over his forehead and brushed the collar of his light teal T-shirt, made his eyes even more vibrant and striking.

Her mouth fell open slightly as her breath left in a rush. His skin had a golden hue despite the season, as if he'd recently spent some time on a tropical island. He was tall, and she was sans heels so he towered over her. His broad shoulders, muscled chest, and sinewy arms said he worked out a lot. He was cut, but not so huge that Becca would classify him as a meathead. His clothes were casual, but expensive, though she barely registered what he had on, mesmerized, as she was, by his oozing sex appeal.

Somehow when these eyes landed on her, her reaction was completely opposite of the store clerk's appraisal. Her body quickened, and she had no desire to stop him from admiring her. In fact, she felt worked up with just this very brief glance, and she felt unnerved. She blinked and licked her lips; her mind searched for something to say but came up with nothing. The surreal moment consuming her senses, she shook herself mentally. She didn't swoon over men; she kept herself under carefully guarded control, and she wasn't about to start now. The man lifted something above the partition full of paint accessories that separated them. Automatically, her hand reached out to take it from him and she pulled her gaze away to see it was a canvas drop cloth. She'd need one of those, her mind acknowledged. He'd obviously taken stock of the contents of her cart.

Mutely, she took it from him and her fingers brushed ever so slightly against his. Electricity skittered through her entire body, and her eyes bolted back up to his.

"Thank you," she murmured softly.

He gave a nod, two seconds before the older man, who Angel assumed was his father, glanced over his shoulder toward him. "What do you think about this color, son?"

His mouth lifted in a slight smile like he wanted to say something, but he didn't.

Angel's lips curved in answer as heat infused her cheeks. *What the fuck is wrong with me?* she wondered. Yes, he was gorgeous, but it wasn't just his looks that drew her in like a helpless moth. It was the intelligent amusement behind those amazing eyes that rendered her speechless.

"Son?" his father called again at the same time as the ringing of a phone pierced the air. He reached into the pocket of his khaki shorts and pulled one out, glancing briefly at the screen. The smile faded from his face.

Angel put the drop cloth in her cart, before turning it away slightly, unsure if she should wait or go. She felt ridiculous. Obviously, he wasn't going to say anything, and now he had a phone call. She couldn't hang out in the paint department staring at him without feeling and looking like an idiot, so she started to push her cart away. She could feel his gaze follow her and heard his dad call him again, more forcefully.

She swallowed and wandered slowly up to the check out, hoping that if she lingered long enough, she might see him again, and he might take the chance to talk to her. However, her logical mind argued that if they were buying paint, that moron would have to mix it and it, would take more time than she needed to pay and load her items into her car. She sighed heavily as she drove out of the parking lot.

Saddened that, for the first time in a long time, a man held her genuine interest and he hadn't said a goddamned word. She didn't want to believe he was just another schmuck and hoped it was only his father's interruption that prevented him from speaking. Yes, she was strong, and she believed women should be self-sufficient and not rely on men, but she still wanted the man to be the man when it came to sex, initiating a conversation or making plans for the dates. When she was sincerely interested, at least. And something deep inside her didn't want to believe the handsome stranger was any less than perfect.

*****

Alex ran a hand through his hair in exasperation as the beautiful girl wheeled her cart away. *Fuck!* His mind screamed.

Reluctantly, he walked over to his father and brother, glancing over his shoulder as she disappeared down another aisle wishing he could follow. He'd wanted to talk to her so goddamned bad, but he had two problems: his voice was destroyed from yelling at the Blackhawks game with Cole the night before, and he knew he'd come across with a creepy rasp that would be off-putting. And of course, Whitney. Inwardly, he cringed. Her phone call in the middle of his stare-fest with the gorgeous brunette brought him back to reality.

*Goddamn it to hell!*

Whitney was his girlfriend of sorts, but it didn't stop his dick from getting hard when presented with someone as beautiful as the girl that just left him. For Christ's sake! He was gawking after her, looking like a jerk in the middle of the paint aisle.

His father held out some paint samples for him to inspect. He didn't give two shits about the difference between Almond White and Creamy Vanilla; he doubted his mother would even be able to tell the difference. He didn't get why his dad didn't just hire a designer and be done with it. Instead he had to drag him and Cole out on a Sunday afternoon.

He sighed. "Dad, I don't care," he rasped out in a whisper. "They're both white. What does it matter?"

Alex knew this little home improvement project was his father and mother's attempt to get his brother to spend more time with the family. Cole was the family's black sheep, lacking responsibility and direction. He'd rather sleep all day than be productive and frankly, Alex was sick of being party to their attempts to make him change. Their father refused to cut him loose despite Alex's urging. His little sister, Allison, was the princess and Alex was left with the majority of the responsibility.

He glanced around again, hoping he'd catch a glimpse of the woman's purple shirt between the aisles. His heart stopped when he'd seen her; she was extremely pretty, despite her simple dress and lack of make-up. He felt inexplicably drawn to her and couldn't resist walking closer, leaving his dad and Cole behind him to select the swatches. His heart sped up, and naturally, his dick woke up in instant arousal. She was perfect. Her breasts round and full, her hips gently swelling and her long, shapely legs, bare. There was a softness about the stranger that Alex found extremely appealing, like he could sink into her and they would melt together, yet there was a tiger behind her expression. Alex found the combination intriguing and unpretentious, which made Whitney seem fake in comparison.

With Whitney, it'd become like fucking a Barbie doll; hard and grasping. He found himself wondering how this beauty in Home Depot's skin would feel under his touch, how she would smell up close, and if her lips were as luscious as they looked. Maybe his intense interest in this random meeting signaled it was time to end it with Whitney, but he liked the convenience of their arrangement.

Alex had a moment's pause at how callous that sounded, even in his own mind, but their relationship was not about feelings and never had been. But the sex accomplished what he needed, and she provided arm candy when he had an event to attend. He was always so hellish busy, that romantic complications were not something he needed to take on.

His father and brother's chatter with the clerk faded into the background as he considered trying to find the woman and strike up a conversation, maybe get her number. His hand swiped over the dark stubble on his jaw. As much as he wanted to, it wouldn't be right to do so while he was still technically committed. It wouldn't be fair to Whitney, another woman, or frankly, to himself. That wasn't the type of man he wanted to be and he had little time for those who were. He may not be in love with Whitney... maybe he didn't even believe in love, but he'd be damned if he'd break his word or be a cad.

# 1

## Good Advice

DR. ANGELINE HEMMING pushed the headphones off of her head in agitation and threw them down with a clang. The damn things itched, they were heavy and terribly awkward. She felt like they were three sizes too big.

"Ugh," she groaned. She'd been doing the weekly radio show for six weeks already and sometimes questioned her decision. This wasn't her. She was a clinical psychologist, for God's sake. She spent her days getting paid $450 per hour to help people deal with real life problems, not make spectacles of themselves in a public forum.

She'd worked her ass off to get where she was, literally and figuratively. Growing up poor, she had few prospects and opportunities like Northwestern University didn't just happen for girls from Joplin, Missouri. Her father, Joseph, was the janitor at the high school and Angel's mother had run off when she was a baby, leaving a broken man without the skills needed to handle an infant. Angeline had her share of bumps since then, but with a lot of smarts and guts, she'd managed to make something of herself. Now, she was in a position to take care of her father financially and to use her education to help people. Really help people. This radio gig… this was fluff, but it served a purpose, and it helped take her mind off of the more dangerous characters she dealt with on a regular basis.

"Angel, what's the problem?" her producer, Darian Keith, asked. He was clearly impatient with her as she ran her hand through her long dark hair, scratching her scalp in reaction to the headphones. Darian was a great guy and professional, as far as she knew about him, which wasn't much. A slender African American, he was dressed in jeans and a light blue T-shirt under his dark blue blazer. He had an easygoing demeanor that Angel instantly liked.

She smirked at his mocking tone, as she pushed the necessary buttons on the computer to play the commercials and cue up the next song. The phone lines in front of her began blinking red.

"It's just… Well, so many of these callers are so freaking *naïve*! Most of them are women, which I know is to be expected, but it burns my ass how they let men treat them the way they do! Gah!" She reached for a big sports bottle full of ice water that she kept on the desk at all times and took a long drink.

Darian chuckled softly, causing Angel to shoot him a caustic look.

"What?" she asked impatiently.

"As we promote it more, men will call, and you'll have perspective from both sides. Guys struggle with relationships, too."

Angel rolled her eyes. "I *know*, Darian. I do have a doctorate in clinical psychology. I get that men and women are equally screwed up; don't worry."

She was a slight young woman with delicate facial features, luminous skin, and thick, flowing chestnut locks that had a soft auburn sheen to them in certain light. She looked too young to be a high-powered force in Chicago's child abuse network, yet her evaluations of suspects and victims could make or break a court case. Angel was proud of her work and had been somewhat hesitant when Darian proposed she host a late night radio show about relationships on his soft-rock formatted station. At first she'd scoffed, tapping her expensive high-heeled Prada's on the gleaming cherry wood floor and crossing her arms over her navy blue Givenchy suit, openly mocking the opportunity.

It had taken some convincing, but eventually she'd given in, thinking it would be fun and much more lighthearted than her nine-to-five gig. Mostly, it was his promise to donate airtime to domestic and child abuse public service announcements that clinched her decision. It was a damn good thing she'd agreed to the trade. The station would go broke paying up, despite the advertising revenues increasing during her time slot, 10 PM to 2 AM every Friday night.

"Lighten up, Angel. This is all in good fun and to improve ratings." He smirked.

Christina Michaels, the rookie production intern, knocked on the window, and Angel glanced her way. She was blonde and spunky, a tomboy of sorts with short hair and a turned-up nose. Holding up two fingers, she indicated that they would go back on air in a couple of minutes. "Line three, Angel."

As Angel grabbed the offending headset and mashed them down over her ears, Darian admired the way her firm breasts pressed against the front of her white T-shirt as her arms lifted. She looked a million miles away from the polished, aloof woman he'd met five months earlier in her office downtown. He mentally shook himself. She *was* damn sexy. So confident and self-assured, yet her curves were soft and womanly.

Darian was slightly chagrined because Angel seemed untouchable and too good to be true. It didn't matter anyway; he was her boss, and there was no way he could date her, even if she allowed it. He consoled himself by considering that looking at her alone made missing his normal Friday boy's night out worth it. After she and Chris got the hang of what he expected, he'd be able to skip being in the studio if he wanted. Somehow his buddies weren't as appealing as they once were. He sighed in regret.

Darian adjusted his own headphones. "Okay, counting down: five, four…" He held up his hands and used his fingers to communicate the rest. Three, two, one, he signaled for her to begin.

"Hello, it's 12:35 AM and this is Angel After Dark, taking your calls for advice and dedications, here with Christina Michaels, screening your calls and our producer, Darian Keith." Angel's sultry voice purred into the microphone as she pushed one lit-up button on the phone in front of her. "Hello, you're on the air. Do you have a question? Or, maybe a confession?"

Darian's ears perked up, and he began to write furiously on the legal pad next to him. Jesus, she was hot.

"Hello, is this Dr. Hemming?" a woman's timid voice asked on the other end of the phone. "Am I on the air?"

"Yes. This is Angeline. What can I help you with tonight?" *Dr. Hemming* seemed so formal for this type of venue and somehow, being called Angeline or Angel made it more acceptable that she was using her education in a less professional way. She inwardly cringed at the thought.

The woman's voice cracked as she sobbed softly into the phone. "My boyfriend… I found out—he's *married!*"

*Oh, hell!* Angel thought and pointed to the headset, mouthing the word 'See?' to the man sitting opposite her. Darian smiled and plopped back in his chair with a sardonic look on his face as he carefully watched Angel's facial expressions change from disgust to calm acquiescence.

"What is your name, honey?" Angel's voice took on the reserved, placating tone she used on the air.

"Celeste. What should I do?"

She sounded very young. Angel was only 28, but hell, this girl sounded like she was barely out of high school. Angel's heart ached for the young woman's plight, wondering how any woman would ever get involved with a man who wasn't available.

*Oh, that's right. Men lie.*

Her professional alter ego mentally bitch slapped her to reinforce she wasn't supposed to stereotype. This wasn't about her own experiences with men, it was about this poor girl on the phone. She swallowed before continuing.

"That's a very pretty name. I'm very sorry you're going through that. I could ask you a lot of background about the situation, but it won't change the fact that he's married. He had no business messing with you under these circumstances. It wasn't fair to you or his wife."

"But... but, he said he loves me... I didn't mean..." she cried—"I didn't know!"

"Celeste, I know this isn't what you want to hear, but this is a self-destructive position you're in. People say things in the heat of passion to get things they want, but deep down they may not mean them." Angel winced as the sobbing on the phone increased but she pressed on. "How did you find out?"

"His wife called me. She found my number in his cell phone. I thought it was him when I answered, and it was horrible." Angel sat back in her chair and sighed heavily. She wanted to rant at the girl for being so fucking stupid. "She called me a whore. But he said he was going to leave her."

"When did he tell you that?"

"When I confronted him."

Angel's eyebrows raised in an expression of incredulity. Then she shook her head in disbelief. *Oh, for Christ's sake,* she thought.

"And you're *still* seeing him?" When met with silence, Angel continued. "Celeste, I'm here to help you. So, I want you to see that he is making a choice, just like you are. You have a choice here, too."

"Ye—yes," the caller stammered.

"He's still with his wife, isn't he?" It was more of a statement, which was confirmed when Celeste didn't answer. "Please stop listening to his words, and start looking at his *actions*. He's got it made. She's not leaving, you're not leaving, so what's his motivation to change and give either of you what you need?" Angel tried to keep her voice even, but an angry flush was coming up under the skin of her face and neck. "It's both of the women in this situation that are being hurt. You have to step back and look at this objectively. How does he make you feel? And I don't mean during sex or when he's trying to convince you that you're the love of his life. I mean when you're sitting in the dark alone, and he's gone home to his wife."

"Horrible. Lonely. I'm heartbroken. It hurts." The girl snuffled.

"I know it hurts, and you deserve so much more. You deserve to be the *only* one, to be cherished and loved. Not used when it's convenient."

"You're right," Celeste admitted reluctantly.

"Good. So what are you going to do?"

After a pause, the woman answered. "End it."

"Good girl. You're doing this for yourself, Celeste. He'll probably beg and plead, that's how men like him manipulate women. But stay strong, and don't give in to his bullshit. Go find someone who deserves you. Okay, honey?"

"Okay. Thank you, Dr. Hemming," she sniffed.

"You're welcome. Call me in a few weeks to let me know how you're doing. Be strong, Celeste."

Angel took a deep breath. The anger on her face was clear in the tight line of her mouth and the furrow between her neatly waxed brows. She shook her head, and Darian wondered if she was going to say something derogatory about that last caller's guy. He waved his hands and shook his head. One thing he'd learned in the short time he'd known Angeline Hemming: she took no prisoners and spoke her mind without thinking about it first.

*No, Angel. Don't cuss out the bastard,* his mind raced. *Not on live air.*

"Well, this is Dr. Angeline Hemming," Angel said as she took the next call, "What is your confession?"

Darian breathed a sigh of relief.

"I confess that I'm sick to death of my boyfriend's arrogant, offhanded manner and the way he treats me!"

"What's your name?"

"Whitney," the woman spat as if she hated her own name.

"Well, Whitney, you sound pretty sure of yourself, so I bet you already know the answer that you're seeking," she laughed into the microphone. "It's refreshing, actually," Angel said dryly, the corners of her mouth turning up in amusement.

"He's turned into such a bastard! He totally takes me for granted. I mean, I give him everything, and he doesn't even know I exist! He works all the time, and we never go anywhere that isn't a company obligation or charity thing. He spends most of his free time with his damn friends, and when we do have sex, he leaves right after."

*Ugh. I know the type,* she thought and leaned her chin into her hand, elbow resting on the desk. The index finger on her other hand absentmindedly drew patterns across the smooth surface. "Do you live with him?"

"No. He, uh, well, I have my own place. Lately, I feel like we hardly see each other and when we do, it's because I've asked to see him. And, then he turns it around on me... saying I nag him."

"Um, yes, I can see why you'd be upset. So... I don't get it. What's in it for you?" she asked flatly. Darian threaded his hands together behind his head as his face twisted in a weird way. Angel shot him a questioning look. He shook his head and pointed toward the phone.

"Exactly. He's out with his rat pack tonight, and I'm stuck in my apartment. He'll probably come back and expect me to service him."

Angel sat up in her chair. "Oh, boy's night out? Well, I think that's good for men on occasion—male bonding and all— but not if he disrespects you in the process. Except, why are you *stuck*? Why aren't you out yourself? Let him know that you're not sitting around waiting. You should show him you have your own life."

Whitney sighed heavily and her voice was flat. "He wouldn't care."

"Whitney, I don't understand. You seem to be a very smart woman. You clearly see the problem; so why aren't you doing something about it? Why would you want to be with a man who doesn't care about you? Take back your power."

"Are you kidding? He's got the power in everything! It's just that... well, he's everything I want in a man!" the woman whined.

"That's not what it sounds like to me. You have to figure out what you need and what you're willing to accept. What's his first name?" She liked to have names to put with personas in her calls. It somehow made it more real, more personal.

"Alexander." The answer was detached, and Angel wondered if the man was the only one to blame.

Darian ran a hand over his mouth. "Fuck!" he said under his breath and sat up straighter.

"Well, have you told Alexander how you feel? What you need? I think as women, we tend to want men to anticipate our every need, but that's not always realistic. Sometimes they need to be told. They don't process things in the same way we do. You can't expect to get what you want if you don't ask for it."

"Ugh, that's so unromantic! I want him to know what I need and provide it for me. I want him to *want* to provide it."

"Whitney, you need to talk to him, but don't sound whiney or needy when you do it. Tell him what you need and then go from there."

"He's been so withdrawn from me. I hardly know him anymore," she said miserably. "He makes me feel... *invisible*. But I can't seem to leave him."

"What do you like about him?"

"He's gorgeous, successful, and wealthy. He's an executive of a huge company, and he takes care of me. He's the type of guy I need to be with."

Angel's brow dropped and her eyes narrowed in understanding. This woman wasn't all she pretended to be.

"Whitney, forgive me, but is this about love or *status*?" There was silence on the other end of the line, so Angel continued after a few seconds. "What would make you feel *visible*?" Angel asked while secretly cringing, waiting for the unwanted answer she knew was to follow.

"It *is* about *love*!" she retorted sharply, a little too sharply for someone supposedly heartbroken. Angel's eyebrows shot up in doubt, and Darian sat as still as a statue. "He just needs to pay attention to me, take me out, and come over more."

"Well, then try to work it out. Ask him what he needs from you as well. Chances are he's not getting all he needs either. Men stay with women who make them feel good about themselves."

"He's not leaving... he's just distant."

Darian was cranking his right hand in a circle, motioning for Angel to wrap it up before another commercial break.

"I have to go to commercial, Whitney, but if he's checked out of the relationship, maybe he has a reason. If you think he's insensitive or disinterested after you discuss this with him, then maybe you should consider your options. If you love each other, he'll want to talk to you and work it out, but you have to tell him the truth.

Good luck." She ended the call. "I'll be right back with more calls and dedications."

As the commercials played, Darian sat in silence.

"What were those faces about?" Angel asked.

"Mmmm—I think I know her. And if that's who I think it is, she's not telling the whole story." His expression filled with disgust.

Angel smiled at him. "There usually are two sides to everything but I'm at a disadvantage here. I only get to hear one."

"In this case, that is *too true*. She's dating my best friend. He will be so pissed when he finds out she's calling and talking about him on air. I hope that not many people put two and two together, because he's not exactly low key in this town. All she wants is the status, the material shit he represents, and his dick."

"Nice! Why does it always come down to someone's dick, huh?" she laughed. "Is she telling any part of the truth? Be honest."

He bristled. "Well, Alex doesn't get involved like that. He's very focused on his work, and he's successful because of it."

"Sounds like every woman's dream guy. Truly," she scoffed. "So she *was* telling the truth."

Darian rose in defense of the faceless Alex. "It works for him. He's very clear going in that it's not going to be a love affair, and if the woman enters into it thinking that she can change him, that's not his fault."

Angel stopped and shot him a warning look, her dark brown eyes flashing sharply.

"You didn't just say that did you, Darian?" She shook her head and huffed. "That's *so* typical! Nice attempt to justify using someone. What do you and Mr. Perfect think happens to a woman who is with a man for any length of time, hmmm? I'll tell you. She either falls in love or walks away. Clearly, your friend knows how this shit works; hence his carefully laid out escape clause. I mean, if he's as brilliant as both you and this Whitney woman would have me believe, he knows full well what he's doing and what will happen eventually," Angel retorted with a sly smile.

Darian thought Angel was too damn smart for her own good, and pair that with her sexy little bod and business suit—watch out. She was like napalm.

"No. Whitney isn't in love. She's a greedy bitch, and I think Alex may pick them based on that particular feature, because he has the means to fulfill that need. His relationships are all about convenience. They're consenting adults that both get something they need from the other."

"Keep telling yourself that, Hans Christian Andersen. Maybe if you repeat it enough your little fairy tale will become reality. In anything beyond a fling, someone falls in love, and if the other doesn't feel the same way or acknowledge it, there's a big pain-fest. It's not some cataclysmic secret of the universe. It's a big, 'duh.' Your friend wants someone who needs him financially, because it gives him all of the control."

Darian really couldn't argue her point, and he didn't want to. Alex did like to keep control. Of everything. "What about you? Do you have a man? You're a beautiful woman, Angel."

"You're kidding, right? The guy would have to be *wow*."

Darian huffed, put off at the thought that this woman he'd placed on a pedestal, would be lowered to a level the likes of the nefarious and money-grubbing Whitney.

Angel's eyebrow shot up at the expression on his face, and she put a hand up.

"Hold up. Not necessarily in looks, but certainly in character. I'm not saying I'm against having a relationship, but after listening to all of this crap? Ugh. I know what I want and what I will accept. My boundaries are firmly established and I have no problem walking if my needs aren't met. I certainly wouldn't be so insecure to put up with this type of one-sided bullshit."

"What about *sex*?" His dark gaze settled on her face, and his eyes narrowed. She knew that look. She'd seen it many times before. It was the predator, sizing up its prey, trying to figure out if the kill was worth the chase.

"I'm not sure this is an appropriate convo to be having with my producer, but since this show is what it is, I'll answer. Sex is sex," she shrugged. "I'm not a *prude*. Physical release is part of being healthy on many levels. Men aren't the only ones that can leave emotion at the door for some good old fashioned bump and grind." She bit her lower lip, trying to hide a smile at the shocked look on his face. "When I need it, I have… options."

Darian opened then shut his mouth again.

*Good. Serves you right, asshole,* she thought. "Not all women can handle that. Some can. Generally speaking, it's like I said, short-term is okay with no strings attached, but that's it."

"What an intriguing image, Angel. Thank you," Darian answered cautiously.

"Well, don't get too excited, boss. You'll be disappointed."

Darian doubted that he would be. In fact, if he wasn't careful, his imagination was going to give him a very tangible problem, so he decided it was time to change the subject.

"I got the promo images back. They look hot. The phones will be ringing off the hook next week."

"I have to get back to work, you know? My boss will have my ass if I screw this up."

He was pulling out his cell phone and leaving the sound booth. "You do that. Do you have it from here? I'd like to go meet my boys."

"Another boy's night aficionado?" Darian nodded. "It's sort of late, but go ahead." Angel waved him out and glanced at the clock. Only five minutes to go.

"It's Friday night in Chicago, Angel. The clubs are open until four in the morning. You really should get out more," Darian said as the door closed behind him.

"I'd like to dedicate *Between the Lines* by Sara Bareilles to Celeste and all of you who have realized that the truth has been staring you straight in the face but you didn't want to see it. We've all done it at one time or another, but we need to learn from our experiences." Angel drew in a deep breath and cued up the song. "It's important to take care of yourself, because ultimately, it comes down to you. Thank you for all your calls and dedications. This is Angel After Dark on KKIS 105.4 FM. I'll see you next week. Peace and love."

*****

Alexander Avery was leaning up against the mahogany bar of one of the most popular clubs on Rush Street. His brother, Cole, was hitting on some trashy looking babe at the end of the bar, and Alex was bored with the whole scene. The scotch burned in his throat as he casually looked around. The interested glances of the many women there did not escape his attention, but left him unmoved. He ran his hand over the soft layer of scruff on his jaw and sighed.

*Maybe I'm getting old,* he thought, *but Jesus Christ! I'm only thirty-two.* There was a time when he would have jumped on that shit. Now, while it flattered him, it offered limited stimulation. He had yet to find a woman who moved him as much mentally as she did physically, which could be the huge source of his apathy, he admitted.

Maybe it was Whitney's incessant whining that made his dick go limp, or maybe it was his mother's demands that it was time he settled down. Between the two of them, he thought his fucking head would explode. Alex glanced in Cole's direction again and rolled his eyes at his brother's expression. Cole raised his head from the woman he was talking to and nodded as if to *say 'oh yeah, I'm gonna hit this'.*

As for Alex, he wasn't into one-night stands. Not anymore. He hadn't been that careless since college, preferring to have monogamous relationships but yet, unemotional. It was a tricky situation and a fine line to walk, but he was a man, and he needed sex. He just preferred it without all the emotional bullshit that came with it, and he made that clear to every woman he got involved with. The problem was; they always seemed to have a hidden agenda, no matter what they agreed to up front. Whitney had turned from being a confident, aggressive sexual partner into a whining, mewling mess he could barely tolerate. That situation had to end, but he wasn't looking forward to the actual confrontation.

As if on cue, his phone vibrated in his pocket, and pulling it out, he saw that it was a text from her.

*"Where are you? Come over. I miss seeing you."*

He was still looking at the screen when Darian finally arrived. They met in graduate school, both pursuing MBAs and had been friends ever since. Alex's degree was in economics and finance and Darian's in marketing and communications. Alex's family owned a conglomerate of businesses, and he was CFO of the parent company. He'd come back to Chicago after a short stint in New York City at a huge investment firm, and he'd been very smart about investing at Avery Enterprises as a result of his experience. The company had new resources and was able to acquire several smaller companies under his watch. Some observers might call it luck, but his father and the board of directors knew it was shrewd business dealings and rock solid negotiation skills combined with know-how to turn failing businesses around.

"It's about damn time, man. Where have you been?" Alex growled as he shoved his phone back in his pocket without answering Whitney's text.

Darian leaned in casually and ordered a beer from the bartender. "If you'd listen to your friends, Alex, you'd know that I have that new radio show at the station."

Alex vaguely remembered Darian mentioning a hot psychologist that he was trying to land for that gig several weeks back, but had lost track of when it was supposed to happen or even it if materialized.

At the time, Alex had been skeptical and teased him. *"How can a psychologist be hot? Probably wears Mary Janes and bifocals, and can freeze ice in her vagina,"* he'd mocked.

*"Dude. She is. Trust me,"* Darian had retorted with a laugh, but the subject had been dropped.

"Oh, sure. How is that going?"

"It's doing well. The promotion is starting Monday, and I expect the phones to ring off the wall. Dudes will be clamoring to talk to her when they see what she looks like, but she is one tough cookie. She'll make hamburger out of them. I'm expecting to laugh my ass off." Darian smiled as he took a long pull on his longneck beer.

"Hmmph," Alex scoffed, unimpressed. "Whatever."

Darian just stared and shook his head at his friend's disbelief.

"What's your problem?" Alex asked at Darian's expression. He ran a hand through his thick midnight hair and took a swallow from his glass.

"You mean... what's *your* problem, don't you?" Darian scowled.

"Listen, if you have something to say, I wish you'd just say it. I've had a rough week, and I'm wound too tight to have you dancing around something you clearly want to say."

"Ah. Things not so good with Whitney?" Darian's eyebrows shot up in mock inquisition.

His relationships weren't something Alex discussed in great detail. His friends knew he saw women as a convenient way to sate sexual urges and fulfill business obligations, but he never talked about them much. Darian was aware that Alex had yet to meet a woman that he actually wanted to spend time with outside of the bedroom. It was cool, though, because Alex took full responsibility and was honest about his intentions.

Alex was so focused on growing the family business he didn't have time for romantic distractions. Even if he would have had the inclination to seek it out, he didn't, not because he was a cold bastard, but it was just a choice that worked.

"Why do you say that?" Alex asked with sincere interest, pulling out a stool and finally sitting down. *Where is he going with this?*

"You'd better get prepared for a shit storm, man. That's all I'm saying." Alex glanced at his friend and Darian's eyes widened, but only very slightly. "Whitney called in to the show tonight."

An angry flush rose up underneath Alex's skin at the implication of Darian's comment. His expression hardened and the muscle in his jaw started to twitch. Part of the bargain was that he'd provide Whitney with an apartment and bank account, and she'd keep her mouth shut about the true nature of their relationship and not try to turn it into more than it was.

"She did *what?*" His tone was quiet, but edged in steel.

They were both seated at the bar, facing in, and Darian glanced at his friend's tense expression in the mirror. Alex set his glass down hard enough to have the liquid swishing over the rim, which prompted Darian to answer.

"She called the show." Darian shrugged, trying to hide a smile but glanced at his friend from the corner of his eye. He never liked that fake bitch, and the sooner Alex walked, the happier he'd be.

It was clear that the news made Alex angry, but he was good at keeping his cool; years of practice being detached and indifferent helped him regain his composure quickly. He ran a hand over the lower half of his face. "Really? What did she say?"

"That you make her feel invisible." Darian set his beer on the bar and shifted in his seat. The bartender approached both men to see if they needed another round, but he held his hand up and shook his head, quickly letting the man know that this was not a good time. The savvy bartender took the hint and turned away in a hurry, silently nodding in understanding.

Alex felt a slight twinge of regret. He cared about Whitney, as much as he'd ever cared about a woman, and he didn't want to hurt her. Maybe he did make her feel invisible, but then, she made him feel like a bank account. "Well, that's about right." Alex said quietly and shrugged. "I'm getting ready to end it anyway. I'm just not interested. It isn't working anymore. She's always on my ass for more time, more money, more... shit."

"More sex?" Darian asked in wonder. "I agree, you could do better on many levels, but in that one aspect, you're such a poor bastard. I feel so sorry for you, Alex."

"I said more *shit*, dickhead. But, I suppose she'd want more sex if I were so inclined." He shrugged nonchalantly. "I don't find her exciting anymore. I'm not sure I ever did, but lately, she gives me a fucking headache." Darian chuckled. "I'm aware she wants more, but she knew what to expect from the first time I took her to bed." Alex knew that sexually she was satisfied. He could make her moan like a bitch in heat, but even in their most intimate moments, it was nothing more than screwing and he knew it. "On the other hand, she cares more about herself than she does me."

"I thought that was what you wanted—no feelings."

"It was. It *is*. But not when the desire is gone. And she pretty much douses that whenever she opens her damn mouth. So, what did your doctor tell her?"

"Basically, she told her to dump your sorry ass."

The bartender came over again, and this time, Darian ordered another round as his friend sat on the bar stool in contemplative silence. "So I guess we'll see if she takes Angel's advice." He dipped his head to hide the smirk that was spreading across his face.

*Angel.*

Alex felt a jolt at the sound of the name, and he turned it over in his head a few times, trying to get a picture of her to form in his mind. He wondered if everything Darian said about her was true. Alex pictured a stodgy, passionless shrew that got off by analyzing other people's lives due to lack of one of her own. But the *name...* maybe there was something to Darian's description of her. Suddenly, he was intrigued and the hair on the back of his neck prickled.

*Who the fuck does she think she was to tell my mistress to end things without knowing both sides of the story? And why the hell do I care anyway?* he asked himself. He wanted out so however that happened, didn't matter.

"I wonder if she would've told Whitney the same thing if she'd known my side of the situation."

Darian watched as Alex got lost in his thoughts and spoke as if he were talking to himself.

"Yes, I told her. But only after Angel ended the call, of course. I couldn't say anything while she had Whitney on the phone."

Alex sat back in his chair and turned sharply toward Darian. "What? You didn't use my name did you? I don't need my personal bullshit under public scrutiny, Darian."

"Relax, Alex. I'm not stupid. Whitney used your first name, and I didn't mention your surname or Avery Enterprises. I told Angel that you're a very focused individual and you were upfront when you got into one of your arrangements."

"Arrangements? She probably thinks I'm a dick."

"Yeah, so?" Darian's tone was sardonic and he smirked. "Aren't they? Arrangements?"

Alex couldn't argue, but that didn't mean he wasn't chagrined, but he was amused by the direction of their conversation and, against his better judgment, intrigued by the faceless Angel. "And? What was her opinion?"

Darian's lips lifted slightly; amused that his friend seemed so interested in something he professed not to give a shit about.

"She doesn't believe that you don't know that you're hurting these women. I think her exact words were: *'your friend clearly knows how this shit works, hence his carefully laid out escape clause,'*" Darian mocked with a quirk of his lips.

Alex leaned his elbows on the bar as a slow, devious grin spread across his face. "It's too bad she's probably stiff, closeted, and frigid as hell. I think my dick just got hard." He looked down at his glass and chuckled out loud.

Darian burst out laughing. He knew that intelligence was what Alex needed in a woman. Maybe he'd open up his heart and mind to more than just a sexual relationship if he could find someone to stimulate him above the belt. If there was anything that turned Alex on, it was a challenge.

"You don't even know what she looks like. God help you, then, because, you'll be in a world of hurt. And, her wit is sharp as hell."

"Whatever," Alex dismissed, but his phone intruded into his musings again. He pulled it out of his pocket and flipped it open.

*Alex, get your ass over here now, or it's OVER!*

"Ugh, fuck. D, I have to go. And, Cole is in danger of getting his cock cut off by that banshee. Can you make sure to get him home? They're doing some serious damage to each other down there." Alex nodded his head in Cole's direction and shook it in disapproval. "The family doesn't need any bad publicity because he can't control his johnson. I love my brother, but he doesn't always think with his head."

"Oh? The text must have been from your lady," Darian speculated and took another long pull on his beer. Alex outwardly cringed at the words 'his lady', not really sure how to classify her anymore, but surely the screaming shrew she'd become certainly didn't fit that profile.

"Apparently, she isn't taking your girl's advice. I'm being summoned or *it's over*," Alex said with blasé sarcasm. He was not looking forward to that conversation. With a roll of his eyes, he slammed the rest of his drink and walked over to Cole, putting a hand on his shoulder. "Cole, I gotta bounce. See you on Sunday."

"Dude! Don't go, Alex. Things are just starting to happen. This is Ruby," Cole said happily, his speech slurred by the amount of alcohol he'd consumed in the past two hours. Alex's eyes drifted over the redhead that was draped around his brother's neck and took note how her blue eyes looked him up and down. He felt disgusted as he acknowledged the woman. She was elegantly dressed with bright red polish on her long fingernails, but Alex felt bile rise in his throat. She might look expensive, but Alex knew trash when he saw it. Her blatant appraisal of his dark good looks made it clear that she'd move on to a better offer without thinking twice.

"Nice to meet you. Goodnight, Cole."

*It's bitches like that who make me avoid relationships like the plague. Just like Whitney.* If Alex were honest with himself, he had to admit it. *So fake, so grasping and calculating,* Alex thought as he turned and walked out. It was obvious that Ruby wasn't interested in Cole. *He was just her next victim, and she would have dropped him like a hot potato if I'd snapped my fingers.*

"It's no fucking wonder I'm the way I am," he muttered under his breath as he walked the four blocks to the garage where his car was parked. "No fucking wonder."

*****

As he drove the few miles to Whitney's apartment, Alex tried to dig up some feeling for the woman he'd been sleeping with for the past year and a half. Sure, she was beautiful, but she was shallow. She was more interested in shopping than what was going on in the world, and she bored the shit out of him. He sighed heavily for letting her physical attributes sway him in the first place. He'd desired her and so he took her. It was easy, like everything else in his life. Sure, he worked his ass off, but making money out of nothing was what he loved best, and he was good at it. That was easy for him, too.

After leaving his Audi with the valet, he swiped the key card in the security door, and the doorman greeted him.

"Good evening, Mr. Avery."

"Good evening, George. How have you been?"

"Good, sir. It's been a while. Nice to see you."

Alex nodded. Yes, it had been a while. At least a month since he'd been there. "You, too."

He straightened his suit jacket and pulled on the cuffs of both of his sleeves as he watched the lights in the elevator climb to the eleventh floor of the upscale apartment building.

He'd met Whitney through his sister two years ago, and after several phone calls and a couple of obvious occasions where she'd dropped by his office, he'd finally asked her out to dinner. Alex shook his head, remembering. He should have his head examined for being so easily called into play. She had a great body and the sex had been good, but they had nothing of real substance to talk about. Whitney worked at an art gallery downtown and was constantly trying to get Alex to purchase some god-awful piece from whoever her newest client was. One of the closets in his spare bedroom was shoved full of the damn things.

Alex ran a hand over the back of his neck as he approached the door and sighed heavily. For what he hoped would be the last time, he took out his key and put it in the lock. As he pushed the large oak door open, he heard music coming from the bedroom. A lone light in the hall cast an eerie glow into the living and dining rooms. The apartment was small but very expensive, and he'd shelled out loads of money on the furnishings that Whitney wanted. Alex glanced around and quickly moved across the room to the bar, taking off his black Armani suit jacket, and loosening his green silk tie as he went.

He pulled out a glass and added ice and two fingers of scotch before he heard Whitney behind him.

"Well, well… to what do I owe this *honor*?" she asked snidely.

Alex's mouth tightened. He had no time or inclination to play games. "You asked me to show up. I'm here." He glanced over his shoulder before he slammed his drink and picked up the scotch bottle to refill it. "Or was that message meant for someone else?" He laughed coldly. "The closing led me to believe it was for me, and if you're expecting me to play nice, your greeting was sorely lacking." Alex was numb. Not uncomfortable, not nervous, not… moved. He just didn't give a fuck.

He tensed when she came up behind him and started to slide her hands around his waist. Considering her pissy demeanor, this wasn't what he was expecting, but her nearness did nothing for him as she molded herself against his back.

"What is it you wanted?" His voice was flat as he twisted out of her hold and moved to a chair in front of the big glass window

in the living room. The lights of downtown Chicago flickered as he
sank down into its softness. Alex's mind raced with what to do
about an almost unbearable situation. He itched to get the fuck out
of there and never deal with this shit again. Or, it could be just like
the hundred other nights he'd spent in this apartment. A few
drinks, they'd fuck, and then… nothing. He'd get up and leave and
that would be the end of it… but tonight, he wanted it to be the
end. For *good*.

She followed him and knelt down behind the chair.

"Whitney. Answer the goddamned question. What—do—
you—want?"

She reached around and ran a hand down his chest, turning
her head and pulling his earlobe into her mouth and raking it with
her teeth, trying to get a reaction out of him. If he closed his eyes,
he could let it happen, but did he really want to? He pulled away
just enough for her mouth to leave his skin.

"So, you want to fuck?" Alex asked bluntly over his shoulder.
His tone was sour and it sounded harsh, even to his own ears. He
felt dead inside, indifferent. He could take it or leave it.

She froze. "No. I want you to give a shit about me. I want you
to stop fucking around with your friends," she said harshly.

"We've been over this countless times. The conversation is
getting old." He lifted her hand off of his body and flung it aside,
and she gasped in response.

Her voice turned sickeningly sweet as she changed her tack,
and her hands returned to his chest again. "Alex, I want you to
make love to me…" she purred, as she started to pull his tie completely undone and open a couple of the buttons on his white shirt.
His hand came up to cover hers and stop her movement. He stood
up, effectively breaking the contact and took a few steps toward the
window, away from her.

"When have we ever made love? *We fuck*," he dismissed.

She gasped, a shocked expression flashing across her face. "Do you have to be such a bastard?" she rasped out loudly. "You think because you're rich and good-looking, you can treat me like trash? You're such a prick!"

He turned and looked at her for the first time. She was dressed in some outrageously expensive lingerie with ridiculous feather trim on the robe that hung open to reveal only lace panties and a matching bra underneath. His eyes traveled down her body indifferently, and he took another sip from his glass. Her body was beautiful—there was no denying that—with voluptuous curves in all the right places. Except for those silicone tits that she'd insisted on getting last year. They'd cost him thousands and he couldn't care less. Alex watched her with his eyes, but his fingers and lips wanted soft, warm, and real. Not hard, plastic, and fake. Maybe he *was* getting old, like his mother had warned him about. He shook off the thought as quickly as it came. He needed to get this shit out of the way.

"How am I a bastard?" he asked flatly, waving his hand casually around at the elegantly furnished apartment. "You have everything you need. I told you in the beginning that this was a physical relationship for me. That's what fits into my lifestyle. You *agreed*. I never lied to you about my intentions, and nothing has changed. I still don't want more than that. But lately, even sex... It's like fucking a Barbie doll. If I wanted a blow-up doll, I'm sure they're a hell of a lot less expensive than what you managed to suck out of me every month." He was cold; he knew it and he didn't care.

Her blue eyes hardened, and she scowled at him. "It's the least you can do, you lousy bastard." Her voice finally broke on the words, and Alex felt a twinge of regret despite himself. "After all this time, don't you care for me at all?"

"Not in the way you want. I don't want anything to happen to you. I want you to be safe and happy, but I'm certainly not in love with you, Whitney. I'm not sure I'm even capable of those types of feelings. I won't apologize for being the way I told you I'd be."

She huffed, and her eyes welled with angry tears at the cold tone in his voice. "I don't believe you, Alex. You show up here maybe once or twice a month for sex and that's it?"

"No, that's not it. We do things. I take you places and on trips… it's known in my circle that you and I are together. I don't treat you like a whore. What the fuck do you want from me?" Alex said shortly. He felt suffocated, caustic… like a caged animal that wanted freedom.

"More," Whitney said, simply.

Alex sighed. There just wasn't more.

"I'm very busy running the company, and I don't want or need romantic bullshit!" Alex's voice took on a harsher tone. "Shit, half of the time I'm not even in town, for Christ's sake! I'm not going to argue about this, and I don't feel the need to repeat myself. This is how it is! Take it or leave it."

*Fuck! Did I just give her a choice?* He wanted to kick his own ass.

She put her hand over her mouth and turned away. "Is there something that you need from me, that I don't give you, Alex?" Her voice was smarmy and evil sounding. "Don't I make you come hard enough? Isn't my pussy tight enough or my tits big enough?"

He sucked in a deep breath. There were *many* things he could add, but he wasn't going to add insult to injury. "Shut the hell up! You sound like trash when you talk that way! It isn't that complicated! It just doesn't feel right anymore! For either of us. Just see it for what it is."

"What is it?"

"What. It. Is. Nothing more, nothing less," Alex said shortly. His tone was dull, devoid of absolutely all emotion.

She pursed her lips and looked at the floor, nodding her head slightly. "I guess I'll *leave it* then. I want to get married and have kids. I wanted that with you." She let out a shaky breath. "I know. Who would have thought it? Me. Wanting to be a mother?"

Alex moved across the room and set his glass down on the end table so he could pull her lightly into his arms, and she laid her head down on his shoulder and cried softly. Children weren't something he considered, but he did know that if he ever did, it wouldn't be with this woman.

"Alex, I love you."

Instantly he stiffened, her words reminding him that she was not what he wanted, and he couldn't give her what she needed.

"Stop. I know you think saying that will change my mind, but it won't. It has the opposite result." All these months of her demanding money and incessantly hissing in his ear had left him with no emotions for her. It showed in how he spoke to her, his cold demeanor, and his stiffness as he pushed her gently away. "I'm sorry, but this is over. You can stay in the apartment. I'll keep paying for it until you tell me you're settled or… whatever."

He pulled her arms from around him and left her standing in the middle of the room. She followed after him, wrapping her hands around his body and pulling his unresponsive form as close to her as she possibly could. "Don't go. Make love to me, just once. Just one more time. Then you can leave—" she begged, desperation hanging heavily on her words, "—if you still want to."

Alex inwardly cringed. As virile as he was, as much as he loved sex, the thought of it with Whitney in this circumstance left him cold. He stilled and pulled her arms from around his body once again. "I'm not trying to hurt you, Whitney. But I'm just… not into this anymore. I'm sorry if that sounds harsh, but I don't want to drag this shit out. Just let it go."

Her face became hard and filled with anger. "So this is it? Just like that?"

"Hardly just like that. Be honest. It hasn't been exciting for months. We want different things out of relationships, and you're materialism has killed the desire for me." He turned and picked up his tie and jacket as he made his way toward the door. "Call Mrs. Dane if you need anything and she'll make sure you are taken care of." Alex wanted nothing more than to be done with her but felt a certain responsibility. His personal assistant could take care of any loose ends. That was her job and she was excellent at it.

"You dick! I hate you!" She picked up the glass he had left on the table and flung it at him. "I hate you! Do you hear me? You're a fucking bastard, Alex!" she screamed after him, but he kept walking as if she hadn't uttered a word.

"So you've said." He always hated this part of it, but it was inevitable. Every woman he'd ever dated had ended up wanting more, and the more they wanted, the more he pulled away. He didn't just get bored and lose interest, he felt suffocated.

The door shut quietly behind him. His usual pattern was repeating itself yet again.

No emotion, no anxiety, no remorse—just *relief.*

# 2

# Phone Sex

ALEX PINCHED THE bridge of his nose. His head ached, and he was exhausted from the week. Avery Enterprises had been losing money on one of its hotels in Munich, and his father sent him to audit the books when a couple million dollars went missing. This wasn't a big concern in the big scheme of the business as a whole, but it was the principle of the thing. Even a company the size of this one couldn't afford to have employees who were skimming off the top.

Several food and liquor expenditures from the restaurant couldn't be substantiated with the appropriate receipts, and Alex was able to find the discrepancy easily. Both the CFO and the executive chef of the property had been fired as a result. It was the chef that was padding his pockets, but if the CFO had been doing his job, it wouldn't have been Alex who found the error from half a world away during a semi-annual audit. He wasn't even angry when shit like this happened anymore, but he was fucking sick of all he traveling.

The first class cabin was dark as the Boeing 737 taxied onto the tarmac toward the terminal at O'Hare International, which sometimes felt like it literally took hours. So many planes waiting to take off on the numerous runways made Alex impatient. He leaned back in his seat and checked his watch for what seemed like the hundredth time; 9:45 PM on Friday night. Cole and Darian had both called asking him to meet them at a local club. He pulled his tie off and shoved it in the front pocket of his laptop case, before running a hand through his hair. Between the two of them, and Whitney's unending attempts to get him to call her back, it left 20 unheard messages on his cell phone. All since he'd taken off from his connection in London.

He sighed heavily. Really, all he wanted was a drink, a hot shower, and his bed. The question was should he go to his apartment downtown or his estate? Either one was about the same distance from the airport, but at least he'd be able to hang with his Golden Retriever at the house.

His phone rang again, and he reached for it from the front pocket of his dress pants, glancing at the faceplate as he did so.

"Yeah? Miss me bad, huh, D?"

"Save it, asshole. Where are you?"

The plane was just pulling up to the terminal, and the jet walk was moving into place. "Just got in. I'm gonna have serious jet lag, man. I'm out for tonight."

"Okay. I probably should go to the station anyway, unless you need a ride?"

"No. I'm having a car pick me up." Alex stood up and pulled his laptop case from under the seat with one hand and slung it over his shoulder. "I'm good."

"Maybe we can get together to play racquetball or something next week?"

"Sure, sounds like a plan." Alex made his way to the front of the jet, and the flight attendant gave him a warm smile, her eyes roaming over him in slow appreciation. His lips twitched slightly in amusement, but he kept walking through the jetway and into the terminal with casual purpose.

"I sent you something, Alex. Are you going to the apartment tonight?"

"I was considering going to the house. Max will be missing me, and my housekeeper has earned some time off after this week. Why?"

"Uh, well, I sent you one of the promos from the show," Darian said with a chuckle. "Thought you might like to see how fucked your perception of the lovely doctor really *is*, but it can wait. Just let me know if you've changed your mind after you see it."

Alex smiled tiredly. His curiosity was piqued despite his insistence that he was totally indifferent to Darian's continued baiting about this woman. It had become something of a game between them, and he chuckled. "Well, it won't make any difference. She's probably frigid. And, Whitney has been damn relentless this week. It's enough to make my dick shrivel up in defiance so I'm useless to the opposite sex. Why are you on my ass about her, anyway?"

"Because you won't believe how unbelievably hot she is, man. Despite the fact that the radio show is doing well and it's really helping me professionally, I'm waiting with baited breath until she doesn't work for me anymore. Then I can make a move on her *myself.*"

"Mmmm... Well, if I'm to believe what you say, she'll bite your dick off for you." Alex laughed as his driver pulled up and took his bags from him. "Then where would you be? You won't be able to show her who's boss."

Darian burst out laughing on the other end of the phone. "Well, I'm thinking it just might be worth it, Alex."

"Not likely. You know how I feel about that. I'd never let any woman lead me around by my dick. *Ever.* You need a distraction in a bad way." His phone beeped as another call came through and interrupted. *Fuck, it's her again.* "Hey, man, I have to go. Whitney's calling again. I either have to talk to her or get my number changed. I'll call you in a couple of days and we'll set up the game."

"I vote for the new number. Later, Alex."

Alex slid into the back of the limo and clicked over to the other call. "Alexander Avery." The impersonal greeting was deliberate.

"Hey, baby," she purred on the other end of the phone.

"Hold on." He put his hand over the phone so he could speak with his driver. "Martin, to Water Tower, please."

He made the decision to spend the night in his downtown apartment, one of the most expensive and prestigious establishments in all of Chicago. It was right in the middle of the city, and it made getting to the office ten times easier than commuting from Evanston. However, at the moment, it was the promise of those photos that lured him there. During the conversation with his best friend, maybe he'd gotten just a tiny bit interested in the intriguing picture that Darian had painted.

"Okay, Whitney. What can I do for you?" Alex's tone was unemotional and businesslike; his mind went blank as the lights of the interstate and other cars reflected off of the darkened windows.

"Come over. I'm lonely," she said softly. He rolled his eyes in disgust. He wasn't in the mood to repeat this scene.

"Uh, were you not there last week when we ended it? That *was* you, right?" he asked, his voice turned ice cold and dripping sarcasm.

"Alex…" she began pleadingly, but he cut her off.

"No. Whitney, I'm beat, and I'm not interested in a repeat performance."

She didn't say anything, and he grew uncomfortable with the silence.

He sighed. "Look, I thought we decided this was best, didn't we?" He really didn't mean to be a prick, but he had to be damn careful of what he said because if the door opened even a crack, she'd be through it so fast his head would be spinning.

More silence followed, except for the sniffling on the other end of the line. He decided to distract her, even piss her off a little bit, so he could get her off the phone. He was already thinking about Darian's radio prodigy and used it for fodder.

"I heard about your call to that radio psychologist last week. Let me remind you of the delicate nature of my position on this. It had better not result in nasty rumors being tossed around in tawdry gossip rags. Keep my name and my company out of it, Whitney, or there'll be hell to pay. If you need to see a shrink to feel better, then see one, but don't distribute my private business all over town. You'd do well to get more respect for yourself as well."

She audibly gasped on the other end of the line. "I didn't call," she lied, and Alex was exasperated.

"Look, cut the shit. I know all about it, and I expect you to handle yourself with more decorum."

"How… how did you find out?" she stammered.

"It's irrelevant." Obviously, she was oblivious that his best friend ran that station. It only solidified his decision. "Just don't let it happen again, or I'll yank all the money immediately. Is that clear?" he said coldly.

"You never cease to amaze me how cold you can be, Alex. I should have listened to that host when she told me to dump your ass instead of trying to make things better. I'm such a fool!" She was angry, but her voice held some semblance of pain, too, and he just wanted to be done with her.

"No, you're not a fool. But you're trying to salvage something that isn't worth saving, Whitney. Goodnight."

*So, Angeline Hemming told you to dump my ass, did she?* Alex was tired, and now he was agitated as hell. *Who does this bitch think she is, giving advice on situations she knows nothing about?* Not that he was upset that things were over with insidious Whitney, but he'd be damned if he'd be painted as the villain in the whole thing.

It was after eleven by the time Alex walked into his apartment, and he tossed his suit jacket and laptop on the dark brown leather sectional. It sat opposite the large windows that composed the North and East walls of the room; one of them was fitted with a sliding glass door that led onto the balcony of his 23rd floor penthouse. He grabbed the remote and pulled his shirt free of his slacks as he flipped on CNN then walked to his well-stocked bar. He pulled down a glass from the cabinet and poured some scotch, downed it, and filled it again before he went in search of Darian's little *gift*.

He found an envelope on the dining room table labeled KKIS FM 105.4. The building concierge was instructed to put his mail inside the apartment whenever he was traveling, and the large, white envelope easily stood out from the smaller ones.

He took it, with his scotch, and wandered back into the living room, sinking down into the luxurious couch cushions. He took a swallow and then ripped the end of the envelope open; anxious to be able to call Darian and tell him he was full of shit.

His full lips lifted in a mocking smile as he pulled the photos from the confines of the envelope and he was left looking at a black and white photo of a woman's face, but only the lower half of it, her full lips pursed and her finger vertical against them in a shushing motion. The long dark hair draping down on either side of her smooth face fell in full, silken waves. The photo was cropped at the top of her cheeks and Alex found himself feeling very cheated that he didn't get to see the rest. She had a perfect nose and high cheekbones accenting the flawlessness of her skin and those amazing lips begged to be kissed. Darian had succeeded. His interest was piqued and he definitely wanted to know more about this woman. Air left his lungs in an irritated rush, pissed that he'd fallen for it so easily.

The only color on the photo was her lips, the nail polish, and the lettering, *Angel After Dark, Fridays 10 PM–2 AM, KKIS FM*

*104.5 and* the scrawled slogan below it, *What's your Midnight Confession?* All in blood red.

"Hmphhh." He expelled his breath and carelessly tossed the photo on the coffee table. Alex frowned, just as upset with himself for being sucked in as he was with his friend for setting him up.

*Screw Darian,* he thought.

This gave barely a glance of what she really looked like, and Alex was still skeptical that it was even her.

"Pfffttt…" he muttered and then pulled out his phone and quickly banged out a text to his friend, never intending to tell Darian he actually liked the hints of what he saw in the promo piece.

> *D– Was this shit was supposed to get my dick hard?*
> *Seriously?*

In thirty seconds, his phone vibrated in his hand as he walked into his bedroom, intent on a hot shower. He laughed aloud at the message.

> *Those are VERY luscious lips, asswipe. You should see*
> *what they're connected to!*

Alex was still smirking when his thumbs hammered out his response.

> *It's probably not even HER. If you wanted me to squirm,*
> *you should have included a real picture, dickhead.*

Darian quickly replied.

> *Just turn on the fucking radio, Alex. Listen and then we'll talk.*

Alex threw his phone on the bed, wandered into the bathroom, and flipped on the radio built into the marble wall, reluctantly tuning to Darian's station. This was a very masculine room, just like the rest of his apartment, done in neutrals and darker tones, but warm and comfortable. The bathroom was as luxurious as the rest of the place with a large, glass-enclosed walk-in shower with nine shower heads, eight of them in the walls and all adjustable, a large sunken whirlpool bathtub, which had never been used, track lighting, and gleaming, deep brown marble everywhere. The fixtures were a burnished gold rather than silver and the porcelain, a rich cream.

He shed his clothes and left them where they landed on the floor as he turned on the shower and adjusted the water temperature. The music from the radio filled the room, and he wondered if he had the right station. The acoustics in the room were incredible, and sound would fill the space even with the water running.

Alex didn't recognize the song but soon a couple of commercials played, and he was well into shampooing his hair and letting the hot water take away the strain of the day before the talk show came back on air.

"This is Dr. Angeline Hemming with you After Dark on KKIS FM 104.5. How can I help you tonight?"

Alex paused at the sound of the soft and soothing voice echoing around him. Definitely sexy and not what he'd allowed himself to expect considering the original image he'd created. The voice did fit his friend's photo much better than the unresponsive librarian-type he'd conjured in his own mind. He smiled slightly and turned into the spray to rinse his hair until it was squeaky-clean.

*She could still be seriously unattractive*, even with the smoking hot voice, he reminded himself. He'd had a friend in college who was a DJ at the college radio station and he'd hung out with him a couple of times. It'd been his experience that most radio talent was in radio, and not TV, for a reason. If he were honest, that voice stirred something deep down inside that made him want to hear it again, even if he was still arguing with himself. "Probably a hag *and* a nag," he muttered under his breath.

He grabbed a towel and stepped out of the shower and started to rub his hair dry.

"Dr. Hemming?"

"Yes. What's your name?"

Again, that sultry voice prickled the skin at the back of his neck. Alex threw the towel aside and ran his hands through his hair, trying to remove the unfamiliar feeling, and deciding that it definitely needed to be cut within the next week. *Mental note: ask Mrs. Dane to make an appointment for the barber to come to the office—soon.*

"What's your situation?"

"I'm Mary. I've been with the same guy for more than five years, and we still aren't even engaged!" The other girl had a mousy little voice that Alex strained to hear as he moved around his room pulling on a pair of black silk boxers. He lay down on his bed and propped himself up on four pillows, resting the cold glass on his hard stomach. God, he was exhausted, mentally and physically.

His phone buzzed beside him, and he glanced at it briefly. Whitney again. *Christ!* He put it on silent mode and tossed it on the bed.

"Hmmm… well, have the two of you actually talked about it? Did he ever mention marriage, Mary?" Alex perked up at the response.

*Bingo. The guy never fucking said it.*

Maybe she was going to be logical and realize that women assumed too damn much. *Intriguing. A logical woman in a sea of emotional goo.* Suddenly, he found himself hoping that was really Angeline Hemming in those photos he'd left in the other room.

"Well, yes. I mean we talk about things like what we'll name our kids, so that means..." Mary's voice dropped off in uncertainty. "Doesn't it?"

Dr. Hemming sighed. "Not exactly. Mary, that's the problem. Most men are literal in what they say unless it's in the heat of passion. If he hasn't proposed, gotten you a ring, or come right out and said he wanted to marry you in a lucid moment, then no, I wouldn't assume anything." She sighed in exasperation. "However, it irritates me that he would discuss children. That's ignorant. He had to know how you'd interpret that."

"But—" the caller began and she was cut short.

"There really are no buts, Mary. Have you *asked* him?"

"Are you suggesting I give him an ultimatum?"

Alex swallowed the last of the scotch and set the glass aside as he listened. His lips thinned to a firm line and his eyes narrowed. *Here we go, he thought. Here is the meat of it. She'll probably tell this woman to corner the poor bastard.*

"No, Mary. That would never work long-term. He might marry you because he wouldn't want to lose you, but later, if there were problems, he might blame you and accuse you of forcing the issue. He'll say he felt trapped. That is not in your best interest, is it?"

There was silence from the caller so Angel continued. *Angel.* Alex ran the word over in his mind again as he realized she was turning into a real person; an elusive woman with full lips, high cheekbones, and the sexiest damn voice he'd ever heard. So oozing, it was like honey covering him in a warm, molten layer. If she was intelligent, savvy, *and* beautiful, it was definitely a lethal combination and not a one that came together readily.

"Mary, are you still with me?"

"Yes, Dr. Hemming. It's just not what I was hoping you would say."

"I'm afraid that's the downside of this gig. I don't get to say what you want to hear. I tell you the hard truth."

"So, what should I do?"

"You need to figure out how to take care of yourself first. Your boyfriend does have choices, but only those you give him." Alex sat up abruptly and pulled his knees up to rest his elbows on both knees. *Holy shit!*

"What do you mean?" the girl asked hesitantly.

"You can choose to let him continue along this path of least resistance, or you can alter the course, Mary. Tell him that it's clear that the two of you want different things, and that you're going to go out and get what you want. He'll ask you what that is if he hasn't before, giving you the opportunity to tell him. Not because you're nagging, but because he *asked*. He will have the ball in his court. He gives you what you need, or he risks losing you. Then, even though it boils down to basically the same thing as an ultimatum, you'll be relating to him in ways he'll respect and understand. The thing is, Mary, he'll think that it's *his* choice, so he'll own the decision. Do you understand what I'm telling you?" Her voice was so assured, and she was completely right. *Completely right.*

Alex was stunned. "Fucking hell," he said softly into the dark.

Mary chuckled softly over the radio. "I think so. That's amazing. *You're* amazing."

Alex's phone lit up on the bed next to him, but this time, it was a text from Darian. Alex smirked as he read it.

*Is your dick hard NOW?*

"Hmmph!" *That smug asshole.* Alex chuckled.

"Thank you. I hope this helped. Just stay calm when you talk to him. And, be prepared to follow through. If he won't commit, walk." Angel's voice was sure and steady, but still velvety smooth.

Alex ran a hand quickly through his damp hair. "If you don't, he'll never step up."

"Thank you, Dr. Hemming. I will. I feel so much stronger after talking with you! I guess men can be like children. You have to stick to your guns or they never learn, right?" She giggled.

Dr. Hemming responded with a low chuckle that shot right through Alex's body and into his cock. What was it about that voice?

"Mmmm. You said it, I didn't. We have to take a short break, and then I'll take another call. Stay with us. This is Angel After Dark on KKIS FM." Alex could hear the smile behind her words, and he pictured those red lips on the poster in the other room. He texted a response to his friend.

*Like steel. You are such a motherfucker!*

**Don't want to say I told you so...**

**but... I told you so.**

*Yeah, yeah. Give it a rest or I'll come over there*

*and beat your sorry ass.*

**LOL!**

While the commercials played, Alex went into the other room, refilled his drink, and paused to look out at the city lights before walking over and picking up the picture. He fought with himself for a minute or two until he went back to the bedroom and grabbed his phone. Probably not the smartest decision he'd ever made, but he wanted to speak to this woman, now silently hoping that incredible voice was truly spilling out of that gorgeous mouth on the poster. His fingers lightly outlined the image. Would she be as responsive as she looked? As delicious as she sounded? His cock hardened at the thought, and he tugged at the front of his boxer briefs in protest, unbelieving that he'd be so affected without so much as a glance at her.

Someone called in with some sappy dedication, and while the song played, Alex wrote down the number that Angel had announced before the music began. He was nervous for some inexplicable reason that he couldn't put his finger on, and it pissed him off, but not enough to change his mind. He never got nervous. Especially when it came to women, and never due to one that he hadn't even laid eyes on. At this point, he didn't know what he was doing or what he was trying to accomplish, he only knew that he wanted to learn more.

*Darian is clearly into her, so it makes no sense that he's taunting me like this.* He thought as he dialed the number. One thing Alex was sure of, if he was interested after speaking to her, he wouldn't be letting Darian's sensibilities interfere with getting what he wanted, friend or not. He should have kept his damned mouth shut.

"KKIS, you're calling Angel After Dark. What is your comment?" A younger, less sultry voice asked the question and Alex hesitated.

"Are you Dr. Hemming?" he asked.

"No, sir. I'm Chris, her assistant. I screen the calls and decide which ones to put through to Angel. Will you tell me what you're calling about, please?"

*Angel.* There was that name again. He wondered what her voice would sound like saying his own.

"Sure. I want to give her some perspective on a caller from last week. I'm the other half of the situation, and I wondered if her response would be different if she had both sides of the story. She told my girlfriend to dump me."

"Really? Yes, I'm sure she'll want this call. You'll need to turn down your radio or the feedback will hurt everyone's ears. Please hold."

"Line 2, Angel." Christina's voice flowed through the intercom on the other side of the glass and Angel glanced at her. She was fanning her face with her hand in mock drama. "This guy sounds hot."

Angel huffed, thinking about the half a dozen DJs at this station who had amazing voices along with pot guts and thinning hair. At least it was a man. *This will be a nice change of pace.*

"He said he was the other half of a call you had last week. Should be interesting."

"What's his name?"

"He wouldn't say. He said his name wasn't important."

The commercial break ended and she leaned forward to click the appropriate icons needed on her computer screen.

*****

"Hello, this is Angeline. Do you have a confession?"

"You could say that…"

Angel's back stiffened at the sound of the caller's voice. Something in the silky tone told her to be on guard, and her eyes shot to the other side of the desk where Darian was seated. Something flashed across his face that she couldn't read, and he tossed the cell phone he'd been using to text down on top of the desk. Angel bristled in her seat and picked up a pen, nervously tapping it on the legal pad in front of her.

"Yes, and what is your name?"

"Names don't matter. I liked your response to the last caller. It was… unexpected."

"Yes, well, I'm glad you were entertained. Christina tells me that you are party to a previous call?"

"Mmmm, yes," he said smoothly, but not exactly giving anything away. Jesus, his voice *was* amazing and Christina was all grins on the other side of the glass, mouthing *I told you so* and wagging her eyebrows up and down for emphasis.

Angel's own eyebrows shot up at the other girl, and a small smile graced her bowed mouth. Darian was frozen in place, one arm crossed over his chest supporting the other, which left that hand to support his jaw. He was all dressed up, and Angel was surprised he was even at the station this late. She knew what she was doing and didn't need him to babysit during the show anymore.

"Well? Are you going to tell me?" Her tone held the slightest bit of annoyance, and the man on the other end laughed softly. He was enjoying making her work for it.

"She called and told you that I was, let me see… selfish and made her feel, I think the word was, *invisible*."

Angel sat back in her chair and adjusted the microphone attached to her headset. No wonder Darian was acting like a scorpion crawled up his ass.

"Ah, yes. Whitney, right?"

"Good memory."

"And I take it that you don't agree with her assumption, right, *Alex*?"

There was silence for three seconds, and Angel smiled in satisfaction, realizing it meant he caught that she knew the name he didn't want to share. Darian was watching intently and he shook his head slightly, but Angel wasn't sure why and she wasn't in a position to ask him.

"Good memory, but no. Our relationship wasn't like that. Not even from the start. She mislead you, I'm afraid, Miss Hemming, so your advice to *dump my ass* was hardly warranted," he said calmly. A little too calmly. Apparently, Whitney told the truth when she said he didn't care about her.

"Mmmm, it's *Doctor* Hemming, but you can call me Angel. I don't remember telling her to dump your ah… *you*, at all. I told her to talk to you."

"Whatever you said, the effect was the same. It hardly matters since it was already over as far as I was concerned. In effect, you did me a favor. She's still calling me, begging, by the way."

Angel rolled her eyes in disdain at the caller's smugness and Darian's face split into a brilliant smile, his white teeth flashing brightly in the dark room. *A likely story.* "So, if it wasn't like that, then what was it like? From your perspective, I mean?"

"Mutual convenience, nothing more," he answered shortly. "I'm a very busy man, and I don't have time for romance. She wanted someone to pay the bills, and I wanted safe sex on a regular basis, so it worked well for all concerned."

"It sounds very cold and business-like, Alex. Whitney didn't share that opinion, as you know. Do you see how she may have felt like a kept woman?"

He laughed out loud. "That was what she wanted, to be *kept!* I never treated her like a whore, and I didn't screw around. We were a couple, but we both went into it with clear expectations. It was simple."

"Clearly, things changed over time, though. From what she said, she wanted more."

"Except, I never offered more, and if she implied otherwise, she was lying. She was trying to change the rules, and I didn't want them changed. End of story."

Angel contemplated for a couple of seconds before she continued. This was a man who always wanted to be in control. "How long was the, um… affair?"

"About a year and a half. So what? Are you going to tell me that everything has to be hearts and roses? That no woman can have sex, for sex alone? If so, it's a great disservice that you're doing to your own sex. Or, is that just how *you are?*" he challenged and his voice dropped two decibels. "Do you get all moist and gooey, Angel?"

She sat back in her chair, starting to get pissed off. *Who in the hell does this asshole think he is?*

"This isn't about me, Alex. It's about *you*, so, my gooey-ness, or lack thereof, is not up for discussion," she retorted shortly and then took a deep breath to calm herself. She needed to remember that she was the one in control of this call, not the arrogant prick on the other end of the phone. "I'm just telling you that for most women, sex is physiological. It's a bond; a chemical reaction, if you will. Yes, it can happen just for the sake of physical release, but I feel if the affair continues for any length of time, some form of emotional feelings will develop. Sex, especially good sex, is a connection, and intimacy on that level has consequences. I'm not saying you've been dishonest, Alex, but, even if Whitney had a clear picture of your expectations in the beginning, she came to care about you, which changed *her* expectations." *Dickhead,* she added mentally.

"And I'm telling *you*, it wasn't like that." His voice was cool and unemotional, which grated on Angel's nerves. "Whitney isn't the type to care about anything other than shopping and material things. She cared more about who made her drapes than she did about me. Trust me. We fulfilled needs for the other and nothing more. Good sex isn't a fluttery heartbeat. It's coming hard—and often." The amusement in his voice was palpable. He was baiting her and it was working.

"How utterly irresistible," she shot back sarcastically. "Did you leave some money on the nightstand when you blew through the bedroom?"

"No, but she had everything she needed. I was the one left wanting. All she did was nag and complain. Talk about dousing a fire. She made the reason I was with her at all vanish."

"You gave her money but no love. You clearly have a deep-seated phobia of intimacy."

"*That's a load of crap!*" Alex paused to gather his thoughts and then continued. "At best, love is overrated. It's a pipe-dream pumped into little girls' minds by Disney movies and fairy tales. You just don't get it. Let me tell you, lady, *intimacy* has never been my problem."

Angel smiled, glad she was finally able to ruffle his feathers. *Whatever, dude.* "There are many *levels* of intimacy, and clearly, you are clueless."

"Clearly, *you* are closeted," he huffed in disgust.

The skin on Angel's face began to flush with heat as her anger grew, and her hand clenched around the pen she was holding. She cleared her throat and continued as if Alex hadn't commented.

"Hardly. Men have to have sex to become emotional and get their protective vibe on. Women, and I'm not saying all the time, but in general, have to feel emotionally connected to really enjoy sex. It's an ageless conundrum. Blame evolution, if you will. Men want to bang their chests and, in effect, impregnate as many women as possible to make sure that the species survives, while women are the nurturers. Their emotions run amok, kicking in, so that the family and the children flourish."

Her caller burst out laughing at her analogy. Darian was doing a good job of keeping it in, but his shoulders were shaking violently and his hand was covering his mouth.

Angel couldn't help but join in, laughing softly. "Before the phone lines go wild, I feel I should add a disclaimer here that points out that in no way am I saying that men do not nurture their children. I'm just talking about base physiological differences between men and women as way of an explanation here."

Alex grunted. "Nice generalization, even if you do frame it as physiological. After that last call, I actually believed you understood men better than most women do. Should I generalize that all women are grasping, money-hungry, bimbos who can't have orgasms without batteries? I mean, if I follow your line of thinking."

He shut up and waited for her to answer, but it was obvious he was angry.

"If a woman can't orgasm with you, it's because she was not properly motivated to do so!"

Darian's eyebrows shot up in shocked surprise at her response while Alex burst out laughing.

"What about you, Angeline? Answer my question. I *dare* you." His voice was teasing, sexy, and totally sucking her in. She never could resist a challenge, and she could tell this man was a panty dropping, sexual predator that could leave a trail of panting women behind him. If she was honest, her body was reacting to his words and his voice alone.

"Can you have sex for the pure animal release of it? Just for the pleasure of it? *Lots* and *lots* of pleasure, Angeline." His voice purred through her headset and a thin veil of perspiration broke out on the surface of her skin in response. She was becoming sexually aroused at his taunting, and it unsettled her. "Have you ever been attracted purely on a physical level?"

She felt her skin prickle at his words, and she wanted desperately to yank the damn headphones off and run her hand through her long hair. How in the hell did he just take control of the conversation and turn it back on her? He was so fucking full of himself!

"Alex," she said his name softly and with purpose. "If you want me to answer, you'll have to answer me first. So, how badly do you, um... *want me* to answer?"

"Go on with your question." He wanted her answer enough to answer first.

She smiled slyly, satisfaction overtaking her expression. "Do you go through life without any real connections? Other than your bank account and your professional life, do you have anything *real*? Has anyone ever touched you on a deeper level? Motivated you to really *want*? Want so much with your heart and body that it left you literally *aching* if you couldn't be with her?" she oozed slowly, her voice throbbing on purpose.

*Fucking men!* she thought. Especially one that was so full of sexuality and a very pompous point of view. *Use that to get your dick hard, you bastard!*

Darian and Christina both watched her in absolute silence until, finally, Darian loosened his tie and tugged at the collar of his shirt, releasing two of the buttons and running a hand over the back of his neck.

Alex cleared his throat.

*That's right, baby, come to Mama.* The corners of Angel's full lips lifted in amusement at his hesitation. *Sucker!*

"No. That kind of feeling doesn't exist for me, and I wouldn't want that kind of emotional slavery even if it did. I like my life the way it is." His voice was melting around her and she smiled. "Your turn to answer my question, Angel."

Clearing her voice of all the sexual teasing she'd just used, she didn't hesitate. "Yes. Of course I can," she said flippantly. "I'm a grown woman. I take full responsibility for my life both in and out of the bedroom, but I have rules just like you do."

"Mmmm, it appears we're on the same page," he said softly. The suggestion in his voice was clear, and Christina's mouth fell open as she listened intently.

Angel laughed softly, the sound smooth and warm. "Not exactly. You deny deeper feelings exist, and I acknowledge the possibility of them but know my boundaries in situations like you describe. I don't think it's healthy to stay in a purely sexual relationship for any length of time. Someone eventually gets hurt. So while you live in denial of real love, I just... *control* my outcomes."

"As do I. I set my boundaries well in advance and communicate them clearly. Are you inferring it's better to screw a bunch of different people than to be monogamous? I find that hard to believe."

She huffed in agitation. "Don't put words in my mouth! All I am saying is that being monogamous is dangerous if you want to remain detached. Personally, I don't think that's even possible. I hope that someday you meet someone who changes your perspective." *And knocks you on your arrogant ass.*

"My pers—"

She interrupted, disconnecting the call to make a point. She smiled to herself, knowing that being cut off would infuriate this man. It unsettled her that she found herself wondering about him more than a little, and she actually wanted to know what he'd say. He seemed dangerous; very, very sexy, and truthfully, that was the most fun she'd had on a call since she started this damn gig. She glanced at the clock, knowing she had to get on to the next set of spots, but hoped he was still listening.

"Thank you for your call, Alex. Someday you'll meet a woman who controls her own orgasms. Not all of us are at the mercy of men, you know. Have fun... banging your chest or whatever it is you... *bang.*"

A bright smile split across her beautiful face, leaving Darian breathless and stunned. Thankfully, Christina was out of the studio because she was laughing so hard the tears were rolling down her face.

"This is Angel After Dark on Kiss FM, and I'll be right back." Angel pushed her headphones off, looking pointedly at Darian. "Did you put him up to that? That was your friend, wasn't it?"

He quickly shook his head. "Nope. I didn't do anything. Don't look at me!"

Angel's eyebrows shot up. *Yeah, right,* she thought. "Why don't I believe you?"

"What did you think of him, Angel? Uh, I mean, of his situation?"

"I'm trying not to," she said wryly and shook her head, getting up to stretch. "He's so full of his own sexual power. I mean... *Shit!* He's obviously been a bad, bad boy and needs a serious lesson."

Darian's eyebrows shot up in surprise, but he didn't say anything, just let out a low whistle. Angel smirked but ignored it. "Aren't you supposed to be out of here? Really, you don't have to come in here every week." Darian's eyes followed her movements and flashed over her stomach and the small strip of skin that was peeking out between her jeans and her T-shirt as she moved.

"I know. I just want to make sure you have it down before I leave you to your own devices."

"My own devices? I've been left to my own damn devices practically my entire life. You don't need to worry about me. I can handle things."

Darian's phone rang, and reluctantly, he picked it up from the table.

"Yes? Uh, yeah. No. No!" His eyes roamed over Angel, who was standing there with her right hand on her hip, looking at him pointedly. "Um, Angel, he's pissed that you cut him off and wants to finish the conversation."

"It is finished," she scoffed with a short laugh. *Poor baby, not used to someone else controlling anything. Hilarious.*

"He asked if he can call you," Darian said hesitantly, already knowing the answer, and her eyes widened.

"Not interested," Angel said carelessly and picked up a stack of promos from the desk to glance through them. "Not at *all.*" But, she *was* interested, and she found herself hoping his face and body would live up to that sexy voice. Men like him were dangerous to women like her who had a strong need to be in control. She was smart about steering clear of anything that would make her lose even one shred of her carefully constructed world.

Darian's mouth fell open in astonishment. "Uh, Alex, she's not here right now. She went to the bathroom. Okay, sure. Completely, Alex. Later." He closed his phone without saying another word to the beautiful woman sitting in front of him.

Angel looked up and wrinkled her nose at her boss. "Chicken-shit," she admonished with a grin.

"Angel, he, uh," he began.

"Yeah. I know." She shrugged slightly. "I'm sure his hard-on is all about the challenge he's feeling right now. He wanted the last word. He's used to getting what he wants, but now there's something he can't have, and he's left holding his dick in his hand. Naturally, he's uncomfortable."

"There's a better chance he's pissed."

"So? Maybe you should introduce the word 'unattainable' to your boy's vocab, yeah?" She sat back down and adjusted the damn headphones. She still had half an hour to go. "Now, get the hell out of here! You're bothering me."

*****

Alex was left sitting on the edge of his bed looking at his now silent phone, stunned that she'd cut him off. He had to admit that he was more than a little aroused by her words and her sassy wit. Damn, he wanted to know what she looked like! As if on cue, his phone vibrated with a message from Darian. It was a photo message, and Alex held his breath as he opened it, somehow sure he was about to get knocked on his reluctant ass.

His thumb ran over the screen as the photo loaded, and his breath caught in his throat. It was a picture of a woman with long dark hair, flowing in thick waves nearly to her waist. She was wearing ratty jeans, the kind that cost hundreds of dollars because the holes were in all the right places, and a small white T-shirt that clung enticingly to her body. She was stretching, her arms extended over her head, and her hands laced together. He couldn't see her features, only the side curve of her face and chin. She was angled away from Darian's camera, but the photo was sufficient to give Alex a glimpse of the line of her body, the soft curve of her hip, the narrowness of her waist, laid bare as her shirt lifted with her movement, and the full side curve of one breast. "Shit, what about her face?"

He wanted to plunge his fingers into the holes in those jeans, to feel the warmth of her skin that was teasing him under that shirt, and to kiss that smartass mouth. Alex's mouth went dry as blood engorged his body to the point of pain, and he licked his lips. He wanted her, and he made up his mind that he would have her.

Alex's breathing quickened as he contemplated this mysterious woman with her biting intellect that was in such contrast to her soft appearance. He dialed Darian's number impatiently. "Uh, yeah?" his friend answered.

"Put that sexy little shit on the phone, Darian."

"No."

"No one cuts me off, D. Put her on the damn phone! I want to speak to her. Either that or give me her number. I'll call her myself."

"No! Uh, Alex, she's not here right now. She went to the bathroom."

"Stop fucking around, D! I know she's right there." Alex waited, but Darian didn't respond. "Call me when you leave."

"Okay, sure."

"And Darian, from what I see, I concede, she's gorgeous," he said softly as he ran his hand through his mop of hair. "Fucking beautiful."

"Completely, Alex."

"Look, I know you can't talk, but this is not over."

"Later."

Alex flopped down on the bed and let his arms fall to the side as he waited for Darian to call him back. *Angeline Hemming, you certainly are intriguing.*

A few minutes passed before his phone rang, and he answered it quickly, not moving from his position on the bed.

"What'd I tell you? She's amazing, right?" Darian said smugly.

"What was your goal here, Darian? You're obviously a walking boner for this woman yourself, but now... Well, let's just say, I'm not sure you're a good enough friend for me to back down."

"Yes, I do think she's hotter than hell, but unfortunately, I can't date her. It blows, but I can't, at least for now," Darian groaned.

"I'm not sure what you were toying with, but I'm worked up now, and want to know more. I want to see her face. I want... hell, I just *want.* I've never been so aroused by a conversation in my entire life. Thanks for that."

"Hey, I didn't make you pick up that goddamned phone. That was all you, so don't blame me, brother! Mark my words, Alex. You're in for a big surprise when it comes to Angel. She won't be like the women you're used to. She's beautiful, smart, and tough as nails."

"What's her number, Darian?"

"Sorry, man. No can do. She'd cut my balls off."

"Stop being such a pussy. You're her boss, for Christ's sake!"

"Not really. She's doing this for her own reasons. She could walk tomorrow and not blink twice but I need her for the ratings. She's only doing this for the public service announcements she's weaseled out of me."

"If you won't tell me, fine. It isn't like I don't have the resources to find out anything I want to know, which will be much more than her phone number."

"Dude, don't get your hopes up. She's untouchable, even for the great Alex Avery. I have faith that she'll kick your ass from one end of Chicago to the other, which is why I've baited you this way. I'd love to see you work for it, just once."

Alex snorted as his mouth lifted in a smirk. As if that was possible. He was more than ready to take on the challenge that Angel Hemming presented. He was more excited by the prospect, and by this woman, than he'd been since he couldn't remember when. Maybe even, ever. "Well, you started this shit. If you want her, you'll have to beat me to it, and I won't play fair. I don't give a shit if you are my best friend."

"I wouldn't expect you to, Alex. You wouldn't be you if you did, but like I said, Angel is untouchable. She's different than most women."

Alex laughed, not doubting his ability to win her over and get his way. "Mark my words, D." He was up to any challenge, especially one with rewards as delectable as this. "I'm telling you now that I *will* touch her. In all sorts of places. And if anyone is gonna be in control of her orgasms, it will be me. *Me.*"

# 3
# Enigma x2

ANGEL ROLLED OVER at the sound of Christina Aguilera's song, *Dirty,* coming from her phone on the nightstand for the third time. Her best friend, Becca James, was no doubt calling to remind her of their gym appointment. It was a standing thing every Saturday, but ever since Angel began at KKIS, it was harder and harder for her to drag herself out of bed.

"For God's sake!" she mumbled as she finally peeled away the pillow she was holding over her eyes, flung it brutally toward the foot of the bed, and glanced at the clock.

Reluctantly, she leaned over and grabbed the phone just as the ringing stopped. "Oops. Too bad, Becs."

Angel flopped back onto her plush pillows and dropped the phone on the bed, closing her eyes in hope of a couple more hours of sleep. Her hope was short-lived when the phone immediately started playing the song again. Angel picked it up and answered with unveiled irritation. "What!"

"Are you still in bed? You have twenty minutes to get to the gym or your ass is mine," Becca answered shortly.

Angel and Becca both had studied social science and liberal arts at Northwestern, which quickly led to becoming fast friends. A study in contrasts; they complimented each other well. Angel was subdued and focused, while Becca was outgoing, wild, and easily distracted. They balanced each other over the years; each adopting some of the other's traits.

Angel continued for two more degrees while Becca had taken her physical education and nutritional science bachelor's and became a personal trainer. And boy did she train! There were times Angel wished Becca had done anything else, but that. She was merciless in the gym and literally worked Angel's ass off. She rolled over and scratched her flat stomach beneath the lime green cotton of her pajama top.

"Becca, I'm so tired. How about we just meet for brunch?" Angel sat up and ran a hand through her hair, squinting in protest at the bright sunlight streaming in around her tightly drawn blinds.

"Uh... *no*! Get. Your. Ass. Here. Now!" Becca punctuated her words with a giggle. "Angel, you owe that tight little bod to me, so suck it up. Don't punish me because you've suddenly taken to giving advice to the lovelorn until all hours of the night."

"It's not just the lovelorn, you Nazi trainer bitch!" Angel groaned. "It's also the codependent, dysfunctional, and mentally unbalanced. Why can't I just run five miles on the treadmill here?"

The apartment that she lived in was first-class with a well equipped-gym where residents had twenty-four hour access; so, it was more for friendship than for necessity that made Angel trek to the Bally where Becca worked. Angel overpaid her outrageously for their sessions since it was the only way that Becca's pride would allow Angel to help her financially.

"Because, I said so. Get moving."

"You have no idea how long these nights are," Angel lamented while she hugged one of the huge white pillows to her, wishing again that she could just sleep. "I hate you."

"I know you love me," Becca teased. "You can whine to me at the gym. I need to hear all about that guy you talked to last night. Holy hell, that was hot."

"Seriously? You heard the same thing that I did, so what else can I tell you? He's an arrogant prick who thinks he can get his dick wet whenever and with whomever he wants. I wanted to reach through the phone and strangle him on the spot. He was so friggin' infuriating."

She flushed at the memory, the heat infusing beneath her pale skin in a hot rush. In truth, his confident arrogance turned her on in a big way, and she bristled at the thought of his sultry voice and the way he'd made her feel. He pushed every one of her invisible buttons. She'd actually been aroused.

"Whatever. Just get here. Jillian wants to see you, and I have to pick her up by ten-thirty."

Angel smiled as she thought of the beautiful little girl with golden blonde curls and sparkling blue eyes, whose chubby little cheeks got even chubbier when she giggled. Her heart swelled with love. Becca had the misfortune of getting pregnant, and her loser boyfriend left her to deal with the hardships of single parenthood. Now, Jillian's father saw her only on rare occasions. It was harder on the poor thing than it was worth, and the little girl suffered terribly from separation anxiety from her mother. Angel had stuck by Becca's side, been her birth coach, and was now Jillian's godmother. The two shared a very special bond and simply adored each other.

Angel got up out of the bed and went to her dresser to select her clothes. She pulled her gym bag down from her closet shelf and packed the street clothes she would need after her workout.

"Okay. I won't shower since you're gonna make me sweat my butt off anyway. See you in twenty."

"Angel... 20 extra squats for every single minute you're late."

"You whore," Angel said, but she was laughing out loud as she padded back into the bedroom. Becca joined in, her high-pitched laughter tinkling over the phone. "I have to go now or my slave driver best friend will kill me."

"The clock starts now."

"Guh!" Angel giggled and shut the phone off, carelessly tossing it on the bed. She hurriedly dressed in black yoga pants and a lavender top, grabbed some socks and her New Balance trainers. She rushed to pull her long, thick hair up into a messy knot on the top her head before grabbing the bag and darting down to the parking garage in the basement of her building.

She glanced at her watch and tossed her gym bag in the passenger seat of her Lexus HS hybrid before sliding in behind the wheel. The car was luxurious without going overboard. Angel's conscience wouldn't allow her to spend unnecessary money when she didn't have to. She'd rather send it to her dad or give it to one of her causes than waste it on things she didn't need to be happy. Her three bedroom apartment was her one splurge. It was more than she needed, but it had extra room for Becca and Jill in case they needed to stay with her, and it offered convenient access to her office and the courthouse. In Angel's hectic world, time was much more valuable than money.

She still had 14 minutes to reach her destination; as she merged onto the 290, her phone rang in her purse. The ringtone this time was her father's and she happily picked it up.

"Hey, Daddy!"

"How's my baby?" His deep voice was gruff and scratchy from years of smoking. Each time Angel thought of it, her heart fell a little. He hadn't had an easy life, but he somehow managed to be so happy all the time. She often wondered how he did it after her mother split. Angel had tried numerous times to get him to pack up and move to Chicago to be closer to her, but he liked his friends and his life in Joplin. The lack of bustle was what Joe enjoyed, but Angel had felt claustrophobic in the little town, and she was never really accepted at high school. Kids were mean due to her position as 'the janitor's daughter'. "I'm good. Becca has me on the way to work out. What are you up to?"

"I'm headed to pick up William and Benjamin. We're going to the Ozarks for the weekend. The weather's nice and the fish should be biting."

Inwardly, Angel groaned at the memory of how lame she'd found those trips. Joe dragged her along more times than she could count, and sitting in a boat, waiting for the fish to bite, was boring as hell. William's son, Ben, was the only real friend she had in high school, but even he went over to the dark side when it came to fishing.

"Dad! Do something *fun!* Go to Branson, at least! See some shows." Branson was a bustling tourist trap with lots of musical shows, amusement parks, restaurants and golf courses. She'd abhorred the golfing, but the rest was something Angel had enjoyed the two times they went there together.

"Fishing is fun! Besides, Will's been a little under the weather, and this is what he wants to do."

"Oh? Is he okay?" Angel was concerned. "Why haven't you mentioned this before?"

"Sure, Angel. He's not one to talk about his troubles. He had some stomach problems, that's all."

"Okay. I hate to run, Dad, but I'm at the gym, and Becca threatened me with extra squats if I'm late. Tell the guys hello for me."

"Love you, hon. It wouldn't kill you to come see your poor old dad sometime, ya know?"

"Yes, I know. I will soon. Love you, too. Bye."

Angel took her bag and rushed through the doors of the club, stopping briefly to swipe her membership card at the desk before rushing to the locker room to stash her things. Becca was waiting for her on the bench in front of their lockers and glanced in exaggeration at her watch. Angel pursed her lips and rolled her eyes in response. Becca was pretty, with shoulder-length blonde hair, a very muscular build, a pert nose and bright green eyes. Physically, she was sturdier than Angel's waif-like frame, but emotionally, much weaker.

"Stop with the watch watching. I'm here, aren't I?" Angel scoffed, closing the locker and quickly pushing the padlock in place. "Lead on."

"Barely." It didn't take Becca long to begin drilling Angel about her late night caller once she had her on the elliptical to warm up. "Angel, ten minutes at 3.5." She leaned on the frame of the machine as she looked expectantly into Angel's face, who tried not to make eye contact but bit her lip to keep her smile at bay as she started the machine.

As she worked out, Angel kept her mouth shut and waited for Becca to crack, wondering just how long it would be until she couldn't stand it anymore. It didn't take long.

"Well?" Becca said with her hands outstretched in front of her, palms up, and Angel burst out laughing. *So predictable.*

"Well, what?" Angel teased.

"Stop fucking around and spill!"

"Bec, you heard it! What are you expecting me to say?"

Becca was exasperated. "Shit, Angel. Am I the only one with a vagina? I almost came at the sound of his voice. Alex, right?" She raised her eyebrows suggestively as she repeated his name, and Angel smiled despite her attempts to keep a straight face. Becca had a wonderful sense of humor and wicked wit that often left her laughing so hard she cried. Angel wasn't sure why, but she didn't want to admit that she was definitely aware of her vagina last night, simply from speaking with the faceless caller. She felt ridiculously out of control, and it was disconcerting, to say the least.

Her warm up completed, Angel reached out and pointed at the timer on the machine. Becca nodded and increased the speed and the resistance. Angel ignored her but her mind raced, wondering if his face and body matched that silken voice.

*Fuck, yes, Alex!* She felt a flush spread beneath the skin of her neck and face, thankful for the workout so Becca wouldn't notice how this guy affected her. "Was that his name?"

"Angel," Becca admonished. "If you don't think he was hot, I might as well call the morgue to come and collect your corpse."

"Stop being so over-dramatic." Angel wrinkled her nose at her friend. "*Yes*, he sounded hot, but he could be a slug, for all I know. It's like that joke Kyle used to make about those phone sex girls on the late night commercials. Remember?"

Kyle was Angel's boyfriend while they were attending Northwestern; a music major and a bad boy, complete with tattoos, a rock band, and a vintage Les Paul electric guitar that was his pride and joy. He was smoking hot, but even he hadn't shaken her like this.

"Sorry, no."

"He used to say that they were probably overweight trolls in hot pink, velour track suits, shoving bonbons into their mouths and reading Tolstoy while they pseudo-moaned with over-exaggerated pants into the phone."

They both chuckled. "Angel, if you're trying to convince me that this Alex is anything but breathtaking, I won't believe you."

"You always were the more delusional of the two of us. I keep my head on straight; less disappointment that way."

"Please don't confuse delusion with optimism! What's his story?"

Angel could see that Becca's curiosity would not be denied, and she sighed in defeat as she climbed off of the elliptical and used the towel hanging around her neck to wipe the perspiration off her brow.

Out of habit, they walked into the room that housed the free weights next; usually they were the only women in there and surrounded by several men pumping iron. Angel found it funny how the men always stared at themselves in the mirror while they worked out. She didn't particularly like all of the ogling they did either, but Becca insisted that if you got the form right, free weights worked the muscles harder in a shorter amount of reps. Angel was all for expediting.

Becca nudged her shoulder when Angel didn't answer right away. "Hello?"

Angel shrugged. "I don't know that much. His girlfriend called in complaining that he was gone all the time and she wanted more. I told her to toughen up and get it or get out. He called in a week later to tell me his side of the story." Angel shrugged as she picked up a seven pound dumbbell in each hand.

"Okay, 3 sets of 20 reps each arm, rest fifteen seconds in between."

"Jesus, Becca. I got it. I know the drill. You only need to be here to irritate me, not tell me the basics, all right?" Angel tried to transition the conversation away from Alex. *Alex, whatever-his-name is*, she mused.

"What aren't you telling me?" Becca asked and picked up a barbell to start lifting beside Angel.

Angel shrugged. "I really don't know much about him, other than he's rich, and he wants his relationships all business."

"Mmmm, well if he fucks as good as he sounds, I'd want to get down to *business* and fast."

"Becca! You've got a one-track mind." Angel smirked in helpless response to the humor. "He was a caller. Nothing more." She hesitated, wondering if it was wise to say the next words. "Even if I was curious about him, he's my boss' best friend."

Becca was steadily pumping iron, her toned arms taking the weight easily. She stopped as her eyes widened. "Darian knows him?"

Turning, Angel walked back to the weight rack and replaced the dumbbell where she'd found them, took a deep breath, and answered. "Yes. But that's all I know."

"And you have no intention of finding out about this man? Are you dead?" Angel rolled her eyes while Becca helped place a barbell across her shoulders for the legwork.

"He sounds sexy, sure. So what? It means nothing. If he's attractive, no doubt he's a heartbreaker. Those types of men are a dime a dozen. I don't need to turn into one of the desperate women who call the show. I'm not going down that road."

Angel dropped down into a squat as Becca started counting them off with a frown settling on her face.

"Maybe it's a trip you should take, Angel. At least, check out the travel brochure. What could it hurt? Your wheels have to be getting a little rusty, girlfriend."

"Ugh! I told Darian last night that I wasn't interested, so it's really a moot point, Becca. Can we move on? I want to get this shit knocked out and go get my Jillybean."

Becca's features softened at the mention of her daughter's name, but she wasn't distracted from the subject at hand. "Is Darian trying to set you up?"

"Not exactly." She grunted as she began another set of squats, the sweat starting to bead on her forehead and seep through her top on her back and under her breasts.

"Oh, for God's sake! Will you just come out with it?"

"He called Darian's phone and asked to speak with me after I cut him off. I said I wasn't interested loud enough for him to hear me." Angel rolled her eyes and kept up the squats without breaking her rhythm.

"He called. He fucking *called*." It was more of a statement than a question. "You didn't even talk to him? He's obviously interested. Aren't you even the slightest bit curious? If his dick is anything like his voice... I mean, *shit*."

Angel burst out laughing. "Becca, take this, please. You're incorrigible!"

"And you're insane!" Becca removed the bar from Angel's shoulders and set it along the mirrored wall. As usual, there were a number of men eyeing the two beautiful girls, one of them even moved closer, clearly interested in Angel. His eyes roamed over her small, well-toned frame in appreciation. Becca glanced his way and caught what he was about to do and waved a finger at him. He was tall, blonde, and muscular, but too meaty for Angel's taste. "Oh, no, honey, this girl is a vegetarian. You're wasting your time."

The man got a perplexed look on his face. "What? Are you two dykes or what?"

Angel bit her lip, trying to keep the hysterical laughter at bay while Becca huffed in response, looking over the man in disgust, taking in the thickness of his legs, body, and especially the neck. *Dude, we don't like men whose neck circumference exceeds that of their skull,* she thought and wished she could say it aloud.

"Uh... no!" Becca's blue eyes flashed to Angel and then back again. "Apparently, she has a new aversion to meat. If she's not up for filet mignon, she's not interested in ground round."

By now, Angel was shoving Becca back toward the cardio room again, both of them laughing uncontrollably.

"Shut up, Becca! Oh, my God!"

The man stood entranced, watching them move away from him. "Huh?"

Another fit of laugher shook Angel's shoulders, and she wiped at the tears leaking from her eyes.

"Exactly!" Becca quipped to him over her shoulder as they disappeared through the locker room doors. "I know steroids shrink their balls, but I guess the brain goes, too."

"Stop, Becca. My sides hurt!" Angel threw out, and it was Becca's turn to laugh. "Is it just their balls?"

"No... you know teeny peens never were my fave! I mean, seriously, all that muscle except where it counts. Dumb asses."

"How much, um, *research* have you done on the subject?"

"*Enough*! And Angel, you need to research that sexy voice."

"Yeah, yeah, okay. Running or stair-stepper today?"

"Running. Three miles at intervals. Start with a jog."

Angel pushed the start button on the machine and began a slow jog while Becca joined her on the treadmill next to hers. "You could use a good bone. Maybe Mr. Velvet Voice can throw you one. Just sayin', Angel."

Angel smiled again. "You're the one who won't let go of the bone. You're like a rabid dog. Why don't you concentrate on getting yourself a good man, and let me worry about me? Let's run. Maybe if you're out of breath, you can get off my ass about this guy. Do you want to meet him? I'll ask Darian to set you up."

"He called *you*. You can't tell me that doesn't make your panties at least a little bit damp. What are you afraid of?"

"I'm not afraid, but I'm not an idiot. Men like him are dangerous to women in general. I'm not looking for a relationship, but if I were, he'd be the last type of man I'd want. He's too detached. You heard him. He needed sex and having a monogamous relationship was a convenient way to get it. Call me crazy, but if you're only fucking for a fling, okay. But I already have someone for that. I don't need to complicate my life with someone like him."

"Oh, yes. How is Kenny?" Becca crinkled her nose in distaste, took a big swig from her water bottle, and then wiped the moisture from her mouth with the back of her hand. "He's just so... bleh."

Angel shook her head. "He's a nice guy."

Kenneth Gant was a lawyer that Angel met when she first starting working as guardian ad litem for the Cook County Circuit Court. He'd taken a strong interest in her from the first time they'd met. Angel dated him for a while, but now it was mainly a sexual relationship once or twice a month. Even that was getting too much. Her rule—sex with no strings for short-term only—was sorely stretched on this one. Funny though, he was the one with feelings, not her.

Angel sighed. When she thought about it, it was about scratching an occasional itch. Maybe it wasn't so different from Alex's situation, except he treated the girl like they were in a relationship, so the boundaries got blurred. With Ken, she was honest and told him, in no uncertain terms, that they had no future together. Kyle had hurt her badly when he cheated on her with one of the band's groupies, and she wasn't about to open her heart like that again. No man was going to control her, or her life, or her emotions ever again. It wasn't worth it to her.

"Nice is girl code for *bleh*," Becca pointed out with a cringe, and Angel shrugged.

"He's been good to me. I'm not seeing him that much anymore, anyway. I felt like I was leading him on. I know he wants more and I don't."

"No shit? Probably the bleh factor kicking in," Becca deadpanned. "He's not bad looking, but his personality—not so much."

"He's not *that* bad. He's sweet." Angel shook her head and chuckled.

"Yeah? There you go with more code-speak again. Translation? *Boring*. You need to get out more, Angel." Becca shook her head knowingly. She was well aware that Angel was not into this lawyer at all. "When you start using adjectives like amazing, fuckhawt or magic peen, *then* I'll know your vag is at attention."

"Magic peen is an adjective *and* a noun," Angel pointed out with a smirk.

"Yeah, well, I think you get my point."

*****

Alex paced back and forth in front of his desk, impatient for Cole to call him back. It was Saturday and the office was empty, most of the lights were off, and it was eerily silent. Avery Enterprises had three entire floors of the John Hancock Center, and Alex's office was on the Southeast corner of the top floor. Of course, it was the best view of the city and the waterfront, and it was more like a small apartment, with luxurious furniture and a full private bathroom, sitting room, and closet. The sofa was oversized and Alex had found himself asleep on it many times while working late on an acquisition deal or schematics for a new hotel.

Ever since that damn phone call last night, his thoughts were consumed with the incomplete glimpses he'd seen of the mysterious woman named Angel Hemming. He didn't have her face, but he had her words. Just that sultry voice intrigued him more than he was willing to admit, and he was compelled to know more about her. Words were the only thing between them, yet he'd been more aroused than if she'd grabbed his cock and begged him to fuck her.

He huffed in disbelief at his own weakness as his mind darted to the picture Darian had sent and the mystery surrounding the woman attached to it. She was intelligent and seemed to understand how a man's mind worked. Which, in and of itself, was a huge turn-on and something he hadn't come across before. Topped off by that damn snarky, teasing banter, and he was captivated. Alex wanted to know more. Much more.

He hadn't slept much and dawn was breaking over the horizon, shining into his penthouse. As coffee brewed in the kitchen, Alex was already in his personal gym. He spent an hour rowing and running until he'd exhausted himself; the sweat casting a thin sheen on the skin of his muscular chest and arms and running lightly down his face. His original plan had been to drive out to his house and pick up his dog, Max, before going to his parents' acreage on the north side of the city. Instead, he found himself in front of his computer Googling Angeline Hemming.

He shook his head in utter astonishment. *Alex fucking Avery Googling a woman? Pathetic.* The worst part was, he found almost nothing. A nod to her chairing some women's empowerment organization, and small mentions about her in articles surrounding a couple of the highest profile abuse cases that Chicago had seen in the two years since she'd gotten her PhD. The nature of her work kept the details quiet as most of the case files were sealed, but it was apparent that she was well respected and sought after. Alex was impressed. She was professional and she had ethics. The only other thing he found was a press release issued about the new radio show being a platform for her charity work. Nothing personal. Not one damn thing. And what burned Alex's ass more than anything was that there wasn't a single picture to ease his burning curiosity.

He moved across the room, raking both hands through his thick hair, and stopped in front of the windows. It was a clear day and the water of Lake Michigan sparkled in the sunlight, contrasting its dark hues against the light blue, spring sky.

"Fucking hell," Alex muttered to himself. He felt irritated that his thoughts were consumed by a woman he'd never met, and he was angry at Darian for taunting him. He shook his head in disgust. He hadn't even seen her face. *Stupidly, I fell for the goddamned bait!*

It had only been minutes, yet seemed like hours when his brother finally called back.

"Cole, what the hell took you so long?" Alex admonished sharply. He was younger than Cole by two years, but of the three Avery children, Alex was, by far, the most responsible. Cole worked because his father and brother forced the issue, but if he had his preference, he'd be laying on a beach in the Bahamas or Bali instead.

"I'm not home. Otherwise engaged, dude."

Alex grimaced at the slang term. *Ugh.*

"Uh, can't say I give a shit what your state of engagement is, Cole. What's the name of that investigator? The one that Dad has on retainer?"

"Whoa. The CFO doesn't remember the name of the investigator?" Cole teased lightheartedly. While Alex was serious and focused, Cole could make any situation into a joke. "I mean, if I was in charge of all the money, I sure as shit would know who the head of security was."

Alex sighed and ran his hand impatiently through his hair again, his fingers stopping to yank on the strands. "Cole, if you want to be in charge of the cash, I suggest you take it up with Dad. For now, can you help me out?" His voice was flat and resigned, like a parent dealing with a disobedient child.

They shared brotherly love, but there was a decided competition between the two. Cole held a degree of resentment toward Alex because he was technically his boss. Their parents, especially their father, Charles, didn't trust Cole's slacker nature. It was always Alex who stepped in to clean up the mess, and it didn't go unnoticed. He was the model child; always excelling, always doing what was expected and more.

"Bro, forget work. Let's go to the Cubs game this afternoon. Get Darian and Dad, and I'll call Josh, too," Cole rattled on. His complete lack of focus made Alex's mouth tighten in annoyance.

Joshua Franklin was their sister Allison's husband. Ally met Josh on a spring break trip to Cabo San Lucas six years earlier. His family was from a small town in Oklahoma, and though he wasn't wealthy, Allison loved his gentle charm and easygoing nature. Charles hadn't accepted him easily; at first thinking no one was good enough for his youngest child and only daughter. But with fortitude and grace, Josh eventually won him over. Josh refused to take a job within the company, preferring to be self-sufficient and started a small insurance agency. Alex ensured Josh's success by running all of the corporation's insurance policies through the Franklin agency. The Avery account and the connections with the family soon had his agency well networked and extremely lucrative.

"Can you please just give me the. God. Damn. Name?" Alex enunciated every word.

"What's got your shorts in a wad up your ass? Jesus, Alex, you need to lighten up. Have some fun for Christ's sake."

"Someone's got to earn the money, and between the two of us, we know who jacks off. If you want me to go to the game and front the beer, stop pissing with me and tell me what I want to know. I can get my business done while you call the rest of your little playmates."

Cole laughed softly in response. "Fuck you."

"Maybe later, dickhead. The *name*?" Alex wasn't laughing, but he was grinning from ear to ear, and the amusement in his voice told Cole he was joking around.

Alex heard some rustling on the other end of the phone. "Fine. I have to look in my contacts. Hold on."

Alex went to his mahogany desk and sat down in the large leather chair, waiting. He put his phone on speaker and set it on the desk.

"Uh, Bancroft. Jason Bancroft."

"Yeah, that's right. Okay, get tickets and text me with the game time. I'm taking Max to the folks, so I'll grab Dad and meet you there." Alex was already looking up the phone number for the Bancroft agency online.

"Sure. Alex, what's this about?"

"Probably nothing. I'm curious about something, and I can't find much on the net. I'll tell you about it later but not in front of Dad."

"You can get anything online, but it takes time. You need to get some patience."

"I'd rather just have it done. Besides, I don't have time to fuck around on the internet."

"If you're keeping it from Dad, it isn't about the company. And the plot thickens."

Alex laughed without answering. "Don't drown in the quagmire. It's not worth it. See you later."

"Yeah, later."

Alex ended the call and immediately dialed Bancroft's number, groaning when he got the answering service.

"I need to speak to Bancroft immediately. This is Alexander Avery."

"Mr. Bancroft is out of the office. Would you like to leave a message?" The bland female voice on the other end of the phone inquired.

"Just tell him to call me please. It's very important." Alex grimaced; angry he felt such impatience over something that, two days ago, was insignificant. It isn't an emergency, no one was dying nor millions of dollars extorted, but yet he felt anxious, clammy, and his heart rate elevated. *Get a grip, Avery. What the fuck is your problem?*

"I understand, sir."

"I'm not sure you do. He's on retainer for my company, and I need a call back in the next ten minutes."

"I'll try, sir. I'll page him. Can I please have your number?"

Alex complied quickly as he left the office and headed toward his late-model, black Audi convertible. He was soon on his way out of the city, traveling north toward his estate with Aerosmith playing loudly in Dolby Surround Sound. The epitome of a rich, young executive, Alex had all the toys that one would expect in his position but gave little thought to it. He could drive a Lamborghini or live in a mansion with a full staff, but considered both obnoxious and unnecessary, though he liked luxury. He was confident and even arrogant on occasion, but it was a fine line measured by a certain degree of class. Yes, he'd grown up in a family with money, but Charles made him work for every damn thing he had and he was expected to excel. It became second nature to own responsibility for everything and everyone, and he never failed. He'd worked hard, and didn't waste his time or energy feeling guilty. When he wanted something, he made it happen.

*Would Angel Hemming be different?* So far, she wasn't like anyone he'd ever met and he was acting out of sorts. Alex was stimulated beyond belief, vowing that after they met, if he wanted her, he'd have her. She fascinated him in many ways. She was beautiful from what he'd seen, but it was her intellect and sense of humor that drove his desire. He wanted to know if she was as sexy as she sounded; if the incredible confidence she exuded would carry over into the bedroom. His dick twitched at the thought.

He smiled to himself. She certainly seemed luscious in every sense of the word. The brief twinge of guilt at the prompt end of his last relationship was quickly forgotten as the phone rang and he grabbed it from the passenger seat.

"Hello?"

"Mr. Avery, it's Jason Bancroft. How can I help you?"

"I need information about someone."

"Yes, sir. Is this a security matter for the company?"

"No. The reason isn't relevant to the investigation. Find out everything you can about Dr. Angeline Hemming. She's a psychotherapist or something, works with high profile abuse cases, and has a radio gig on Friday nights."

"Do you want the basic rundown? Background check, credit, criminal record?"

Alex laughed. Even he realized how absurd that sounded. "No. I mean, sure, but I want the real *guts*. Where she grew up, family background, education, resume, connections, places she goes, names of her friends. I want to know her routine and if she's seeing anyone."

"Yes, sir."

"If she is, find out about him as well," he said with a wicked grin. Knowing a competitor's weakness always made them a vulnerable target.

Mr. Bancroft chuckled. "How detailed should I get?"

"*Everything*. Down to the name of her fucking dentist."

Jason Bancroft laughed out loud, understanding Alex's real motivation. "Ah. But, what if she doesn't have teeth? Have you considered that?" he joked.

Alex flashed a big smile in response as he changed lanes and floored it. "Oh, *she does* and they're sharp as hell. I've already been bitten."

# 4

# Temptation and Gravitation

*THROP!*

The manila envelope landed on the mahogany desk with a loud thud. Alex threw his assistant, Mrs. Dane, a dirty look at the abrupt gesture. She'd been his right hand since he'd taken the helm alongside his father and had earned a certain measure of Alex's respect. It entitled her to get away with things that someone else might not and cemented their professional relationship with a good measure of friendship. She smirked at him and patted the back of her tightly coiffed chignon with her right hand as she turned to leave the room. She was a robust woman with graying dark hair, perfectly groomed, and steadfast. *Sturdy* was the word Charles used to describe her.

"Wait, Mrs. Dane. What's in this package?" Alex ran a hand down his navy blue and red silk tie and raised his eyebrow at her.

Mrs. Dane was older than Alex by probably thirty years, and she was impeccable in everything she did. He'd never asked her age because his mother told him it was impolite to inquire that of women. Especially one that was older than you. She stopped and turned toward him, brushing an imaginary fleck of lint off of her purple brocade suit. "I have no idea."

He smiled. "Well, *where* did it come from?" He picked it up and looked at the logo on the envelope. *Bancroft Investigations.* "Never mind, Mrs. Dane. Thank you." He looked up at her from his seated position behind his desk. "Did Dad say what this urgent meeting is about?"

"I'm sorry, Mr. Avery. He only said that you were to meet him in his office at 4:30 today. Have you signed the checks I left for you? If so, I can get them in the mail before I leave." Most of the checks from Avery Enterprises were signed with an electronic version of his signature, but when they were over half a million dollars, Alex deigned to sign them personally.

"They're done." He reached in his drawer and handed them to her. It was Friday afternoon and Alex balked at a meeting this late in the day, even if it was with his father. "You're free to leave after you get these in the mail, Mrs. Dane. Have a great weekend."

"Thank you, sir." A genuine smile spread across her gentle face as she walked toward his office door. "You as well."

"I will. Thank you." Alex opened his top drawer and used his letter opener to slit the top of the envelope then pulled out a thick folder. Angeline Hemming was printed on the front, and it was held closed with rubber bands in both directions. There was a note clipped to the front.

*Dear Mr. Avery,*

*Dr. Hemming has a flawless record, near-perfect credit, and impeccable credentials. Nothing stood out as a red flag, but I did include everything for your review. Small town girl from a poor family who excelled academically, she put herself through school with scholarships and a variety of jobs, none of them questionable. She is well respected professionally for her work in domestic abuse cases and active in some of the local charities that are relevant. She owns a condo less than two miles from your apartment downtown.*

Alex's eyes widened. *That close? Maybe I've seen her somewhere.*

*The only photos that I was able to find were her high school yearbook. I've included the scans inside, but they're kind of grainy. She's been seeing a lawyer by the name of Kenneth Gant, but not much evidence of the relationship other than a couple of fundraisers they've attended together. He's clean as a whistle, too, so I hope that is what you were looking for.*

*Her father still works as a janitor in Joplin, Missouri. I found her mother, as well, but there is nothing to substantiate that she is part of Dr. Hemming's life at the present. She resides in Houston, Texas and has since remarried.*

*Regards,*

*J. Bancroft*

Alex had just removed the letter and the rubber bands when the phone on his desk began to ring.

"Alex Avery," he answered, and then flipped through some of the documents as his father's voice came through the phone.

"Alex, you're late. Can you come up now?" Charles Avery asked.

"Yeah, Dad. On my way. Unless we can put this off?" Alex asked hopefully.

His father laughed. "It won't take long."

"Dad, listen, I was going to meet Darian for a few drinks. I promised him I'd play racquetball this week and had to blow him off because of the Toronto trip."

"You can't give your old dad five minutes?"

"All right." Alex wasn't due to meet his friend for almost two hours but was exasperated that he had to delay looking in the folder in front of him. He sighed, closed it, and put it in his right hand desk drawer, then carefully locked his desk. "I'll be up shortly."

On the walk to the elevators, he searched his mind for what his father might want to discuss. The Wellington takeover was going well, he'd taken care of the situation in Toronto, and an offer of employment had been made for the replacement of the incompetent CFO in Munich. *Not bad for a week's work, so what in the hell could it be?*

Charles's office was two floors above, and Judy, his young assistant, smiled at Alex as he walked out of the elevator. She flushed and straightened her hair. Alex smiled at the obvious nerves he created in the girl. She was pretty, but a little shy. Light brown hair and slim figure. Not beautiful. Not memorable, but competent. He lifted his hand and pointed toward the door. Judy nodded and Alex walked into his father's office, closing the door behind him.

Charles was on the phone, presumably with Alex's mother, if the content of the conversation was anything to go by. Alex settled himself in one of the leather wingback chairs in front of his father's huge antique desk and waited for the call to end. This office was a great deal more old-fashioned than his. The furniture was collectors' items, and the walls were well-lined with Charles's classic book collection. Alex's own taste was more modern, more open, and a good deal less cluttered.

"Okay, darling. I'll be home in an hour." His father was dressed similarly to himself: expensive designer suit, custom-made Egyptian cotton shirt and silk tie, Italian leather shoes. They both looked like they stepped out of a GQ magazine and right into the corporate world. Alex released the button of his suit jacket as he waited. "Alex just came in. Yes, I'll tell him." Charles smiled and then replaced the phone into its cradle.

"Your mother said she expects you for dinner on Sunday. Cora loves Max, but she wants to see *you*, too."

Alex rolled his eyes in mock aggravation and then joined his father's laughter. "She sees me all the time. I suppose I can manage dinner, providing she doesn't invite one of those simpering women from the country club."

Charles's eyebrows shot up and his face sobered. "Your mother just wants to see you happy, Alex. She thinks you need someone to take care of you, and you know how much she dislikes Whitney."

Alex sighed. "Well, Whitney's history, so that's no longer a concern."

"Oh?"

"Yes. We broke up a couple of weeks ago… old news. Why isn't Mom on Cole's ass? He's so busy screwing around, his dick is about to fall off, so why am I the focus of every one of her matchmaking attempts?"

His father sighed and nodded in understanding. "Amazing you should bring up Cole, Alex. He's what I wanted to talk to you about. He needs guidance. He seems a little out of control lately."

*Here we go again*! Alex thought and ran an impatient hand through his full head of hair. "Not just lately. Why now? And, why am I always assigned with babysitting duty? '*Out of control*' is Cole's middle name, Dad." Alex's impatience with his older brother was clear and Charles' brows dropped in a frown as he contemplated his next words carefully.

"You don't give him enough responsibility."

"That's because I'm in charge of the bottom line. I don't enjoy flushing millions down the toilet because you want to give Cole some leash, and I'm the one in the hot seat with the board of directors. He isn't focused and you know it."

Charles shook his head. "I know in the past it's been a problem."

"No shit, it's been a problem," Alex interrupted his father shortly. "I love Cole, but all he wants to do is show off and fuck around. You asked *me* to take responsibility and I have, so will you just let me do my job?"

"Alex. Please, just listen. I'm very proud of you. For both stepping up to take the helm and the incredible growth you've at-tained for the company." Charles got up and went to the sideboard, pressed on the top, and the cabinet opened to reveal a complete wet bar. He pulled down a glass and filled it with two fingers of Chivas. He turned toward his son and offered it to him before pouring one for himself. "It's much more than I or the board ever expected. You've done exceedingly well and so quickly."

Alex accepted the glass and pulled at the knot of his tie, loos-ening it, and then reaching in and unbuttoning the top button of his shirt. "Thank you."

"All I'm asking is that you help Cole. I want to put him in charge of something, even if it's small. He feels useless."

"Maybe because he *is* useless. He's the epitome of *lazy*. Has he expressed interest in being productive or is this just another at-tempt to get him to get his head out of his ass?"

Charles eyed his youngest son as he considered his words carefully. "I think if we can figure out what motivates him, we'll have better luck."

"Ugh," Alex groaned. "How the hell am I supposed to do that when he doesn't even know? It's just easier to run the company and give him money to screw off. Believe me; it will be more cost-effective in the long run. I'll just put him on the payroll and have accounting direct deposit into his account."

"Alex," Charles said sternly, "he's your brother, and you will help get him involved."

"You can't force Cole to get involved, even if I do agree… and being involved isn't the same thing as being productive. Hell, who gives a shit about productive? I'll settle for not *destructive*."

"Like I said, find something he has an interest in."

Alex's eyes narrowed, and he ran a hand across the dark five o'clock shadow on his strong jaw.

"Okay, I'll try to find a project that he can't fuck up. A merger or something where we can't help but make a shitload of money, but you realize that if I do that, it's still *me*. He won't learn a goddamn thing. Cole has no ambition to invest the time it takes to find deals like that or figure out which businesses are worth more in pieces, which to acquire, and which to leave on the table. It isn't something someone learns overnight or without sincere interest!"

"Alex!" Charles retorted sharply. His son's blatant honesty was one of his more prominent traits, and sometimes he would benefit from a little more tact in his delivery.

"What? You know I'm right, Dad. This business… it's a gut feeling and research and seeing the big picture. It's *finesse*. Cole lives in the moment. I can show him the processes and where to look, but he has to want to learn, and he has to be hungry. You may have to face it; he might not have what it takes. Why don't you just put him in charge of procurement or something, for Christ's sake? Let him order the fucking paper clips." His full lips lifted in the start of a wry grin.

Charles put a hand on his youngest son's shoulder and squeezed. He knew the expression on Alex's face was teasing. "Thank you, Alex."

"Can you promise me something, though?"

Charles nodded slightly. He knew his son and the way his mind worked—the two of them were so much alike. Alex always got the job done, could always be counted on, even if it meant putting his own life and needs on hold. "Sure, son."

"If he doesn't take it seriously this time, if he blows a bunch of money or worse, makes Avery a laughing stock, this will absolutely be the last time you will ask this of me. I'm done after this."

Charles shook his head sadly. "That's a reasonable request."

Alex stood up and re-buttoned his jacket before striding over to the bar, rinsing out his glass, and setting it on the marble countertop. He sighed heavily and then moved toward the office door.

"Okay, and can you please speak with Cole first? Let him know this is it and that he will follow my instructions exactly. I will drop him on his ass before I'll run around after him and clean up another one of his messes."

"Alex, before you go, how are you doing after the split from Whitney?"

"Seriously? I'm golden." He smiled, thinking of the new challenge sitting in his desk drawer. "Right as rain."

"I'd like to see you settle down, son. Let some nice woman really know you. You deserve the kind of relationship that I share with your mother. There really is nothing to compare to being in the arms of the woman you love."

"Sure, Dad. I'll keep that in mind," Alex scoffed, throwing the words over his shoulder as he left the room. "Have a good night. I'll see you Sunday."

Judy looked up from her desk and cast an admiring glance over Alex as he passed.

"Goodnight, Mr. Avery."

"Goodnight, Judy. Enjoy your weekend."

*Fucking hell*, Alex thought to himself as he walked quickly back to his office to pick up the file from his desk. He glanced at his watch and started to make his way out of the building, racking his brain for something he could give Cole to do that wouldn't cause too many issues if he failed. Alex dug for his car keys and made his way toward the elevator. It opened to find Darian walking out and catching him off guard.

"What are you doing here, man? I thought we were meeting at Murphy's at 6:30?"

"It's damn nice to see you too, Alex! Change of plans." Darian's dark eyes glanced over the thick red folder in Alex's hands. "Taking work home? You dedicated motherfucker." He shook his head as he backed up into the elevator again and waited for Alex to join him.

Alex chuckled. "Hardly. But I'll let you believe that."

*Yeah, whatever,* Darian thought. Alex was the most workaholic son-of-a-bitch he knew, but it had paid off in spades. His focus had made a lot of people a lot of money, and Darian was one of them. He took stock tips from his friend and also purchased stock in Avery whenever Alex had a particularly profitable deal in the works. Alex never gave him the details because that would be considered insider trading, but Darian paid attention to what was going on at his best friend's company. He kept track of Avery Enterprises in the trade magazines and watched how the stock was trending. When Alex bought stocks for his personal portfolio, he would let Darian know and he would follow his lead.

"Seriously, what's in the folder?"

Alex frowned, not sure he wanted to tell Darian that he was investigating the lovely Dr. Hemming. He was itching to read every last report, but he'd have to wait a few hours until Darian got rid of whatever wild hair was currently up his ass.

"My father's on my case to keep Cole busy, and I'm trying to come up with something that won't cost us out the ass." The tone of his voice was amused, but Darian was well aware of how serious the situation could become.

"Yeah. I know how pissed you were last time when he let that merger with Sullivan fall through. Why don't you put whatever that is in your car and I'll drive?"

Alex was perplexed. This was unexpected. "You didn't turn gay on me, did you? Because I'm not really dressed for a date, and I don't want you to be my bitch."

"Shut up, dickhead. You'll be kissing my ass in about 40 minutes. I'm about to give you a gift." Laughing, Darian shook his head, silently admonishing himself for what he was about to do. Alex closed his passenger door and used his remote to relock it.

Alex slid into the passenger side of Darian's Cadillac Escalade and stopped to watch the other man's expression as he buckled in.

"Really. Where are we going?"

"To a karaoke bar in Schaumburg."

Alex sat further back in his chair and burst out laughing. "Yeah, right. Sure we are."

"No, we are, Alex."

"Is this payback for my blowing off the racquetball? I'll give you a thousand dollars if I don't have to watch you sing karaoke. And, in the suburbs? Are you fucking kidding me with that shit?" He was still chuckling as he leaned an elbow on the door and brought his right hand up to his mouth. "You know I don't drink in the suburbs."

"You're a snob, Alex."

Alex considered this for a moment, the amusement clearly written all over his face. "I can live with that." He paused for a few seconds then continued, "This isn't the type of joint with jizz all over the walls, the waitresses have 5 inch fake nails, and you get STDs just from sitting on the bar stools, is it?" Alex was smirking as he said the words, and then his straight, white teeth flashed in a huge smile as he took his sunglasses out of his inside breast pocket and slid them over his vibrant green eyes. "Because my mommy warned me about places like that," he mocked dryly, tongue-in-cheek.

A deep laugh burst from Darian's chest. He couldn't wait to see the look on his friend's face when he saw her. *Fucking priceless.* "This is a *very* special establishment, Alex. You're going to really love it, even if it is lacking the tasty accouterments you just described."

*****

The man at the end of the bar nodded in Angel's direction. He was attractive in a slick, snarky sort of way, wearing an expensive suit and linen shirt that he left open at the neck. Angel inwardly cringed at the mass of dark hair on his chest that looked grotesque against the fake tan and glitter of gold around his throat. She had a feeling that if she went over and squeezed him, oil would literally ooze out onto the hardwood floor. There were several other men eyeing her as she stood at the bar in her stylish designer suit and Jimmy Choo's.

She hated coming into places like this alone. Becca's parents lived in Schaumburg, so the girls would sometimes go out near their home so they could watch Jillian. It was Becca's twenty-eighth birthday, and Angel had agreed to meet her at one of her favorite hangouts.

She turned back to her drink, trying desperately to keep her nose from wrinkling in disgust and silently praying that the man wouldn't make a move. It had been a rough day, and this place, with its fast-talking men who thought they were God's gift to women, wasn't anything she really felt like dealing with.

Wine glass in hand, she looked around, taking in the details of her surroundings. It was dark; an array of black marble and mahogany hardwood floors, deep red upholstered furniture, and low lights. There were speakers along both sides of the room and opposite the entrance, a stage with a small dance floor directly in front of it. The music was loud and the talent was, well... marginal, at best. Angel didn't understand it, but Becca loved this place, and it was her birthday after all. It'd been a while since she'd stretched her vocal cords, and she highly doubted that she'd imbibe as Becca would desire her to do today.

The shark at the end of the bar raised his chin in a nod at the same time as he lifted his glass. *Ugh.* Angel tried her best not to visibly grimace and simply let her lips smile slightly before she turned around in her chair, only to be faced with an array of the same from different sources. Some of them were attractive, she had to be honest, but it took a lot for her to look twice at a man these days. They were more work than they were worth. Her mind darted to the day in the paint store with longing. That would have been a man worth meeting.

Angel was aware that she was attractive, but she worked at it and didn't take it for granted. She had been plain growing up, mostly because she had no mother to show her how to do make-up or take her shopping. Although Joe tried, what did he know about guiding his young daughter on her journey into womanhood?

She'd since made up for it in spades. Her skin was flawless, her nails perfectly manicured, wardrobe impeccably tasteful, yet, hinting at sexy, and hair and make-up meticulous in every detail. When she was working, it mattered, but when she was alone or at home, she didn't think twice about her appearance.

Angel thumbed through the karaoke menu as she waited; opening to the page and artist where she knew Becca would gravitate. Her phone rang and she retrieved it from her purse, glancing at the faceplate as she did so. *Darian.*

"Hey, Darian."

"Hi. I'd like to meet you for a drink tonight before the show. Can you do that? I have some ideas for promotion and wanted to talk to you about it."

"Can't we do that at the studio later? It's my best friend's birthday, and I'm meeting her tonight."

"I see. Well, can I just meet you there? I won't intrude long."

"Umm…" Angel glanced around, not sure if Becca would be pissed at her boss crashing their girl's night out or if the establishment was particularly the place for a business meeting. "It's a karaoke bar out west, so I don't think it would be a good place to talk. It will get loud in here soon."

Darian laughed. "Karaoke! I didn't take you for a singer, Angel."

"Ha, ha." She rolled her eyes at the jab. "I told you. It was Becca's choice, not mine."

"Look, I've had a hell of a day and wanted to unwind a little. I thought we'd kill two birds with one stone, and maybe I'll even let you fly solo tonight."

"Well, when you put it that way." Angel smiled as Becca finally walked in the door, and she waved her over. "Okay. We're at Red. It's out by Woodfield Mall. Do you know where it is?"

"Sure do. Can I come now?"

"Okay. I only have a couple hours until I have to get home and change before the show, so the sooner the better."

"I have to make one stop first and then I'll be right out. You know rush-hour traffic though; it might take me a good hour."

"No problem. See ya in a few." Angel hung up the phone and hugged a smiling Becca in greeting. "Happy Birthday, you gorgeous bitch."

The two women laughed together as Becca stole Angel's drink from her hand and took a sip. "Looks like a tasty crowd tonight." Becca turned toward the bartender. "Steve, can you send over a couple of Cosmopolitans and keep them coming?" She grabbed the music binder from the top of the bar and lead Angel toward a table near the front. Many of the tables were already filled with various men and women, some of whom Angel recognized from other times that they'd been there.

"No one hit on me while I was waiting, so maybe it's better than average."

"Hmmm," Becca said as she pulled out a chair and sat down, watching Angel as she did. "Jesus, girl, you always make me look like such a slog. You had to wear Chanel?" Her eyes skirted over Angel's fitted black suit and lime green blouse. The skirt was a few inches above the knee, the jacket angled in and ended just below the black leather belt that cinched in her waist below the flowing silk of the blouse.

"I came straight from work, and I had court today. I mean, look at this spinster hairdo!"

Becca was in jeans and a cute top, her long blonde hair tossed as she huffed at her friend. "Right, Angel. Is that why that sleaze at the bar is looking at you like he could eat you?"

Angel's hair was in a loose knot at the top of her head, soft tendrils flowing around her face, a rosy blush rushing over her cheeks. "He's harmless."

"Agreed. Creepy fucker, though. But look, there's your boy-friend," Becca giggled, nodding in the direction of another table behind Angel. "He's practically drooling."

Angel smiled, already knowing that when she turned around she'd find someone completely opposite of anything she would normally be attracted to and probably downright offensive. It was a game they played often. She glanced over her shoulder, trying to keep a straight face to find a short, rotund man dressed in a busi-ness suit openly gaping at the two girls. His mouth was hanging open, and he was obviously taken with them both.

Angel bit her lip to keep the laugh from bursting out of her throat but couldn't help a soft chuckle. She looked around, locating a tall, gangly man on the other side of the bar. He was keeping to himself, staring down into this glass, his head covered in a gro-tesque corkscrew comb over, he looked in his mid-fifties.

"So what?" She giggled. "He's yours." Angel's hand was hid-den by Becca's body so she was able to point slightly in the man's direction before she picked up the drink that the waitress brought over. Becca giggled and wrote down a song choice on one of the slips supplied in a pile on the table.

They were both in a fit of controlled laughter when the wait-ress brought their drinks. "So, Angel, will you sing for my birthday?"

Angel wrinkled her nose. "I haven't picked up a real mic in over two years." Her fingers played with the rim of her glass as she contemplated her past. It had been a great part of her life, but it was over. Her eyes lifted and she smiled. "I'm here to listen to *you*."

"Eh, it's like riding a bike. Maybe we can do a duet?" Becca's eyebrows wagged and a smile split across her pretty face. "Besides, gotta give our boyfriends a show. Let 'em know what they're really missing."

"Mmmm..." Angel shook her head at her friend's silliness. "I forgot to tell you, Darian called and needs to talk to me about something for the show. He said it couldn't wait, so he's stopping in here for a one drink. I hope you don't mind."

Becca's mouth quirked a little. "Sure, but he's coming all the way out here? Shit, maybe you're getting fired." Angel grinned at her friend's teasing. "Is he hot?"

"Oh God, Becca. Just go sing, already!" Angel was exasperated. As if dealing with this shit for four hours on Friday nights wasn't bad enough, now she had to deal with Becca's perpetual state of manhunting.

"No, really. Is he?" The blonde girl persisted, eyeing Angel with a small amount of skepticism.

"Yes, he's attractive, and no, we aren't involved. If you're interested, you should go for it."

Becca flipped open the binder to the exact section of the song menu that Angel had predicted: Christina Aguilera. She perused the songs while Angel sipped her drink and tried not to pay attention to the stares they were getting. Even the women were checking them out. Becca read her mind. "It's bad enough when the men hover like vultures. Is my left tit hanging out or something?"

Angel burst out laughing. The woman on the stage was just ending an excruciating version of Katy Perry's *Hot and Cold,* and Angel leaned over to see what Becca was writing down.

"You *are* serious about teasing these hacks."

"Well, go big or go home, right?" She grinned at her friend and then pushed her chair back to take the request to the DJ. It was early so there wasn't a waiting list, and she got right up on stage as the first bars of *Candy Man* started to play. Angel laughed and settled in to listen as her friend dove into the song with gusto.

"Sweet, sugar, Candy Man!" she whispered into the microphone as the big band horns joined through the speakers. Angel was smiling so hard her face hurt as the music filled the room.

Angel couldn't help the small pang drawing her toward the stage. After all, old habits die hard, and those had been some of the best times of her life.

Angel sighed as she let the good memories of Kyle and the guys permeate her thoughts. The band... They started it with a few of their friends the second semester of sophomore year. Angel minored in classical piano, and Kyle had been a bad boy majoring in music. They used to jam in the music conservatory on a regular basis. They were good, and it seemed a natural course to form a real band and try to make some money. Kyle was incredibly talented, and they dated for a couple of years. So many of Angel's happy memories revolved around music, but it all crashed and burned her senior year.

Angel was roused from her thoughts when something touched the sleeve of her jacket.

"Are you going to sing for us, beautiful?" He had a low, raspy voice, clearly caused by years of smoking. His cologne was sickening and overpowering in an attempt to hide the reek of still lingering cigarette smoke, but he was dressed well and screamed money. Angel stiffened; her back straightened in a ridged line. She recognized him as the dark-haired man with the jungle of chest hair who had leered at her when she'd first come in. Her eyes fell pointedly at the hand resting on hers in silent demand that it be removed.

"Um, no. I don't think so."

"I bet you have a beautiful voice. You sound like an angel when you speak." He pulled out the empty chair on her right and sat down without an invitation.

"Listen, I'm here to celebrate my friend's birthday, so if you'll excuse me," Angel began as the man made no attempt to hide his glances down the deep V of her blouse. It was ruffled and elegant, showing just a hint of cleavage.

"Come on, honey…" he persisted.

"I said take your hands off me!"

\*\*\*\*\*

The two men just entering the bar drew some obvious attention, both of them tall, and carrying themselves with a strong sense of assurance. The women all stopped and did a double take. Darian was more aware of the attention. Alex had enjoyed it when he was younger, but had since become immune to fawning females. He was well aware that he was attractive to the opposite sex and while he'd used it to his advantage on multiple occasions, he didn't feel the need to preen or prance under their observation.

This was the first time that either had been to this particular establishment so, no doubt, the regulars were wondering about them. Both were very striking men, one of them almost embarrassingly so, oozing confidence, power and quiet swagger. Commanding in his presence, Alex scanned the room.

"This is nicer than I expected, man. I didn't know you were a singer. If you're hoping to be discovered, I'll front the money to produce you. All you have to do is ask."

Darian's eyes scanned the bar, looking for Angel's slight form as he responded to Alex. "Ha, ha, Alex," he stated dryly. "You're fucking hilarious, but that's not why we're here."

Alex ran a hand through his hair and tried to ignore a chubby redhead to his immediate left, staring at him from her seat. The tight polyester material of her electric blue top was cut low and showed way too much of her overly ample tits. She nodded at him and smiled boldly through brightly stained lips. *Christ.* He broke eye contact hoping she'd take a hint. "Then what are we doing here?"

His friend nodded toward the stage, and Alex's eyes followed the path he indicated. A pretty blonde was doing a decent job of singing and was having a very good time doing so.

"Do you know that woman?" Alex asked.

"Not that one. Look there." Darian pointed toward a table in front of the stage to where a young woman was being approached by a greasy-looking, older man. Alex stiffened involuntarily at her obvious discomfort. The man was a little too flashy to be taken seriously, but he obviously had money.

The woman's back was to him, but Alex could tell by the elegant way she held herself—the upswept dark hair above the graceful slope of her neck and high fashion clothing—that she had a great deal of class; very polished and chic.

She turned angrily against her agitator, the words rushing from her mouth in protest to the man's hand on her arm. Alex caught sight of her profile and a long expanse of leg above a sexy stiletto shoe, and instantly he knew who she was. She was flawless, and his breath caught in his throat, his memory rushing back to that day six months ago in the Home Depot. This had to be fate.

Unthinking, he moved forward, and Darian spoke up to stop him. "Alex, she won't want us to intrude. She can handle herself."

Alex paused briefly. "Is that Angel?" His eyes narrowed at the realization of their real purpose being here. Darian gave a slight nod, though Alex didn't really need confirmation. "I'm not going to stand here and watch that bastard manhandle her," he said firmly and continued his trek toward the table.

"Listen, Oscar Meyer, I don't have a wit of interest here. I would suggest that you take your hand off of me immediately, or

I'll be forced to waste this perfectly good drink by dumping it all over your sorry ass!"

Alex smiled because he couldn't help himself. That *voice*. And even though Angel was pissed and on the defensive, she was incredibly funny. Her breathtaking features were bored, her voice flat and devoid of emotion.

"Come on baby..." the man whined, still not willing to give up. "Just one drink? What do you have to lose?"

"My self-respect, and quite possibly, my lunch," Angel retorted, her anger finally filtering into her tone as she forcibly lifted the man's hand from where it rested on her sleeve.

Alex pulled the chair out on her left, and when she glanced up at him, he finally had full view of her face.

*Jesus fucking Christ, she is beautiful!* he thought.

Porcelain skin, deep red lips, high cheekbones, delicate nose, and those eyes... he could drown in those eyes and be completely happy to do so. The one time he'd seen her when her warm chocolate eyes left their indelible stamp on him, she wasn't made-up, but still amazing. Now... Holy hell, he could barely breathe. He'd never been so intensely or immediately affected by a woman in his life. Based on Darian's description, he reluctantly acknowledged she'd be stunning and more. Before he ever laid eyes on her, he'd known that she was going to shake him to his very core, and now to realize she was the one image he'd struggled to forget and who most likely made distancing from Whitney inevitable.

Angel's shocked eyes widened as she looked into his beautiful face and recognition shot through her. What was he doing here? His dark green eyes were mesmerizing as they locked with hers; a soft, confident smirk on his masculine mouth; his wild mane of hair was lightly mussed, like someone had run their hands through it a hundred times. The top buttons on his white shirt were open and there wasn't a tie, but he was dressed in a navy blue suit.

Armani, if Angel's trained eye pegged it. He was tall like she remembered, with broad shoulders that tapered to a narrow waist shown off by the expensively tailored shirt. Based on the home improvement project, his appearance now was certainly a conundrum. Something inside Angel stirred at his nearness and everything seemed to be moving in slow motion. Her mouth dropped open to speak just as Alex gathered his composure and sat down next to her.

"Sorry I'm late, honey," he said smoothly, a small smile gracing his full lips. "Rough day at the office."

"Uh…" Angel just looked at him while his hand settled on the back of her chair. The other man, clearly taken aback by Alex's presence, finally let go of her arm.

Alex leaned forward, closer to Angel, so he could speak to the man on her opposite side, and she was assaulted by the clean, male scent of him highlighted by expensive cologne, even as her eyes were still unable to look away from his face.

"As you can see, the lady is otherwise engaged. I'm not amused that you're hitting on my girl. Touch her again, so help me God, I will pull your balls out through your nostrils. Understand?" Alex's tone was quiet and level, as if he were doing nothing more than ordering breakfast. He waited as the man's mouth dropped open to speak, but finally nodding in mute silence. "Good. Please excuse us. Immediately." His voice oozed over her skin like warm honey, and she felt a sudden familiarity. That voice. His tone was biting, but still like silk, and the monkey-man rapidly stood to leave them alone. Angel smiled and bit her lip, praying that she wouldn't burst out laughing.

"I'm sorry. She never said she wasn't available. You're a very lucky man."

Angel's heart thumped in her chest as she listened, unable to move a muscle as the scene unfolded before her. It was completely ridiculous. This dark-haired Adonis was a stranger, simply stepping in to help her with an annoying problem, and nothing more... but there was a part of her that wondered what it would be like to really be *his girl*. She'd wondered about those green eyes on multiple occasions, but now to put that voice in this man... could it really be?

"Too true. If I were you, I'd learn that when a woman says 'no', that's what she damn well means." Alex's eyes hardened and then softened when he looked back into Angel's eyes as a giggle burst from her chest while the man retreated. "I'm sorry, but I couldn't let that continue. Are you okay? Did he hurt you?"

She shook her head, still laughing softly. "No, I'm fine, thank you. I was about to throw my drink on him."

"Yes, I heard. Very amusing. I almost let you, just so I could watch." They sat for a few seconds, just looking at each other, neither one able to tear their eyes off of the other. "It would have served the bastard right."

Out of the corner of her eye, Angel caught a glimpse of Darian just as Becca was coming back to the table after finishing her song, clearly checking out the two men. "Oh, I have to speak with..."

Angel stopped and looked from one man to the other, realization of why the voice rang familiar and who the man sitting next to her was, quickly dawning on her. Her happiness at seeing him again soured as his identity hit her square in the face. Her brow dropped and her mouth set into a firm line.

*Fucking Darian. What the hell is he playing at?* She was overcome with disappointment and fury.

"Hey, Angel." Darian greeted her, but she said nothing for a few seconds, silently seething in her seat.

"Darian, you asshole!" she said finally. "And, *Alexander*, I presume?" she asked astutely. "*Whitney's* Alexander?" Her mouth compressed further and the perfection of the last minutes evaporated into thin air.

"Not anymore." Alex winked. "How could I resist the opportunity to meet the woman responsible?"

Angel's mind cranked around the question... did he realize she was the girl from the paint department that day? If he didn't, she wouldn't be the one to point it out. The situation was already embarrassing enough.

Becca's eyebrows shot up and her lips pursed. "Oh, shit," she said as she sat down across from Angel. She searched her best friend's expression trying to determine if she was going to stand up and walk out.

"Oh, let's give credit where credit is due," Angel scoffed angrily. "From what I understand, the ruin of the relationship rests solely on your pompous shoulders. I did nothing more than validate her decision to cut her losses. It's obvious you only think of yourself. I mean, here you are, when I made it clear that I didn't want to speak with you beyond the call the other night, right?"

"Angel, it was—" Darian began but Alex held up a hand to silence him, shooting him a look.

"An error in judgment; nothing more." Alex smiled slyly, which only infuriated Angel further. "I thought you deserved another chance." She sat fuming as he shrugged out of his jacket and hung it over the back of his chair, then unbuttoned his shirt sleeves and began slowly rolling them up, exposing a good portion of his lightly tanned forearms. Angel could easily see the strength as the material tightened over his muscular frame as he moved, and his authoritative demeanor made her pulse speed up.

Becca cleared her throat. "Oh, shit," she murmured again under her breath, and Darian turned toward her.

"That's an understatement. I'm Darian, by the way. Angel works with me at Kiss FM."

Becca smiled, biting her lip as Alex and Angel continued their volatile banter. Darian lifted his arm to signal the waitress as a middle-aged man with a large paunch took to the stage and began rendering a painful version of *New York, New York.*

"Yes, I know who you are. I'm Becca James. It's very nice to meet you."

"I believe it is you, who had the error in judgment, Mr—?" Angel turned decidedly bitchy, her tone harder. She had certainly regained control.

"Avery, but please, call me Alex."

"Well, *Mr. Avery,* thank you for your, um... *interference* a few moments ago but I believe I have some business to discuss with Darian." Her eyes shot to the other man. "What the hell were you thinking bringing him here? Did you really need to talk to me about the show or is this some sick joke?"

Darian didn't answer right away because the waitress was at the table, and he was ordering a round of drinks. When he did, his tone was blasé.

"Angel, are you *dying*? Is this a catastrophe? And yes, I do have some things to discuss with you, but we can do that at the station."

"It's Becca's birthday, and I don't want to ruin it for her, so I'm not going to bitch slap you right here and now, but believe me, this is not the end of this. I should drop you on your ass with the radio show, you arrogant prick!" Angel's anger was causing a flush to rise on her cheeks.

Alex placed his elbows on the table, leaning toward her a little until he could literally feel the heat radiating between them. He longed to reach for her hand, to brush his fingers along hers, or lean into her just enough so their shoulders would touch, but he didn't want to ruffle her feathers any further. He wanted to soothe her, to calm her, and get her to talk to him. "Are you certain that meeting me is such a bad thing? Weren't you even the least bit curious about me?"

"Pfft." Angel laughed sharply and lied through her teeth. "Not at all."

"Oh, really? So you always remember the names of your callers?" Her face was flushed, and he could see she was royally pissed. "Look, after our conversation on the phone last week, I was… well, let's just say intrigued. Don't blame Darian. He's my best friend, and he knew how much I wanted to meet you, Angeline." His eyes bore into hers, and the electricity between them was tangible. The sound of her given name rolled easily off his tongue. It felt good to say it, and he found himself longing to hear his fall from her lips in the throes of passion. He'd certainly dreamed about her enough… but then he didn't know the true seduction that he'd find in her voice. He'd dreamed about her as two different women and was delighted to find she was one and the same.

Darian and Becca simply sat there observing the other two who had all but forgotten about their presence.

"I wanted to see for myself if the chemistry I felt on the phone was as palpable as it seemed," Alex continued. His eyes moved over her face and dropped to her mouth unwillingly. The last thing he wanted to do was disrespect her, but damn if he could help himself.

"Mmmm… and what are you finding out?" Angel leaned into him slightly, her eyes dropping to his mouth and then back up to his eyes seductively.

His lips quirked, and he wanted to reach out and touch her… to see if her skin was a soft as it looked. "I think it's definitely worth exploring further," he said so softly that only Angel could hear him. "And so do you. But we felt that the first time we ran into each other, hmmm?"

Angel audibly gasped. He did know they'd met before, however briefly. Her heart pounded in her chest, the seconds ticked by without a word being said as they stared at each other, neither one wanting to be the first to look away because it would be the same as surrender. Angel felt an obvious pull from this man, but she wasn't enjoying it. It pissed her off that she had been manipulated into the situation, and she wasn't stupid enough to allow his obvious charm to fuck her up. He was the type that could leave a woman in a boneless heap, sobbing after him when he was ready to move on. She had to admit she was still as attracted as she had been the day in the paint aisle. More, since both fantasy men were combined into one. Who wouldn't be, but the warnings in her head were screaming loud and clear.

Darian finally cleared his throat. "Angel, are you planning on singing?" He broke into their conversation, knowing that if something didn't give, Angel would probably go ballistic, and it would be he and not Alex who would get the brunt of it. Really, he couldn't blame her. He'd basically ambushed them both and was beginning to wonder if bringing Alex here was such a good idea after all.

"No," she answered shortly. "I'm plotting murder right now."

Becca coughed and ignored Angel's comment. "She did say she might do a duet with me tonight, though."

Alex was still leaning on the table. He reached forward and picked up the scotch that the waitress must have placed in front of him during their exchange, but he was too caught up in the woman next to him to notice. "Yes, I would enjoy that. It will give me an excuse to look at you."

Goose bumps broke out on her skin despite the close crowd and the heat within the bar. *That damn voice, obviously very practiced in saying things women loved to hear.* He was so sexy he was dangerous, and her worst fears were confirmed. The body and the face were perfect compliments to it and far better than she could have hoped.

"Hmmph," Angel huffed. "You don't seem like the kind of man that needs excuses for anything you do," she retorted sharply.

"See how well you know me already?" he said suggestively, as his white teeth flashed in a perfect smile, and Angel's heart thrummed inside her chest. She pushed the hair on her forehead back hoping her hands weren't shaking so badly that they would give her away.

She ignored the intimacy in his remark but her insides melted despite her anger at both of the men for manipulating her this way. "Well, I don't sing *karaoke*."

"Oh, only in the shower?" He couldn't help letting himself imagine her delicious body, naked in the shower. It was fucking impossible to avoid thinking about sex when he looked at her. Desire surged through him with a force he'd never known.

"Something like that."

"Now that's a picture..." Alex let his words drop off suggestively.

"Angel used to si—Ouch!" Becca grunted when Angel kicked her under the table, shooting her a warning look.

"Surely, for your friend's birthday? She seems to want you to. Come on, I dare you." Alex played with her, and she couldn't help but smile. Becca laughed out loud.

*Of course, he'd have to dare me. Okay, you fucker. Just get a hold of yourself, Angel,* she told herself sternly. *Stop swooning over this bastard. And, now!*

"Well, when you put it like that..." she purred sweetly. Alex got a satisfied look on his face until her tone changed to all business and her arms folded across her chest. "Are you willing to put your money where your mouth is, Mr. Big Shot? I'll do it, but for $5,000 to a charity of my choice."

"Angel's a big philanthropist, Alex," Darian interjected.

"So you've said," Alex answered, his eyes still locked on Angel's face.

Angel shot Darian a warning look that asked him how much he had shared about her with Alex and then challenged Alex. "Well?"

"Done." Alex didn't hesitate, his brilliant green eyes never leaving Angel's.

*Why does he have to be so beautiful?* Why did it have to be *him?* Angel asked herself as her heart plummeted like a boulder in a landslide. *It fucking figures.*

Becca perked up and pushed the song menu in Angel's direction, her eyes dancing with laughter. It was still open to the same page. Angel pulled the book forward, and Alex used looking at it with her as an excuse to lean closer to her once again. He could feel the sexual tension between them, his body was reacting to her nearness, and there was little he could do to stop it. It was damn embarrassing, and he shifted uncomfortably in his chair. She smelled incredible, her perfume wafting around him in a delicious cloud that he'd gladly get lost in forever. If everyone else in the bar dissipated into thin air, he wouldn't have noticed. She made him hungrier than hell, and he felt like a gift from the gods had just been dropped in his lap. Only she was snarling instead of purring like he'd prefer. No matter. He'd overcome. He always did.

Angel glanced at Alex over her shoulder, a question clearly on her face. "What do you think you're doing?"

Alex looked perplexed, and he shook his head and shrugged slightly, like it should be obvious to her what he was doing. "Looking at the songs with you, of course."

"Oh, *no*. If you pick the song, the price goes up."

Alex laughed out loud, and, to Angel's chagrin, she found the sound very pleasant.

"You drive a hard bargain, but I'm willing to concede if it gets you up on that stage. Money is no object. Will double do?"

"Are you hoping to humiliate me by picking something completely ridiculous?" She leaned back and opened both hands toward the book, indicating that he should have at it.

"Not at all. Consider it nothing more than a birthday gift for the lovely Becca. I'm simply buying." Alex glanced at Becca and shot her a panty-dropping smile that went all the way up to his eyes. He was obviously enjoying himself, which pissed Angel off even more.

"Fine."

Angel focused on Becca, who raised her eyebrows and bit her lip in an attempt to hide a mischievous smile.

"This one." Alex pointed to a song in the middle of the page, not even looking to see what it was. He couldn't seem to rip his eyes away from Angel, and he didn't really care what the song was. Any would serve his purpose

"Wow. Is that your version of the scientific method?" Angel mocked sarcastically and leaned forward to see which one he selected. Alex found her response amusing, and his smirk became more pronounced. Her brown eyes darted between the two men. "Are you shitting me with this? Do you even know what this fucking song is about?"

This incredibly intelligent and beautiful woman had such a potty mouth. It was a conundrum, another paradox about this stunning creature, and Alex loved it. He felt sure that he'd discover more and more that he would enjoy about her as time went on. He found himself unable to consider that he might not have that option.

"Look, if you *can't do it*, just say so," he challenged with a lop-sided grin, and Angel's heart bounced around the inside of her chest in response.

"Fuck you," she shot back.

A laugh burst from his chest, and Angel knew that her quick temper unwittingly set her up for the glib reply. "Whatever you say. It would be my pleasure."

A laugh burst from Darian's chest but he quickly tried to stifle it when Angel shot him a dirty look. She quickly grabbed a song request form and began filling it out with the song Alex had chosen.

"Yes, it would be. You have *no idea*," she retorted which only made the others laugh even harder. She smiled because she couldn't help it, silently admonishing herself and working up a glare for the rest of the tables occupants. To look at Alex Avery, it was obvious to every woman present that he'd be an incredible lover. How could he not be? He was so goddamned confident. The way he moved spoke volumes. He was more than comfortable with his body. He literally oozed sex, for God's sake! At least getting up on stage would put some distance between them, which, she inwardly admitted, she needed space to regroup.

This was like nothing she'd ever felt upon meeting someone for the first time, other than the first 20 seconds with him when they hadn't even really met, only shared a smile and light touch. *Oh, Jesus.*

No doubt things would be explosive between them between the sheets. The pull between them was tangible and she was certain that if the eye contact and body language was anything to go on, Alex felt it every bit as strongly as she did. If that didn't give it away, the fact that he was here, in this bar, his sole intention to meet her, was telling. Her heart raced at the thought. It would be a dangerous game to get involved with someone like him, and if she believed what he told her on the phone, he didn't believe in love. The combination of ruthless sexuality, the incredible face, sense of humor, and smooth demeanor was dangerous to any woman. Even Angeline Hemming.

"Oh, I've got a pretty good imagination, and it's working fucking overtime right now. You've just thrown down a challenge that I'm more than willing to accept if you want to play," he said suggestively. "But know this, I play to win."

"Alex," Darian admonished and shook his head, but Alex wasn't listening, he was watching Angel intently; waiting for her response, but she didn't answer.

"Angel, what song did he pick?" Becca asked, and Angel pushed the slip of paper in her direction so that she could read it. Becca picked it up and smiled. "Holy. Shit."

"I know, right?" Angel smiled devilishly at her friend. The men had no clue what the joke was and looked at each other, perplexed. "*Should Have Known Better*. The only one more apropos would have been *Stupid Girls* by Pink."

Darian held out his hand for the slip of paper, and Angel scowled at him as she allowed him to see it.

"Did you put him up to this?" she wanted to know.

He shook his head and let out a low whistle. Being in radio, he was obviously familiar with the lyrics.

"Well, let's get this shit over with, shall we?" she said, holding out her small, elegantly manicured hand, until Darian gave it back to her.

She stood up slowly and, for the first time, Alex was able to get a complete view of her body. He sucked in his breath, glancing quickly toward Darian who mouthed, *I told you.*

Alex's eyes couldn't help but follow her every move. The lime green blouse accented the black of the suit, and the short pencil skirt showed off long shapely legs while hugging the gentle swell of her hips. He couldn't help but stare as she walked up to the stage. The skirt was short enough to give a hint of her firm thighs, yet long enough to be professional. Elegant stiletto pumps fit her style perfectly. The fitted jacked hugged her upper body, emphasizing the enticing swell of her breasts. *Perfect.* Everything about her called to him, and he found himself wanting to peel back those layers of clothes to discover every inch of delicious flesh underneath. More than that, she was extremely intelligent, and he loved the playful banter that they seemed to fall into so easily.

*Fucking hell.* She was delicious in every sense of the word. *Are you fucking kidding me with this woman, D?* Alex thought. To say it aloud would be disrespectful to the other woman at that table, who was, herself, extremely attractive. "So, Miss James, how long have you known Dr. Hemming?" Alex used any opportunity to learn more.

"We met at Northwestern about six years ago. She's a good friend. My little girl adores her."

"You have a child? How old is she?"

"She just turned two last month."

Angel came back to the table and started to remove her jacket, revealing that the blouse underneath was a halter style that left her shoulders and a good portion of her upper back bare. If Alex wanted to look at her, then she'd damn well give him something to see and put him in as much pain as possible.

Angel was done fucking around. Two could play at this game.

It was obvious to Angel that he desired her, and damn it all, she couldn't help herself... he was so unbelievably sexy. It was insane, but it was exciting and frightening all at the same time, but she wanted him as well.

Watching his face as she hung the jacket over her chair, Angel noticed how his eyes narrowed in desire when he looked her over. Satisfaction spread through her like liquid gold, heat racing like fire along her skin. She reached up and pulled out the two pins holding her hair up, allowing it to tumble down her back in all its glory. Alex's mouth opened in surprise. *Bingo!*

Becca winked at Angel in approval of her blatant teasing. "This should be good," she said under her breath, but Darian heard her. "She's gonna chew him up and spit him out. I *love it.*"

"Yeah, that's what I'm afraid of," he replied just as subdued, the two of them having their own conversation.

"Jesus, you don't fight fair," Alex said softly, his eyes sparkling. "You're just gorgeous."

"Aww! Stop or you'll make me feel special," Angel scoffed with a sexy half-smile.

She was shaking on the inside but, outwardly she was in complete control. This man affected her in ways she wasn't comfortable with, and the compliment thrilled her more than she cared to admit. She had to remind herself that this man was a selfish prick who used women for sex without strings. She took a deep breath to center herself.

Alex sobered. "I'm serious. You are extremely beautiful, and you are well aware of that fact. You use it well."

*Like you don't?*

"All's fair, as they say." Angel leaned down toward Alex to make sure he could hear her over the din, and her hair fell forward over her shoulders. His hand reached out to touch the silken strands carefully. "I can count on you to follow through, right?"

"I'll never disappoint you, Angel."

"Mmmm... we'll see. Buckle up, boys."

She walked back to the stage, pulling her skirt up slightly, which allowed her to stand with her feet some distance apart, and then wrapped both hands around the microphone that she stood behind while the 16 bars of intro began to beat to life.

"Here we go," Becca said smugly.

The song was fast, and her legs and hips rocked in time with the music. She looked straight at Alex and he couldn't rip his eyes away even if it would have saved his life. Becca simply sat back like a satisfied cat, mouthing the words to the song as Angel sang.

A slow grin spread across Alex's face as she owned the song, hammering home the words. If he hadn't made the decision before, he made it then. This was going to happen if it was the last thing he did.

As she whispered the last words, their eyes locked. It took everything he had to fight the urge to pull at the front of his pants. He was so engorged it was uncomfortable, but he wouldn't have changed it. He was captivated and completely lost in the woman commanding the attention of the entire room.

Darian's gaze shot from the stage back toward his friend and reversed again. He recognized the look of determination on Alex's face and resigned himself to what was inevitable now. Alex would be relentless in his pursuit. Angel was strong; but was she strong enough to withstand Alex's guile? Darian had yet to witness a woman who could.

When the song ended, she marched back to the table and coolly retrieved her jacket. Alex stood up immediately and took it from her, holding it and then slipping it easily onto her shoulders.

"Allow me," he murmured close to her ear, and the heat of his breath rushed over her skin and she shivered, hoping he wouldn't notice. "You were amazing, Angel. Your voice…"

"Just write the check to Harmony House in Becca's name and send me a copy of the receipt," she said softly over her shoulder, their mouths only inches apart, and his hands squeezed her shoulders after the jacket was in place.

"You fascinate me. That dirty little mouth of yours is so sexy. And to find out it belongs to those amazing eyes…"

She chuckled with an aloofness she was far from feeling. "I wouldn't get too attached," she said softly, pulling free of his grasp before moving around the table to hug Becca goodbye, leaving Alex standing there speechless. "Love you, baby. Sorry I can't stay longer, but I'll make it up to you. Darian, your ass is grass. Stay out of my studio tonight if you know what's good for your balls."

Alex stood still as stone as Angel walked out of the bar. His eyes, like those of every other male in attendance, followed her every step.

# 5

# Push and Pull

BECCA GLANCED AT Alex Avery. He was standing, with his straight back to her, tall and elegant. Easily six foot two, and the way he carried himself; *Egads.* He was the epitome of tall, dark and handsome... with a dangerous edge. Not in a bad, criminal sort of way, but his demeanor screamed that he was someone with power, money, confidence, and not to be fucked with. Becca covered her mouth with her hand to hide a smile. Except her best friend... *she* fucked with him and fucked with him good.

He stood motionless, watching Angel until she disappeared through the door and then finally turned back and sat down, picking up his glass and downing his drink in one gulp. He was clearly affected, and Becca's eyes narrowed as she tried to figure him out. Her blue eyes shot over to Angel's boss who was also studying his friend.

*What the hell?* It was her birthday and she was sitting at a table with two men that she didn't know. *Shit,* she thought. *Happy fucking birthday!*

Alex was studying his empty glass with rapt fascination until Darian cleared his throat and spoke. "I'm sorry, Becca. I didn't mean to chase Angel off like that. It wasn't fair to you."

Becca sat back in her chair and folded her arms across her small bosom. "Well, it was interesting anyway." Her attention turned to Alex, who was still sitting silently in quiet contemplation, but he shifted in his chair and raised his hand to flag the cocktail waitress. He certainly was gorgeous, and Angel couldn't have been unmoved. Her eyes raked over the polished GQ perfection of the man sitting opposite her. She shook her head in amusement. She had to give Angel credit; whatever she was feeling, she hid it well, and Becca couldn't wait to get out of there and call her.

When the waitress made it to the table and eyed both men with undisguised interest, Alex pretended not to notice and was a perfect gentleman.

"Miss James, can I offer you something? A chocolate martini, isn't it?"

When Becca nodded in the affirmative, he ordered a round for all three of them and took out his wallet from the inside breast pocket of his suit jacket and handed over some bills to the waitress without many words. Becca couldn't help but notice the alligator wallet and the perfectly manicured fingernails on his long, elegant hands.

For himself, Alex's first instinct was to get up and follow Angel out of the bar. He was not in a place he was comfortable with or ever found himself in. His mind raced, and he was much more invested in the lovely Dr. Hemming than he wanted to be. What started out as intrigue and curiosity had quickly turned into a need for something more. He wasn't sure if he was grateful to Darian for bringing him here this evening, or just plain pissed off.

Admittedly, he wanted to meet her. Yes, he was insanely attracted to her beautiful face and luscious curves, and yes, her quick wit and intelligence were readily sucking him in. The smartass remarks falling out of those amazing lips made him laugh. She was funnier than hell, and he found that extremely intriguing. It was all good, but he would rather it have been under different circumstances so Angel wasn't on an immediate defensive. He wanted her willing to allow him closer, and now, that possibility was royally screwed. He had some major hills to climb before he'd have the opportunity to know her better, but he was more than willing to do the work.

His body quickened at the mere thought of her, but, before, when he'd seen her the first time, he'd wanted her body; now his interest went far beyond the physical. The realization was amazing and left him reeling. He wanted to *talk* to her, to learn about her, and to have time to get to know her.

"So," Darian began, and Alex shot him a sharp look over the top of his full drink as he took the first swallow.

"Yeah, *so*. What the hell were you thinking, D?" Alex's demeanor was cool and his expression relaxed, but there was a hard edge to his voice. To Becca, it seemed nothing more than a casual conversation. No big deal. But Darian knew Alex well, and he recognized the steel behind his gaze.

"I thought you wanted to meet her. You did, didn't you?"

"Not like this. Now she's pissed. Not exactly the result I was after."

"I don't think she was mad at you, Alex, but, she was angry with you, Darian. Yep. Seriously pissed at you." Becca pointed her index finger in Darian's direction. "She'll probably chew you a new one the next time she sees you. My advice would be to give her a lot of space."

"She can't do anything to me. I'm her boss."

Becca laughed out loud. "That's hilarious! You really believe that shit? Angel is her *own* boss. She'll fire your ass and walk off the show. Just saying, give it some time." Her eyebrow went up and her mouth thinned out in mocking consternation.

Alex's mouth lifted at the corners in the start of a smirk. He liked this girl. She was spunky. Not as feisty as her gorgeous friend, but he could understand why they were close. Both of them were beautiful, vivacious, and full of life. Alex found Angel utterly mouth-watering and the connection he felt was immediate. Dressed down or up… it didn't matter, but now his interest was even stronger, and if it was possible, he found himself more curious than before.

Darian had been dead-on in his description of Angel. Maybe she was too good to be true, but he'd enjoy finding out. Darian's interference made it more difficult, but still, it didn't occur to Alex for a second that he wouldn't be able to overcome Angeline's defenses. *In fact, I think I might even enjoy the game of cat and mouse immensely.* He was smiling to himself when Darian laughed at Becca's warning.

"Nah, Angel's a pussycat. All hiss and spit on the surface, but underneath, I'll bet she purrs like a kitten," Darian retorted and picked up his beer.

"Man, you don't know what you're talking about. She'll put you down. *Hard.* She didn't used to be that way, but well, she's *evolved.* Don't you hear that when she's on air?"

Alex sat listening intently to everything that Becca said and wondered what could have happened to change her. Did she used to be all soft and giving? *Mmmm…* Alex's thoughts were very titillating, and he let his imagination run rampant, enjoying the fantasies that filled his mind about how he would indeed make her purr and what he'd do to get her to put those claws away.

"Where did she learn to sing like that? She's almost professional," Alex asked, scooting his chair a little closer to the table.

"Yes. *Almost*. I can't tell her stories. They're hers to share if she chooses, but don't hold your breath."

"You make her sound harsh but she doesn't seem that way to me. She just seems," Alex searched for the right words, "strong and confident, but I do sense a softer side lurking underneath." *One I've glimpsed before.* Alex was swirling the amber liquid around in his glass as he spoke, more to himself than the other two. "Very engaging. She's really stunning."

Becca studied his face, taking note of his contemplative expression, and smiling softly at his obvious fascination, she looked down at her drink and nodded. He did have a good feel for Angel. He was pretty much right on.

"Engaging and stunning, huh?" Her blue eyes snapped back up to lock with Alex's. "Yeah, that she is. I sometimes think she takes on too much, but she's Angel. Alex, I heard about you and your girl Whitney. The thing is, I like you, so I'm gonna cut to the chase. Angel's no twit like that. She doesn't give two shits about material things or superficial bullshit. Her outward appearance is for her job. She'd just as soon give every dime she has to charity, and your power or money won't matter. She's a great person, and she has the biggest heart of anyone I know, but she protects herself. She's guarded."

Alex sat back in his chair and contemplated his words carefully. "I just want to get to know her. She seems... I enjoy..."

"Yeah, I saw you *enjoying* her earlier. She's better... *more* than most women, but she's not invincible or ambivalent, even if she likes to give the impression she is. So *don't fuck with her*. If you want to get to know her, then let her get to know you. She might play with you for a while, but make no mistake about it, it will be your chain that gets yanked, not hers."

A deep guttural laugh burst from Alex's chest, and Darian looked embarrassed. "I think I might enjoy having my, uh... *chain* yanked, if you will." Alex nodded his head in her direction and took another drink from his glass.

"Whatever. If you think you leave 'em in heaps behind you, so does she. Don't say I didn't warn ya." The pretty blonde pushed away from the table and stood up, both men rising with her. "I gotta go get my kid. Thanks for the birthday drink, Alex. And Darian, glad to finally meet you, but remember what I said. Give Angel her space for a bit if you don't want to start singing soprano."

After the girl left and they sat back down, Alex's hard gaze settled on Darian.

"What the hell is your problem? I just gave you a gift."

"I can't figure out your motivation for throwing us together. You want her. I can almost smell it on you."

"I can't have her. It seems such a waste of a beautiful woman. And you want her more. She'll make you chase her, and maybe I'm tired of seeing women fall over for you. She'll teach you to appreciate the finer things in life."

"It isn't like that."

"Yeah, sure it isn't. Take a look around, for fuck's sake! You're a smart guy, Alex."

He glanced around nonchalantly and noticed three or four women openly sizing him up. "D, they're looking at both of us."

"Man, give it a rest. Admit it. Everything I told you about Angeline is the truth. She's beautiful and amazing."

Alex's fingers of one hand traced around the top of his glass and his eyes followed their movement and his brow creased. "Incredible, yes," he agreed.

"You need someone like her. She'll make you fall in love, and when you take her to bed, you can tell me what it's like."

"It won't happen." Alex's mouth turned down at the corners as he shook his head.

"You have so little faith in your ability, bro'?"

"Not that, asshole. *When* it happens, I won't share the details. Every touch or thought about her, will be mine alone. But, I won't fall in love."

"We'll see."

"I should kick the shit out of you for doing this to me."

"No, you should thank me. But a steak dinner and a few beers will do."

*****

Angel's mind was still reeling when she walked into the radio station two hours later.

*Damn Darian to hell!*

She didn't know what she was thinking or feeling about the gorgeous man she'd met earlier, but she was sure of one thing: his confidence had a presence of its own. Was she pissed, excited, shaken, or stunned?

*Good. Fucking. Question.*

One thing was for sure, Alexander Avery wasn't like anyone she'd met before, and it wasn't because he was so dangerously good looking. It wasn't because that face had haunted her, had become the fodder of every one of her fantasies, and pushed a bigger wedge between her and Kenneth. He was brilliant, successful, funny and probably a plethora of other things that would scare the shit out of her if she took the time to explore it.

*If I'm stupid enough to get sucked in,* she told herself. He's the type to leave them crying in the aisles, begging, while he walks away without a backward glance. Whitney was evidence of his reality, and Angel's mental constitution and resolve were only intensified by her obvious attraction.

She sighed and threw her purse under the desk as Christina bounded through the door in her usual youthful exuberance.

"Hey! You're here early!" she said, setting a full file folder in front of Angel. "Here are the real juicy emails from this week. I went through 'em and the top five are here. It seems like we've been so busy lately with live calls, you may not get to them all. These four hours blow by!" She shoved her hands into the pockets of her khaki shorts.

Angel, having gone home and changed out of her business suit, was dressed in old jeans and a Habitat for Humanity T-shirt that she'd gotten the previous summer. She and Kenneth had taken a week off to help build a home for a woman with seven children whose house had burned to the ground in an electrical fire.

She wound both hands through her long chestnut hair and looked around the desk, letting out her breath in a rush. "Yeah, okay," she said quietly, clearly preoccupied and unfocused.

Christina frowned at Angel's uncharacteristic behavior. It was routine to go over the emails before the show went live, but clearly the other woman's head wasn't in the game. "Angel, do you need anything? Do you still want to go over these emails?"

"Can you give me a minute or two to get organized, Chris? It's been a really long day, and I'm a little scattered right now. I'm going to get some water, and then I should be good to go." Angel looked up at the young woman briefly and then flipped open the folder before letting the flap fall closed again.

"Will we be blessed with Darian's presence tonight? He hasn't called, so I'm not sure if he'll show. Have you heard from him?"

Angel rolled her eyes in disgust, huffing. "He won't, if he knows what's good for him!"

Christina's mouth fell open and her eyes widened at Angel's shortness and tone. "What? Why?"

"I've had enough of him tonight, that's all."

"Ah..." Christina began but it was clear she was filled with trepidation at asking the questions she wanted the answers to.

"O… kay." It was obvious to Christina that if she wanted more, she'd have to push.

"Thanks," Angel answered.

The other woman's brows shot up and she pursed her lips as she turned to leave the booth and take her place on the other side of the glass. Angel sat down and leaned back in the chair.

Christina continued talking but Angel wasn't listening. She nodded in response to something about Glenn, the scruffy jock who just ended his shift, and then moved out of the booth to get a bottle of water from the refrigerator in the small break room at the opposite end of the building.

*What the fuck is my problem?* she asked herself with a slight shake of her head, glancing at her watch. Only ten minutes until she had to be on air.

*Alex Avery.* The name bounced around in her brain along with images of the crooked grin and mischievous look in his deep green eyes as they sparred with each other at the bar. The contrast against his almost black hair was striking. And that fucking voice, even more mesmerizing in person than it was on the phone.

"I should have known that bastard would be freaking perfect," she mumbled as she made her way back into the booth again. Was it too much to ask that he'd be bald or fat with pockmarks covering his face? Did he have to be the dream guy? He was even more killer in a suit.

Despite Alex Avery's charisma or his incredible looks, Angel was more affected by how her body involuntarily responded, her heart racing and her skin flushing with heat. She sighed in disgust as she sat down at the desk once more. She prided herself on her self-control, in both her personal and professional lives. She sure as hell didn't fall into a quivering pile of goo at mere words or sight of a man. *Ever.* So the events of the evening were leaving her somewhat shaken.

She flushed as she remembered the electricity that raced through her as his heated gaze raked her body or how he never took his eyes off her as she sang that stupid song. When he touched her while helping with her blazer, the tangible connection was impossible to ignore. It was all she could do to keep her voice under control. She felt vulnerable and unsettled.

And, his body! Her imagination ran wild with pleasurable possibilities. The broad shoulders that tapered to the slim waist and narrow hips and those goddamned sinewy forearms were enough to make her mouth water, even without that glorious mane of hair that begged for her fingers to rake through. He was tall and rock hard. Rock *fucking* hard. *Rock hard fucking*, her brain protested. She huffed and pulled the file toward her and took out the top sheet of paper, trying to get her mind on anything other than Alexander Avery. At least she could understand the poor girl's plight that had called in two weeks ago. No woman with hormones stood a snowball's chance in hell against all that blatant masculinity and polished confidence. It was no wonder.

Even as Angel tried to maintain her bravado and banter back and forth with him, there was a palpable undercurrent she couldn't deny and it was obvious Alex felt it as well. He hadn't tried to hide it, but she'd be damned if she'd allow him to reduce her to another notch on his very long list of conquests. *No*, she admonished herself; she would remain in control if it was the last damn thing she did. "Why do all the beautiful ones have to be pricks?" she said, still mumbling to herself, sorry now that her fantasy might be dashed. At least before, she could build him up as perfect and not some slick womanizer. She should be glad this happened. She hadn't thought about that bastard Swanson's court case since last week when Alex called into the program. She sighed. On the other hand, she wasn't sure one bad boy was easier to deal with than the other. Just different.

"What?" Christina had returned and overheard Angel's quiet musings.

"Oh, nothing. Darian lambasted me tonight, most likely thinking I'd go all wet and weak like his stereotype of the typical woman."

"What happened? If you don't mind my asking?"

"Yeah... that guy. The *voice*. Remember?"

Christina sat down slowly on the other side of the desk as her eyes widened. "Oh, shit. It was like warm honey. I wanted to take a bath in it; he sounded so damn good."

"That's the one." Angel nodded. "I was out for my best friend's birthday and Darian, that bastard, showed up on some bullshit pretense of talking to me about the show, with this guy in tow."

"Holy crap. He's not Alex Avery? Darian's friend?" The younger girl's face lit up in obvious interest when Angel flashed her a look. "What's he like? Does the voice match? I mean, is he as beautiful as his voice?" She leaned on her fisted hand toward Angel over the desk and the series of questions tumbled from her eager lips. "Um... maybe I don't want to know? It will ruin a fantastic fantasy if he's a schlep."

"Ugh. Not you, too," Angel lamented.

When Christina didn't respond but only stared at Angel with rapt interest, she pushed her hair off her face and kept talking. "Oh, you know... able to leap tall buildings in a single bound." Angel smiled and was rewarded with a small chuckle from her companion. "Hell yes, it all fits. Unfortunately. He's..." she shook her head, "gorgeous, confident, and extremely intelligent, sexy as hell... man candy personified. Just the type of guy that can fuck up a woman's life in a gargantuan way and make her think he's Santa Claus in the process. He's a taker, and from what I can gather, he thinks he can have anything he wants, whenever he wants it. I'm sure he leaves a trail of women crying in his wake."

"You obviously talked to him then."

"Chris, I deal with relationship bullshit every day. We talked a little, but nothing that meant anything. My observations are simply that. Nothing more."

"Did he move you in any way?" Christina and Angel weren't friends, per se, but she'd gotten to understand Angel's controlled demeanor. She'd expect Angel to kick the shit out of any man whose attentions she didn't want, and she knew she could do it, hypothetically speaking. Angel was the female version of the man she'd just described, and Christina had seen the way Darian drooled over her when she wasn't looking... however, Angel was completely indifferent.

"I'm human. He's hot, and after I got over being pissed, he was sort of disarming. There's no getting around it, and as my friend, Becca, so aptly points out to me constantly..." Angel paused, her eyes widening for emphasis and she smiled. "I *do* have a vagina. Good thing I have a brain to go along with it. His relationships are purely physical but at least he's honest about it. If he lied and made promises, now that would be unforgivable."

Christina burst out laughing. "Yes, my vagina is talking to me about him just from your description! But, I thought Darian, I mean—" she stopped.

"Darian, what?"

"I thought he was into you, so why would he introduce you to Superman?"

"Eh... no, he's not. Besides, he's my boss." Angel shook her head. "I like him, but I don't want to date him."

"What about his friend?"

"I'd be lying if I didn't say I find him more than a little tempting." Given how silly she already felt she sounded, Angel didn't feel the need to fill Christina in on their earlier encounter. "I'd literally have to be dead not to notice. He's quite disarming and he knows it. It's not even a matter of opinion; every woman there was practically touching herself, just looking at him. But, he's not dating material. He's not someone you mess around with if you want to come out unscathed. I'm not one of *those* girls. I hope he got that message tonight."

"What do you mean 'those girls'?"

"You know, the kind he's used to. The mewling, needy, '*I'll do anything, just please don't leave me, baby,*' kind."

"Yeah. I get that about you. You're more the, '*don't let the door hit you in the ass on your way out,*' type."

Angel flashed a big smile and nodded. "Am I that bad? We can talk more about it later. I have to start the show."

"Okay. Alex Avery, huh?" Angel nodded again and cued up the first song of her set. "Google, here I come."

Angel smiled and shook her head as she settled the headphones in place. "If Darian calls, tell him to fuck off."

"All righty, then," Christina spouted happily, as she flounced out of the booth to her position behind the glass partition with the phone.

"This is Dr. Angeline Hemming and this is After Dark on KKIS FM. I'm waiting... so give me a call at 800–555–6900 and let's talk."

As the song started to play, Angel couldn't help but wonder if Alex was listening. Part of her wished he was, but she wasn't conceited to think a man like him would take the time. Tonight had been a fun bit of interaction, but that's as far as it would go. She'd made it clear it wouldn't go any further, and he wasn't the type of guy that wasted effort or resources on a dead end.

As the song played, Christina pressed on the intercom. "What if the voice calls? Do you want to talk to him?"

Angel made a rueful face. "He won't," she said, matter-of-factly.

"Are you sure?" Christina paused, with a soft laugh and Angel's head snapped up. "Line two."

Angel's stomach lurched, and she could feel her cheeks start to burn as a flush infused the skin of her face and neck. This was unexpected, and she hesitated and then sat up and picked up the phone, pushing the correct line. "This is Dr. Hemming."

*****

"Angel, I thought we were at least on a first name basis now."

"Hardly, Mr. Avery. What is it you need?"

"Well, that's a loaded question if I ever heard one."

"That isn't what I meant, and you know it. I'm working. I don't have time for this."

"I only called to apologize. Darian shouldn't have launched us on each other like that. He didn't even tell me that you'd be there until I saw you in front of me. And, what a sight you were. You're the most beautiful thing I've ever seen. *Again*."

Angel flushed but remained silent, processing everything, until Alex continued. "I'd like to make it up to you. Have dinner with me tomorrow night." It sounded more like a command than a request, no doubt because he wasn't used to anything other than blatant adoration from his female friends.

"I appreciate your apology, but no. Thank you."

"Why not? Are you afraid you might like me?"

"I have my own reasons, and I don't intend to share them with you." She already liked him. That was the red flag.

"Angel, don't be difficult. I really want to see you again."

"How inconvenient for you, since what you want doesn't really concern me." She bit her lip, trying to hold in her amusement. Why did she enjoy this so damn much?

He laughed. "Are you sure about that?"

"Very."

"You're such a bad liar, Angel; a trait I find extremely attractive. Your face is very expressive. So is your voice. And I'm very happy to pick up the challenge you're throwing down. It will be my pleasure to make what I want become of *major concern* to you."

"Do you have a genie in a bottle or some magic potion that I should know about? No? Then go away. I have to work." She was smiling so hard her face hurt. This was so damn fun.

"You know I won't give up. All I'm asking for is to share a meal with you. I always, *always* get what I want." His voice was husky, and Angel swallowed hard.

"Men like you never ask for anything. You just expect it to be served up on a silver platter. It's utterly repulsive. I'm not the airhead-type so you're barking up the wrong tree entirely," she quipped.

"Don't assume things about me, please. I know what type you are and what type you aren't... That's why you intrigue me so much. I want to *talk* to you."

"Wow. How original. Hey, baby, I want to get into your pants... uh, I mean your *mind*. That's just brilliant. I don't hear an ulterior motive in there *at all!*"

Alex couldn't help a chuckle. "Why are you always busting my chops? I'm a man, you're a woman, and I want to know more. What's the damn mystery? Yes, I'm attracted to you. Extremely. And, I've thought about you several times since the home im-provement store. At least I have the balls to admit it." He was laughing his ass off, and she couldn't help but smile in response.

"Believe me, there's no mystery. I have a feeling that you wouldn't be so interested if I had *any* sort of balls. Look, I have to go. Chris has a caller on hold for me and the song has 15 seconds left."

"Okay, since you said my name in your silky, little voice, I'll let you go for now, but you will hear from me again. Just because I know what I want and how to get it, doesn't necessarily classify me as a player. I would have thought your psychology background would have made you a little more open-minded to the possibili-ties. And, Angel, I'm listening tonight."

With that, the line went dead and left Angel scrambling with her computer to start a commercial break before she took her first caller. As the night wore on and she spoke to her callers, both men and women, about their problems, it was always in the back of her mind that Alex was somewhere listening to every word. It excited her more than she wanted to admit; but, to give her credit, she kept her wits about her.

It didn't help when Christina came in during the first set of spots with her eyes flashing and a flush on her cheeks. "Holy crap! Angel!"

Angel huffed in understanding. "Ah," she said calmly as she wrote notes on one of the emails she planned to address when she went back on air. She smiled and shook her head slightly as she scribbled roughly on the paper. "Google did its work, I guess?"

The younger girl rushed into the room and sat down at the desk across from Angel. "You know I never cuss but… Are you *fucking* kidding me? This man is like… Gah! He's so *hot*! Is his hair really like this? And he's a big corporate dude? Oh, my God! Delish!"

Angel cringed at the slang term, so indicative of someone so young, but hardly a good description of Alex Avery. *Smooth operator. Now that was more like it.*

She looked up and met Christina's stare. "You need to keep your eyes open, girl. He's too beautiful and he knows it. You heard him. He admitted that he avoids emotional commitments. He's dangerous."

"Angel!" Chris exclaimed in exasperation, gazing down at a picture she'd printed out of the man in question. Angel couldn't help but glance at it. It was a cover shot from Forbes for Christ's sake. He was in an impressive office, sitting on the edge of his desk, with one arm resting on one knee, in a dark blue suit, light yellow shirt, and striped tie. "Even if he only wanted sex, who could say no? He's so dang sexy. Just look at him!" She held out the picture.

Angel stood up and crossed her arms across her chest. "Believe me, Chris. I've seen him." *Up close and personal*, she thought as a shiver ran through her. "Do me a favor… just don't start licking the ink off the page, will you?" she scoffed. "Medical insurance doesn't cover stupidity."

Christina shook her head in response. Angel was impossible.

"What did he say on the phone?"

"He asked me to dinner tomorrow night."

Chris's eyes widened. "You have to go!"

She ran her hand through her hair. "That's just it; I don't."

"You're insane. Absolutely bonkers! What could be the harm in a dinner?"

Angel let out an exasperated breath. "I don't need to get tangled up with Alex Avery."

"Not even between the sheets? God! I wish I were you. I wouldn't tell him no, that's for sure." She did an anxious little jig, turning in a tight circle.

Angel's heart thudded heavily. *Well, maybe between the sheets would be fun.* God knew sex with Kenneth had become mundane. Despite her thoughts, Angel admonished Christina's tendency to careless behavior. "You, little girl, need to make wiser decisions."

"Come on, Angel. I hear you every week! I know you're not a prude, and I know you're not against having sex for sex sake."

"If you're an adult and you can protect yourself; physically and emotionally, Chris, then, sure."

"Okay, so… find out more about him."

"We have to get back to work. The phones are lit up like Christmas trees."

When Christina was firmly ensconced at her post, Angel replaced the headphones on her head and took a sip of her water as she watched the last ten seconds of the commercial tick off on her computer screen.

*****

Alex sat on the leather couch in his great room with his Golden Retriever, Max, sprawled out across his lap. The dog was eighty pounds, but he was a huge baby and Alex adored him. They were inseparable when he was in town. He even took him to the office on occasion. Mrs. Dane refused to walk him, saying, in no uncertain terms, that she was no pooper-scooper and he didn't pay her enough to be one. Alex liked her immensely and so allowed the tirade. He'd good-naturedly offered her a raise if she'd do it.

*"Pfft. You can't afford me. If that dog's shit were made of gold, I wouldn't touch it. Are we clear?"* The next day, she'd called a dog walking service to be on retainer and that was that.

It was dark in his house, and he'd discarded his tie, belt, and jacket. His shirt was unbuttoned and left hanging open over his bare chest. His father would chastise him for not wearing an undershirt, but the Chicago summer had been so fucking sweltering.

He was still reeling that Angeline Hemming was the sexy little thing from all those months ago; the soft little girl who invaded his thoughts so much he no longer found the plasticity of Whitney exciting.

Alex listened to Angeline as he threaded his hands through Max's luxurious coat over and over again. He leaned his head back on the couch, letting her voice wash over him. He wanted to hear her words, but since they weren't for him, he was more into the sound of them than the content. *What is it about this woman?* He closed his eyes and let out his breath in a long sigh. *Everything.*

Darian wanted the two of them to go out downtown, and Alex was certain that, if they did, he could be fucking some willing woman instead of spending the evening alone with Max and Angel's dulcet tones. He was somewhat pissed at his obvious weakness. Could he be that gone over her already, even though he knew nothing about her? Just the sight of her, the sound of her voice, her scent... was more than enough to affect him in painful ways.

His mind wandered to the contents of the file folder sitting on leather upholstery in the backseat of his Audi. Probably everything he wanted or needed to know about her was in there, but damn if he didn't find himself resisting it. From what he'd seen and heard, she was utterly incredible, and he wasn't worried that he'd find anything remotely untoward within the reports. More than that, he wanted to get to know her, *really know her*, not read a cold dossier. Suddenly, to do it the right way seemed important to Alex. If things evolved as he hoped, she'd be angry, and it would no doubt ruin any real chance he had of getting close to her.

He shook his head in amazement. In a matter of a few short hours, the contents of the investigation didn't mean a goddamn thing. Physically, she drove him crazy. It was a blatant, tangible thing between them. He knew she felt it, and it excited him enough to make him shake. His cock hardened just remembering the urge he had to place his mouth on the pulse of her neck and touch her hair as he helped her with her jacket right before she walked out of the bar. Uncharacteristically, he'd been helpless to do anything other than watch her leave and feeling out of control in any situation was disconcerting. When she was singing that sexy song, he felt like it was only to him—because it was.

"Fuck," he said into the large room and shifted uncomfortably. Max whined in protest at Alex's movement. "Oh, Max. I'm so seriously screwed."

"Welcome back, this is Angel After Dark... and I'm here for you. What's your name?"

Alex's pulse quickened when Angel's voice filtered through the speakers and filled the air around him. His left hand went to his chest and he started to rub it, just slightly, at the unfamiliar feeling.

"Joanie."

"Hey, Joanie. What can I help you with?"

The caller was crying softly, but as Angel waited for her to answer, he swore he could hear her breathe.

"My... my husband just left me. He's screwing his secretary. Oh, God, it hurts so much! I mean, what about my children? They're so young."

"Oh, Joanie, I'm so sorry, honey." Angel's voice was sympathetic and sad. "So sorry."

"Everyone is giving me all the bullshit clichés. You know, 'you're better off without him, you have a choice to feel better, just move on,' and I can't take more of that. Please don't say that to me."

Alex listened intently and reached for his beer, waiting for Angeline's answer.

"Joanie, people are just trying to help you, and they think, by making less of it than what it is, you will begin to see it that way and it will become less painful. They're hurting because you're hurting, and truthfully, there is nothing they can say or do to take this away. This may be a cliché, but it's true; you will begin to feel better, but it will take time. I won't belittle your pain by telling you it will happen overnight, because it won't."

The caller sobbed harder, and Angel waited for it to lessen a bit before she continued.

"I am not a believer in that bullshit about feeling better being a choice. That's impossible. Things happen in people's lives because of choices other people make. Choices you had no control over. He made the choice and now you and your children are left to deal with it. I don't believe you can just choose to feel better, and it pisses me off when people spew that crap. The best thing I can tell you is that the choices you do have are how you take care of yourself and your children. You have choices about how you react to his choices. Focus on doing what is best for you, and, eventually, you will feel better. And, remember, the children had no choice in this either, and I know you'll put their needs first. Whatever he did, he's still their father."

"I understand." The caller sniffed.

Once again, Alex was impressed by Angel's level-headed ability to see both sides of the situation, and his admiration for her only increased. If she ever had children, she'd never let bitterness keep them from their father. He grinned into the darkness. "Max... she's just about fucking perfect, even if she is a pain in the ass."

Angel continued, "It happened. It won't, or can't, be undone; so you need to decide what you want moving forward. I'm sorry I don't have a magic wand to take the grief away for you. I wish I did. If your friends and family are only adding to your pain, even though their intentions are good, take a break from them as well. Tell them you just need some time to deal with things on your own. Take your kids on a trip somewhere that you have no memories with your husband, or move somewhere that you've never lived with him. All of this will help, little by little."

"Thank you, Dr. Hemming. Can I call you again if I need to?"

"Of course, Joanie. Take care. You're listening to Angel After Dark, and I'll be answering an email from James in Des Plaines after the break. Be right back."

Alex remained where he was on the couch with Max for the remainder of Angel's show; at times pissed at himself that he couldn't pry himself from the spot, and, other times, completely content with the sound of her voice filling the space around him.

He pulled out his cell phone and hit redial, ignoring the missed call from Cole. He had no desire to talk to his brother until the little heart-to-heart that they'd be having on Monday.

"KKIS, this is Chris."

"Good evening again, Chris. Can I please speak to Dr. Hemming?" The giggle from the other end took him aback. "Hello?"

"Um, sorry. Do you wish to speak to her on air, Mr. Avery?"

"How did you know it was me?"

"We've spoken twice now. I recognize your voice, of course."

"I'll tell Angel how competent you are, but no, this is personal."

"Hold on, please."

Alex moved his dog off of his leg and stood up, pacing in front of the stone fireplace. He'd just had his house built the past spring, but the architecture and features were decidedly classic, reminiscent of his parents' estate with dark hardwood floors, lots of marble and stone, and solid wooden beams. Masculine, but refined.

"Mr. Avery, Dr. Hemming has regretfully declined this call. Personally, I think she's nuts, but it is what it is."

Alex was disgruntled. *Shit!* But at least this girl seemed to be on his side. "Thank you... I'm sorry. I don't remember your name."

"Christina."

"Thank you, Christina. Can you please give Angel my number and tell her I'll be waiting for her call."

The girl sighed. "I'm afraid, if I know Angel, you'll be waiting a while, sir."

"Well, tell her, whatever it takes." His voice was low and he surprised himself. When he said those words, he actually meant them.

He could hear Christina's breath rush out. "Crap, hold on."

He heard the phone rustle, and then Angel's impatient voice greeted him. "Alex. I can't talk now. I have to go on."

"Just say you'll have dinner with me."

"It won't get you what you want," she said quietly, and he smiled in satisfaction.

"How do you know what I want? Unless, it's what you want, too."

She sighed, her exasperation clear. "*Fuck.*"

Alex couldn't help it, a surprised laugh burst forth at Angel's expletive. She was so incredible.

"Okay," he said in his most sultry tone. "If that's what you want, you won't get an argument from me. But I was only intending dinner," he teased. "Say yes."

"Ugh. I have a big case to work on this weekend; I need to focus."

"Excuses. You have to eat. Eight o'clock. I'll pick you up at your apartment downtown."

"But… how do you know?"

"Please. You're kidding, right?" Alex waited with baited breath for her to answer and then decided not to push his luck. Things were going well. "You better go, gorgeous. See you tomorrow."

"Put up your dukes, Alex. This shit is on." She tried to make her voice hard, but he caught the amusement behind it.

"This is one fight I'm looking forward to, Angeline. More than you know."

He hung up his phone and looked at it for a second while he waited for her to come back on the air. He couldn't wipe the stupid-ass grin off his face, even if he'd wanted to. He was feeling very pleased with himself.

At the end of her show, Alex was still hanging on every syllable.

"Did you ever meet someone and something indefinable happened? I mean, you felt an instant shock run over your skin at just a look from this person or the slightest touch from his hand? You couldn't control it. Immediately, all your girly parts stood at attention, despite the fact that you knew things about his behavior you didn't particularly like? Yet, he sucked you in with his eyes… something about him was irresistible? Oozing sex and muscled perfection… Were you a helpless, quivering mess?"

Her voice was soft and sultry, dripping desire, and Alex's body hardened immediately. She was speaking to him and he knew it. Teasing, describing exactly how she'd affected him earlier. She

would be the biggest cock-tease of his life, and he loved every
second of it, but was more determined than ever to turn the situation around until she was begging him to take her. His mouth almost watered at the thought, completely in sync with his aching
body. His breathing sped up in an involuntary response.

Her voice changed, laced with laughter as she tried her
damnedest to deadpan. "Yeah... well, that *didn't* happen to me tonight. This is Angel After Dark. See you next week, babies. Be
safe."

The sound of Alex's laughter reverberated through his empty
house combined with the song Angel played at the end of her set;
*Maneater* by Nelly Furtado. He wasn't familiar with the song, but
Angel's message was loud and clear.

*Fucking priceless!*

# 6
# Sexy Bastard

"I TOLD YOU this would happen, Angel!" Becca laughed as she walked through the door of Angel's condo. She was carrying the little girl Angel adored. "Your ass owes me, girl."

"Anja!" the baby squealed as she opened her arms and was immediately transferred from one woman to the other. Angel giggled and put her mouth to the fat little cheek, planting a motorboat series of kisses, ignoring Becca's comments. Jillian wrapped her plump arms around Angel's neck and hugged her tight.

"Jillybean! How's my baby girl?" The two of them laughed together as Angel carried her into the apartment. The little girl's eyes were alight with pleasure. "Thank you for bringing Mommy to Auntie Angel's. I missed you!"

"Meesh you," Jillian copied Angel's words in her little-girl-ese. "Stay."

Angel's eyes widened and her face curved into a bright smile. Her nerves had been on edge, driving her insane at the prospect of dinner with Alex Avery, so a good shot of Jillian was just what she needed. "You want to stay?" The toddler nodded and put a hand out to touch Angel's cheek. "Of course, you can stay, baby. Do you want cookies?"

"Angel!" Becca groaned.

"Oh, can it, Becca. I have oatmeal raisin. At least they have some nutritional value."

"You blow off the gym and then eat cookies. Must be planning a sexathon workout tonight," she said with a grin. "I can't believe he's *the* guy!"

Becca had laughed her head off when Angel had revealed that Alex was the gorgeous missed opportunity from Home Depot.

Angel pulled a big cookie out of the package she'd gotten from Truly Scrumptious earlier in the day. Easily the best bakery in downtown Chicago, and, bonus, they delivered. "Like I said, *can it.* I'm considering bailing, but I don't know how to get in touch with him."

Becca laughed loudly, mocking Angel's words. She sat on a stool across the counter with an arm on either side of Jillian, who Angel perched on the marble counter top. Jillian held her cookie with both hands as she happily munched away.

"You don't expect me to believe that shit, do you? Angeline Hemming, brilliant doctor, can't find a phone number? Please." Her eyes followed Angel's movements. "You dragged my ass around Home Depot three times looking for him, so I don't get your attitude. I mean, how many times did fantasies of him give your vibrator a workout?"

Angel glanced up at Becca from beneath her lashes and sucked in a big breath. She was filled with a mixture of curiosity, apprehension, and just plain lust. Her fingers tapped on the counter in uncharacteristic nervousness that didn't go unnoticed by her friend. "Will you shut up?"

"What's the big deal? You go out with him, play the banter game you guys are so damn good at—tease, tease, tease—drive him crazy, and leave him with a raging boner. That's the plan, isn't it?"

"Maybe; if I wasn't so damn nervous. There's just something about this man that…"

"There's just *a hundred* things about him, you mean. I don't think I've ever seen a hotter guy. I bet his, uh, junk is effing perfect, too. Mmmmmm." Her eyes flashed with wicked amusement.

"Not helping!" Angel had done more than enough thinking about his junk and the many pleasures she'd find underneath his clothes. She had fantasies about that mouth doing unspeakable things to her, hot melding of bodies and passionate kisses. She swallowed. God, she wanted him. Alex made it crystal clear he would go there, so it wasn't like Angel was counting her chickens. There was so much more to this man than sexual magnetism.

Fuck, he was the sexiest bastard she'd ever laid eyes on, but it was more than his looks. Confidence… and *brilliance* oozed out of him. It was easy to resist an attractive man, she'd done it often enough, but Alex Avery punched all of her buttons intellectually, too. Angel knew she'd have to be on guard every minute of their time together. It would be too easy to let the fun they had teasing each other, and the overwhelming attraction, cloud her judgment.

Jillian held her saliva-soaked cookie up, silently offering to share. Angel ran a hand over the little girl's golden hair. "Thank you, baby. That's so nice of you to share." She bent and took a small bite from the least mushed-up edge. "Yum!"

"I know how badly Kyle hurt you. Is that what are you afraid of? You're much stronger now. You can handle him, Angel."

Angel bristled. "I'm not afraid, exactly. I just don't know if it's worth it."

"Well, it will be if you fuck him. Except, I sort of picture it as *him* fucking *you*. Hard." Angel shot Becca a hard look as she gasped in surprise.

"Becca!" Angel picked up Jillian and walked with her into the living room. "For God's sake!"

"*What?*" Becca asked incredulously. "Don't tell me you haven't thought about it! It's likely he's a sex god. I bet he makes women come just by breathing on them." She smirked and followed Angel into the other room. "Let alone his co…"

"Stop, Becca!" Angel burst out laughing but her insides did little flips. It wasn't anything that she hadn't considered herself. "Yeah, you're probably right about his God-like status, but I'd never let myself become a receptacle. Oh, no, if I decide to go there, I want to shake him."

"My Anja, dance!"

Angel hugged the little girl. "In a few minutes, sweet pea. Auntie Angel wants to talk to Mama for a minute. Then we'll dance, okay?" Jillian nodded and shoved the cookie back in her mouth, gnawing at it with her little white teeth.

Becca sat on the couch next to her friend. "Shake him how?"

"Just… I don't know! But he's so confident in his abilities, in bed and out of it. I'd like to see him wanting and uncertain he'll get it."

"Angel. Don't you think he'll get it? Because personally, I think he will," she said tongue-in-cheek.

Angel chuckled. "So, now I'm easy? Alexander Avery will make mush of me, and all my convictions mean nothing?"

"This has little to do with your convictions. Why does taking some pleasure from the man you've been thinking about for months make you a slut? Men use women for sex all the time, and this particular man has admitted that he doesn't do emotions. So… what's wrong with turning the tables? And, he is hot, no denying it. I'd hop on that, if given half a chance."

"He is gorgeous, that's for sure." *But I like him, which makes him a risk,* Angel thought.

"Do you think he's all show and no go? Some attractive guys don't deliver the goods. Know what I mean?"

"I think we've all been there, honey." Angel rubbed the baby's back and bounced her knee slightly underneath her. "Somehow, I'd be extremely surprised if Alex is lacking, in *any* area. That's why he's so dangerous." A shiver ran through her at the thought. She tried to clear her head of the man who had occupied her mind for the last 18 hours. "Plus, I have to work this weekend. I should be at the office transcribing a clinical report right now."

"Which case?"

"You know I can't talk about who it is, but I wish we could put this guy away forever. My gut tells me he's guilty as sin, but if he's managed to cheat the tests, my hands are tied. Effing tests. They're not foolproof. Sometimes, I hate this job."

Jillian climbed down off Angel's lap and started toddling around. "Dink?"

"Sure, sweetheart." Angel got up and walked into the kitchen.

"Water, Angel. She's had too much juice today."

"Okay." Angel filled a sippy cup that she kept for Jillian with water and one ice cube from the door of her refrigerator, returning to the room and handing it to the baby.

"So? Tell me *something about it.*"

"Just a creep accused of raping his stepdaughter. The poor kid was so terrified, she didn't come forward with it right away. By the time they did a physical exam and rape kit, there wasn't enough evidence."

"They're not prosecuting? Kenny's office isn't involved?"

"Yes, but he isn't working on it personally. It basically comes down to this girl's word against the defendant's. Her hymen was broken, but she's sixteen, so it's likely the defense will try to smear her and say she'd had sex with a bevy of boys. Kenneth thinks they'll drag her through the mud badly enough that she might never recover. Ugh, it's a mess. The dude is fairly successful, so the judge slapped a gag order on everyone involved in the case, and the files are sealed. That bastard's rights matter more than the victim's. I hate how the system works. It makes me sick."

"Is her mother on her side?"

Angel nodded. "That's the blessing. She took her child out of the situation immediately, so at least this man can't abuse her again. I only hope I can do enough to get him behind bars."

"What does Kenny say?"

"It will depend on her credibility as a witness and what I can document. The problem is, I have to put down what the tests show. That's the curse of being a clinical psychologist and not a therapist. It's not about my opinion. It's about what I can prove."

"I know you'll do your best, Angel."

"I have a deposition on Tuesday morning, so I have to examine the transcripts. The lawyer is a viper, and the guy himself is pretty scary. That's why I don't need Alex Avery consuming so much grey matter. I can't afford this right now."

"So? Move him out of your head and into your bed, babes. The solution is a four letter word. F. U. C. K."

"Yeah, I get the picture, Becca. I think you're delusional, but thanks." There was no way in hell a night in his bed would banish thoughts of him, would it? More likely, she'd be even more consumed... unless the sex sucked. "Humph!" Angel huffed. Like that was even a possibility.

Jillian toddled up and put her gooey hand on Angel's knee. "Anja, dance!"

"Yeah, *Anja*," Becca deadpanned with a grin. "Dance!"

Angel's face lit up and she giggled, scooping up a squealing Jillian and hurrying over to the stereo. "Dance? Okay, let's dance! What should we dance to, honeybun?"

"Boogee Jooze!" Jillian said happily, and Becca burst out laughing.

"*Boogie Shoes*, it is!" Angel flipped on Jillian's favorite music and immediately the little girl began bouncing in her arms, giggling in delight. Angel sailed her around like an airplane during the horn bridge and the two of them fell into fits of laughter.

Becca settled back and watched her baby giggle in the arms of her best friend as they bounced to the music. Angel and Jillian adored each other to the point that Jillian almost forgot about her mother when Angel was in the room.

The doorbell rang and Becca jumped up to answer it while Angel started the music over again at Jillian's insistence. When she opened it, she was faced with a big bouquet of deep purple Canna lilies topped off by a Yankee's baseball cap, which was all that was visible of the deliveryman behind them.

"Delivery for Dr. Hemming," the boy said.

"Uh, just a second. Angel!" she called. "ANGEL!" she shouted again over the music and then took the square crystal vase from the boy. "She'll give you a tip. Hold on."

Angel hurried to the door with the baby attached at her hip. "Pretty!" Jillian exclaimed and reached toward the flowers. Angel gasped at the beautiful bouquet of at least 3 dozen of the gorgeous blooms. "Hi. Who are these from?" Angel asked, already knowing the answer.

"Alexander Avery, ma'am."

Angel inhaled deeply. "Of course. Just a second, I'll get my purse."

The boy shook his head and put up a hand to keep her from walking away. "That's not necessary, Dr. Hemming. Mr. Avery was very generous. But, there is this, too." He reached out with a small box wrapped in silver paper with a dark purple organza ribbon that matched the flowers.

"Thank you. Is there a card?" Angel asked. Becca came and took Jillian out of Angel's arms.

"No, Anja!" The little girl protested. "Anja!" She started to wail, big tears rolling down her cheeks as she reached out for Angel.

"With the flowers, ma'am. Have a nice afternoon."

"You, also." Angel closed the door and walked back into the kitchen where Becca had set the bouquet on her marble-topped, kitchen island. Her hands trembled as she pulled the white card free. Her name was handwritten on the envelope, but that would be from the florist, no doubt. Angel glanced up at Becca, who looked amused. Jillian still struggled in her mother's arms.

"Anja! Anja!" she cried.

"Just a minute, sweets. Angel will take you soon," she soothed the little girl and then opened the card.

> **These reminded me of you… So unique and**
> **distinctive, beautiful on the outside, but**
> **deeper shades, even more brilliant, inside. I**
> **can't wait to discover more about you.**
> **Looking forward to tonight,**
> **Alex**

Angel was speechless as her hand reached out to touch a delicate bloom. Chocolate Canna lilies were very expensive—deep purple in the center fading to deep lavender around the edges. *He doesn't do anything half-assed, that's for sure.*

She picked up the box then pulled the purple ribbon and ripped the paper away. Inside was the newest version of iPhone. *A fucking iPhone?*

Angel laughed even as the phone rang and Alex's name appeared on the screen. She held it up and showed it to Becca.

"The man's a genius and he's gorge. Now if his peen measures up, I'll have to kill myself."

"Quiet, Becca," Angel said shortly, rolling her eyes, and answered the phone. "Thank you for the flowers. They're lovely."

"It's my pleasure. I hope you don't think the phone is too over the top, but I didn't have your number, and I wanted to hear your voice." Amusement laced every one of his words. Angel could picture the smug expression on his handsome face. "Plus… I couldn't have you helpless if you needed to get in touch with me."

Angel laughed. "Alex, one thing I never am is helpless. Don't you know that yet?"

Alex chuckled on the other end of the line, his voice low and velvety. Angel's heart hammered in her chest when he ignored her comment. "I've planned a very special evening, so don't go getting cold feet."

"I assure you, there is nothing cold about me." She smiled secretly as she thought of her dress, her preparations for the evening, and his audible intake of breath. Her words were meant to seduce and tease. "So a cocktail dress, then?"

"Mmmm… please. I can't wait to see you. Eight o'clock, remember?"

"Yes." Angel wasn't sure what else to say. Her pulse was hammering and her palms were sweating. The man affected her like no one ever had.

"We're going to have a nice time, Angel. I'll be good."

"Is that a promise?" she teased softly. Alex was laughing when she turned off the phone before giving him a chance to answer.

Becca was leaning up against the counter with a now-sleeping child curled into her shoulder and neck.

"What did he say?"

"That he'll be *good*." Angel's eyes flashed with laughter.

"Wow, that bastard is smooth, I'll give him that. You better get your big girl panties on."

"Or off, you mean," Angel said with a confidence she didn't feel. Alex Avery wasn't someone to tangle with unless you expected to get burned. *But in what way?* That was the delicious question that Angel needed answered. "Not sure if he's playing hardball or softball."

Becca rolled her eyes. "One thing is certain, there is definitely going to be some kind of balling going down tonight."

The room blurred before Angel's eyes as she lost herself in her thoughts. Yes, she had to bring out the big guns so that she remained in control of the situation. The more prepared she made herself, the more likely she would come out the victor in this game of cat and mouse. But how would she get the taste she wanted so badly and come out unscathed? *How, indeed?*

*****

Everything had to be perfect. Alex shook his head in self-admonishment. He kept hammering himself. This was a fucking date, nothing more. No different than any other he'd been on in his life. Hundreds of dates and he'd never been nervous. Until now.

As Alex rode the short distance to Angel's apartment in the company limousine, he smoothed down the front of his silk shirt. He'd dressed with more care than usual. His deep brown Armani suit was tailored to perfection, downplayed with no tie, but the expensive cream shirt gave his skin a golden glow where the top two buttons were left open. His hair was its usually messy perfection, his jaw clean-shaven. If he were honest, he had serious intentions of getting more than close to Angeline tonight. He remembered how she smelled and how soft her skin was and suddenly found himself pulling at the crotch of his pants as his cock swelled and his heart raced in anticipation. He'd never been so turned on by the mere thought of someone before. It was an uncomfortable problem to have.

"Fuck, Avery. Get some control."

"Did you say something, Sir?" the driver asked and glanced in the rearview mirror.

"Nothing, Martin. Thank you."

The sun was still up but low on the horizon. Alex glanced out the window, watching it flash between the buildings as it set. He pulled in a deep breath. He wasn't sure how the evening would end, wasn't even sure how he *wanted* it to end.

He'd argued with himself for the past 24 hours since he'd come face-to-face with her again. He had to be honest with himself and with her. Angeline Hemming was not a woman who settled for ambiguity or unanswered questions. And there was no question, when it came to his desire for her—he wanted her... *badly.*

The question was, could he control the want long enough to get to know her? Alex was certain fucking her would only make him want more. To get what he truly wanted, he'd have to treat her with kid gloves. Angel stirred something deep within him that, for the first time, didn't originate in his groin, but it ended there.

Martin pulled up in front of Angel's apartment building and came around to open the door for his boss. The formality of it grated on Alex's nerves, but he forced himself to remain in the car until Martin completed the task. Alex Avery was nervous. He was actually nervous. It was a rare occurrence, only happening when he had a particularly precarious and huge business deal on the table; when the stakes were particularly high. For some reason, he felt the same way now.

Pulling on the cuffs of his sleeves under his jacket, he ran a hand through his thick mane on his way through the doors, the light bit of hair gel he'd used resisting his fingers.

"Jesus Christ," he muttered to himself under his breath. The doorman stepped aside and pulled the door open so Alex could enter. There was a concierge and security in the lobby. He took in the marble floors and brass handles on the doors, the dark wood and eclectic furnishings. All very elegant.

Alex walked to the desk to speak to the concierge. "Alex Avery. I'm here for Angeline Hemming." His breath hitched as he waited to hear the man tell him to go straight to hell. It certainly was something she would do. Just to show him who was boss.

"Ah, yes, Mr. Avery. Dr. Hemming is expecting you. Apartment 315. I'll let her know you're on your way up."

Alex's breathing eased as the elevator made the short trip to the top floor. When the doors opened, he quickly found the cherry wood door with the brass numbers and rang the bell. There was soft music coming from the other side, and he tented his fingers as he waited.

When it opened, his surprised eyes fell on Becca. She leaned against the door in ratty jeans and a pink T-shirt from the fitness club where she worked, her eyes raking him up and down in apparent appraisal.

Alex smirked at her. "Hello, Becca. Nice to see you again. I'm here for Angeline."

"Hi, Alex. Come in." Becca moved out of his way so he could enter the apartment. The lights were low, but Alex's eyes drank in the details, longing to know Angel better. The space had clean, elegant lines; classic furniture, more gleaming cherry wood on the floors, and dark marble in the kitchen greeted him. The artwork was tasteful but sparse; a large fireplace took up most of one wall in the living room, topped off with a large flat screen mounted over it. The vase of lilies he'd sent sat on the coffee table in the living room.

Becca followed him in. "Can I get you a drink? Angel usually keeps a nice assortment."

Alex glanced at his watch. Five minutes past eight.

"Actually, I have reservations at TRU for 8:30." He glanced around and Becca used the opportunity to check him out. Her eyebrows rose and her lips pursed. TRU was a classy French restaurant; extremely exclusive and pricey.

Just as he said it, the door down the hall opened and high-heeled shoes sounded on the floor. He turned toward the sound and froze in place, his breath catching in his chest.

Angel looked amazing. Her legs went on for miles in strappy platform heels accented by a bow around the ankles and a short, little black dress. It was simple and elegant, with a deep halter neckline leaving the inside swells of her breasts bare, but just barely; her shoulders and arms completely so. Hair piled up, accentuating the long line of her neck, with soft tendrils falling around her face; her only adornments were diamond and onyx drop earrings and a thick matching bracelet. Her make-up was subtle and her soft, pink lips glistened softly.

She stopped 10 feet in front of him, soft, alluring... so tempting. Her perfume softly surrounded him as he drew breath into his suddenly tight chest. He couldn't take his eyes off of her, his heart racing. Add to it that, for once, she wasn't busting his chops, and she was absolutely irresistible. His hand came to rest on his chest as he struggled for what to say, torn between looking at her, listening to her voice, getting into her head, or getting into her pretty little panties.

Angel was equally breathless. She'd steeled herself for this moment, but she was still left gasping. He was the most beautiful man she'd ever seen, his suit impeccable and perfectly tailored to his lean, but solid form.

"You're... luminous, just... radiant, Angeline. I... have no words," he said softly, his green eyes alight with desire.

Angel blushed. "Those are pretty good ones. You look very handsome, too. I didn't know what your plans were so... I wasn't sure what to wear."

"You're perfect. Shall we go?" He smiled softly. "The car is waiting."

"I just need my bag." She walked into the kitchen where Becca was watching silently and picked up her clutch from the counter. When she did, she passed Alex and he was presented with the rear view of her dress. It hung loosely on her small body and the back was completely bare down below the waist. He could just see the beginning of the little dimples at the top of her ass.

"Holy hell," he said in surprise. Angel smiled softly, her eyes meeting Becca's, who laughed out loud.

When Angel turned and came back to him, she smirked and glanced up into his eyes. "You didn't expect me to play fair, did you?"

"You're just…" he began.

"Half-naked?" she teased, her eyes challenging him. "Yeah, I know."

Alex smiled and offered his arm. She took it and soon the two of them were in the elevator. "What do you think you're doing to me? I promised to be good, but you make it impossible." He leaned down closer to her ear. Her perfume was intoxicating, and he longed to press his lips to the soft throb of her pulse in her neck. "What do you have on under that dress?" he asked softly, his warm breath dancing on the top of her shoulder.

A slow smile spread out on her face as heat spread out in the pit of her stomach. This wasn't going to be easy. "That's for me to know," Angel stated simply.

"Mmm, and for me to find out." His voice felt like a warm caress on her skin. "I love a challenge."

Angel laughed nervously, the electricity of his gaze and the implication of his words skittering across her skin. It could be that she wouldn't be able to resist the undeniable sex appeal of this man. Fuck, the pull was strong.

"You can dream." She bit her lip to keep from laughing out loud.

"A fact which has been proven in the past few months," Alex admitted, both of them clearly enjoying themselves. A shiver ran down her spine at his words, skittering outward over the surface of her skin. The fact that he hadn't forgotten their first almost-meeting was not lost on her.

Martin was waiting with the car door open, and Alex's hand fell to the back of Angel's bare waist as he helped her inside. This was the first time their skin touched and it rocked them both.

Alex's eyes connected with Angel's when he slid in beside her. She held his gaze. "What?" she asked.

He shook his head and ran a hand through his hair. "Nothing. I'm glad you agreed to join me this evening. You look absolutely stunning." His eyes roamed the bare skin of her shoulders, over her face, and down her cleavage to her crossed legs. "Thank you, for that."

Unexpected pleasure surged through her. Surely such words meant more from this man than from any other. She expected to feel mad attraction and for Alex to launch a full frontal assault, prepared to resist at all costs, but instead, he was seducing her with nothing more than words and an innocent touch. She was in big trouble and she knew it, yet he excited her more than she'd ever been. Either Alex was a much-practiced predator or the mutual attraction was dangerous and tangible... with a life of its own.

Alex told himself that he'd be content to just look at her all evening, talk with her, and learn about her past through conversation and questions. He loved how her eyes lit up with amusement when he teased her and how much it thrilled him when she teased him in return. And, of course, his body was on fire.

"Is Becca your bodyguard tonight, Angel? Is that why she was at your apartment?"

"Will my body need guarding?" she quipped with a smirk. She looked at her lap, playing with the clasp on her purse.

"My intentions were the best of the best, but that dress... damned if I know now."

The sexual tension vibrated in the air between them, and they were both bristling in the plush leather seats of the limousine. It was all Alex could do not to reach out and run his hand down the smooth skin of her arm. Angel felt his glances like a physical caress.

When Martin pulled up in front of the restaurant and walked around to open the door, it was Alex that offered his hand to Angel as she exited the car. She trembled slightly when his warm fingers closed around hers, and as she stepped from the car, he tucked it into the crook of his arm again.

Angel smiled coyly. *The perfect gentleman. No one would know that he was an emotionless cad*, she scoffed mentally. She knew of this restaurant but had never been. It was extremely upper class, and it was almost impossible to get a reservation. Kenneth tried several times but had never gotten the job done.

"I hope you like French cuisine, Angeline. If not, we can go somewhere else of your choosing," Alex murmured softly as they walked through the large mahogany doors, manned on both sides by attendants.

"This is wonderful. Thank you, Alex."

The black-haired hostess lit up like a Christmas tree when she saw Alex; her eyes scanned the woman beside him, darting over Angel from head to toe—the once-over not escaping Angel's educated gaze. She smiled sweetly at the other woman, something like pride surging through her because she was the one on Alex's arm. Angel shook herself mentally. *Snap out of it, Hemming.*

"Mr. Avery! When I saw your name on the reservations list, I made sure to reserve a table by the window. It's such a clear night and the view is fabulous!" the hostess gushed.

"Thank you, Karen. May I introduce, Dr. Angeline Hemming."

"So nice to meet you," Angel said with a polite smile.

"Good Evening, Dr. Hemming. Right this way, please," she said pleasantly.

She led them to a small table at the west edge of the dining room. The sunset through the windows was breathtaking, and Angel took it in along with the simple, open floor plan: white linen, crystal, flickering candles, mahogany floors, and a huge mixed floral

arrangement on a table in the center. There were camellias floating
in crystal bowls on each of the tables, surrounded by six votives.
The whole effect was quite exquisite.

"This is a beautiful restaurant," Angel said as Alex pulled out
her chair, the scent of his cologne was a heady mix of musk and
freshness. She couldn't help but inhale deeply and was intoxicated.
Angel shuddered slightly, hoping Alex would miss it.

"Angeline, are you cold?" His voice was concerned. "Would
you like my jacket?"

"No, thank you. I'm fine."

"I suppose it's the whole half-naked thing you've got going
on, hmm?" His face split into a crooked grin, and Angel's heart
flopped around in her chest.

"Yes. How's that working out for you?"

Alex was seated and he leaned back in his chair, his head
cocked ever so slightly as his eyes raked over her again. "So far, so
good."

She flashed him a smile. Damn if she could help herself. The
waiter was there to take the elegantly folded napkin, unfurl it, and
lay it across Angel's lap.

"Good evening, Mr. Avery, Dr. Hemming. I am Dustin and
I'll be your server this evening," said the young blond man in a
white shirt, tuxedo vest, and bow tie. "Davis, our sommelier, will
be with you shortly for your drink order, and I'll return in a few
minutes." He opened a leather-bound menu and handed it to Angel
and then one to Alex.

"I guess you come here a lot," Angel stated. "Since the staff
knows you."

"Some. It's an excellent restaurant. We use it for business
lunches at times, too."

"Mmm…" Angel's mind was racing, wondering if he brought
Whitney here and if that was the cause of the hostess's curiosity.

She wanted to ask, but decided not to speak about Whitney unless Alex brought her up.

Alex appeared calmer than she felt. "I want to apologize again for Darian's misguided matchmaking ploy. It wasn't fair to you. Angel, I didn't know what he was up to, so I hope you'll forgive me."

She sighed. "Apology accepted."

"I must admit, however, that at this moment, I'm damn glad he was so insistent. You… intrigue me."

"You're just not used to a woman with brains, I guess," she said, amusement lacing her voice.

Alex's lips lifted at one corner but he didn't smile; his eyes serious. "Not one so beautiful," he said honestly. Their eyes locked and the amusement left Angel's expression.

Suddenly, another tuxedo-clad gentleman was standing at the table. He was older and distinguished; his full head of hair, stark white and perfectly in place. "Good evening, Mr. Avery." He nodded in Alex's direction.

"Good evening, Davis."

"Who is this beautiful young lady with you tonight?"

Alex smiled. "Angel, this is Davis, the sommelier here at TRU. Davis, may I present, Dr. Angeline Hemming."

Davis offered his hand and brought Angel's to his mouth for a small kiss. "It's my pleasure, Dr. Hemming."

"The pleasure is mine, Davis. Please, call me Angel." Angel was at ease with this man, and Alex was enjoying the exchange between the two. She was perfect, articulate, classy… comfortable in his environment.

"Angeline." Davis repeated the name Alex had used. "What a beautiful name. It suits you."

"Yes, it does," Alex agreed, his green eyes narrowing and a smile playing on his full lips. Angel had a hard time taking her eyes off of him to speak to the other man. "Angel, would you like champagne or wine with dinner?"

"Wine would be nice, thank you."

Alex was a conundrum. They had bantered back and forth, had very heated exchanges, teased and prodded each other with sexual innuendos, but this version of him was sophisticated and restrained.

Alex looked up at Davis. "We'll be ordering our meal first, Davis."

Over the next few minutes, they perused the menu, and when Dustin returned, Alex gave both his and Angel's meal preferences. After they settled on seafood, he ordered a very expensive bottle of white wine from Davis.

"Montrachet 2002, please, Davis," Alex said without consulting the wine menu that was offered.

"Very good choice, sir. This must be a very special occasion." He left with a wink at Angel.

"You know, Alex, that could probably feed a small village in Africa for a year."

"I doubt that there is much nutritional value in wine, certainly not enough for an entire year," he mocked with a gentle smirk.

"You know what I mean." Angel rolled her eyes.

"If you will enjoy the evening more, if I agree to feed a village in Africa for a year, consider it done. Now... can we move on?"

Angel laughed despite herself. The look on his face was adorable, and she had to kick herself mentally to keep her wits about her. "What do you want to talk about, then?"

"Tell me about yourself—your home and family. Where did you grow up?"

Dustin brought the first course of crusted bay scallops and corn soup with crab. "Thank you, Dustin. This looks delicious," Angel smiled up at the young man and he beamed at her.

"My pleasure. Enjoy," Dustin said and promptly left.

Alex picked up his fork. "So?"

"So, it's boring. Nothing like your glamorous upbringing, I'm sure."

"Tell me. I want to know."

"Well, I grew up in a small town in the middle of Missouri. Nothing much to tell. It was just my father and me. My mother left when I was only six."

Alex remembered from the cover letter with Bancroft's file that her mother was in Texas, but since he hadn't explored it, he didn't know more. Sadness briefly crossed Angel's features, and Alex quickly changed the subject.

"So, no siblings." It was a statement, rather than a question.

"No. You?"

"Yes. I have an older brother and younger sister."

"How come your brother isn't working at Avery Enterprises with you?"

Alex's eyebrow went up and Angel had the grace to flush.

"Er... Christina Googled you." She wrinkled her face. "Sorry."

He put a scallop in his mouth as he watched her quizzically. "I see."

"Look, I was on the phone with you when she did it. I specifically resisted doing it myself." Angel felt a hot rush in her cheeks as his eyes narrowed and then he smiled, obviously pleased that she would wonder about him as he had her.

"Well, Cole's somewhat of a fuck-up." Alex cringed when Angel looked up from her soup. "He'd rather someone else do the work, take the risks and responsibility. He's been a disappointment to my parents, and he always expects me to just give him money. I love him, he's a good guy deep down, but I get very frustrated."

"You being the chosen one; the golden child, right?"

"I guess you could say I was the one who stepped up when I was needed. Avery is a huge conglomerate and we employ thousands of people throughout our various subsidiaries; people whose wellbeing can't be risked on the decisions of someone like Cole. My father needed me, so I switched schools and did what needed to be done." Alex's voice was calm, matter-of-fact, and Angel strained to hear the regret in his voice, but didn't find any.

"So… where were you studying before?"

The courses were changed and the conversation continued. "Julliard. I wanted to be a classical pianist."

Angel gasped. *Wow.* She'd been a music minor at Northwestern, classical piano and voice. They had something in common. "That's um… sorta hot." She smiled across the table.

"I'm surprised your assistant didn't find that out. It's no secret. I've done several interviews and it always comes up. I think I mentioned it in the Forbes article last year."

"Well, I didn't look through her Google pile. She just told me basic information. She was more concerned if your face matched your voice."

Alex smiled and offered Angel more wine. She nodded and he filled her glass. The wine was delicious, and it was making her feel more relaxed. "And?" he asked.

"You'll have to ask her."

He laughed out loud and refilled his own glass. "It's okay, Angel. I Googled you, too."

Her eyes widened as she forked a bite of her salmon. "You did?"

"Of course. I wanted to see if the face and body matched the voice, too." He mimicked her words and they both laughed softly. The sound of her laughter pleased him very much.

"And?" she prodded, tongue-in-cheek.

"I didn't find out much. You're somewhat of an enigma."

"Because of my work, I have to lead a very private life. I'm always under one gag order or another and can't speak about my cases. Sometimes, the perpetrators involved are less than desirable, if you know what I mean."

Alex's heart seized and something that felt like panic made a subtle surge through him. "It sounds dangerous." His voice hardened slightly.

"Sometimes. I suppose it can be when they don't like what I have to say. Many times it's my testing or testimony that puts them behind bars when the victims are too scared to talk or the physical evidence is less than convincing."

"Has anyone ever threatened you?"

She shrugged. "Once or twice."

Alex didn't like the way he felt hearing about the possibility of Angel being in danger. It was foreign and unsettling.

"Surely you could do something else. With your voice and your looks... you could be a super model or get the radio show syndicated. I can talk to Darian."

Angel's face tightened a little. "Like all the other airheads you're used to?"

"That's not what I meant, but why take risks? You're dealing with rapists and abusers, for God's sake. Someone could hurt you. These bastards are dangerous."

"Well, maybe I don't see how I can make much of a difference in the world by sucking in my cheeks and trotting around with my head in the clouds."

"Angel, I didn't mean to offend you, or imply that your work wasn't important, but..." he began, a surge of protectiveness welled up inside him, and he was angry and upset that someone might hurt her.

"Good, because it *is* important. I should be working right now, but instead I'm here with you. The case is a girl that was raped by her stepfather, and the bastard is cheating the tests. I know in my gut that he's guilty, and my hands are tied unless I can find something incriminating hidden in his answers. I've been working on it for months. I was actually taking a break from it the day I was buying paint."

"Who is it, Angel?" Alex asked seriously.

"I can't say. It's a matter of professional ethics."

"I can help if I know who it is," he said shortly. Certainly Bancroft could find something incriminating. There had to be a mistake somewhere that could be uncovered.

"I appreciate your, um... concern, but there is nothing that you can do."

*The hell there isn't*, Alex thought. He wasn't going to push it right now, but he wasn't done with this subject. Not by a long shot.

Dustin came back to clear away the remnants of Angel's fish and Alex's lobster and then set a spoonful of mango-mint sorbet in front of each of them. "Dessert?" he asked.

Angel smiled. "That was delicious, but I don't think so. Not for me." She picked up the sorbet. "To be honest, I think the sorbet between each course was my favorite part of the meal."

Alex leaned across the table and took her hand. "Let's share something. I rarely indulge in dessert, but I feel like it tonight." He wanted to talk to her more, to get closer to her physically as well.

"Am I not sweet enough for you? You have to fill me with sugar?"

Alex chuckled softly. *Oh, beautiful girl, what I would love to fill you with.*

"Yes, sweet and sour. My favorite flavor, so come on," he coaxed. "Just a couple of bites. I love the almond cake with vanilla custard, but if you'd prefer something else..."

His eyes implored her and a small smile played on his full lips.

*Thud.* Alex was lethal. No woman could deny him anything, if her own reactions were anything to go by. "Okay. A couple of bites."

He placed his napkin on his chair as he stood and offered Angel his hand. "Dustin, in the lounge, please."

"Yes, sir. Right away."

Alex's hand fell again to the small of Angel's back as he led her into the bar area. While the dining room was light and filled with white, the lounge was plush black velvet seating, gleaming marble tabletops, and very low lighting. Again, votives twinkled everywhere, and there were splashes of magenta and white in the extravagant flower arrangements.

Just before they were seated, Alex ran his thumb down her bare back from her neck to her dimples, and then spread his hand out on her lower back. It sent electric shocks through Angel instantly. She stiffened in response and felt his breath dance on the back of her neck as he leaned down to whisper to her. "Sorry, I absolutely couldn't help myself. I've been aching to touch you all night."

Angel wasn't sure what to say, or if she should say anything. The pull between them was palpable. She wanted him to touch her... even if it wasn't smart. Alex was already making her feel things that she didn't want to feel, and knowing it, she still couldn't help herself. This was one time when her head wasn't in complete control. Not even close.

They were ushered to a half-moon booth, and when Alex moved in beside her, her pulse quickened. Dustin came back within a few seconds and set the dessert down on the table along with clean wine glasses and another bottle of the expensive white wine. It was wrapped by a linen napkin in a silver ice bucket near the edge of the table.

Angel smirked at Alex. "Now it's two years for that village in Africa." She was nervous at his nearness, could feel the heat radiating between them, and she didn't like feeling out of control.

"Done. Anything you want." The velvet quality was more pronounced because his voice was quieter. She closed her eyes briefly, suddenly imagining that voice making love to her in the dark, his body moving over hers, filling her, his mouth exploring her skin.

*Anything I want?* Her imagination took off like a rocket, and she felt slight heat rush to her cheeks.

Alex picked up a fork and dug into the white cake with chocolate ganache, cherries, and almonds. It looked delicious and he held a bite in front of Angel's mouth, his eyes dropping to her luscious lips at the same time. She opened her mouth, watching his face as she took the cake from him.

It was delicious. The almond cake was slightly bitter, which was a perfect foil for the sweet milk chocolate. *An exquisite and sinful balance.* The words raced through her mind as Angel applied them to her situation with Alex, like the war between Heaven and Hell, angels and the demons. *Was* there a balance? Could she spend time with this man as she ached to do, without losing herself or her heart?

Alex's pulse was pounding equally hard. He took a bite of the cake from the same fork he'd given to Angel. It wasn't much, but the small intimacy made his heart race.

She turned toward him slightly. "What is it you want from me, Alex? Are you trying to get back at me?" she asked boldly, needing the answers.

Alex set the fork on the plate, picked up his wine glass, and met her eyes with his own. "For what? Running out of Home Depot before I could get your number?" He smiled softly, a devilish glint in his green eyes.

"Well, for speaking to Whitney; for the end of that relationship."

*So much for leaving Whitney out of the conversation,* Alex huffed softly. "She didn't end things, Angeline. *I* did. So, no, I'm not mad at you."

She was surprised. "You did?"

"Yes. It wasn't working. I was bored, and Whitney wasn't happy either. I hadn't touched her in more than a month. I had someone else on my mind, I suppose."

His arm was leaning on the back of the booth and his fingers brushed along Angel's shoulder in the lightest of touches, gently tangling in the silken strands of her hair. It might as well have been a lifeline surging energy from one to the other. "Seriously, I've thought about you so much."

"Why didn't you speak to me? You just handed me the tarp. I felt silly standing there waiting for you to say something."

"I had laryngitis, but I wanted to. Badly. But also, I was with Whitney, and you know my rules. No point in starting something I wouldn't be able to finish. It would have been torture."

Angel swallowed and drew in her breath before she nodded. Integrity didn't fit into her womanizer idea of him, and she didn't know how she felt about that. "So what do you expect out of this?"

"I'm trying not to have any expectations, Angel. I find you extremely stimulating—" He paused when she smiled and looked down at her hands. "—in so many ways."

"So..." she paused just a beat before taking the plunge. "You want to fuck me."

Brilliant green eyes contemplated her for a few seconds. "Wow." Alex ran his free hand through his hair. "You cut right to the chase, don't you?"

He leaned in closer to her, the gesture so intimate, like they were a couple and he had every right to invade her space.

"Well?" Angel demanded. "Do you?" She knew the answer but wondered if he'd be honest.

"I'd be lying if I said I haven't fantasized about it ever since I heard your voice the first time. Even without a visual, I was fascinated by just the thought of you, imagining how you'd feel under me and having you moan my name as you came." Alex smiled when she gasped. If she was going to cut to the chase, so was he. "I can sense that you are just as fascinated. This thing between us is stronger than I've ever experienced. And yes, I'm dying to know how it would feel to be with you. But..."

Again, he surprised her. Was this real or some ploy to suck her in? "But?"

"You're amazing, and I don't want to screw this up."

Dark brown eyes starred into his brilliant ones. He met her gaze without flinching and soon she felt his fingers brushing against her cheekbone, his face only inches from hers. Angel drew in a deep breath and still Alex's fingers slowly explored her cheek and then her temple. She was losing the battle.

"Angeline... you're *so* beautiful. What *do* you have going on under that dress?"

Warmth was flooding her body and settling in a tight throb in the pit of her stomach. Her hand reached out for the front of his shirt and he slid in closer. The lounge was dark and intimate and the booth that they were in was in a back corner, completely secluding them from others.

"A blush silk and lace thong and a Brazilian wax," she breathed out, knowing full well the effect it would have on him.

"Oh, my God..." he groaned and leaned his forehead on hers, his arms gathering her close, his fingers burning the skin of her back. "And is your body reacting like mine is right now? If I reached up under your dress, would my fingers find that silk damp?"

"Uhhh... Alex..." she breathed. Suddenly, they were alone, with no comprehension of anyone else in the room and totally consumed with each other.

"Let's have a taste. Just a little taste..." His voice was raspy and rough in his desire.

Angel's mouth parted and she licked her lips, lifting her chin so her mouth was a mere whisper away from his. It was all the invitation he needed. His lips brushed over hers, nudging them apart and licking at them softly until she moaned and she opened to him fully. He groaned into her mouth as they both gave into the want, the kiss deepening, and their tongues sliding against each other again and again.

Angel thought she'd died and gone to heaven. Her chest tightened up and her heart felt like it would fly from her body. He was divine; his mouth devouring and then ghosting, lifting and coming back for more, like he couldn't get enough. His hand slid up her thigh and just underneath the edge of her dress, and her hand moved up into his hair to pull his mouth closer, forgetting where she was.

"Jesus, Angel," he breathed against her mouth and then dragged his lips up to kiss her temple. "We have to stop. It's getting out of control. We have to remember where we are."

Angel's hold on him loosened, but she didn't let him go, her glazed eyes looked into his. "Uh huh…"

"Shit… I've totally screwed my good intentions."

Angel was left trembling, and Alex was clearly moved. "Didn't you expect to kiss me tonight? We both knew this would happen, Alex," she breathed.

Would this insatiable preoccupation go away if they had sex? Would the want go away? She sure as hell hoped so, because she couldn't afford to risk her heart on a man notorious for not falling in love. Not when he was so incredible. Every minute she spent with him only shattered the image Whitney's words planted in her mind. Was he really the selfish, unfeeling user the other woman described? Was his behavior with her tonight an act? Or was this really him?

*What the fuck am I doing?* She made the decision. She wanted him but she didn't want him to own her. She had to take control of herself and of him or she would lose huge.

"Let's get out of here, yeah?" Alex asked and ran his index finger down the side of Angel's face.

She nodded. "Yes. But, we have the wine." *A $3400 bottle of wine just barely opened.*

"So? It's only money, and I can't wait to be alone with you."

*****

In the limo, Alex held Angel's hand, his thumb rubbing over the top of her fingers. The briefest of touches between them was enough to set them both ablaze. She sat close to him in the middle of the seat, and electricity raced between them like a closed circuit.

"Angel, I want to kiss you, but I'm just going to take you home tonight." Alex pulled her hand up and ran his nose from her palm up her middle finger, then placed his open mouth on her palm. She couldn't pull her eyes away from his and her mouth fell open.

"If you want to kiss me, then do it," she urged softly. *"Do it."*

"No." He shook his head and inhaled deeply. "The next time my mouth is on yours it's going to end in an orgasm or two. Otherwise, I can't go there."

"Oh, God." Angel's fingers closed tightly around his as her bones turned to jelly.

"That's why Becca's at your apartment, isn't it; to keep us on the straight and narrow, tonight?"

"I keep a room for them at my apartment because I love seeing the baby, but tonight... I thought it was wise to have her there, yes," she admitted.

He sighed again. "Yes. I'm wishing we would have stayed at TRU and finished the wine now. I'm not ready to let you go yet."

"I do have to work tomorrow, so I should be home in a couple of hours, but... we could always go to your place," Angel suggested, the words ripping from her chest almost against her will. Her eyes closed, not believing she'd just said it out loud. It had taken her six months to go to bed with Kenneth, and with Alex, she was acting like a wanton.

"Um..." His body was tormenting him—heart racing, groin aching, mouth going dry. He wanted her, but as a rule, he didn't fuck at his apartment. Women weren't allowed to invade his personal space. He always went to them so he could get up and leave whenever he wanted. It kept the control in his court.

"Angeline, are you sure?" This woman blew all his rules out the window and he didn't give a flying fuck. "I've made no secret how much I want you, but I'm trying so hard to take this slow. After that kiss, I can't promise I'll be able to resist." Alex's eyes searched hers.

"I'm not asking you to promise... or to resist. As you said, we're both adults."

His eyes burned into hers, searching to see if this was truly what she wanted, because amazing as the revelation was, what she wanted mattered. "Martin, take us home, please."

"Yes, sir," he answered. Alex resisted the urge to close the partition that separated the couple from the driver, also the urge to pull her onto his lap and explore the treasures beneath her dress. His hand still held hers and he lifted it to his mouth again. It was important that she know that he respected her and wanted more than just sex.

"Angeline, this evening was not intended as a seduction. It was intended to make up for Darian's bullshit and to get to know you. Truly."

Angel saw the sincerity in his expression, and she reached out to touch his face with gentle fingers. The slight stubble was already felt under her fingers and pointed out the level of testosterone that surged through this man. He was all man. He was fucking perfect; so male and strong. He made her glad she was a woman.

Unable to stop herself, she leaned forward and pressed her open mouth to his. Instantly, he pulled her roughly against him and his mouth opened to play with hers. She expected him to be demanding in this kiss, but he was tender, his mouth worshiping hers. He was irresistible.

"Oh, baby… Angel," he whispered as his mouth lifted off of hers.

And something inside her did somersaults.

*****

They didn't speak as they rode up in the elevator after Martin dropped them off in the underground garage of his building. Alex swiped his keycard that would give access to the private level where he lived. His fingers were entwined with hers, and the anticipation throbbed between them.

Alex was struggling. He didn't want to treat her casually. He always respected the women he was with, made sure they were satisfied, but with Angel, he wanted to worship her, and he wanted her beyond this one night. The truth of that rocked him to the core.

When they walked into his apartment, he didn't turn on the lights, but pulled her gently to him; his hands now free to roam her naked back and hips. Angel leaned into him, reveling in the feel of his hard muscles pressed into her softness.

Her hands pulled his shirt free of his pants and started to unbutton it, silently begging him to kiss her. Still he resisted. His hands closed around hers to stop her.

"Angel…" he groaned and finally lowered his mouth to the curve of her shoulder. "Ugh, God… we don't have to do this."

"Don't we?" She backed away from him, not taking her eyes off of him.

His chest, revealed by the open shirt, was magnificent, as Angel had known it would be; the hard muscles moving in a beautiful dance as Alex removed his jacket and threw it over a chair. "No," he answered quietly.

"Don't you want me?"

"Without question, but I find myself in unfamiliar territory. I want to see you after tonight, and I don't want you thinking I'm a cad."

Angel, on the other hand, was silently praying that a good roll in the hay would purge this man from her system. Could she be bold enough to take him down and leave him shaken to the point where he couldn't resist? She decided to be honest about her intentions.

"Here is where I stand, Alex. I hate how confused I feel and how out of control I am in this. Believe me... this isn't me." She was trying to get clarity on Alex. Surely he had been with women this soon before.

He drew in his breath. "And you think sex will put it into perspective?"

"The only thing I know it will do for sure is ease the aching." Her words shot straight to his cock as she moved closer again and ran her finger down his bare chest, across his abdominals to the waistband of his pants. His body was as perfect, as hard as she imagined. The muscles rippled under her fingers.

Her perfume and the smell of her skin assaulted his senses.

"You *are* aching, right?" Her voice was seducing him, sultry, and she moved her hand lower, brushing the bulge in his pants. "Mmmm... *yes*," she whispered against his jaw.

*Fucking hell. Is she really all that she seems?* he wondered. Aching was an understatement. Her closeness, her hands on him, the warmth of her breath against his skin, and her mouth so fucking close, was killing his resolve.

Everything in Alex screamed for him to take her. She wanted him; he felt it in her response and heard it drip off her words. He knew that fucking her would be earthshaking, and his body throbbed and shook with anticipation like it never had before. His eyes burned over her, taking in the long expanses of bare skin and imagining more.

Angel moved away from him into the living room, letting him look at her, and making his heart thunder in his chest, his cock so full it hurt. The only light came in from the Chicago skyline, casting her in shadow and wrapping her in a mystery that he wanted to solve. He only saw the outline of her body, but he followed almost against his will. She didn't speak, but her arms rose to the back of her neck as she undid the clasp of her dress. Alex's heart stopped as he realized her intentions. Angel turned, holding the open neckline to her with one arm, the material now free of her shoulders. She was acting out one of his fantasies right before his eyes, but this was more vivid, more exciting, than any fantasy he'd ever had.

Their eyes met and locked, the room dark and silent. After a moment's hesitation, she let the dress fall to her feet.

He couldn't breathe. Her outline against the Chicago night was everything a man could want in a woman: slim waist, softly swelling hips, full, perfectly round, firm breasts; still in her heels and thong, she was perfection.

His cock was overly engorged and straining against his dress pants to the point of pain, his breathing erratic… he was done. Lost. No way he could resist now.

"Angel…" He moved slowly toward her and traced his fingers lightly over her delicate collarbones and down, until both palms were cupping the outline of her breasts. He closed his eyes as his thumbs brushed the pebbled hardness of her nipples. "Jesus Christ! You're so beautiful."

She let him explore her body, her heart threatening to explode, soft sighs and moans falling from her lips. She never wanted a man's touch so much, even though they barely knew each other, she'd never felt more right with someone. Something about it felt inevitable, like the rushing of water over Niagara Falls, powerful and unstoppable.

His hands brushed her waist and the swell of her hips, over her bare butt cheeks, the contours firm beneath his light touch. He felt that to touch her more firmly might make her evaporate into thin air.

Angel shivered and thrilled at his heavy breathing. He wanted her and it made her feel more powerful than she'd ever been.

"Let's go upstairs," he whispered, his mouth tracing hotly up the cord of her neck toward her ear.

"I don't want to wait that long…" Her fingers slid over his chest and down, her heart thumping wildly at the soft line of hair she felt leading below the waist of his slacks. The truth was; the bedroom was more personal than Angel wanted to risk. "I want to feel you, Alex," she breathed out.

He turned her around and over onto the back of the couch and let his hands explore the front of her body, plunging underneath the silk at her sex. "Ahhhh…" He moaned when his fingers encountered her smooth, hairless folds. He wanted to look at her, wanted to place his mouth where his fingers were. He bit down lightly on her shoulder when his fingers found her hot wetness. He'd hit the point of no return and his movements became less gentle and more urgent, each breath heavier than the last. His mouth dragging over the bare skin of her shoulders and neck, he pressed his swollen hardness into her bare ass at the same time as his fingers stroked her roughly, over and over. Alex left her panting.

"God, it feels so good to have your hands on me," she ground out.

"Uhhh, fuck. I love touching you like this. I need to hear you come. I've lain awake consumed with it, Angel." His expert fingers worked on her, one squeezing her nipples and massaging her flat stomach below her navel and the other switching between direct stimulation of her clit and plunging two fingers inside her to imitate what he wanted to do with his dick.

Her heart thrummed in her chest. He was so fucking sexy: his scent, his voice, his words and his body, the confident way he moved, how he knew exactly how to please a woman. God, she was helpless to stop the delicious tightening that was growing within her. She clenched around his fingers and Alex groaned. "God, my cock is so jealous of my fingers right now."

"It feels too good. I don't want it to end yet," she panted softly. Angel reached behind her so that both hands could close around him. He was long and thick, surging against her hands. They explored each other, their touches becoming desperate and frantic.

"Baby, I'll give you more. You've got to let it go. I'll give you more; as much as you want."

She was unraveling against her will, shuddering and quaking in his arms, and still he was relentless, drawing every delicious twitch from her until her breathing evened out slightly. His was still rough, not yet to his release. Alex was wound as tight as a drum.

Angel turned in his arms and slid her hands up his chest, pulling the remaining buttons free, then moving into his hair, her mouth reaching for his. His arms tightened and lifted her so that her mouth was on the same level as his and her butt was barely resting on the back of the couch, and her legs went around his waist. They kissed hungrily, devouring and sucking on each other's mouths. She moaned into his mouth, and he wanted to haul her up the stairs and throw her on his bed. Alex pressed his pelvis into hers, slowly but in hard repetitions.

"I need to feel you inside me. I need to make you come. Are you ready for me?" Angel asked boldly. She wasn't sure who was talking, but it didn't matter because it spurred him on and that was what she needed.

He moved and laid her down backward over the arm of the couch, allowing him an unobstructed view of her body, her breasts, delicate hipbones, and concave stomach. All thoughts of the bed-room vanished.

"You are so incredibly stunning." Alex decided it was time to take control back. He'd give her what she wanted, but only if she gave what he wanted, and it wasn't just his cock sliding in and out of her delicious body. "I don't think I've ever seen anyone more beautiful." His hand reached out and he dragged it down between her breasts, over her stomach to the edge of her thong. His hands curled around it and he pulled the material free of her body. Her eyes were dark and sparkling, half-lidded with desire. She watched as he brought the fabric up to his mouth and nose and sucked in his breath.

"Oh, Alex," she moaned.

"I bet you taste as good as you smell. I am more turned on right now than I've ever been in my life... but I will stop, Angel." His eyes roamed over her bare sex, only a small strip of hair left and the briefest of tan lines visible over her hips and breasts. "You are so damn sexy, woman."

Her mouth fell open. "So, don't stop."

"I will if you don't agree." He moved away for a few seconds and she heard the zipper of his pants and then the foil wrapper of a condom being opened. Soon, he was standing in front of her, and her eyes froze as she watched him unroll it onto his huge cock. Shit, he was gorgeous. She closed her eyes, imagining what it would feel like to have that fill her. Surely her small body couldn't take it all.

Alex lifted her knees and then pulled her shoes free and let them drop to the floor. She moved her feet up his body to rest flat against him, her toes near his shoulders. He rubbed the engorged head of his penis along her wetness and she gasped.

"Are you going to give me what I want?" he growled quietly, continuing to tease them both with the rubbing up and down of the head of his cock against her clit. His eyes closed when he slipped in a little and her heat burned him alive.

"Anything… Just fuck me," she insisted in a breathy whisper.

"This will not be the only time, Angel. Tell me that we'll see each other again, or I'll stop. Say yes and I'll give you every inch of me."

Her hand reached for him and his fingers threaded through hers. "For Christ's sake, say it, Angel! I want to hear it."

"Okay, yes! Yes, Alex."

"Uhhhh…" He let out his breath as he pushed into her. She was wet with desire, the slick heat pure heaven to Alex. "Oh, God… uh, shit." He thrust into her hard and deep—five or six quick strokes—because he couldn't help himself, then slow and long, wanting Angel to feel every thick inch of him as he spread her open. Even as erotic as it was to watch his body slide in and out of hers, he wanted more contact; her skin on his, tasting her breasts and mouth. Again he was shocked at how different this experience was. Normally, he'd be content to fuck and slake his desire without closeness, but not this time. He pushed the thought away as he pulled her up to him. "Come here, babe."

She was slight and he took her weight easily, turning around so he was the one half-sitting on the arm of the couch, her knees coming to rest beside his hips. Her arms wrapped around his shoulders and his around her hips and back. "I want you to ride me," he whispered against her skin, his mouth hot as it dragged wet kisses from the cord of her neck to her breasts. He pulled a nipple into his mouth and suckled it, grazing it with his teeth. Angel gasped, the sensation connecting straight to her clit. He worshiped her flesh as her hips rocked against his, taking him in as deeply as she could. He felt her clench around him and he almost died. His own climax was building and building.

"Angel, God, you feel so good. I could fuck you forever." She wasn't sure if it was moments or forever, but she loved every throb and thrust.

Finally, their mouths crashed together, their tongues delving deeply into each other's mouths as their bodies moved in unison. Angel's heart was full, too full. She closed her eyes against the keening sounds of their arousal coming to a climax, concentrating on what she needed to do to pull him over the edge.

"Angel, I'm gonna come. Fuck, I can't stop." Alex's guttural moan finally tumbled her over the edge. His mouth went back to feasting on hers, swallowing up the soft sounds she made as she climaxed with him. Alex's arms wrapped around her, rocked her against his body, even as he burst inside her, tensing and stilling as she quivered and jerked in his arms. His arms tightened around her and she turned her face into his neck as she surged against him one last time. Now the only sound was the rhythm of their heavy breathing, coming and ebbing in unison.

Keeping their position, their connection, his muscles flexed under her hands as he picked her up and carried her up the one flight of stairs to his bedroom. No woman had ever slept in that bed, but he wanted Angel there. He was totally spent, his muscles shaking, but he wanted to curl her up into him, unwilling to lose the connection.

Angel knew where he was going, and she told herself she should get up and walk out. Show him it was only sex for the sake of sex, but her heart wanted to stay in his arms as long as she possibly could. She felt safe and taken care of, blissful with his heart hammering next to hers. Warm and relaxed still curled around him.

He pulled back the black down comforter and laid her down, holding the edge of the condom as he pulled out. He touched her cheek with his other hand. "I'll be right back."

Angel rolled onto her side, willing herself to get up and go downstairs, get her things, and disappear. She closed her eyes, unsure of what would happen next. What did she want? What was this? He'd made her promise to see him again, but would he be open to more than sex, or were the words he spoke to her that first phone call the real Alex? It was a big risk. *Fuck... I'm in so much trouble.* She closed her eyes, her body already craving his touch, her mind in turmoil.

The edge of the duvet lifted and soon a warm arm was pulling her back against his hard body, and warm breath assaulted the back of her neck seconds before his open mouth settled on her shoulder. Her hand traced the arm around her, unable to stop herself from touching him.

"I should go. I have so much work to do tomorrow."

"That was... mind-blowing. You are iridescent, Angel. Breathtaking." His voice was low, sultry.

"Mmm..." Angel was torn. She didn't want to feel close to him. He would break her heart. So much for her theory.

"Hey," he said softly and rose up on an elbow, pulling her so she was flat on her back. "So? Is the ache all gone now?" Angel glanced up into his face but couldn't hold his gaze.

"You're an excellent lover, Alex."

He sensed the change in her demeanor and frowned. "That's not what I asked... because I'm only left wanting more. I'm aching more than before. You promised you'd see me again, Angel."

"I'll call you," she said and pushed his arm from her, struggling to sit up and trying to remember where her dress and shoes had fallen. *Oh, yes, downstairs.*

"If you need to go, I'll take you. But I want to see you again."

"Alex, can you just let me go? It was a wonderful evening, but I just... am not feeling like myself. I need to get home so I can work tomorrow."

"Fine, but I don't feel right not taking you home," Alex protested.

"Really, I'd rather it be this way," she said softly and reached out to touch his cheek. "Tonight was amazing. Really." Her heart knocked around in her chest when his expression softened. "All of it."

His hand closed around hers and he brought it to his lips, pressing his open mouth so he could leave a lingering kiss on her palm. "Okay," he said against her skin, his eyes on hers. "Can I call you tomorrow?"

"It's your phone," she said softly. Her emotions were confused, she was torn between running away and diving into his arms; part of her willing to risk the heartache however much her mind screamed that she would hurt over this man if she let this go any further. And what was the truth? Was Whitney telling the truth? Was he cold and unemotional? Even Alex had said so himself. Tonight certainly indicated otherwise, but maybe he was just playing games. She was scared because when she was with him, she was weak.

She had to get away before she lost herself even more.

# 7

# Sweet and Savory

ANGEL TIPTOED INTO her apartment, careful not to wake Jillian or Becca. She was completely shaken by the events of the evening. So much for her resolve to keep control of the situation, her theory that sex with Alex Avery would quell the ache was screwed. It only made her hungry for more. He was sexier than any man she'd ever seen. So hot, so practiced, so confident, and so vocal about what he wanted.

Angel was physically quaking and mentally rattled. She didn't even remember the short cab ride home after she'd bolted down the stairs, threw on her dress, and gathered up her shoes. She was out the door and racing down the stairs well before Alex could follow.

His voice still echoed in her head. *"Angel! Stop!"*

She sucked in a deep breath, filling her lungs to capacity as she tiptoed down the hall to her room. His scent was all over her—on her clothes, on her skin—and her heart felt heavy when her bedroom door clicked shut behind her. She dropped her shoes and threw her purse on the bed. With trembling hands, she undid the clasp on her dress, the same one she'd so boldly let loose two hours earlier in front of Alex's huge window in the great room of his apartment.

"What the fuck are you playing at, Angel?" she said with a ragged breath. "He will eat you alive." *How in the hell could I think I'd be immune to all that blatant masculinity and smoldering sex appeal?* Her dress fell in a pool on the floor and she left it where it landed, pulling back the covers, crawling beneath them and folding her body in on itself. She should take a shower, but she was unwilling to wash his essence from her body just yet. Her throat ached, her mind raced, her eyes burned, and her body... felt empty. The physical imprint of Alex was still there, holding her open, aching. Never before had she been left wanting like this, with her mind refusing to shut off. Her breath came hard and deep as she struggled to get her heart and pulse under control.

The phone in her purse started playing *S.E.X.* by Nickleback and Angel started in the bed. Of course, it was Alex calling the phone he'd sent with the flowers. Her brow creased. She should run and keep on running, but she craved the sound of his voice. She wanted him to prove Whitney's accusations wrong and to believe he was so much more than that... wanted it so much that her heart squeezed and iron bands tightened around her chest, making breathing difficult. She gasped as she finally reached for the phone and the music stopped.

"Uhhhh..." *Will he leave a message?* she wondered, angry at herself because she wanted to answer, but conversely that she'd been too slow about it. Seconds ticked by and the beep of the message being recorded never came. Her heart sank. The screen on the phone blurred before it went black.

*Shit.*

Angel clenched her teeth and rolled onto her back, confusion left her off-balance. Did she want to see him or run as far from him as possible? Did she want to fuck him or make love to him? She stopped dead and pulled in another deep breath, her fist slamming hard against the mattress. Those thoughts had no place in the same space as Alexander Avery.

She started violently when the phone in her hand rang again. The words of the song he'd picked for his ringtone burned into her cognizance. How in the hell did he know how she felt? How did he connect with her like he did? Was he some sort of superhuman that got off on screwing with her perfectly organized, safe life?

"*Is* sex always the answer for you?" she breathed into the phone, repeating words used in the song.

Nothing but silence followed.

"Is it?" she asked again softly. The sound of his breathing washed over her, making her body quicken as if he was right there next to her. She closed her eyes. She could feel his breath—the heat; the passion—rushing like a physical caress over her skin.

"I used to think so. Until tonight," he said honestly. His voice was low and velvety smooth. "But I don't know anymore."

It was her turn to be silent as she rolled onto her side and pulled her knees up to her chest. The safest thing… the smartest thing, was to hang up the phone, but she just couldn't.

"Don't say things like that just because you think it's what I need to hear."

He sighed heavily; slightly sad she would have that thought after the magical evening they'd just shared. "I'm not. I wanted to make sure you arrived home safely. Have you?" He was lying on his bed in the dark, moved beyond words by the woman who rocked his fucking world and then evaporated like a ghost in the night.

"Yes."

Neither of them was willing to end the call, each searching for words, reliving the amazing evening they'd just spent together.

Finally. Alex sighed. "I wish you hadn't left. I wasn't ready to stop touching you."

Angel bit her lip, shivers rocking through her body, sending bumps scattering along the skin of her back and limbs, making her nipples hard and her clit throb. "Your voice... Alex, you're giving me goose bumps *without* touching me."

Alex ran a hand down his face, his heart pushing blood all around his body, his cock full and aching. "*Christ*, Angel. Tonight was momentous. I've never felt so... completely connected this fast." *Or ever*, he thought.

"It scares me."

"Is that why you ran away?"

"I didn't run away."

"Didn't you?"

"It's like I told you. That wasn't me."

"Which part? The smart, snarky part that mind fucks me at every turn, or the soft, so sexy part that drives me insane with desire? When you came for me... I've never felt so powerful. It was incredible."

"No, Alex. The part that drops her dress on the first date." She groaned, so softly it made his dick twitch. "I've never done that before."

"That makes it even better. You know, this isn't how I operate either. I usually take it for what it is and don't think twice about it once it's over."

"Yes, like you said that first night on the phone. I remember."

"I've never been left wanting more before it even ends, until you. Will you give this a chance, Angel?"

"I'm not like Whitney. That could never be me"

He replied sarcastically, clearly annoyed. "*Like Whitney?* Are you even listening to what I'm saying? You're *nothing* like her. I didn't give her a second thought. But you? You're all I fucking think about! Everything I never knew I wanted."

Angel gasped. They were only words, but they were so powerful. Pulling her heart, making her body ache in ways she never knew possible. This man, whom she barely knew, moved her more than anyone ever had. "Please, stop."

"Stop what? Being honest? I thought that's what you wanted and I have been. Completely."

"I want to believe that."

His voice, soft and warm just seconds before, turned angry and exasperated. "Why can't you? Haven't I treated you with respect? Didn't I ask to see you again? Can you trust your instincts instead of the brief synopsis you got from that plastic bitch?"

"I'm sorry, Alex," Angel said softly, meaning it. Her heart was already aching over this man, and she didn't want to hurt him or disrespect him. "I'm... With my profession, I see all this shit, and I know it's not fair to project it on to you." He sighed heavily and she heard some rustling in the background suggesting that he was pulling back the covers or moving underneath them. "I've had my own issues in the past, and I just... It's hard to let myself be vulnerable, but that is definitely how I feel with you. How is that for honesty?"

"It's good, and it means a lot to me you'd admit that, Angel. Really. But you have no reason to mistrust me, other than what Whitney said. So, if this gets screwed up, I'd prefer it was because of the two of us, and not someone from either of our pasts. Is that fair?" He was so sure of himself, like it was a done deal, but his voice was soft and persuasive.

It sounded logical enough. But, whoever or however it got screwed up, one thing she was already certain of; when it ended, it was going to hurt... if she let him get any closer to her. If she let herself get closer to him. But the scary part was that she *wanted* to get closer; *so* much closer. She wanted to lose herself in the fluttery feelings, the blazing passion, and in him.

When she didn't speak, Alex bristled, his mind seizing in panic. It was important that she give him a chance to get to know her. For the first time in his life, he actually gave a shit, which definitely wasn't his normal M.O.

"Look, I've had relationships that, for whatever reason, didn't work. It doesn't mean I'm a man-whore or disrespectful to the women involved. I'm always monogamous and safe." He huffed and then changed his tone to one of amusement. "I mean, I don't want my dick to fall off, for Christ's sake! I've grown rather attached to it."

Angel laughed softly. She had such a hard time keeping him out. Their sexy banter was fun for both of them.

"I was hoping it was starting to mean something to you, too," he said, lowering his voice, the amused tone replaced by the sexy teasing.

"It's growing on me, yes."

"Mmmm," he moaned softly and her body responded. "It's just growing, period."

Fuck, he was hot. "Mmmm... is right," she agreed. "So, are you saying that you aren't in this just for sex? You made no bones about that before, so..." Angel hesitated.

"I'm not sure what this is yet, Angel, but it's very exciting, and I want to explore it further. That's all I'm asking of you right now, other than that we be completely honest with each other. I want you. Physically, it's insane, but intellectually, I find you're on my level, and you're funny as hell, which is extremely sexy." He was laying it all on the line. "Where are you with it?"

"The sexual attraction is vicious. I feel torn. We could have a great time with no strings for a bit, but I worry about the consequences. I'm not someone who makes decisions without considering all the angles. One of us could get bloody on this."

Angel was already feeling vulnerable. Maybe it was the wine that was allowing her to be freer with her words, but more likely it was how connected she felt to Alex, and it felt like he was pulling her through the fucking phone.

Alex sighed. "I know. I heard every word that you said during our first phone call and since. I get it. It's a risk, but one I'm willing to take."

"Coming from Mr. I-don't-get-emotionally-involved, that's no risk at all."

"Neither one of us knows what will happen." Alex struggled between his need to keep his hand close to the cuff and his desire to spill his fucking guts. It felt like there was no choice. "It feels different with you. If you said we could only talk on the phone for a month, I'd be okay with that. This isn't just about sex. You're in my head." He closed his eyes. That was the biggest admission he'd ever made. It gave her all kinds of power, but there was nothing for it. It was what it was.

"Would you be able to keep from seeing other women in the interim?"

"Without question. It would just make it more explosive when we finally do come together."

Her heart thumped and she smiled at his choice of words and the amusement in his tone.

When she didn't answer, he strained to hear what she was doing on the other end of the line.

"Angel? Tell me what you're thinking," he demanded softly.

"I'm thinking that you're dangerous, and I need to be careful." *I can't let you melt me and turn me into a mindless pile of goo.* "But, I do enjoy talking with you."

"And being with me?" His voice was sultry bait, drawing her out.

She smiled and laughed softly, running a hand through her hair. "Would you believe me if I said *no*?"

"Not after tonight. No, I wouldn't believe that."

"Then why ask?"

"Because I want to hear you say it. I need to know that you are as fucked over this as I am."

"I'd say I was pretty thoroughly fucked, yeah."

He laughed softly. The sound so low and sexy, Angel clenched her thighs together in an attempt to stop the throbbing. "So when can I see you?" Alex asked.

"When do you want to?"

"Now. I'd come this minute if you'd let me."

Angel's pulse pounded in her ears. *I wish,* she thought. "I can't. Becca and the baby are here."

"Jesus, Angel!" Her response let him believe that if she were alone, nothing would prevent her from asking him over. Alex found himself wanting to wrap her up close to him all night. Something he never even contemplated before. He'd never wanted to be close to a woman but if he were honest: he was in just as much peril of getting hurt as she was. He brought his fingers to his nose and inhaled deeply. "I can still smell you on my fingers and on my skin. Mmm."

Angel bit her lip and squeezed her thighs even tighter. "God, Alex…"

"He can't help you like I can."

He was turning her on and making her smile at the same time. "Stop. It's starting to hurt."

"Fuck, yeah, it does. I'm like steel right now, but it's so good."

"Yes." Her heart skipped a beat.

Alex knew he'd have to do something about his problem, his hand moving below the sheet to close around his aching flesh. "So, can I call you tomorrow?"

"You mean today?"

"Whenever. Can I?"

"I have to work, so can you wait for a day or two? You distract me too much."

His breath stopped and joy filled him even as his body screamed for release. "That's a good thing. I'll do my best to give you some time. But I *will* call."

"Okay. Thank you again for this evening. It was…"

"*Magical.* I'll talk to you soon, baby."

*Baby.* Why the hell did that excite her so much? She struggled to keep the tremor out of her voice. "Goodnight, Alex."

Angel cshut off the phone and set it on the nightstand, knowing that she wouldn't be giving this number to anyone. No one would be calling this phone but Alex. It was fucking sexy as hell to have the private connection with him; the one-on-one access. It was all kinds of hot.

Mind racing, body aching… sleep was slow to come.

*****

Alex couldn't sleep. His mind was reeling. Elation and something that he couldn't categorize flooded through him.

*Angel.*

He was still amazed that she'd stood in the middle of his living room, almost naked and so tempting. Not that women hadn't dropped their clothes without so much as a touch from him before, but for this one to be so open about what she wanted, threw him for a loop. Her motive wasn't to use sex to weasel her way into his life; it was just simple wanting on both of their parts. He'd almost died. She was so sexy and surprising. He was even more amazed at himself for bringing her back to his apartment in the first place and then feeling anxious when she fled like the fires of hell were on her heels.

He rolled over again. The bedclothes tangled angrily around his limbs as he kicked at them roughly, finally banishing the offending material to the floor in a heap next to his big king-sized bed. His Egyptian cotton sheets offered little comfort. A soft sheen of sweat shone on his body in the dawning sun through the window in his room, and he huffed in frustration.

"Fucking hell," he muttered. "It's hot in here."

He put his hand over his eyes, one leg hanging halfway off of the bed, his foot flat on the floor. The whole night, after the call with Angel ended, had been a mixture of Heaven and Hell. Now, as Angel's naked image rushed through his mind once again, his traitorous body stiffened and he groaned, bringing his hand to the offending member. While very exciting, at times, this obsession was annoying.

He had to get his head on straight and his body under control. For fuck's sake, he was responsible for billions of dollars in assets, hundreds of jobs, and ran a huge corporation. Surely, he could get his cock under control. She was a woman, nothing more. He kept telling himself that over and over. Except he knew he was lying to himself.

Padding into the bathroom and scratching his bare stomach on the way, Alex turned the shower on full blast, adjusting the temperature as cold as it would go. He steeled himself against the icy spray, and just as he was about to step into the water's stream, there was a buzz on his intercom from the lobby concierge.

Alex quickly wrapped a towel around his middle and hurried into the other room to answer the buzzer. "Yes?"

"Alex, it's me, Darian. Can I come up?"

Alex glanced down at the lessening bulge under his towel and moaned. The last thing he wanted was to have to explain to Darian. Also, for some inexplicable reason, he felt the need to keep Angel and what happened between them quiet. "Shit."

"What?"

"Uh, yeah. Come on up."

Alex walked quickly into his bathroom, dropped the towel, and stepped quickly under the cold water. "Son of a bitch!" he ground out, turning the front of his body into the water and lifting his face to completely drench it and his hair. It had the desired effect; his erection disappeared instantly through his shivers.

In less than a minute, Alex was pulling on a pair of old Levis and rubbing his wet hair dry as he made his way to the door to let Darian into his apartment.

When the door opened, Darian breezed past, dressed in knee-length shorts, athletic shoes, and a loose T-shirt with the sleeve unceremoniously cut-out to halfway to his waist. "I thought we could hit the gym. You up for it?"

Alex continued to dry his hair and preceded the other man into the kitchen. A heavy workout would be just what he needed to clear his head and focus on the coming week's obligations. He still had to decide what he was going to do with his father's instructions for Cole. He left the towel hanging over his bare shoulders as he pulled the orange juice carton from the refrigerator and took a long pull on it without getting a glass.

"Okay," he answered shortly.

"Where were you last night? I called three times. Cole and I were at Excalibur, and he was doing damage to some little twit. I was bored." Darian flashed a smile and pulled out a chair at the kitchen bar despite the table in the far corner of the large, modern kitchen. Alex moved around digging in the refrigerator and the cupboards for the beginnings of breakfast.

"I wasn't around. Sorry," he hedged.

"No shit. Where were you?"

Alex hesitated. "Went to TRU for dinner. Then I was home. Why the twenty questions?" Alex asked casually, throwing a bagel in the toaster. "Want one?"

"Yeah, sure. What ya got to put on it?"

Alex tossed two tubs of flavored cream cheese on the counter and then some cherry preserves that were his particular favorite.

When they were both eating and Alex was still moving around the room as he gathered the things to make cappuccino using the machine on his counter, Darian's eyes narrowed. Alex was much too quiet.

"So? Have you talked to Angel? She must really be upset." He chuckled. "Won't give me the time of day."

"You're damn lucky she didn't quit on your stupid ass."

"Alex." Darian said his name to get his attention diverted from the coffee he was making, all the while wolfing down the bagel and popping another in the toaster.

Alex's eyes lifted to land on Darian's.

"Have you talked to her?"

"Yes," he answered cryptically, not willing to share much.

"And?" Darian set his cup down and raised his eyebrows. "What's going on?"

"I don't want to talk about it."

"That bad, huh? Did she rip you a new one?"

Alex smiled softly and shook his head. He didn't look at Darian, but continued steaming the milk and then poured it into both of the cups after the espresso had been added. Darian's curiosity was piqued and he pressed on.

"Alex, *what?*"

Alex shrugged nonchalantly. "She wasn't upset with me. She sure was pissed at you, though."

A shocked look settled on Darian's face as he studied Alex's expression. "You took her to TRU? It was her, wasn't it?"

"Yeah and she is freaking amazing. So *gorgeous*. But that's all you get." He took a sip from his mug and turned his back on his best friend, making the pretense of straightening up after the meal.

"What the fuck?" Darian leaned on the counter as his eyes widened in surprise. "Tell me what happened."

"We had dinner and talked." A reluctant grin split his face. "So what?"

"Alex, there is nothing *so what* about Angel and you know it. And since when do you spend an entire evening talking to a woman? Normally, you'd tell me something."

"Not this time."

"Avery! Did you take her to bed? Already?"

Alex couldn't help the lazy smile that lifted the corners of his mouth. *Technically, it was the couch,* he thought. "I said drop it, D." Alex picked up his cup and began to leave the room. "I have to go to my parents for brunch at noon, so if you want to hit the gym, I have to dress."

"But…"

"Drop it." Alex rolled his eyes as he went up the stairs, though Darian missed it. He had no intention of sharing last night with anyone, not even his best friend. Sure, in the past he'd thought nothing of giving Darian some of the details, but this time, he intended to keep the relationship between himself and Angel private. They were so intimate—with words, with their bodies, with their minds—sharing it with anyone else was unthinkable. He felt like he'd known her all his life despite just meeting her and not knowing much about her. He looked forward to finding out more, as slowly as necessary.

He dressed, reluctant for more of Darian's third degree. Alex ran a comb through his thick midnight mop and chose to forego the tedium of shaving. He rubbed his shadowed jaw and smiled. If he saw Angel later, he'd want to shave just before. *WHEN I see her, dickhead. It's going to happen, Avery,* Alex admonished himself, glancing in the mirror one final time before leaving his room.

When Alex was halfway down the flight of stairs, he looked up to see Darian twirling a scrap of blush silk around the index finger on his right hand. He sucked in his breath. *Fuck!* In her rush out last night, Angel must have forgotten her panties. A hot flush infused beneath the skin of his face and neck. Alex knew his face would give him away.

"Lookie, lookie, here!" Darian teased.

Alex's heart pounded inside his chest in panic as he quickened his pace down the rest of the stairs, eager to snatch them away and wipe the smug grin off his friend's face. "These are very sexy, Alex. The woman attached to them must have melted your cock off," he said.

"Give them back. *Now.*" Alex's voice was ice cold and hard.

"Whoa, hold up, dude." Darian held both hands in front of him in an effort to ward off Alex's advance, the panties dangling from one hand. "I found them on the floor. What's your probl—"

Alex grabbed the panties and scowled at him. "I said give them to me, Darian!" Sucking in his breath, he moved quickly into his den and opened the lower left drawer where the red file was hidden. He ran his fingers over the fine material and lace, remembering how he'd peeled them off Angel, before leaving them in the drawer and returning to the living room.

Alex gathered the keys for his Audi from the coffee table. "Let's go."

"Dude. Are you seriously not going to tell me about those panties? Shit, they're sexier than hell!"

"Sorry to disappoint you."

"Why? Dude, it's killing me! I can't believe Angel gave in on the first date. Man, you're my hero."

"Shut the fuck up. It wasn't like that. She didn't give in. I did." Alex grimaced when he said it, revealing more than he intended.

"*What?*" Darian burst out happily. "I think I just came in my shorts."

Alex ran his hand across his jaw in exasperation. *Jesus Christ.* They were out of the apartment and taking the elevator down to the garage when he made the decision that he would drive separately from his friend. "I had no intentions of sex last night. I respect her, and I didn't want her thinking that Whitney's twisted description of me was correct."

"Alex. Of course Whitney's description was right. You've been an unemotional prick and you know it."

"Well, I never gave a shit before. End of interrogation."

"Wow. The mighty Alex Avery is being led around by his dick when he said it'd never happen. If that isn't classic, I don't know what is."

Alex chuckled to himself. Well… at least it was a happy dick. Fucking ecstatic!

*****

Angel threw her dictation recorder down on her bed and flopped back on her pillows as her stomach rumbled. It was after seven and she'd been poring over the case files for the past eight hours. Once Becca and Jillian left after a late breakfast, she'd turned off her phone and immersed herself in the task of analyzing the tests and listening to the interviews again and again.

Mark Swanson was an evil bastard. There was no getting around it. He was well known and had a successful chain of dry cleaners that his grandfather had started fifty years earlier. He was connected with important people and his businesses were located all over the greater Chicago area. Everyone knew his smarmy face because it was plastered all over the advertising for Swanson Cleaners. Angel shuddered just thinking of that face. He was guilty as hell and she knew it in her gut. She had a sixth sense about scum like him, but she didn't have a thing to pin on him.

Angel ran both hands through her long hair and took a deep breath. She was frustrated, listening to his calm tone, methodically describing his relationship with his stepdaughter; completely different than how she described it. He was cold and emotionless. An icy shiver ran through Angel in reaction, the hair on her arms standing straight up.

The girl, on the other hand, was emotionally broken and terrified. It was obvious which of the two was telling the truth. The problem was, the prick had mastered his answers to the standard tests, completely fooling them. Even the polygraph that he'd taken he passed with flying colors. The fucker didn't profile like an abuser or rapist, and her professional reputation rested on her honesty in what she found in the results. When he left her office the week prior, he'd been smug and condescending; threatening.

*"Make sure to get your notes all organized, little lady, and the results are what they need to be. Right, honey? Then we'll all live happily ever after."*

*"Just get out of my office. You can't fool me."* Her voice had been cold as ice, but deep down, she was scared. He was dangerous and thought himself untouchable.

*"And you should hold your tongue if you know what's good for you, eh?"* He'd reached out and touched her chin with his index finger, to which Angel had immediately batted his hand away and glared. Swanson simply grinned and walked out like he hadn't a care in the world.

Her chest tightened in disgust. He had no fear of being caught or he wouldn't be so forthcoming with his threats. He had no conscience, no remorse. "Slimy bastard. This is when I hate my fucking job. Uuughhh!" she screamed into the empty air.

The hearing was in two months, but her deposition was Tuesday. There was nothing left to do tonight, and her plans included getting a bath and making something simple to eat. Her apartment was quiet as she walked through the living room on her way to the kitchen. Her eyes fell on the large bouquet of purple lilies on the square, dark wood coffee table in front of her plush olive green suede sofa. The apartment was clear of clutter, but the furniture was a mixture of modern lines and lots of luxurious comfort; plush cushions, dark wood, and slate tiles in the entryway and bathrooms.

Becca wasn't happy when Angel brushed over the details of her date with Alexander Avery, but all she shared was that he was charming and a few elegant details about the restaurant. She ran her hand over the marble countertop as she passed; thoughts of the more intimate moments came flooding to the forefront of her mind. She wasn't ashamed of what happened, but something inside her wanted to keep those surreal moments to herself. Maybe it was because she didn't want Becca to know she'd succumbed just like every other weak-willed woman in Alex Avery's sights. Maybe it would hurt less when it ended if she could pretend it never happened, and she wouldn't be able to do that if her best friend knew the details.

The two phones were sitting on the island and Angel stopped herself, a strong urge to turn them on just to see if he'd called. She left her phone where it was and picked up the one from Alex. As she looked at it, knowing she was about to give in, her heart started to hum. What if he didn't call? As hard as it was to admit, she wanted to see him, hear his voice. She closed her eyes and turned on the phone. Even if he did call, she wouldn't be able to get the message. What was the password to the voicemail? He hadn't said.

The screen lit up as the phone turned on, and there were no missed calls. Her heart fell and her cheeks burned with a flush.

*This is what I get for fucking him last night! I should have trusted the logic and not given in to the goddamn lust.* Angel was angry at her weakness… for allowing the faintest hope that he was different. Until that second, she hadn't really known how badly she wanted him to be more than Whitney said he was. She really wanted him to be as perfect as he seemed.

Angel sucked in a deep breath and scowled, trying to push down the disappointment that left her reeling. She went to the cupboard and pulled out some angel hair pasta, then to the refrigerator for parmesan cheese, fresh garlic, tomatoes, parsley, and butter. She decided she needed some wine to take the edge off of her emotions and she opened a bottle of chardonnay that was chilling in the refrigerator.

As she poured, she was startled when the Nickleback song blasted behind her, but even as she spilled the wine all over the counter, her face split into a happy smile. "Crap!"

Alex, the display announced the caller, and she smiled, happiness rushing through every cell in her body. "I am so screwed here," she muttered as she picked up the phone and answered. "Hello?"

"I waited as long as I could stand. Are you done working?" Alex's velvet voice ran over her like warm silk. A smile softened her face, memories of the night before warming her skin and throbbing through her body.

"Just finished."

"What are you doing?"

"Well, I was just going to make some pasta."

"Pasta sounds good. What kind?"

A wicked giggle burst from her lips. "Hot naked."

"You're shitting me, Angel," he said in a deeper tone, chuckling. "You're a naughty tease."

"No, seriously," she laughed softly, moving to get a rag to wipe up the spilled wine. "I'm making hot naked. It's really yummy. And super easy." She was smiling so hard her cheeks were starting to hurt.

A low laugh preceded his words. "Yes, I'm sure it is. I can make hot naked, too. But my version is hard."

*Fuck, he was sex personified*, she thought with a grin. "You have no idea."

He laughed again and her nipples actually hardened at the sound. "Oh, but I do. Those are my three favorite words."

She frowned slightly and bit her lip. "Hot, naked, and yummy?"

"No, hot naked, *Angel*."

"Want some?" she teased, knowing full well what she was implying. Her eyes were sparkling with excitement, so much pleasure in just talking to him, imagining what her words were doing to his body.

"Some hot naked Angel? You don't have to ask me twice."

She was giggling by now, so hard she almost snorted. "No, hot naked *pasta*. It's only fresh garlic sautéed in butter, poured over angel hair with fresh Parmesan. If you want it a little more dressed, I can add parsley and chopped Roma tomatoes."

Alex laughed with her. "No, babe, I want all naked, all the time."

"Okay."

His voice sobered and deepened slightly, his tone inquiring if this was an invitation. "Okay?"

The implications were clear. This was decision time. Should she give herself a chance? Should she give Alex a chance? "Yeah, okay."

"Now?"

"Alex, just get your ass over here. But I warn you, I'm not fancy tonight, so don't go getting all beautiful." She looked down at her jean shorts and plain white T-shirt. Quite a change from how he'd seen her last.

"Should I bring anything? *Dessert?*" They both laughed softly together, so in sync; knowing exactly what the other was saying and the sexy game that they played so well.

"Nope. I got this." She felt mischievous and delirious all at the same time. Knowing he'd be in front of her in a fraction of an hour excited her more than she wanted to admit.

"Yeah… you do. But we'll negotiate the dessert later. But I warn you, I have one hell of a sweet tooth of late."

# 8

# Hot and Not So Naked

EXCITEMENT FLOWED THROUGH Alex as he
waited outside Angel's door. There was something between them
that made it impossible to resist.

His heart pounded heavily in his ears as he pressed his hand
to the cherry wood. The smooth, elegant surface gave no hint as to
what lay behind it. So much like the woman who lived there. Angel
held herself in such control—sophisticated and subdued—but
underneath there was passion like Alex had never experienced. Her
sharp wit and potty mouth were unexpected. He shook his head in
amazement at the juxtaposition.

Stepping back slightly, his eyes widened in surprise as the door
swung open. Gone was the polished business suit and elegant
cocktail dress, replaced by tattered jean shorts and a non-descript
T-shirt, similar to the first time he'd seen her. Her legs were long
and golden, and Alex took in every inch as he worked his way up
her body. Her chestnut tresses were piled atop her head in a messy
knot, held in place with some sort of elastic band, and she had
some rectangular metal glasses sitting on her pretty nose.

Angel leaned on the doorframe, her arms crossed and one foot crossed over the other. "Hmmph." Her left eyebrow shot up above the charcoal-framed glasses. "Take a picture, it might last longer," she scoffed with a teasing smirk. "I told you I was a mess."

Alex himself was casually dressed in jeans and a black V-neck T-shirt, which lightly clung to his muscular torso. He was ripped, and all she could think about was how it felt to be in those strong arms. It created vivid recollections in her mind of how the muscle played beneath her fingers and how his breath came in uninhibited pants the night before. His jaw was dusted with just a smattering of stubble, and his hair was the same perfect disarray that she ached to thread her hands through.

He put a hand on his chest. "Um…" he began as her eyes raked him over in a similar fashion. Angel stepped aside and ushered him inside. He grinned and her heart did somersaults. "Take a picture, it might last longer," he retorted.

She laughed softly as he moved past her. "Hey, what's good for the goose, is good for the gander."

He turned to watch her close the door and bolt the lock; the gentle curves of her hips, the slimness of her back, and round fullness of her rear, getting his full attention.

"What?" he asked incredulously when their eyes met.

"Oh, nothing." Angel shrugged slightly. "Just something my nana used to say when I was growing up. It means…"

"Yeah, I know what it means." His green eyes burned, and her full lips lifted at the corners in the start of a smile. "That you give as good as you get. I like that a lot."

Alex longed to grab her and press his mouth to hers but somehow managed to resist the urge. He needed her to trust him. It was the only way she'd open up and he wanted that for the first time in his life. He actually wanted to *know her*. The thought stunned him, and Alex tugged on the hair at his right temple in agitation.

Angel sauntered back into the kitchen, shooting a look over her shoulder indicating that he should follow. He did, but before she got far, he reached out and slid his hand down her arm until his fingers closed warmly around hers, pulling her gently back toward him. Her free hand came up to rest on the solid wall of his chest and she felt the heat of his skin radiating through the material of his shirt.

Angel tried to mask the shivers running through her; to hide the electricity she felt at his slightest touch. The firm muscles under her hands did little to calm her down. Angel's mouth dropped open slightly as her lids became hooded and Alex couldn't help but register the implications. Still holding her hand, he cupped her cheek with the other and brushed the pad of his thumb over the fine bones in her cheek and then gently across her full lower lip.

"I told myself I wouldn't touch you tonight, but I can't seem to help it," Alex murmured softly, his forehead coming to rest gently against hers. Her breath rushed out and he sucked it into his lungs. He wanted every nuance of her, and the knowledge rushed over him in waves, but he held himself firmly in check. He was used to taking what he wanted, but this time, what he wanted was Angel to *give*.

Angel's body pulsed and her breathing quickened. She longed to press into him; to feel his hardness against her soft curves and have his mouth and tongue inflicting the sweet torture she knew he was capable of.

"Mmmm…" Involuntarily, her face lifted, offering Alex access to her mouth but his hovered without making connection. Eyes closed, his breath was hot as she waited. "Maybe I want you to touch me," she whispered against her will. "Just a little."

Alex's thumb continued to rub over her hand while his fingers tightened around hers, and he moved to place a soft, open-mouthed kiss on the corner of her lips. "Okay. Just a little then."

Angel was left bemused when he released her suddenly and moved around her into the kitchen, leaving her flustered and confused.

"So… tell me."

Her face twisted in consternation and amusement. "Tell you what?"

"Anything." He shrugged and leaned casually against the counter near the refrigerator at the far end of the kitchen. "Everything."

She moved about preparing the pasta, and trying to avoid his eyes. "Um, I'm thinking that this is not such a good idea. You're… well, you're you and I'm…"

His soft laughter filtered through the room. "Yes. Last night, I think that worked out quite well for both of us. I'm not asking you to lose your identity, Angel. Only share a meal and your thoughts."

"Come on, Alex. We both know you don't give a damn about my thoughts. But, if you must know, I'm considering that last night was a mistake." She was chopping something on a hardwood board with her back to him. Alex didn't like that he couldn't see her face as she said the words. "I wanted to talk to you about it in person."

"I do care about what you're thinking. I've said it. Can you look at me?" His tone took on that of Alex Avery, CFO: man who commanded respect and one that didn't like what he was hearing.

She threw something into a pot and the sizzling mixed with the rumbling and hissing of the water boiling in the other pot, and then turned to face him.

"Look—" she wiped her hands on a white towel and threw it aside carelessly, "—last night was nice."

"Nice? Hmmm, not the adjective I'd use, but continue."

"I guess I'm curious what you want from this?"

"I told you. A meal and your thoughts. I didn't come here to seduce you or fuck you into submission." His eyebrow quirked and a sexy grin split his handsome face. "That is what you think happened last night, right?"

She chuckled softly as she resumed cooking, unwilling to admit how much this man got under her skin. "Um, actually I sort of see it as the other way around."

"Touché." His grin widened. "So how about we agree that we won't go there tonight. We'll eat, talk—"

"Touch?"

"Only a little," he said with a mischievous grin. "I've already made that commitment. When you know me better, you'll realize I always keep my word."

She bristled slightly, not sure if it was an implied promise to keep his distance or that he wanted to be closer. She poured the sauce over the pasta and picked up a block of cheese and began grating it over the top. "Hmmph," she snorted, disappointed at the lack of contact that seemed to be her fate tonight. "That remains to be seen. Do you want it dressed?"

"I thought we agreed we liked things naked," Alex teased.

"Yes, well, use your imagination," she shot back without missing a beat, and Alex burst out laughing. She was so different, so refreshing, and he couldn't tear his eyes from her face as she used the back of her hand to push a stray lock away from her face.

"Uh uh. No teasing, miss. I promised to be good, so play fair, please."

This time it was Angel's turn to laugh as her eyes widened in mock exaggeration. "What's good for the goose…" she reminded as she plopped a well-laden plate filled with garlic-scented pasta and a light salad down in front of him. "And, stop fishing. You are good. Very good. So let's just get that off the table right now, okay?"

Alex's body reacted to her words and to her nearness… to the luscious memories from the night before as she took the seat to his left and the soft scent of her perfume wafted in his nostrils.

The light in her apartment was low and the soft jazz playing from somewhere in the living room echoed off the walls. Alex felt comfortable in an unsettling sort of way. His body reacted, but he felt at ease in Angel's home. Talking with her was nice, and their easy bantering was completely stimulating in a number of ways. He chose to ignore her comments lest he give in to the need to reach out again, but his eyes stole glances at her as she offered him some bread.

"What?" she demanded when she caught him staring.

"Nothing. I'm not going to let you trick me into anything. Did you get your reports finished? Were the results what you'd hoped?"

Angel shook her head and shrugged almost imperceptibly. "I can't really say."

Alex's brow dropped as he wound some pasta onto his fork. "It just seems dangerous, Angel. What made you choose to do this type of work?"

Angel's eyes lifted to meet his and what she saw there was earnest concern. He truly wanted to know. "I wanted to help people who couldn't help themselves, to become a voice for those without one."

Something in her voice made Alex push. "Sounds like there's more to it."

"The pasta will get cold. We should eat," she murmured, but Alex had already taken a bite.

"It's delicious. Is gourmet cooking another of your many talents?"

"Hardly. Only the bare essentials. I'm surprised Dad and I survived. This is so easy, though. I make it a lot." Angel was thankful he moved to another subject, praying silently that he wouldn't revisit the previous one.

"So?" he persisted. "Why psychology?"

"Um." Angel hesitated as she played with the food on her plate. She'd never discussed it with anyone other than Becca and not for years. "Well…"

A warm hand closed around hers and the heat traveled up her arm and infused her face.

"It's okay if you don't want to tell me, but I really hope to know you better," he said gently, his fingers brushing back and forth over her knuckles. "I want you to trust me. I get that I have to earn it."

Something about this man caused an upheaval of her insides and all of her carefully laid plans to resist him came tumbling down. Suddenly, she found herself longing to open up, but what would his reaction be? Did she dare tell him?

"Well, my freshman year at Northwestern, someone was... well, she was assaulted at a frat party and it... changed me."

Alex's fingers were still around Angel's hand as he replaced his wine glass by his plate and turned his full attention on her. "Oh, I'm sorry. Was it Becca?"

"Mmmm, uh uh." She shook her head, and then stopped, eyes flashing up to his. His face was concerned, interested, focused.

"What happened?" he asked softly.

"We were at a party, we had drinks, and someone drugged her." Angel looked away quickly. "She was raped."

Alex ran the back of his fingers across her wrist. "Oh, my God. I see."

His touch was comforting and his company wrapped around her like her favorite quilt.

Angel shook her head again as she regained her senses. "She was too scared to call the police, afraid that her friends and family would be ashamed of her, afraid they'd think it was her fault. So, I wanted to be in a position to put bastards like that behind bars, or help anyway, with situations like that."

Alex nodded silently and reached out to brush her cheek the same way he had her wrist. It was so gentle and surprising. She wondered if he understood.

"Alex, tell me more about your parents and sister. You only talked about your brother last evening."

It was clear to him that she wanted the subject changed and he sensed she was hedging. Some nondescript emotion flitted over her delicate features and it pained him. He quickly cleared his throat. "My father is a brilliant businessman, and my mother is a beautiful, caring woman. She and my sister, Allison, do a lot of philanthropic work when they're not messing in my personal life." He chuckled softly as he continued to enjoy his meal. "Which is often."

"I sense you're all very close. Are they all in the area?"

"Mmmm." Alex nodded. "Allison's husband is in insurance, and though my parents take two extended trips a year, most of the time they are here. They still live on the same estate that they purchased when I was in high school. It's quite beautiful. My father worked very hard, and Mom kept it up perfectly. When I first saw you last spring, we were buying stuff to redecorate the sunroom of that house." His eyes watched her face carefully. "He wants to move, to buy her houses in a few locations worldwide, but she won't hear of it. I told her that she can still nag me wirelessly, but she thinks I'm kidding. Plus, she loves that house."

Angel smiled at his humor, drawn in by the softness of his voice, the warmth of his enveloping nearness. "That sounds nice. My dad," she sighed, "I can't get him to leave the sticks. Joplin was a nice place to grow up, but there is so much more that I'd like him to see."

"You miss him." It wasn't a question, his expression understanding.

"All the time." Angel wasn't eating much of her dinner and it didn't go unnoticed by the man beside her. He could see her mind whirling behind her furrowed brow as she watched her fork push her food around the plate. "Alex... about this—"

He sat back in his chair a little, not liking where he knew her words were headed. "Angel, are we having fun?"

"Fun isn't the issue," she dropped off quietly. "Is it?"

Alex was unsure what to say, wondering how this woman, who always had words aplenty, seemed at a loss in the current moment. "Isn't it?"

She reached for the wine to refill their glasses. "Is it?"

He picked up his glass and concentrated on the liquid as he swirled it in a miniature cyclone, carefully considering his words.

"Why did you agree to dinner the other night if you didn't want to know more? Would I be here if you don't enjoy my company?"

Her eyes flashed to his face. "I do. But—"

"What are you afraid of?"

"Nothing!" Angel answered quickly and then bit her lip. "I'm just realistic, Alex."

"What are you trying to say, Angel? Just spit it out."

"Okay. If you want to fuck for the sake of fucking, I can do it for a while. But if you want to get to know me, we can't have sex." She shrugged and smiled, her brows arching in challenge.

Alex pushed his plate away as he burst out laughing. "What? Intimacy on only one level at a time, eh?"

"Sex isn't intimacy."

Alex instantly sobered. "It is with us." His green eyes bore into hers, unflinchingly daring her to dispute him. "You're afraid of me, Dr. Hemming."

"No, I'm realistic." She knew she was lying to herself and to him. "I don't believe in what you represent. However, against my better judgment, I find you very—" she looked away. "—you're charming and likeable, even though my brain screams you're a womanizer. So if we want to be mutual users for a while, fine."

Alex paused, the laughter dying in his chest. "Is that truly how you see me? I thought I'd been clearer."

"I get it. After knowing you a little better, I understand more. I don't necessarily agree with your arrangements but I can see your point of view, even if it still differs from mine."

"What differs? We're attracted to each other, and we enjoy our time together. Can we just let what happens, happen?"

"Nope."

"Nope? That's it?"

"We *can't* let it happen. I'm attracted to you. Not gonna lie. You're funny and charming and all the wonderful shit dreams are made of; except one thing. You don't *feel*. Call me crazy. That's huge." She flitted between the dining room and the kitchen as she methodically cleared the table, ranting as she went. Alex was amused and mesmerized.

"Do you dream of me, Angel? And I do feel. I love my dog."

*Lucky damn dog.* "Shut up and focus."

Alex grinned and a big smile split out on Angel's face, even though she was trying to be serious. He thought she was the most beautiful, sexiest thing he'd ever seen, glasses and all.

He cleared his throat and sat up straighter, mocking her. "Yes, ma'am."

"I don't know if I trust you."

Alex shut his mouth and looked at her. He knew closing the deal meant shutting down the argument that sprung to his lips. Angel cocked her head.

"I know you could just be messing with me to get me back for the ridiculous notion I made that twit breakup with you, but let me assure you, it wasn't me... it was you."

"Okay. It was me," he agreed good-naturedly.

Angel stopped and glanced back over her shoulder on her last trip to the kitchen, to roll her eyes at him.

"You're agreeing with me? So you will tell me, Alex Avery, what the fuck you're up to."

"Okay." This time it was softer and more persuasive. Her steps slowed on her way back.

"Okay? It was that easy?"

"Yes, *okay*." His expression was sardonic, amused. "Let's take the wine and go in the other room, and I'll tell you anything you want to know."

*****

Two hours, two bottles of wine, and lots of laughter later, the two of them ended up on some big pillows on the floor in front of her sofa, on their sides face-to-face and their feet tangled.

Quiet and serious, Alex's hand finally reached out to touch her, pushing a tendril back behind her ear. She closed her eyes as the back of his knuckles brushed across her cheekbone. She drew in a long breath, reveling in the wonder of the sensation. It was light, warm... electric.

"Alex," she began as her eyes found his.

"Shhh... you said I could touch a little." His open palm moved over her shoulder and then, with slight squeezing massage, down her arm. It was dark with only the glow of the muted television to cast a blue glow around the room. His eyes were darker and more intense. Maybe it was desire that filled his gaze, and she found herself hoping... wanting, her body involuntarily leaning toward his.

"Angel, tell me who did that to you in college," he said it softly, but his tone was demanding. "Who could hurt you like that?"

"How do you know? I mean..." Angel began to withdraw, but his hold tightened, keeping her close.

Alex shrugged slightly and his brow furrowed. The muscle in his jaw twitched. "I just know. Just tell me who it was, so I can kill the motherfucker."

Angel's eyes stung with tears as they began to glisten. Alex hadn't moved other than to keep rubbing her arm and to finally bring her hand up to his mouth for a soft, open-mouthed kiss on the inside of her wrist.

"I can't."

"Yes, you can. Trust me." His fingers continued over the flesh of her arm and shoulder, up behind her neck as he applied gentle pressure and squeezed.

Angel saw understanding and sadness in Alex's eyes that propelled her to share something that she'd never told anyone, save Becca.

"No." She shook her head. The waver in her voice broke as a tear slid from each eye. "I mean I trust you. But I can't tell you who it was. I don't know."

Confusion filled his features. "What? How?"

"I told you. I was drugged. Ruffies. I don't remember any part of it. Except the next morning. I woke up in a bedroom alone, missing my clothes and…"

Alex's chest was feeling constricted and fire rushed under his skin. "And?"

"And, there was blood."

He sighed heavily and leaned his forehead against hers, his hand coming up to cup her cheek. "I'm so, so sorry. You should be worshiped, not abused. Sweetheart, I'm sorry."

"Stop," she whispered. "You didn't do it. I'm sorry about it, too, but at least I don't remember experiencing it. If it hadn't happened, my life would be different, and I would have made different choices. I wouldn't be helping anyone."

Alex studied her face, searching her expression for anything that would signify she was telling the truth about reconciling with it. He was speechless as he stared into her glittering brown eyes, and then moved a soft strand of hair back behind her ear. She was so strong. Alex felt his admiration for her grow even more.

Angel was hungry from his touches, yearning for more even as her brain fought for control.

"After that, I changed. I took self-defense classes, threw my-self into school, and shut-out everyone. Until I met Becca. She had so much bravado and guys didn't fuck with her. She encouraged me to join the band." Angel paused as realization dawned on Alex.

"Ahh... so you *are* a professional," he teased lightly in an at-tempt to comfort her and ease the tightness in his own chest.

Her eyebrows rose and she smiled as he brushed her chin with his fingertips. "Not at all. It was something I did to be in control of men. I was untouchable, if you will. I could get up on that stage and be someone else. Soon, I became that person."

"What happened to the band?"

"They're still together. I talk to them from time to time."

"Help me understand why you're not still playing with them. You're a natural. So good," he said softly.

Angel's hand finally reached toward him almost against her will and her fingers brushed his jaw. The stubble was short but sharp, and she knew if he kissed her, the soft skin of her face would feel the sting. It didn't matter, she wanted it; images of the night before painting vivid pictures and making her body open and moisten. The desire was overwhelming as she scooted closer.

"Mmm... okay, so, we've figured out that we're both *good*. So where does that leave us?"

Alex's body quickened at her touch and words, his arms slid-ing around her, drawing her close to his body. He wanted her. There was no denying it. She sucked him in like a moth to a flame, and for the first time, he didn't care if he burned into nothingness.

"Wanting. Aching." The answer was simple. He watched her eyes, and then as her hot, sweet breath washed his face, his eyes dropped to her mouth. When Angel's little pink tongue came out to caress her upper lip, he gave up. "Ughhh."

"Kiss me," she commanded softly, her mouth tilting up to reach for his, and her eyes began to close seductively.

"I promised myself I wouldn't go there tonight, Angel. More importantly, I promised *you*."

"What were the words you used last night? Just a little taste?" she reminded him as their mouths hovered together and her nose nudged his.

"Yes, and look where that ended up."

"Mmmm…" Her voice was tempting, pulling him down, her breath hot against his lips. "Do you regret it?"

"Would I be here if I did?" His index finger slid down the curve of her face. *So fucking gorgeous.*

Angel reached up and pulled her glasses off, haphazardly flinging them up on the couch. "So don't regret this either, then."

They stared at each other without flinching, each silently daring the other to be the one to break the moment or be the one to give in. He wanted to, so much his breath hitched in his throat.

Alex hesitated a little too long. She pushed away from him and started to get up in a scramble of limbs. "Angel…"

"For Christ's sake!" she muttered in embarrassment as she struggled against the arms that had now closed around her to halt her flight. "Stop! If I have to force you, just—let go!"

"What the hell? I'm trying to show you this is different!" Alex quickly rolled her beneath him and pinned her to the floor, his knees spreading hers apart and his arms caging her head. They were both breathing hard as she struggled to get free. "That *you* are different, Angel! Angel!"

She stopped dead and they held each other's eyes, her look defiant and his slightly amused. She was embarrassed that she wanted this man so much that he could reduce her to the state of being on the verge of begging him to take her. She turned her head to the side to avoid his burning gaze.

"Now," he said seriously, pressing his pelvis into hers and she was left in no doubt he wanted her. She surged up to meet him against her will. "Does it feel like I'm unaffected? I am so fucking turned on I can taste it, but I'm trying to show you that I'm not who you believe me to be. So please stop trying to seduce me. I'm only human." He said the words, but his mouth found hers in a series of hungry kisses, and their bodies moved to create the friction they both craved. Angel's mouth and body were alive under his, and her hands frantically pushed the material of his shirt up and away in search of the smooth skin and hard muscles of his back. Soon sounds of wet kisses and soft moans filled the room.

"This is hard enough as it is," he moaned before coming back for another deep kiss. "I wish I knew what you really wanted." His mouth dragged from hers as he spoke, the confusion he felt not enough to stop him from kissing her again.

Words were lost as their passion took over, panting heavily and rolling around on the floor, bodies grinding into each other. They knocked into the coffee table and sent the empty wine bottle clattering to the floor, followed by the hallow sound of it rolling across the hardwood.

Alex pulled his hungry mouth from hers and pushed the hair, now free of the knot, back from her face in gentle strokes. Her mouth reached for his and he gave her what she wanted, because he wanted it, too. Again their tongues laved and thrust, mouths sucking on and devouring the other. It was magnificent perfection.

"Jesus." His chest rose and fell heavily under her hand. "I need to leave. *Now.*"

Her leg hitched and wrapped around his waist in silent protest, and his hips answered hers. "I want you to stay."

Alex closed his eyes as if he were in pain. "I have to go. I promised this wouldn't happen, but it feels too damn good." His lips found the soft skin beneath her ear and his open mouth left a fiery trail down the cord of her neck, while his hand clawed at the neck of her T-shirt and then moved down to cup a full breast.

"Alex," she breathed his name, and it was all he could do to keep from drowning in her.

"God, you're prefect," he groaned and then pushed away from her. Sitting, he pulled his knees up and he leaned on them, trying to regain control. She stayed where she was, but her hand ran down his back and then up again. She wasn't able to stop herself.

Alex sucked in a deep breath, as much air as his lungs could hold, turned to look at her and then took her hand in his, fingers caressing as their eyes locked. Rising to his feet, he pulled her up behind him and held her hand as he walked to the door, thumb brushing back and forth.

Angel was bewildered, confused, and hungry. Didn't the self-professed sexual predator want her? She wasn't sure if she should let him hold her hand or pull it away.

When they reached the door, Alex pulled her closer as his arms slid around her. "Tell me what you want."

Angel refused to look at him, standing stiff in his arms, her heart still thrumming wildly in her chest. *You*, her mind screamed.

"Angel?" When she still didn't answer, he lifted a hand and tilted her chin up, forcing her to look into his face. "Just tell me what you want and it's yours."

She opened her mouth but then promptly closed it. "I'm... I mean, I don't know." *I want you to stay. I want you to kiss me. I want to be able to enjoy your body and not lose myself in the process.* Her emotions were all over the place and she felt completely out of control. "What I want and what I know should happen aren't the same thing." The fine cotton of his expensive T-shirt teased her sensitive fingertips as she explored the muscles of his stomach.

"Do you want me to walk out of here and not look back?" he asked softly, his lips brushing her temple.

Her eyes closed, knowing what she should say. "Yes."

"You're such a little liar," he said with gentle firmness. "I won't let you cheat us out of this, Angel."

"What is this?" Her head tilted back and her hair fell over the hand that moved up her back to close around the back of her neck and head.

"*This* is amazing. Just let it happen. We'll go slow. I won't touch you until you ask me to."

"I'm *asking* now!" she protested, and he shook his head. "Why are you doing this, Alex? You told me this isn't how you play, so what do you hope to gain?"

"You. Time." He was seducing her with his velvet voice and the lips that felt like languid butterflies on her eyelids, cheek, and then her open mouth, his hands holding her head and kneading her back gently.

"Sex?"

"If it's meant to happen, yes. I have to go to Madrid tomorrow, and I'll be back on Friday. Can I see you?"

"Yes. But I have the show." To deny him seemed unthinkable. Her logic protested but she couldn't give it a voice.

He pulled her close and his mouth staked its ownership of hers again, and her arms lifted of their own accord to wrap around his neck, her hands threading into his hair. The kisses were sublime and they feasted on each other until she felt his hardness press into her and her body answered with moist heat of its own. "Ughhhh," she moaned softly, disappointed when he finally pulled away after placing one last kiss on her neck. "Don't go."

"Baby, I gotta go or I'll never leave. So, I'll see you in five days. Keep the phone handy."

He opened the door and her hands fell from his body.

Angel found herself feeling stunned and bereft when the door closed, and she leaned back against the wood, the cold wood a stark contrast to his warm flesh. "Five days…"

She moved into the kitchen and began to clean up the remnants of the meal, forgotten for the past three and a half hours, thoughts of Alex rampant in her mind. She smiled in spite of herself. Her mind knew he was dangerous. More than dangerous, but damn it, he was funny and sexy and brilliant. Lethal. Surely, she'd suffer in the end but it felt so good, it was hard to deny.

The buzzer to her apartment sounded, startling Angel out of her contemplation, and she hurried to the door, anticipating Alex.

"Hey, *you*. Back already?" she asked with a smile. "I knew you couldn't stay away."

"Dr. Hemming?" a deep voice rasped. It wasn't Alex and Angel was startled, jumping slightly in her skin.

"Yes?" she spoke into the speaker and then released the button for the response.

"If you know what's good for you, you'll be wise about your comments on Tuesday. Mr. Swanson can be a reasonable man, with reasonable people. We know where you live. And now, your boyfriend, too."

Angel's heart fell to her stomach, thudding heavily, and heat flooding her skin at a record pace.

# 9

# Secrets

ALEX THRUMMED HIS hand on the top of his knee, waiting impatiently for Cole outside his apartment. The neighborhood was nice, but not used to limousines, and certainly not the caliber that Alex or his parents lived in. Neither Alex, nor his father, was inclined to provide more to Cole without the benefit of some sort of contribution to the business.

He glanced at his watch impatiently and finally pulled out his phone.

"Yeah?" Cole's groggy voice pissed Alex off. His mouth settled into a thin line.

"Cole, for Christ's sake! I'm *waiting*. Get your ass out here. *Now*! I'm late for my flight."

There was rustling and the clank of a belt on the other end of the line as Cole crawled out of bed and threw on some clothes. "Where you going, again? What time is it?"

"Just get the hell out here. We'll talk on the way to O'Hare." Alex shut off his phone and shoved it in the breast pocket of his suit. The sun had been up for three hours, bright in the sky, but the limo's dark windows made his expensive sunglasses unnecessary. He pulled them off and flung them on the leather seat beside him.

After another ten minutes, Cole's unkempt form slid into the seat directly across from Alex as the driver closed the door behind him. Shaking his head in dismay, Alex watched his brother shove a Cubs baseball cap onto his uncombed head.

"Who dresses you, Cole? Have some respect for yourself and for the family. Jesus. Think about what you represent!"

Cole scowled at his younger brother. "Get off your high horse, Alex. Who the fuck do you think you are, getting me out of bed at the crack of dawn?"

"Apparently, I'm your fucking boss. And my high horse, as you put it, needs a good polishing. Dad asked me to straighten your ass out, but this is it. After this, I'm done."

"Fuck you, Alex. Daddy's little favorite. It makes me want to puke."

"You think you can go through life banging bimbos and relying on others to pay for everything you do? Get your head out of your ass. Life isn't all rainbows and unicorns. At some point, you have to grow some balls and take some responsibility."

Cole had the grace to flush and look out the window as the limo pulled out of his complex. "I'm not a suit. I have no desire to be Dad's clone. Besides... he's got one already."

"If you don't want to be a part of Avery, then tell Dad, so he'll get off my ass. But get a goddamn job."

Cole sighed and twisted his ball cap around. "What does Dad want me to do?"

Alex leaned back in the seat and watched Cole fidget. "It's my call. He suggested mergers and acquisitions, but I have something else in mind. Since it's not in the office, maybe you can stomach it."

Cole's brows lifted slightly. "What does it involve?" His tone was bored and uninterested.

"Supposedly, a local businessman is neck-deep in a rape case. It's all hush-hush. I want to know who it is."

"I don't get it. Why do you give a fuck?"

Alex's jaw shot forward and he stiffened slightly. He couldn't admit the truth to his brother because he hadn't fully accepted it himself. "Just find out. Get Bancroft to help you, if needed, but do it before I get back from Spain."

The limo pulled up to the terminal, and the driver proceeded to unload Alex's bag to the curb as the two men slid out. Passengers and airport workers glanced at them, taking in the stark contrast between Alex's polished black suit and vibrant silk tie to Cole's wrinkled khaki shorts and rumpled white T-shirt.

Alex replaced the sunglasses in one smooth motion and straightened the cuffs of his shirt under his jacket. As always, his dress and demeanor was impeccable and polished.

Cole studied his brother carefully; certain that the hard tone in his voice went deeper than he was letting on. "What's the real reason, dude?"

Alex picked up his briefcase as the larger bag was checked at the curb.

"If this asshole is as shady as I believe him to be, there are holes in his business dealings, too. Find out everything. Who he is, what he owns, his relationships, who he employs, who his lawyers are… I want his weaknesses. Get it all. If you need money, Mrs. Dane is instructed to provide whatever is necessary, but not for bullshit, Cole, just this assignment."

Two flight attendants making their way inside glanced in Alex's direction, clearly interested. The corners of his mouth lifted in a wry smile. He noticed the shapely legs on one of them, but his interest was minimal.

"Hellloooo, ladies," Cole said, lifting his hand in a wave.

The women visibly grimaced as they looked him over. "Eww," one said softly, raising a hand to whisper rapidly to her friend. Cole was a good-looking guy when he gave a shit.

Alex flashed a snow-white grin in Cole's direction. "See? Now don't you wish you had at least showered?" He laughed.

"Hey!" Cole called after the women as they disappeared through the double doors.

"You don't live in the hood, so dress appropriately, please," Alex admonished.

"Well, you smell like a girl."

A smile broke at his brother's smart-ass remark. Despite their disagreements, they were still good friends.

"I need you to focus. This is very important, so no whoring around this week," Alex added as he turned away, trying to squash his grin.

Cole's face crinkled in protest and groaned. "Why?"

"Because I said so," Alex insisted, handing a twenty to the baggage claim attendant.

"No pussy for you then, either. Fair's fair!" Cole retorted loudly, not caring where he was or who overheard. He shoved his hands in the pockets of his khaki shorts.

"Nice. Your eloquence slays me," Alex mocked dryly, but laughing despite himself as he left the curb and turned to walk into the terminal. His thoughts flashed to long silken strands wrapped around his fist and a soft, luscious mouth wild beneath his own, the scent of vanilla and muskiness, and fiery heat wrapped tightly around his cock. *Angel.*

He was astonished that, on this occasion, he was definitely on-board with that restriction.

*Definitely no pussy.*

\*\*\*\*\*

Angry. Apprehensive. Worried. Violated. Scared. All words that described the feelings flooding through Angel and she couldn't ignore any of them. So many emotions convoluted the situation and how she was able to deal with it.

After last evening's surprise visitor, Angel had contacted building security hoping that the attendant could describe him or that he was on lobby cameras. No such luck. All that could be seen was a black fedora as the man kept his head lowered. He was medium height and husky. Not much to go on besides he had the most hideous voice she'd ever heard.

*And now we know where your boyfriend lives, too.*

It ran through her brain again. What would Alex think? He'd laugh at the label. He was no one's *boyfriend*, but he'd be pissed that someone would be throwing threats around. Shivers rushed over the skin of her arms, causing goose bumps to break out under the navy blue Christian Dior suit. Despite his declaration of taking it slow, and her protests to letting it happen, Angel sighed at the inevitable. She liked him. A lot. Her first instinct was to pick up the phone after that asshole buzzed her apartment and call Alex. She didn't. He had enough on his plate, and telling Alex would be too much like admitting they were *something*.

Angel walked through the polished glass doors that led into the government office building across from the courthouse, her high heels clacking loudly on the marble floors. It had been several weeks since Angel spoke with Kenneth, but she needed his advice; he knew the case, even if he wasn't working on it personally. That fact allowed him to speak to her about it, off the record.

"Dr. Hemming! How nice to see you! Is Mr. Gant expecting you?" Ken's assistant popped her head up from her computer screen. She was fresh and pretty, a law student on internship with the firm.

Pain shot through her lower lip as she bit it too hard. "Um, no, Carrie. Is he busy?"

"He has court in about an hour, but it's only an arraignment, so he should be available."

"I should have called first. Please extend my apologies." Angel paced back and forth in front of the desk, uncharacteristic of her usually cool demeanor. The minutes ticked by until a smiling Kenneth came out to greet her.

"Angel! You look gorgeous."

Angel felt the wet warmth of his partially open mouth as he bent to kiss her cheek and his hand lingered as he ran it down her arm. Kenneth was an attractive man. Bright blue eyes, well-kept blond hair, and clean-shaven. He wasn't as tall as Alex and his muscles less defined. He was thinner, less broad through the shoulders. Angel shook herself out of the comparison.

Kenneth ushered her into his office and closed the door behind them. Despite the high-powered position he held, his office was sparse, the furniture dated and cluttered with papers. Angel's brow crooked in sarcastic bewilderment.

"I don't get how you can win so many cases, given your disorganization. How do you find anything?"

Kenneth smiled as she settled into one of the hard, wooden chairs and he went around the desk. "Ah! I love my chaos. I know where everything is."

"I bet your assistant wants to shoot herself."

"So, what do I owe the pleasure? You haven't been around much lately." Kenneth's softly spoken words were loaded with hidden meaning. He knew it. She did, too.

"Yeah. Really busy. The radio show and everything."

"Yes, I heard it once or twice." He threw a pen down on his desk and shuffled some papers out of the way. "Stupid people."

Angel flushed and her back stiffened. He just didn't *get it*. He *never* did. "Everyone has problems, Kenneth. Even you," she said pointedly.

"Pfft. My biggest problem is when I get to see you. I've missed you."

"You're seeing me now," Angel dismissed, not wanting to get into the discussion of why they were no longer having sex. "And, it's me with the problem. I need your advice."

Kenneth leaned back in his chair and studied the beautiful woman in front of him. She was elegant and composed, her dark tresses smoothed back in a professional chignon that her manicured hand reached up to check, make-up perfect. "What's this about? Swanson?"

Angel's eyes widened in surprise. "How'd you know?"

He shrugged and began to roll down the sleeves of his white dress shirt and tighten the red and grey tie in preparation for his court appearance. "The guy's scum. Everyone knows he's guilty as sin, but it only matters what we can prove. That's where little wonder-Angel comes in."

"Wonder-Angel? I can't prove a damn thing as it stands now. The tests aren't infallible, and I can't manufacture answers. The only thing I can think to do is tell him the files got deleted and we need to re-administer them. He cheats the tests, but maybe if we rattle his cage and make him think we're fishing, he'll crack."

"We *are* fishing. Have you spoken to Stacey about this? She's the one prosecuting the case."

"I have a deposition tomorrow, but I'm not ready. If I go in now, I'll have to say the tests were inconclusive at best. It's not enough. We need more."

"His lawyer, Felix Mann, is a shark. He'll eat you alive."

Angel's chin jutted out in indignation. "I can handle anything that bastard dishes out, but there's more. After the test session, Mr. Swanson told me to make sure he was innocent, and now some thug's after me. Last night…"

"What?" Ken exploded.

"Calm down. Nothing's happened yet. Just words so far."

"Angel! Stop being so blasé about it!" He moved to sit in the chair next to her and take her hand. "Tell me what happened!"

"Some guy came to my building, buzzed my apartment, and told me that if I knew what was good for me, I'd make sure Swanson gets acquitted." She purposely left out the threat on Alex.

Ken caressed her delicate knuckles but she itched to pull away. His hands felt sweaty and weak, not strong and assertive, assured in every single movement. She flushed at her thoughts.

"They came to your *home*? We should call the police and have you removed from the case."

"No!" She pulled her hands free and stood, turning back to Kenneth after she'd walked a few steps away. "We have to catch him in the act. I mean… he'd just do it to someone else who is less equipped to deal with him, so it's best to just go with the flow. I needed someone to know what's going on in case something happens, so just tell Stacey I lost the flash drive, all of my notes, and the test results. Have her get a continuance. Whatever! Just help me pin this bastard to the wall." Angel rattled on frantically, a tone that Kenneth rarely heard her use. He felt uneasiness grip his chest. "You know better than anyone… we need something concrete."

"Did you recognize the voice?"

"No." A tremor ran through her and Kenneth noticed, his eyes narrowing. "But it was nasty and unnatural."

"Angel, let's just put someone else on it. There are other cases you can work on." His hands spread out in front of him as he moved closer, his eyes boring into hers. "You're in danger and I won't have that."

Angel huffed and straightened to her full height plus the four inches of her heels. "Well, it's not up to you, is it? You can either help me, or not. Decide."

She crossed her arms across her chest as she scowled at him.

"And it is my decision. This office assigned you." Angel scowled at him. "Have you thought about what it could mean to those close to you? Becca and the baby? Me? Hell, who knows? Even your father? What if something happened to you? He'd be heartbroken."

Angel signed heavily. "Of course I have, Kenneth! What good will it do for me to turn tail and run? Swanson will think he *won,* and I couldn't live with it! This fucker needs to go down before he hurts anyone else. He's slime and he's damn well capable of a lot more than rape." Her tone softened, pleading, "So—*help me.*"

Kenneth's arms closed around Angel's slight form as he pulled her close. "Okay, Angel. Okay."

*****

Alex's chest protested as he pulled in a breath. Exhaustion and jet lag weren't enough to keep him from finding his way to his destination. He stood against his car at the far side of the parking lot of KKIS, waiting. He ran both of his hands through his hair, impatience eating away at his insides.

It seemed like he was always waiting; waiting to call her, waiting to get back to Chicago… waiting for her goddamn show to be over, waiting *to see her.* The past four hours had dragged, even as he listened to her weave the incredible magic of her silken voice over the airwaves. And, the past five days? Fuck, he didn't even want to think about it. *Control, Alex,* he told himself. *You are in control. You control your environment. You. Only you.* Yet, here he was, waiting for her like a dog.

"Fuck!" he muttered in amused disgust.

He crossed his arms over his strong chest, the white T-shirt stretching taut over his broad shoulders as the hot air, now hotter, left his body. It was a muggy night; clear, yet the stars were hidden by the massive light reflection of the city. The air was heavy, condensing in small beads on his golden skin.

Alex glanced around the large parking lot and the surrounding street. It was an older neighborhood, the few business buildings, restaurants, and bars still wearing the clothing of yesteryear—quaint and cozy—where locals lived, worked, and played. A little blast from the past existing in the middle of greater Chicago, untouched by modern accouterments; except for the station. It didn't fit. Like a twenty-first century alien in Mayberry.

The radio played through the open window of the car, a spot for a local car dealer followed by an announcement of a charity event in the park, a battle of bands in the park that benefited childhood cancer. It sounded fun and like something Angel would surely enjoy. He noted the date in his Blackberry as a bunch of kids scuttled across the street toward the station. Some of them were tall, but they were a mix of heights and ethnic backgrounds. Five in all, dressed in black, their clothing and hats way too much for the August weather. The hair on the back of Alex's neck and forearms stood on end. Something felt wrong. His body went rigid as he pushed off of the car, muscles coiling as he watched them carefully.

Alex leaned into the car to lower the volume on the stereo and strained to hear their conversation. They moved with deliberation toward the two cars near the front of the station, Angel's Lexus and an old Ford Taurus. They moved in closer to them, inspecting and looking in the windows, mumbling in low tones. Alex saw the flash of metal reflecting the light from the street lamps.

"Hey! What are you doing?" Alex yelled into the silence, adrenaline rushing through his body, his heart pumping loudly in his ears. "Get away from there!" He walked in long, quick strides toward Angel's car.

The group startled, glancing over their shoulders before scurrying off into the inky darkness, disappearing down a residential street south of the parking lot, amidst a barrage of whispered curses.

"What the hell?" he muttered as he walked around the car, checking for any evidence of vandalism. He glanced in the windows, taking in the dark leather seats, looking for anything that would tempt potential thieves. Her gym bag was on the back floorboard, but there was nothing else. The doors were locked with no sign of forced entry. The other car was older with nothing more than a bag of Doritos in the back seat. "Fucking hoods."

"Thanks for all your calls and dedications this evening. Let me leave you with this… it's one of my favorite songs. I love the rhythm. It just makes me want to take my clothes off. And who needs clothes on a night like this?" Angel's sultry voice lilted out of his car window as he approached. "This is Angel After Dark on KKIS FM. Love and peace." Her suggestive words were underscored by the beginning of the Maroon 5's *Secret*, its pulse tangible, and despite his current state of concern, his body stirred at her sultry suggestion and he smiled softly to himself, leaning back against the car.

*Surely she knows I'm listening.*

As he waited, doubt clouded his thoughts like a heavy fog, rolling everything he knew to be true into obscurity. He'd called her on Wednesday, but due to the time difference, it was in the middle of the night for her and she hadn't returned his call.

*Maybe she isn't interested.*

Alex stopped himself, sighing, and pushed at his hair as the hot breeze caused it to brush annoyingly over his forehead. Never before had he wondered if a woman wanted him. Although it felt mutual when they were together, he could see how much she was fighting with herself, and he didn't like it.

The minutes ticked by, the sultry song speaking of secrets, sweat, and sex until it faded out and the syndicated overnight program began. His eyes searched the front of the station, willing Angel to appear.

When the door pushed open and she finally emerged with her assistant in tow, his heart sped up at the sight. The two women were talking to each other softly as they moved toward their cars. Angel was wearing a short denim skirt and layered tank tops. Alex's hungry eyes drank in the sight of her bare skin, long legs ending in five dollar flip-flops, and the soft swells of her body calling to him. She looked good enough to eat.

"Angel!" he called out, just loud enough to reach her, and immediately her head snapped toward the sound. She stopped. Alex pushed off of his car and began walking toward her as the other woman got in her car and drove away. Both of them watched each other in silence until, finally, he was so close he could feel the heat between them rising and smell the salt and sweet that was her skin.

"Lurking in parking lots is beneath you, isn't it?" Her eyes sparkled as they narrowed. His fingers itched to touch her. "What are you doing here?"

"I told you Sunday, I wanted to see you when I got back. You look amazing."

Angel rolled her eyes and huffed. It was 2 am and she'd worked since 8 am. She couldn't possibly look like she'd want to, given the man now standing in front of her. "Pfft. Flattery will get you nowhere." Her heart thrilled at the sight of him, despite how she'd spent all day trying to squash her hope that he'd appear.

Alex chucked softly, unsure of her demeanor. "Won't it?" he murmured as he moved closer, almost pinning her to the car. He was trying to calm his reaction to her nearness, even as he challenged himself with it. She was so fucking delicious and he wanted to taste. He concentrated on the tendril of hair that the breeze was messing with on the side of her delicate features. She stared up into his face, her brown eyes defiant.

A pout settled on her soft lips and her brows pinched.

"It's dangerous out here. I don't like this set-up. The few cameras are trained on the building and the lot is vulnerable."

Angel ignored the comment. "You didn't call," she accused almost against her will as the soft fabric of his shirt found itself being rubbed between two of her searching fingers. Alex closed his eyes.

"Yes, I did." His head bent toward hers and his open lips found purchase on her cheekbone and then moved to her temple.

Angel pushed away enough to look up into his face with challenging eyes. "No, you didn't."

His fingers closed around hers and his eyes smiled as he pulled her closer, up against his body, his other arm sliding around her waist and up between her shoulder blades at the same time his nose nuzzled her face. "Funny thing about those phones, they ring on both ends."

He knew he shouldn't take for granted that he could touch her, but damn if he could fight it.

Angel had the grace to flush. She had to admit it, as much as she'd wanted to, she made herself resist picking up the phone all week. Besides all the bullshit, he was always on her mind.

"I... I'm the woman." She smiled at the ridiculousness of her statement and enjoyed the shivers his mouth and nose were creating. His face was clean-shaven and he smelled of basil and expensive cologne.

Alex smirked. "Really? How did that escape my oh-so-focused attention?" His hand slid into her hair as he tilted her head so he could place a feather kiss on the side of her mouth, teasing her to give in. *She will give... I can feel her body humming*, he thought. Finally, because he could bear it no longer, Alex kissed her mouth, soft and gentle, a slight suck on her lower lip as he pulled away.

It was ninety degrees outside and yet she shivered in his arms and his body answered hers, throbbing, even as he held himself in check.

"You know what I mean. And I didn't think I should intrude. You were working," she said against his mouth just as he repeated the kiss.

"So were you." Another kiss...

She sighed, but remained silent, letting him kiss her, straining not to give in. Her hands clenched. Alex felt her frustration because it echoed his own. He could lose himself in this woman, his whole neat and tidy life would be fucked beyond recognition and he knew it; all of his carefully placed boundaries, flushed in a moment.

Angel was fighting the same battle, but for different reasons. He mentally shook himself. Were her reasons really all that different from his? He nudged her top lip with the tip of his tongue, their breaths mingling. Alex breathed hers in, wanting her essence.

"Look who is here, begging like a dog. Are you going to kiss me back or what? You don't want me to start humping your leg, do you?"

"Hmmph!" she said as a low laugh gurgled up from her chest. "You're relentless."

"More like defenseless." He smiled against her lips—nudging, teasing—until her arms finally slid around him and into his hair, her eyes finally closed. He knew he'd won this battle, and his mouth finally took hers in the hungry kiss he'd been craving all week. Fuck, she felt good, his long fingers exploring her body: her back and hips, rib cage, and the luscious side swell of her breasts.

His tongue slid like silk against hers, hot and demanding, and Angel thought she'd die any second. They strained together, his hardness communicating his want as her hands wound in his hair, passionately pulling him closer. He groaned into her mouth as he kissed her deeply, their incredible passion igniting like spontaneous combustion. It was a living thing. Undeniable.

Angel wondered why this one man could turn her world upside down, clouding her judgment until she didn't give a flying fuck about her lifelong convictions.

"You're crazy. Don't you have horrible jet lag?" she whispered as he pulled away and rested his forehead on hers, his strong arms still fully around her so that her breasts were flattened on his chest.

"Would you have come to me tonight?" he asked. When Angel hesitated, he lifted his head to meet her gaze. "Would you?"

Her eyes were languid, wanting to close, as she played with the silken strands at the back of his head. "No. Definitely not." She said the words, but was left wondering how true they were.

"Right. So here I am. *Woof.*" His white smile flashed in the darkness and they both burst out laughing. Alex pulled her away from the car and lifted her in a bear hug, still chuckling. "I missed your voice."

"Feels like you missed more than that. Down, boy," she teased, even as her arms returned his embrace and her face turned into his neck.

When he placed her back on her feet and released her slowly, Alex wasn't willing to lose all contact, keeping his fingers laced with hers. "I did miss you." It was an admission; to himself as much as to her.

"Well, you know… it's my sparkling personality."

Alex's eyes settled on her face. She was luminous and he couldn't tear his gaze away. "Yes. Something like that."

"So—" *I missed you, too,* she thought.

"Yeah. Uh…" Alex struggled with the scene from earlier. Should he tell her? He wanted her to be safe but didn't want to worry her. "I'll follow you home, okay? Just to make sure you get there safely."

His thumb brushed across her hand as he brought her fingers to his lips. Alex towered over her and she loved it. So handsome, and so much *man*. So strong, capable, masculine; her body flooded with desire. Business suit or jeans, scruffy or clean-shaven, he was beautiful and so hot. *Fucking unreal*, she thought.

Angel's heart swelled and her features softened. In that second, she wanted Alex to be real more than she'd ever wanted anything and wasn't ready to get in her car without him. Her heart thudded so hard it hurt. She was in serious trouble and it scared her more than Mark Swanson. Much more.

"How was your week?"

"Long," he said simply, his eyes intent, watching to see if she caught the hidden meaning.

"And why didn't you call me again?" Her eyebrow quirked as she shot him a teasing look, his fingers still wound into hers.

"I did. Why didn't *you* answer?"

"The damn phone did not make a peep. The brilliant guy who gave it to me forgot the charger. So, yeah."

"Christ, I'm a moron! I'm sorry! But you didn't program my number into your other phone?" he asked hopefully. "I mean, you have my number, I don't have yours."

"I'll never tell." Heat rushed under the skin of her cheeks in a becoming blush.

Alex smiled warmly, the extent of his pleasure surprising him. "Come on, babe. Let's get you home." He opened the door and her perfume wafted out of the car. "It's hotter than hell out here."

"You planning on tucking me in?" She could see his exhaustion as she slid behind the wheel. "Or are you too pooped to pop?" The dimples in her cheeks were visible as she bit her lip, obviously fighting the urge to smile.

"I'll never be too tired with you. Stop tempting me. You don't fight fair."

"Who says I'm fighting?"

"Oh, you are. I know you are."

# 10

## Touch Me Forever

ANGEL GLANCED IN her rearview mirror as she waited for the door to her underground garage to open. Alex's black Audi was behind her and it was dark. She couldn't see him, but her mind imagined him with his arm leaning on the wheel, waiting; like she was.

Her nerves were shot, her heart pounding. What the fuck was she thinking letting him follow her home? The threat from the weekend prior loomed over her. It was hard to admit, but she was frightened—for him, for her—and for her heart. Alex was right. She was fighting, but it was no longer clear for what.

The visitor parking was near the door, while her parking place was next to the elevator. As she got out of her Lexus, he was already strolling over toward her, hands in the pockets of his jeans. Casual, sexual, gorgeous; like he wasn't even aware of the effect he had on her. His eyes devoured her and she trembled.

*Jesus, God, help me.*

Her throat tightened as his arms slid around her loosely, and his scent saturated the air.

"Alex…" It fell from her lips without her consent as her hands wrapped around his strong forearms.

"Mmm, huh?" Warm and damp, his lips gently brushed her temple and then parted, his breath washing over her skin. As hot as Chicago was, and humid as hell, this type of heat was wanted, craved. "You smell just like I remember." His nose brushed the side of her neck behind her ear. "Absolutely wonderful."

She smiled softly in the dimly lit space as his lips meandered down her cheek to her jaw, softly sucking with each little kiss. It was heaven. She leaned into him; afraid her legs would no longer support her as all thoughts of pushing him away or making him leave, vanished.

"I was just thinking that you smelled amazing, too."

His hands cupped her face, tilting her head as his mouth settled on hers, a low groan erupting. The kiss was gentle, searching, and her lips parted under his, wanting more, the tip of her tongue sneaking out to flick against his top lip. He pulled her lower one between both of his.

"You should sleep," she whispered against his mouth.

"Fuck sleeping. I'll sleep when I'm dead."

"Aren't you tired?" Her hands slid up his chest, her fingers kneading at the muscles under his shirt.

"Not too tired to touch you." He dragged his mouth from her temple, leaving a trail of kisses back toward hers.

"Then come inside."

"Angel, you'll be the death of me."

"Just come."

"Unnnggg. Stop saying *cum*." His voice was low and feral. Angel's body flooded with heat, and she pressed her forehead into the smooth skin on his cheek. She knew she was done.

"It's so late. I have plenty of room."

"In your bed or the room you keep for Becca?"

"Wherever you want."

"I want *your* scent."

"Okay." His arms tightened as his mouth moved in slow deliberation against the smooth cord of her neck. Angel shivered again.

"You know what will happen."

She nodded. "I want it to happen."

Blood surged at her words, filling him further, and he groaned as his hand wound in her chestnut waves. It was like silken water, falling through his hands, and he gasped at it again, his mouth hovering over hers.

"I'm trying not to reinforce your low opinion of me, yet you seem determined to undermine my effort. You'll think I'm a cad if I give in to this."

"No, I won't. Besides, you're exhausted. You shouldn't drive." Her chin rose, her mouth seeking to find his in a kiss. His mouth played with hers, noses brushing and nuzzling, hands grasping at the silk and cotton covering over-sensitive flesh.

*My apartment is 5 minutes from here and I never stay over. But with you... I want things I never hoped to want.* "Maybe I am a little drunk. You're intoxicating. It's insane."

"God, Alex. I'm aching... open."

"Angel," he whispered, a sweet hot wave of breath against her face. Each of them silent, just breathing, not willing to let the other go. Finally, the fingers grasping at the back of his neck loosened and slid down his arms, her eyes finding his, beseeching as their fingers entwined, and she began to move backward toward the elevator that would take them to the place three floors above that would become their sanctuary.

Beyond words, Alex's eyes burned over her as she bit her lower lip, and the elevator doors closed; the cool inside a sharp contrast to the stifling heat of the Chicago night. Her body trembled and tightened, but not because of the chill.

He found himself wishing the trip would be longer, so he could push her up against the wall and press into her. Instead, he turned her and wrapped her in his arms, burying his mouth against her shoulder, knowing he'd have no choice but to give in to the maddening want. He was done trying to deny himself something that was clearly undeniable. As long as it was what she wanted, he'd give her so much pleasure she'd beg him to stop. He'd make sure she was incapable of staying away from him.

Theirs was an unspoken dance of longing, lust, and life force, flowing from one to the other like electricity or oxygen. As they made their way to her apartment, never letting go of each other in the low lights of the corridor, their minds and pulses raced, each fighting their own thoughts.

*I want you like I've never wanted anyone.*

**I'm scared you'll devour me... break my heart and leave me bleeding... still, I can't help myself.**

At the door, she fumbled in her purse for the key, and when she pulled it out, Alex's hand closed over hers, pulling it from her non-resistant fingers before shoving it the lock. Her back was against the door as he reached around her. Her dark brown eyes lifted to search his face, desperately seeking confirmation that he was as helpless as she was. Both of their minds raced, conflicted.

*I am completely out of control with you. I'm lost somewhere in your eyes, your arms, your body, your mind. Lost.*

**What happens when I give to you? Or when I take from you? Will you consume me, body and soul? I can't escape you.**

His free hand pushed her hair back, as his eyes met hers un-flinchingly, thumb brushing her chin.

**You leave me defenseless... it's like I'm drowning, grasping and clawing for every breath. You'll break me**, her mind cried, even as the depth of his desire registered.

*You'll own me.*

Alex's mouth crashed down on hers, and she whimpered as his body pushed her hard against the door, his hungry kisses left her breathless. Her mouth opened further, allowing him the deepest access, and her hands clutched at the back of his head.

Alex's heart pounded hard against her chest, and she felt his arousal against her hip, as their mouths moved in perfect symmetry. One giving, the other taking, passionate and wild and then softening, becoming more gentle.

"Angel, I should go. You don't want this."

Her hands slid from him to reach behind her and fumble with the door. "Don't I?"

His breath rushed out as his forehead pressed down onto hers. He was trembling, fighting to control his desire, and she felt powerful knowing he was beyond control.

"No. You want to know that I'm willing to invest in you. That I'm not what you think. I want you to trust me."

"Unnng," she moaned as the door fell open and she lost her balance, stumbling backward. Instantly, Alex's arms tightened, preventing her fall. "Please, just hush." Her fingers brushed his lips as their eyes met. "I don't want to think right now, so just... shhhh."

Alex stilled, his eyes burning into hers. God help him, he wanted to be with her. In whatever way she would allow. His head moved in an almost unperceivable nod.

Her hand reached for his as her purse and keys landed in a rattling pile on the floor, and the door closed behind him. It felt like slow motion to Alex as she pulled him down the dark hall in silence, the only sound was the blood rushing, pulse pounding in his own body, matching the throb in his groin.

Her room was large and smelled of perfume and vanilla. Alex's eyes narrowed, taking in the looming shadows of the large bed, adorned with a dark duvet and lots of pillows, a chaise in one corner, and a door leading to what must be her bathroom or walk-in closet. The blinds were tightly drawn so only the briefest of rays flickered in from downtown, fully illuminated outside.

"I can't sleep if light shines in," she said softly, moving to pull back the covers.

Alex watched her, immobile, unsure. His hands clenched, aching to feel her flesh under them.

"I like hearing your voice in the dark."

Angel pushed up his shirt, baring his stomach, her chin tilting up to look into his face. The lights reflected off of her eyes, making them sparkle like the moon on a lake. He caught his breath.

"Do you think about me... in my bed... often?" she asked.

He could hear the smile in her voice and his lips curved into one of his own. "Constantly. It's debilitating." As she continued to push his shirt up, Alex finally gave in and pulled the offending garment over his head, letting it fall to the floor. "Angel, come here," he commanded softly.

"Stop saying *cum*." She pressed her open mouth to the pulse at the base of his neck, standing on tiptoe to reach.

Alex chuckled, his hands closing around her waist and beginning to push her shirt up in turn. "You make me laugh. It's so damn sexy."

"I'm going to rinse off, okay?"

"You don't need to."

Angel cringed slightly. Part of her wanted to just melt into his arms, but she reminded herself that she hadn't showered for twenty hours. "Yes, I do. I'll only be a minute."

Angel sighed as he sank down on the bed in front of her and pulled her into him, his mouth closing over the tip of her breast over her top. She moaned and arched as his teeth grazed and her nipple hardened instantly.

"Fuck, you are so responsive..." His words and breath fell on her breasts, and his teeth tugged on the hard bud until she was trembling and panting. "So soft, Angel."

Her arms wrapped around his head, fingers thrusting into his hair, and she bent to kiss his forehead, thrilling that this man was

here, in her room, in her arms, even if it was a fleeting moment...
one that would crush her later.

"I'll be just as responsive after my shower. Even more. I
promise." Her voice was soft and soothing, the sweet seductive
sound he'd come to crave. He pushed the material out of the way
and his lips found purchase on her tender flesh. Angel sucked in
her breath as her body arched involuntarily toward him.

"Mmm... I like it when you make promises." His words muffled as his mouth continued its slow torture on her breasts, hands
roaming her back and hips.

"I always keep them, so let me go for just a few minutes."

"Do I have to?" He kissed along her jaw and up, his mouth
finding hers in a long deep kiss. When her tongue answered his, he
groaned into her mouth, the kiss deepening and their embrace becoming more frantic as his fingers tore at her clothes, freeing her of
her shirt and opening her shorts.

She ripped her mouth away. "Just five or six minutes..." Her
fingers went from his jaw up the side of his face and into his hair.

Alex was reluctant to let her go. He was bemused. He barely
knew her, but yet, she was all he could think about. She made him
hungry for her words, her mind, and her body; so fucking hungry.
His mouth moved down from her chin and over the slender col-
umn of her neck until, finally, to her bare shoulder where he bit
down gently.

"Uhhh." She let out her breath. "Wait for me in bed."

His palm cupped the side of her head and his lips moved
down the side of her face. He sighed in resignation. "Okay. Go."

Releasing her, he began undoing his jeans. As Angel exited the
room, she was left with the visual of strong muscles under smooth
skin and the smattering of fine hair that condensed and narrowed
to a line leading down over his defined stomach.

Angel leaned up against the bathroom door. What was she
doing? Her hands were shaking, her body buzzing, as she turned

on the water and stepped underneath. As much as she knew she shouldn't be with him, her mind a never-ending loop of how much he could hurt her, the longing was too much to resist. When he was near, she was helpless. And now, he was in her bed… waiting.

She toweled off and ran a quick comb through her hair, debating if she should get something to put on. "Who are you kidding? Clothes have no place in what's about to go down," she mumbled softly to herself, lighting the almond and vanilla candle on the vanity and shutting off the light. The mirror reflected how flame glowed on her skin, reflecting amber in her eyes.

Naked, she carried the candle into the dark bedroom and set it on the end table on the right side of her bed. Alex was on his stomach, his arms curled around the pillow his head was resting on, the sheet clinging to his hips. Angel's breath caught at the site. Her queen-sized bed seemed to shrink with his long form angled across it.

The candlelight danced off the walls and his body as she studied him, his face relaxed in repose, his hair appearing darker against the white pillowcase. Damn, he was striking—*stunning*. Angel let out her breath, slightly disappointed that he was already sleeping, but so appreciative of this chance to look at him unobserved.

She bent to pick up his discarded T-shirt and slipped into it. While it was fitted on his broad shoulders and then tapered to his slim waist, the whole thing bagged on her, the V of the neckline leaving one shoulder bare. She brought some of the fabric to her nose and inhaled as she climbed into bed.

Her fingers ached to reach out and touch him, to feel his muscles play as he moved over her and inside of her. Her body flooded with moist heat, aching, and her heart beat faster. *Surely, he must hear it*, she thought.

Sitting on her knees next to him, she gave in to the need, and soon her hands were roaming over his back and shoulders, alternating gentle kneading with soft touches and the light scratch of her nails.

Alex stirred. "Mmmmmm, that feels nice," he said, voice muffled by his arm.

"Just relax, go back to sleep."

He let her continue for five or so minutes but then turned onto his side and reached for her. "I can't sleep with you touching me, Angel. You turn me on too much."

She couldn't help notice his arousal bulging underneath the sheet and her hand closed around him. Alex's eyes closed. "Are you sure you don't want me to touch you?" she teased softly. He thrilled at the tone in her voice.

"Touch me forever." Their eyes locked.

Angel's heart swelled. If only he meant it. "Be careful what you ask for."

Alex rolled onto his back and lifted her until she straddled him, knees beside his naked hips, sitting on his thighs. His gaze burned over her in the candlelight. "As much as I adore your choice of wardrobe, I'd rather you be naked." His hands slid up the sides of her body underneath the shirt and her arms lifted, allowing him to remove it and fling it aside.

"Jesus," he said softly, his hands rising to cup her breasts, thumbs teasing her nipples with practiced expertise. She was perfect, every inch of her visible to him. "You're so damn beautiful." Her skin ignited everywhere he touched, his fingers gentle as if she were made of porcelain, and his mouth began exploring her shoulder and the cord of her neck.

Angel continued to pleasure him with her hands, and Alex's breathing increased. She felt powerful, beautiful, and sexy as he fell back against the pillows with a low growl, helpless to what she was doing to him. He brought it out of her. She was more uninhibited, more wanton than she'd ever been in her life. His eyes devouring her made her ache, darkening as his hand moved down between her legs. Her head fell back as a soft moan left her mouth. He was hard as steel, but smooth as silk in her hands, a drop of clear fluid squeezed from the swollen head and she smoothed over it with her thumb.

"Ugh," he grunted. "I have a condom." He reached under the pillow and pulled the foil packed from underneath.

Angel smiled softly as her eyebrows lifted. "Pretty sure of yourself, aren't you?"

He ripped open the packet and chuckled. "I'm absolutely sure that I can't be with you in a bed and not fuck you. I've thought of little else."

She watched him roll it onto his engorged cock, wondering how in the hell he could be so perfect. "So I guess you've given up on your quest to keep things platonic."

"I can't fight it, especially when I know it's what you want. You do want it, don't you?" He paused, his hands sliding up her thighs to her hips and his eyes met hers in the darkness.

"Yes. I keep saying it. So hear me." It was soft, but it thrilled him. "Fill me."

He lifted her and slid inside her body in one fluid movement. "Uhhh," he breathed. "God." Her hips surged against his as she leaned back, bracing her hands on his thighs, enjoying every inch of his body as it pushed into hers. She was graceful, even elegant in her movements, and Alex could not take his eyes off her, even as his body tightened.

He touched her breasts as she rode him, pulling gently on the rosy nipples until his mouth was jealous of his fingers. He could feel her body tightening around his and his pleasure became secondary to hers. He raked a hand down her body, over her flat stomach, finding the goal of her clit. Her flesh was hot, slick, and the desire to see her come overwhelmed him. He watched her face, the way she arched her back and neck, her eyes closed. When her mouth fell open, he knew she was close. Her voice and the way her body started to quiver confirmed it. "Mmmm, Alex... uhhh... God."

He sat up and wrapped his arms around her, one around her still moving hips, pulling her tighter against him and the other up to the back of her head. He wanted her mouth, wanted her cries of pleasure to pour into him as his would surely pour into hers. The position was so intimate, so close, torsos plastered together, hips surging with a single purpose, hands clutching in desperation and mouths sucking, taking, giving. Alex had never felt this much passion, this much frantic desire. If he could be inside her forever, he knew it would never be enough, and while it thrilled him, it scared the shit out of him too.

Angel's fingers in his dark hair pulled his mouth closer; their kisses intensified between their panting breaths. Their bodies dug into each other's, harder and deeper until he felt her stiffen in his arms and she moaned his name.

Finally letting himself go, his arms tightened. "Angel, it's so good with you..." He jerked hard several times as he poured into her, and she kissed the side of his jaw and then his temple, stroking back his hair over and over. They remained entwined as their breathing calmed down, hands caressing the other.

For Alex, this was like nothing he'd ever experienced. He had no desire to disengage, throw on his clothes, and leave; it hit him like a ton of bricks. He turned his face into her neck and left a trail of kisses to her mouth as he rolled her onto her back, still embedded within her. He'd shot off so hard, he was still quaking with the aftershocks.

"Angel... I don't want to go. Can I stay?" His fingers gently stroked the hair back from her temple and deep green eyes found hers as his mouth hovered. Hers lifted, first nibbling, then sucking his lower lip into her mouth.

"Yes. Stay."

*****

Alex woke with something tickling his nose and snuggled into the warmth next to him. His eyes opened with a start, realizing that he was in bed with Angel, her head resting on his chest below his chin, her long tresses splayed out on his skin, their limbs entwined.

He'd slept with her. He liked it, *more than liked it*, and it left him in awe. Even now, hours later, he was in no hurry to leave. He needed to meet Cole to find out what he'd discovered, but he was reluctant to move.

"Wow," he muttered, running his hand over the hair on her back and down, enjoying the feel of her womanly curves against him. He sucked in his breath as the memories of the past night, well… morning, enveloped him. Angel was so free and giving, unselfish in her desire to please him, which made him want to please her even more.

He glanced down at her sleeping face; the high cheekbones had a slight flush, below the long, lush lashes, her nose, perfect, and her luscious, full mouth swollen with his kisses. She was… resplendent. A broad smile broke on his handsome face as his hand softly kneaded her back. She snuggled closer, her leg lifting over his. Instantly, he pulled her tighter against him, turning slightly toward her and hoisting her leg higher over his hip.

"Mmmm," she moaned softly. "Alex."

His smile grew even wider. "Mmmm, Angel," he agreed in a soft murmur against her cheek and then found her mouth with his in a gentle kiss. "Good morning."

Angel stretched in his arms, which made her body come in closer contact with his, pressing all the good stuff together. She smiled and opened her eyes, her hand coming to rest on his now-scruffy jaw. *So strong*, she thought. "Did you sleep well?"

"Like the dead."

"Did I wear you out?"

He smirked and pressed his hardening erection into her softness. "Never. I never want to leave this bed."

She looked into his eyes, and suddenly they were both serious.
"Um..." She felt uneasy. This was too comfortable; it felt too
good. If she wasn't careful, she'd start feeling shit she didn't want
to feel; if it wasn't already too late. Plus, he shouldn't even be here,
not if she wanted to keep the threats to him at bay. Her chest
constricted.

"What?" he asked, nuzzling with his nose. His breath was
warm on her face, his voice like honey, and her body responded.
She wanted him. Her fingers skittered over the hard muscles of his
arms and shoulders.

"Um... what time is it?"

"Does it matter? It's Saturday." He rolled her over, covering
her body with his, and continued to kiss and nuzzle, pressing her
down on the mattress, hardness against softness.

Angel closed her eyes. She had to move, to get some distance,
and protect her heart. Knowing what he could bring her body to,
stole her breath, but she had to think. *Think, Angel!*

"Becca is coming. I mean, we always work out on Saturday."

Alex pulled back to look into her face, a small smile playing
on his beautiful mouth. Angel's eyes were transfixed on his, her
heart thrumming in her ears. "I'll work you out, better than Becca
can, baby." His hips moved against hers, teasing as his eyes danced
mischievously.

"No, Alex. I'd love to, but she'll be mad at me. She's coming
all the way into town from Schaumburg."

Alex could see the panic in her face, and for the first time in
his life, he gave a shit. He wanted to know what was behind it.

He rolled to her side and propped his head on his elbow.
"What's bugging you? Becca isn't the issue."

"Yes, she is. We promised each other that we wouldn't change
our routine because of a guy. And I'm sure you have things to do,

too." She glanced at him out of the corner of her eye, still lying on her back. "Don't you?"

Alex searched her expression. "I was supposed to meet my brother, but he's never on time. It annoys the shit out of me." He reached for the Rolex he'd placed on the side table. *11:45 AM!* He sat up and ran a hand through his beautiful mess of hair, made messier by Angel during their sex play. "I do need to get going." The woman still in repose, where he'd left her, was hard to leave. The sheet was draped over her and he could see every nuance of her body through it. "Damn if I want to, though. Angel... this is..."

"We don't have to define this, Alex."

"Maybe I want to."

"Well, I don't. I thought you just wanted to have fun, no strings."

His brow furrowed. "I told you that I don't have sex with multiple women. I'd prefer that you weren't fucking around either."

"But... that's a string." She bit her lower lip and Alex had the urge to pull it free with his thumb.

"Are you sleeping with anyone else?"

"Not since we've been—"

He interrupted shortly. "Good. Keep it that way. I'll make sure you're satisfied." He winked.

Angel flushed, rolling her eyes. *No doubt.* "It isn't that; it's getting involved."

"Well, it *feels involved.* I stayed over, which doesn't happen. It felt good so let's just go with it. We'll each have our lives, but no other lovers. We tell each other in advance if that becomes an issue. Okay?"

Angel knew there was no way in hell she'd want to be with anyone else. Not when he wanted her. He was as close to God-like perfection as she'd ever seen, and Whitney's description of him fell incredibly short.

"Yeah."

Could she take that conversation? *"Angel, I want to have sex with someone else..."* She didn't want to think about it.

"Don't worry so much."

Angel watched him as he rose and walked to the other side of the bed to find his clothes, admiring every incredible inch of his amazing physique. She rolled over and gathered the sheet closer. "So you'd have me believe that no other woman has seen that ass in the light of day?"

He chuckled as he pulled on his jeans. "Not since college."

"Pity. It's a fine ass." She smirked and licked her lips suggestively.

Alex laughed. "Not as fine as this one." He slapped her on the rear and she squealed, giggling as he pulled the sheet from her, leaving her naked and sprawled on the bed, eyes wide and staring.

Alex undid his jeans he'd just donned and then pulled her, laughing, by her ankles toward him. "I don't think I'm leaving just yet."

*****

Becca sat at Angel's kitchen bar scowling as she watched her friend pour orange juice into two glasses.

"Sure you don't want some?" Angel asked.

"Yeah. I want to be at the gym," she retorted.

Angel's expression was indulgent. "We're going. Just a few more minutes. He'll be out of the shower."

"I can't believe this, Angel. You said you weren't going to see him again."

Angel shrugged. Her black hoodie was zipped up part way over a white tank and black yoga pants, her hair in a messy bun that had tendrils falling all around, her body still feeling the effects of Alex's possession only minutes earlier. Becca was dressed for the gym, also, but less fashionably than her friend. "I can't help it."

Becca's eyes widened as she bit down on a banana. "What?" she spoke with her mouth full. "You never fall prey to *gorgeous*."

Angel shrugged again. "Alex is... sort if inescapable, Becca. He met me after the show. He was exhausted, just back from overseas, yet he waited for me. I'm beginning to think my opinion of him was all wrong."

Becca finished the banana and threw the peel in the trash under the sink. "Wow. You've known him, what, 2 or 3 weeks? Maybe there's hope for you yet."

"I'm still cautious, but," she shrugged, "I enjoy being with him. I realize the risks, and my head fights with me over it, but damn if I can resist."

"Must be talented between the sheets. Doesn't help your resolve; he's gorgeous."

"Yes. That. I seriously can*not* help myself," Angel agreed pointedly. The girls were giggling just as Alex walked causally down the hall.

Freshly showered, and wearing the same clothes from the night before, Alex's hair was damp, the strands darker and falling boyishly over his forehead. He impatiently pushed it back with his right hand. A smirk lifted his lips as he entered the kitchen. Angel nodded toward the juice waiting for him on the counter and he picked it up. "Hello, Becca."

"Alex."

He walked around Becca toward Angel, leaning down to place a short kiss on her mouth as her hand came to rest on the solid wall of his chest. Angel blushed at his easy display of affection in front of her best friend.

Becca's eyebrows raised and she pursed her lips, nodding to Angel behind Alex's back. "Hot!" she mouthed.

"Do you want something to eat?" Angel asked Alex.

He rubbed her upper arms with his hands. "I just spoke to my brother. We're meeting for lunch, so I'm good. I have to run, but I'll call you later?"

She smiled. "Dead phone. No charger, remember?"

Alex laughed. "Oh, right. I'll remedy that soon. Call me, so I'll have your personal number."

"I like the other phone." Angel stopped herself before she revealed too much. That private line between them was super sexy.

Alex's eyes narrowed but he smiled, understanding. Satisfaction filled his expression. "I do, too. But, just this once." He touched her chin with his fingers and his thumb brushed Angel's jaw. Becca bit her lip and looked away. The gesture seemed very intimate. "Walk me to the door?"

He took her hand and she followed slightly behind him. "I'd like to see you tonight. Are you free?"

Angel's brow dropped, disappointment filling her. She'd made plans to meet Kenneth to discuss the next steps in the Swanson case. "Um, I have a work meeting. Actually, it's just a casual thing, but I have to go."

"Will it take all evening?"

"No, I'm meeting him at six for drinks. So I should be free by eight or so." Inwardly cringing, she wondered how she'd get away from Kenneth that fast. He'd want to pick up where they left off, and she'd be left with no choice but to tell him she was seeing someone else. Ugh.

"Him?" Alex's brow raised and a soft smile lifted the corners of his mouth.

"Uh huh. The district attorney, Kenneth Gant."

The name registered in Alex's mind, Bancroft mentioned that he was the man Angel was seeing, and the hair on the back of his neck stood on end, jealousy burning in the pit of his gut. He looked down at her hands in his, his emerald eyes on fire. "I see. Let's talk later, okay, baby?"

"If it matters, I wish I didn't have to go, but I do." Something inside her wanted to make sure he knew this was business and nothing more.

She waited for his response, and finally, his eyes met hers. He pulled her into his arms for a hug. Leaving Angel felt strange. He turned into her hair inhaling deeply, memorizing her scent. Even though Becca looked on, Alex's mouth took hers in a passionate kiss, his tongue invading her mouth, teasing hers into play. He took his time, enjoying the feel of her mouth on his, her body in his arms, her fingers in the hair at his nape.

When he drew away, he sucked in his breath and kissed her temple. "See ya."

On his way to the garage and his car, Alex shoved his hands into his pockets; his mind racing with questions about the man that Angel would be spending the evening with. For the first time in two weeks, he had the desire to read the red file. While he was confident that the passion between them was unparalleled, he wasn't willing to leave it to fate. That's how he won, by dissecting the competition and knowing their weaknesses.

"Fuck me," he muttered, running a hand through the beautiful, damp mess of hair. He knew he wouldn't read the goddamn thing.

When the elevator doors opened, the garage was filled with a car alarm honking repeatedly and he realized it was his Audi. He hurried forward, slowing as he approached. The windshield was shattered—like someone had taken a baseball bat to it—a huge round break, spreading out from the center, some of the glass littering the expensive leather interior and sleek black paint.

"What the hell?"

He shut the alarm off with his remote and moved closer, pulling a piece of paper from under the wiper and glancing over the rest of the vehicle. There didn't appear to be any other damage, thankfully.

Unfolding the paper, the words sank in.

*Keep away. If you know what's good for you. If you know what's good for* HER.

Alex burned; his heart tightening as anger flooded through him. He began to shake, his fist closing around the note.

"Son of a bitch!" he exclaimed loudly, his voice echoing through the empty space.

# 11

## Without a Net

ALEX SAT ACROSS from Cole as he cracked open the first of his second dozen crab legs, shaking his head and watching in stunned amazement as his brother packed in huge quantities of food. The morning had been a blur; getting his car out of the garage before Angel saw the damage and to the body shop, then the rush to meet Cole as planned. He shouldn't have bothered; Cole was late as usual.

Alex used the time to think about the implications of the vandalism and strengthened his resolve to find out what the hell was going on. Thoughts raced; the group of young men the night before at the radio station, and Angel's comments about her cases getting scary sometimes, had his neurons working overtime. The possibility of it being a coincidence seemed highly unlikely.

"Cole, can you stop eating long enough to tell me what you found out?" Alex leaned on his elbow against the back of the booth, his food untouched, his thumb and index finger plucking at his eyebrow impatiently. His lips set into a thin line when Cole continued to concentrate on his plate. *"Please?"*

Cole shrugged and licked two of his fingers and, at the same time, rolled his eyes.

"Uh, yeah, but I still don't get why this is important to you." Alex's stern expression urged him to continue. "The only dude I could track down that fits the profile is the owner of that big chain of dry cleaners. He's pretty connected; knows a lot of politicians and has distant mob connections."

Alex's face twisted in disbelief. *What the fuck? Investing—maybe, real estate—sure, but dry cleaning?* He could think of none. "How powerful can someone be when his business is cleaning clothes?"

Cole shrugged again. "It's all over the place. The business name is *Pressed.* They've been in operation for more than fifty years, Alex. I know you've seen 'em... Bancroft believes it could be a front for laundering cash. His business grew in one huge spurt after his father died."

Alex vaguely remembered some TV commercials and images of a logo. Obnoxious orange and bright blue with that smarmy bastard's mug attached to billboards and television advertisements. Angel's conversation of the rape of a stepdaughter made him cringe. "Yes, that is suspicious. Did you get financials? Where did the money come from?"

"It's not clear yet. Some loans, venture capital maybe, but it's probably dirty, Alex. Bancroft got pics of Swanson with James Standish, who, apparently, is married to Swanson's younger sister, Carol."

Heat spread under Alex's skin as the threats to Angel's safety took on more urgency. The Standish family was rumored to be marginally involved with the Chicago crime circuit; drugs, dirty politics, and who knew what else. It was known, and yet, business continued as usual. Alex worked on an international level for Avery and remained clear of any businesses the mob was involved with. His mind raced with questions about how solid this bastard, Swanson, was with the mob.

"What about his own family? Does he have kids?" He picked up his Blue Moon and took a long pull.

"Yep. He's been married twice and has a 30-year-old son from the first one. Thomas. He didn't even finish high school and his old man's set him up to take over. There is a stepdaughter from the second marriage. She's the one accusing him of rape."

When Alex seemed lost in his thoughts, concentrating on the way his beer sloshed around in the bottle as he moved it in circles, Cole put down his fork. "Alex, what is this about?"

Green eyes flashed and a muscle in Alex's jaw twitched. "What do you know about his business?"

Cole sighed. "I have the list of locations and whatever was available on public record."

"Is the company publicly traded?"

"Nope, it's still family-owned, but it's incorporated."

"LLC?" Alex searched for a weakness. If the company was limited liability, the bastard's personal finances would be protected.

"Nope."

Cole studied Alex as the corners of his lips lifted in a devilish smirk.

*Stupid bastard*, Alex thought. What idiot would have a business that size tied to his personal assets? Alex almost laughed out loud. "Excellent. I want to know which locations are owned and which are leased. Find out what the purchased properties are worth and what he pays for rent on the others, and get a list of the employees and all of the businesses around the cleaners."

"I didn't know Avery was in the dry cleaning business. Does Dad know about this?"

A scowl settled on Alex's face, but no answer was forthcoming.

Cole shifted uncomfortably in his seat. "This shit is getting old, little brother. Tell me what the hell is going on. I have a right to know why I'm doing this."

"You're having fun, aren't you? Just do it."

Cole pushed his plate away, a stern look on his face. "I won't do another goddamned thing until you explain."

Alex drew in a heavy sigh and his brow creased, uncertain how much of it he was willing to share. "Uh," he hesitated, not sure what label he should assign to Angel. "I have a friend working on the rape case, and I think the asshole is pressuring her to doctor her testimony so he comes out clean."

Cole's eyes widened, his expression incredulous. "You *think*? Surely a friend would tell you for sure?"

"It's a professional ethics thing. Won't discuss it."

"What will fishing around in his business dealings accomplish? If he's in with the mob, even lightly, then…"

"Exactly. The bastard's dangerous, and she doesn't know what she's dealing with."

Cole nodded knowingly, eyebrows lifting. "Ah ha, the clouds are clearing. Your friend is a woman. Didn't take you long to re-place Money-Grubbing Barbie. Are you really interested in this chick, or is this just to keep me busy?"

Alex sat back in the booth, holding his beer casually. "Angel is hardly a *chick*, and yes, I'm interested. Very. And I'm worried."

"Wow." A grin split his face at the obvious discomfort Alex was in. "She must be one hot tamale."

"Shut up, Cole. We've only known each other a couple of weeks—"

Cole interrupted, a knowing look crossing his features. "And already you're this tied-up in knots? I never thought I'd see the day."

Alex was flustered by his brother's perception of something he hadn't even taken the time to analyze. But, the thought made him flush. "I'm not in knots. I just don't want to see her hurt."

Cole's eyes narrowed and he nodded, disbelieving. "How is she involved? Professionally, you say?"

"She's the clinical psychologist assigned to assess Swanson's mental capacity and pathological tendencies, I gather." Even without confirmation from Angel, he knew he was on the right track. She'd shared enough for two and two to equal four.

Cole whistled. "So she's hot *and* smart. She *is* hot, right?"

Alex took a long pull on his beer, and when he was finished, a beautiful smile flashed. "It's *me*, Cole. Come on," he teased. "Besides, when you clean up, you land some hot women. Although, I do wonder about your beer goggles. That redhead a couple of weeks ago? Gross."

"Ruby?"

"Surprised you remember her name."

"Well, she gives great head," he said simply, as if it was a well-known fact.

Alex mocked him by acting like he was going to throw up. "I don't need the raunchy details. She was just nasty."

"Tell me about this new one. How's her bod?"

He was staring at his beer and his lips lifted in a slight smirk on one side. "Ahhh-mazing. She's beautiful and her voice... it slays me."

"Beautiful enough to risk getting involved with the mob?"

Alex looked uneasy and ran a hand through his hair. "We're not involved. We're checking things out."

"Alex, you don't even quirk an eyebrow unless something has your full attention. I know you."

"She is very intriguing. She minored in classical piano at Northwestern, too."

Alex's hand went to his jaw and his features softened, which didn't escape Cole's notice. "She couldn't play as well as you."

"I studied for years, Cole, so I don't know. She was in a rock band in college, not the boring classics."

"Those boring classics kicked my ass. Good thing you and Allison took it seriously, otherwise Mom would've needed smelling salts. I'm just not into all that high-crotch, highbrow bullshit. I wish you'd all stop trying to force it on me."

"No one's forcing you to be *high-crotch*." Alex's shoulders shook as he burst out laughing at his brother's slang-term. "Dad just wants to see you take an interest in something."

"You mean Avery Corp." Cole's features twisted in disdain.

"Well, he worked his ass off. It's only natural he wants us to care about its longevity. It's security for all of us."

"How did you do it? Give up Julliard for a desk job?"

"You do what you have to do for those that depend on you. We employ hundreds of people with families to support. Dad should be commended for that. If you started looking at it like that instead of a ball and chain, you might be more accepting. Even proud to be part of it."

"Dad has so many cronies in place, the firm runs itself."

"Oh, yeah? Then why am I dragging my ass all over the world? Thinking like that will get us bankrupt. The board of directors and shareholders expect a certain ROI. Do you think it just happens?"

"Is that what you have planned for this dude you have me chasing? Are you going to take over his company?"

"Not exactly." Alex's eyes narrowed as the plan formulated. "Since his company's privately held, we can't do it simply with stock purchases. We'd have to buy him out, and it's not my goal to line the bastard's pockets. No…" He leaned forward, playing with the hair near his temple thoughtfully. "You did say it wasn't an LLC?"

"Yeah. I mean, no, it's not." He watched the wheels turn behind his brother's eyes and, for the first time, was excited about something with purpose. This was going to be dangerous and exciting.

"Swanson isn't as smart as he thinks he is. Money equals power, so we bankrupt him. But legally." Alex knew he should discuss it with his father, but this was personal, and he wanted to get his head around the money necessary to take the business down first. "I need the financials, Cole. Avery's going into the dry cleaning business so you have no excuse not to wear a suit. Mom will be so proud," he teased.

"Oh, shit."

"One other thing." Alex took the receipt the waiter left on the table and wrote down the address to Angel's building on the back, sliding it toward Cole when he was done. "I want a list of anyone who works there, who lives there, and who owns it. Find out if anyone has connections to Swanson. I also need the real estate history. What is it worth? We need the trend of appreciation to get an idea of what a realistic offer would look like."

"Alex, now you're buying apartment buildings?"

"Just do it. I was there overnight, and someone bashed the windshield of the Audi and left this behind." He dug the note out of his back pocket and threw it on the table for Cole to see.

"Holy shit!"

"The damage wasn't horrible, and the note is amateurish." He brushed it off. He'd take whatever steps were necessary to protect Angel.

"No, not that. You were there *overnight?* Never thought that would happen, dude. *Ever.*"

Alex cleared his throat as he stood to leave. "You have better things to do then worry about where I sleep. Get on it." He threw some money on the table before grabbing the note and stalking out of the restaurant without another word.

*****

Angel looked at her watch. Kenneth was late, and she was impatient. She didn't think this noisy bar was the best place to have a discussion, but it was obvious Kenneth had other ideas. They'd spent a few fun evenings in similar venues that usually involved dinner and too much wine, and then they'd end up at his apartment near Roosevelt University. It wasn't much, but it was all he needed. If money were his first priority, he wouldn't be in the D.A.'s office. That was part of his charm. He was unpretentious and had good morals. Angel didn't feel a love connection, but she liked and respected him. They had a lot in common. His feelings for her were another matter, and her stomach tightened in protest at the conversation she knew would follow any resistance to the evening turning physical.

She pushed away any emotions that conjured up thoughts of midnight hair, green eyes, and long, beautiful fingers that already played her body like an instrument. She'd resisted the urge to call him all day. He'd asked her to, he said he wanted to see her, and damn it all, she wanted to see him, too. She pulled out her phone and thumbed through the contacts on the touch screen, finding the name and number she'd programmed in two hours earlier. She huffed in resignation, remembering the small battle she won with herself when she resisted the urge to assign a speed-dial. That would be too much like admitting they were more than fuck buddies.

Angel smiled slightly at an attractive man clearly admiring her. She sat at the bar in dark skinny jeans, platform Louboutin's, and a frilly lace button-down, in ivory, over a matching tank that was smattered with a few sequins. Her hair was messy perfection in the way only an hour in front of the mirror could achieve; her eyes full of smoky shadow and lips vibrant red. A shiver ran down her spine. She didn't dress for Kenneth or the many men checking her out. She knew it. She'd known all afternoon she wasn't strong enough to ignore Alex when he made it plain he wanted her.

"Just fucking admit it, for crying out loud," she muttered under her breath, pushing the button that would connect her to her motivation. He answered on the second ring.

"Alex Avery."

The din in the bar was loud and she could barely hear him. "Hey," she spoke loudly and he laughed.

"Hi! Where are you?"

"Downtown at Patty's. It's so loud in here!"

"Why didn't you call earlier? Trying to torture me?"

Angel flushed with pleasure. "Not exactly."

"Oh?" His voice was amused. "Only sort of?"

"No, but I have been resisting."

"Knowing it's a struggle is a step in the right direction," he said, chuckling. "Although I still don't get your reluctance. It feels good, doesn't it?"

She hesitated and bit her lip. To admit it would give him power. "Too good."

"Wow! That was easy. I expected more of a fight."

Angel could practically hear him smile. "I find I don't want to fight tonight."

"Mmmm, me either. When will you be done?"

"Um, an hour or two? Kenneth's late."

"Angel, are you alone at that bar?" His tone took on a harder edge.

"Yeah, but he should be here any minute."

"I'll be there shortly."

Angel gasped as his tone hardened. Alex interrupting her meeting with Kenneth was not something she was looking forward to. She didn't want to answer questions from either one. "That's not necessary, Alex."

"He shouldn't leave you alone there. It's fucking inconsiderate to let you be unprotected."

Angel flushed, suppressing a bubble of laughter that boiled up in her chest. *Unprotected? That's hilarious!*

"I'm fine. Honestly. Don't worry, I won't fall prey to anyone that will distract me from my final destination tonight." She was smiling so wide her face hurt, and the man that was checking her out began to make his way toward her, thinking it an invitation. She jumped down from the bar stool and turned her back on him. "I'll call you when I'm done."

A tap on her shoulder made her turn around.

"Excuse me, what's a beautiful woman like you doing here all alone?" The man was tall and dark. He looked Italian or Greek and was dressed casually but put together well; clean cut and expensive.

She put up a finger to hold him off for a moment so she could finish her call.

"Um, hey, I need to run."

"I'm coming. *Now.*"

Before she could answer, the phone went dead and she scowled. *Fuck!* she thought: as her eyes lifted to the man in front of her.

"I'm actually meeting someone, but I appreciate the offer," she responded with a smile as Kenneth finally walked up to her and slid an arm around her waist, bending to place a kiss on her cheek. "Here he is now."

"Sorry I'm late, Angel." He sounded out of breath. "I had to park six blocks away."

The other man smiled in regret and moved away. "You're a lucky man."

Kenneth smiled. "I am. Thank you."

Angel bristled and moved out of his embrace. The comment made her aware that Kenneth's perceptions weren't clear. She picked up her wine glass as Kenneth took the stool she'd been saving with her purse. "Want another?" he asked, motioning for the bartender to order a drink.

"Please." She'd need it if Alex showed up. It felt ridiculous to worry over the reaction of a man she barely knew. He had no right to get all hot and bothered, and she had no right to get excited by the prospect of his protectiveness. Inside, she thrilled at it but wasn't looking forward to introducing the two men. Silently, she vowed to hurry and get Kenneth out of there before Alex made an appearance.

"Listen, Kenneth, about the Swanson case. The tests are re-scheduled. Thanks for getting the court date moved back."

"I still don't like it. We should just get it over with and move on."

"Mark Swanson deserves to be behind bars. If this case isn't enough, we'll create another one. Sometimes, the system sucks."

"Angel, you know we can't manufacture evidence. It's called entrapment. He'd walk for sure then." He popped some of the pretzels sitting in a bowl on the bar into his mouth. "We'd both lose our licenses."

"That's not what I mean! I'll push him just enough to piss him off. He'll either crack on the tests the second time around or he'll do something stupid." Her eyebrow rose and she smiled. "It isn't entrapment. It's more like capitalizing on someone else's mistake."

Kenneth shook his head and put his fingers in his ears. "No! I'm not hearing this."

"What choice do I have? I have to push his buttons and get a reaction out of him. Bringing him up on another set of charges will help, won't it?"

"Sure, but I'm not willing to risk you getting hurt. This isn't a game, Angel. We shouldn't even be discussing this."

Angel was exasperated by his blasé attitude. "Fine, we won't discuss it then. But, I will do it, Kenneth."

He stopped and looked at her, knowing he wouldn't win. He never did. She left him helpless and he liked it. She was the most beautiful woman he'd ever seen, and tonight, even more than usual. "You look gorgeous. I'm honored."

*Don't be,* her mind shouted.

"Should we go somewhere for dinner?" Kenneth's fingers ran lightly down her arm. "What would you like?"

"Um, actually, I can't tonight."

"Angel, we haven't seen each other for so long. I miss you. I thought tonight we could—"

She inwardly cringed at the hurt expression on his face. "Kenneth, I know what you thought, and I'm sorry, but we both know this isn't going anywhere."

"It could if you'd let it."

She shook her head, her eyes imploring him not to make it more than it was. "We've had a lot of fun but if it was going to be more, then it would be by now." Her fingers touched his cheek lightly in an effort to soften the words that were coming. "You know things have been falling off for a while now."

His expression was hurt when he withdrew his hand, as if touching her burned him. "Angel, where is this coming from?"

"We haven't been together in over six weeks. We haven't even gone out to dinner."

"That's because you're such a workaholic." He looked away, avoiding her eyes. "I've tried."

"I know. It's my fault." Angel reached for his hand. She felt like an asshole for hurting him. "Besides, I shouldn't be dating the D.A.; not when we work on such important cases together."

Kenneth frowned, his blue eyes icy. "That's bullshit. Just tell me the truth. I deserve *that* at least."

She nodded. "You're right. The truth is I didn't want to hurt you. I care about you, but I can't pretend I have feelings that aren't there. I'm sorry."

"Are you seeing someone else?"

Angel bit her lip. "Only just recently."

"I see. Who is it? How did you meet?"

"Kenneth, please. None of that matters. We both know that we used each other. We had fun, we had good sex when we both needed it, but that's all it was. Be honest!"

"Still, if it weren't for this other guy—"

"If it weren't for him then *nothing*! We'd have nothing more than what we've had. I've been thinking about it for a few months, since before he was in the picture. Would you want me to lie and just go through the motions?"

Color flooded his face as her words sank in and his eyes bore into hers, finally. He shook his head and promptly changed the subject.

"I still don't want you to mess with Swanson. Let us do our job in the D.A.'s office and stay out of it, Angel. If you don't mind, I'm gonna take off."

*Wow.* Either he was very hurt or he'd seen the relationship as she had—comfortable and convenient. Angel was stunned. It was like turning the last page of a novel that you enjoyed but weren't dying for the sequel. It was over. No big deal.

"Yeah. So, I'll call you after I get the second set of tests completed next week."

Kenneth loosened his tie as he stood, leaning down to give her a lame attempt at a hug. "Be careful with that bastard, Angel. Just do the tests and leave it at that. Don't take unnecessary risks to incriminate him. I mean it." His free hand moved up to hold the back of her head as she kissed his cheek. "I still don't want anything to happen to you, even if you don't want to be with me."

Angel hugged him back, choosing to ignore the last part of his comment. "Thank you for worrying about me. I'll be careful."

*****

Blood rushed in Alex's ears as he watched the blond man wrap his arms around the woman he now considered his possession, the heat from within causing a thin film of perspiration to break out on his forehead and his heart to race painfully.

*What the fuck was happening to him?*

Patty's was loud, and he was unable to hear the conversation above the din, but Angel looked far from uncomfortable. She kissed his cheek before the man bent to speak into her ear while he threaded his fingers through her dark hair. She was beautiful. Her slender curves accented by the tight designer jeans, legs made longer by her animal-print pumps, full breasts being pressed to the other man's chest. It was too fucking much.

The room exploded around them as Kenneth Gant's hand slid down her back over the top of the sheer lace, over her skin. Alex ran a hand through his thick hair as he stopped dead in his tracks, unsure if he should turn around or stake his claim. The latter won as he resumed his beeline toward them.

"Good evening," he stated coldly as he waited for them to acknowledge him. Angel pulled back from the embrace immediately at the sound of his voice and turned. She looked like a deer in headlights, but Alex soon turned his attention to the other man. Sliding his left arm possessively around Angel's waist and pulling her close to his side, at the same time he extended his right hand. "I'm Alex Avery." Kenneth's mouth opened and then closed without uttering a sound. Alex was Alex. Outwardly confident, commanding, intimidating, even casually dressed in dark jeans and a crisp white V-necked T-shirt that showed a hint of the dark hair on his chest. He relaxed only slightly when Angel's arm moved around him to return his embrace. "And, you are?"

"I'm Kenneth Gant. District Attorney," Kenneth said, finally taking Alex's proffered hand.

*How gratifying for you*, Alex thought.

"Yes, Angel mentioned that," he returned, his eyes narrowing, sizing up the other man. "Sorry I'm late, honey." He turned to capture her open mouth with his, daring her to deny him as he pulled her lower lip between his and then placed another small kiss on the corner. "Are you finished with your business?" he asked against her mouth, carefully pounding the last nail in Kenneth's coffin. He wanted it clear that his own reasons for being with Angel were oh-so-personal. "I wanna play."

Alex was pissing her off. He knew it and he didn't care. He couldn't help it, even if he'd wanted to; the lack of control was infuriating. He should be cool and calm, not giving a shit one way or the other. But, that wasn't happening in this instance.

She scowled at him and stiffened in his arms, defiance jutting out her chin. His own arm tightened as he silently dared her to say she didn't want to convey the same goddamned message to everyone in that bar. *We are together. End of fucking story.*

After a little more uncomfortable small talk, Kenneth left the two of them alone, and Angel plopped down on the stool and crossed her arms. "What the hell was that? Why didn't you just pee on me?"

Alex's lip twitched, but this voice was still hard. "Don't tempt me. We'll discuss this in the car." He pulled out his phone and hit a speed-dial. "We're ready. Be in front in five." Long fingers wrapped around her forearm and slid down to her hand. "Come on. We're leaving."

"No." She jerked her hand free of his, her eyes defiant.

"What did you say?" Green fire burned over her face, his expression blasé.

Fuck him! How dare he think he could order her around? "I said. N. O. Is English your second language?"

Alex's temper was boiling, and the muscle in his jaw twitched impatiently. "Hilarious. Let's go."

"You didn't have to be such a jealous prick to him, Alex! He's a nice guy. We were talking about the case!"

Anger constricted his chest and heat flamed under his skin. *Did she just call me jealous? What the hell do I have to be jealous of?*

"Yes, I saw you *talking.* Now, let's go! I'm not getting into this here."

"Well, maybe I don't want to get into this at all!" She felt like a little brat having a tantrum, but goddamn him! Who did he think he was? She jumped up from the table and started to storm out of the bar.

Alex followed right behind, amused at the looks being shot in their direction. He didn't give a shit. The end result was what he wanted—her on the fucking sidewalk. Charles was there waiting in the valet lane, the back door to the black limo open and waiting for them, but Angel walked past it, put two fingers between her lips, and whistled loudly, clearly hailing a cab. Alex quickly grabbed her arm, and she reacted by smacking him hard with her purse.

He smiled slyly, her show of anger somehow comforting him. "Come on. Get in the limo, Angel." His amusement only infuriated her further.

"Fuck you, Alex!"

"Okay, if that's what you want." He said the same words that he did on the day he met her, his tone softening, his anger fading. She was so beautiful in her rage; it almost hurt. Hair flying in the breeze, her cheeks were flushed, breasts heaving, and eyes glistening in angry frustration. "But you have to come first."

"Oh, shut up!"

He sighed, his mouth returning back into an angry line. "I know you want to be with me tonight, so stop fighting it. Get in the goddamned car, Angel!" He waited ten seconds before taking matters into his own hands.

"You are the most infuriating man I've ever—oof!" She lost her breath as Alex hoisted her over his shoulder in the middle of the busy Chicago night and moved effortlessly toward the car.

"Lover's spat." He flashed a smile at a group of people on the sidewalk who stopped to gawk, acting like it was nothing out of the ordinary as he deposited her in the car like a sack of potatoes and followed her inside.

Angel scrambled away from him as he closed the door, and
Martin pulled the car from the curb. Alex sighed and ran a hand
through his hair. "Go to the house, please, Martin."

"Alex, please take me back to my apartment."

"No." The night before proved she wasn't safe there; at least
not until he had more information, and certainly not without him.

"Poor Alex. Who knew you'd be such a jealous weakling?
Maybe I should have gone home with Kenneth like he asked."

"Like hell! We both know you're where you want to be, so
who are you trying to convince?"

"You are such a conceited bastard. Do you think you're the
only one who wants me?"

Alex didn't speak as the limo moved onto the interstate and
out toward the suburbs, but he pushed a button to close the partition so the driver wouldn't hear them.

"Do you think I'm a bitch in heat and your dick is the only
thing that can offer salvation?" she spat.

Alex moved like lightening to tumble her backwards and pin
her to the seat beneath him, his hands around her wrists beside her
head. Angel stared up at him, gasping for breath in her surprise.

"Stop! Just fucking stop. *What I think* is that whatever *this is*
eats at my guts. When I saw Kenneth's hands on you tonight, you
kissing him, it took all I had to restrain myself. Now, as far as *my
dick*—that's up to you, but I wager, you *want it.*"

Her legs went around his waist as they both panted in each
other's faces, hearts pounding together; blood rushing. Angel
wasn't sure what she was struggling against as his nose brushed
hers and her chin lifted involuntarily. Probably, it was fear he'd
steal her soul. He made her hungry even in this madness, even in
anger there was still this immeasurable lust. This man had power.
Too much power and he knew it.

Alex's hands loosened on her wrists as he nudged her upper
lip with his lower one, teasing a response she was unable to deny

him. The fingers on both of his hands entwined with hers as he pressed into her. Angel moaned into his mouth at the pleasure, and he became even more aroused as his hardness met her heat.

His words rushed out in a whisper just before his mouth staked its ownership over hers. "You are *mine.*"

# 12
# Too Good to be True

ANGEL'S MOUTH WAS alive underneath Alex's, even though her brain searched for the will to struggle, pull away, or keep her traitorous body from responding. God, he tasted good, so perfect in his seduction.

With her chest heaving, she finally managed to break the kiss by turning her head to one side. Alex was not deterred, letting his mouth—still hungry for her flesh—move over her cheek and down her chin before leaving a hot, moist trail on her neck as the fingers of one hand worked at the buttons of her blouse.

"I fucking hate you," she whispered ardently, her voice trembling right along with everywhere he touched, unsure if she was speaking to him or herself. She squeezed her eyes shut as they began to burn, and her fingers wound in his hair. "I really hate you. I hate feeling so out of control."

"I hate you, too," he murmured against her breast before pushing her cream lace bra out of the path of his mouth with his chin and tongue, "for making me want you this much."

Angel drew her breath in a hiss as his hot mouth closed around her rosebud nipple, already hard in anticipation. Alex's lower body surged into hers and made her flush with damp warmth, leaving a delicious ache she knew only he could alleviate.

"Uh… God," she moaned as her body rose up to meet his, and she pushed her hands underneath the hem of his shirt, raking her nails down his back, amazed at the way the muscles flexed as he moved over her. The cool, silk knit was a stark contrast to the fire of his flesh. "Alex, what about the driver? Can he hear us?"

"Don't know. Don't care." Alex brought his head up to look into her face. She was breathtaking: a heated blush on her cheekbones and her hair splayed in a halo around her head on the light grey leather, her dark eyes glittering in the reflection of the lights filtering in from the night racing past the limo. He pushed her hair back as once again, their bodies surged together.

"Christ, you feel so good." Their eyes locked. "Do you want me to stop?" he asked, but he knew the answer.

The back of his fingers brushed over her flat stomach as his eyes searched for the answer in her face. Angel bit her lip and shook her head ever so slightly, but it was all the answer Alex needed. His fingers popped the button on her jeans and slid the zipper down.

*****

Angel was quiet and pensive, after the sex in the back of the limo, and had still not spoken when Alex held his hand out to assist her when they'd reached his gated estate on the north side of the city. Her eyes widened as she took in the large, natural stone, two-story house, elegantly lit in the front and surrounded by lavish landscaping and a curved drive.

The large trees told of either longevity or great expense to create the ambiance, and the hot breeze felt amazingly cool as it evaporated the soft sheen of perspiration on her skin, leftover from the passionate scene that had just concluded. Alex ran his free hand through his hair as he gently and silently tugged her toward the large mahogany door under the chandelier in the front entry. His eyes watched her closely, wondering what she was thinking. He was left unsettled by his own lack of control where she was concerned yet determined to get her to relax around him. Judging from the phone call they'd shared earlier, it would have been a great night if seeing her with Kenneth Gant hadn't caused his insides to explode.

His thumb brushed the top of her hand as he unlocked the door. The house was dimly illuminated from a few lamps that his housekeeper had left on, as was her custom, not knowing when or if the master of the house would show up. He had barely disarmed the electronic security system when Max bounded down the large staircase toward them, barking madly. Angel started at his side.

"He's harmless," Alex said softly, but the woman at his side had already let go of his hand and was moving toward the large dog, kneeling down and ruffling him enthusiastically with both hands.

"Hey! You're gorgeous, aren't you? Such a sweet baby!"

Max whined and licked her face, nudging her chin over and over with his nose.

"Alex, he's beautiful! What's his name?"

Alex threw his keys on the antique table at the foot of the stairs. "Max. He's a good boy." He watched as she continued to stroke the dog, whose tail was wagging madly. "Max, leave her be." He ran a hand over the animal's head as he passed, making his way into the great room and to the wet bar along one wall. Angel followed with Max at her heels. "Can I get you a drink?"

"Sure, whatever you're having, but I shouldn't stay long. Will your driver take me back into the city?"

In the process of adding ice to two tumblers, Alex tensed and lifted his head. He considered his words and then shrugged. "No."

"No?" Her eyebrows shot up and the skin on her arms bristled.

Alex filled the two glasses halfway with scotch, held one out to her, and motioned for her to precede him to the large leather furniture in front of the fireplace. He found himself wishing it were November or December so the fire could be blazing. There was a large antique grand piano near the window, one of his most loved possessions.

Angel reached for the glass but didn't move. Alex rolled his eyes and moved around her. "Come on in."

"Are you planning to keep me here against my will?" One eyebrow shot up. She hated that she couldn't be mad at this man for long.

"Never. I'll simply convince you to stay. Max will help me, won't you, boy?" he said with a soft laugh as the dog nudged his hand for attention.

"How? By starving me into submission?"

Alex motioned for her to sit down. "Oh, sorry, I owe you dinner. Unfortunately, I was planning on being home later, so my housekeeper has the night off. What would you like? I'll send Martin out to pick something up."

Angel was curled up in the corner of one of the big brown couches, her head resting on her hand, looking up at him. "Or, you could just take me home." His green eyes roamed her face in the low light. He liked the intimacy of the moment and didn't turn on more lights.

The dog jumped up on the couch and settled next to her, and soon she was stroking the thick golden coat.

"I'm not taking you home."

Alex grabbed a remote and soon soft music was filtering in from some hidden speakers around the room. Angel flushed, not liking where her thoughts were headed.

"Nice. Will there be a huge round bed dropping from above and a spring-loaded champagne bucket popping up from some hidden hole in the floor?"

Alex laughed. "No, Angel. I like music. I have it piped all over the house. I'm not one of *those*."

"Hmmph!" She let out her breath, her expression clearly doubting his words. "Yeah, sure. If I explore the house, will I find ten other sex slaves, bound in chains, locked up in the basement?"

Alex huffed, sinking down in the chair facing her and downing the rest of his drink before placing it on the end table nearest him. "Hardly. I only have one sex slave at a time," he joked; his beautiful mouth quirked up at one side and Angel had to laugh. He was gorgeous; her breath hitched even though she should be pissed at being held prisoner.

"So, why are we here?" she asked softly, wanting to know his intentions.

His green eyes bored into hers and his finger and thumb tugged on his lower lip as he considered his answer. "Well, because we made plans to be together tonight, and you pissed me off going to that meat market alone. You should know better than that."

"I wasn't alone." Max put his head in her lap and whimpered for Angel to continue stroking his coat. "Kenneth was there."

"He was late. If you can't count on him then get more responsible, uh, *friends*." A new wave of anger rushed up in his chest, heating his skin. He rose and walked slowly to refill his glass. His movements were relaxed, but his tone spoke of agitation.

Angel smirked, unable to hold back the glimmer of hope that this amazing man cared enough to be jealous. "What is all this? We agreed we'd be monogamous when it comes to sex, but otherwise, we'd live our lives. Besides, we had plans later, and you knew it. I don't get why your panties are all in a bunch. I wasn't fucking him under the table, so I wasn't violating our understanding," Angel goaded softly. She bit her lip to hide a smile when he turned back to her from the bar.

Jealousy burned him alive, but it was more worry over her safety and he needed her to understand that. "I feel sure he'd like to be doing some violating."

"So what? He knows where things stand," she said, nonplussed.

Alex tried to read her expression, wondering if she was telling the truth. "All I'm saying is that if the guy can't keep his word, then make concessions to compensate."

"Like what?"

"Like use your goddamned head, Angel! It's not just him! You know what I'm talking about!" he blurted loudly, startling Max, who jumped down to go to him.

Alex moved to sit on the floor in front of Angel when she didn't answer, feeling her eyes burn into him and her perfume wafting around him. After a minute, he turned to her.

"Look, I'm not ignorant or immune to what's going on with you. Last night at the station, there were hoods messing with your car while I waited; I chased them away." Angel's heart thumped in her chest and he reached out for her hand, kissing the tender flesh on the inside of her wrist, his eyes holding hers. "What if I wasn't there?" he asked against her skin.

Angel sighed softly, unable to help softening toward him, and her hand moved to the side of his face. "Nothing, Alex." She shrugged slightly. "If you weren't there, I would have been fine; like I'm always fine. They were probably just some neighborhood kids messing around in the parking lot."

"I won't take chances with you." Alex struggled. Should he tell her about his car and the note? He didn't want to scare her, but he wanted to protect her. The undeniable emotion that moved him to take care of her both enthralled and terrified him. He worried; he wanted to protect, to touch, to taste, and to own like never before.

His fingers closed around the wrist near his chin, and he pulled her toward him until his mouth found hers and his arms encircled, pulling her down onto his lap. He was gentle, the kiss coaxing; not like the passionate assault in the limousine.

"Just give me some peace of mind and be more careful," he pleaded as his lips left hers and she curled into him, his fingers sliding into the silky strands on the side of her head as his thumb brushed her jaw. "What should we order for dinner? You'll need energy later."

Angel chuckled and nodded, her forehead coming into contact with his jaw. She felt safe here in the arms of a man she barely knew. It was nuts but undeniable. Their intense physical connection and his tenderness were at complete opposite ends of the spectrum. That told her that there was more about him she wanted to know—and know well—despite the fact that her heart would bleed when it ended. Her emotions ruled her mind for the first time and it felt too good to fight. She smiled into him. "So will you."

His chest rumbled underneath her cheek as he laughed. "I like the sound of that. Okay, something with a lot of carbs, then." He pulled out his phone. "Martin, please run down to Giovanni's for some pizza and spaghetti. Hold on." He moved the phone away. "Angel, what kind of pizza do you want?"

"Pepperoni and cream cheese."

Alex grimaced. He'd never heard of that combination. "Pepperoni and, uh, cream cheese. Yes, me either. Yeah, I know, it sounds gross to me, too!" Angel punched him playfully in the stomach and he grunted. "Get a large supreme and whatever you'd like, also. Don't forget the hot peppers and parmesan."

Angel was nibbling on his lower jaw when he threw the phone aside. "It's delicious, asshole. You'll be eating your words."

"Mmmm…" Soon, Angel found herself pinned beneath him, his hot mouth on her neck, hands pushing her blouse open, teasing the sensitive flesh under her lace bra. "I'll be eating something, that's for sure. If I'm lucky." He smiled against her skin and she let out a breathy moan that went straight to his cock. "You're delicious."

*****

Alex and Angel sat in the middle of his huge, over-sized bed, in the middle of the disheveled sheets, finally eating the pizza, now cold, that Martin had left on the counter in the large marble and mahogany kitchen.

Alex's eyes widened. "Holy shit! This is... *fucking*... *amazing!*" he mumbled with his mouth full. It was three AM and they were both starving and exhausted. Angel giggled as she picked up a slice and tried to situate herself back into the pile of bedding. She tried desperately not to spill it in the dark, the only light coming from the moon shining in through the cracked blinds. Alex's bedroom was like the rest of the house: stone, massive furniture, dark wood, and all man.

"Told ya," she said, shoving the pizza into her mouth, laughing.

He watched her with amusement as he enjoyed the satiated glow of her expression and her waves of dark curls falling softly across her cheek as she concentrated on her pizza. He delighted in having her with him; their evening spent teasing and exploring each other's bodies to the height of heights. She was the most exciting creature he'd ever known, but yet, so easy to be with.

"Yes, you did." He stopped to take a pull from a long neck Heineken before holding it out to her. "It doesn't hurt that I'm hungrier than I think I've ever been, though."

"*What*ever. Just admit it, Alex. I'm right and you're wrong," she teased, taking the beer from him, her face lighting up in a big smile, her hair in a big mess around her face. "Nana nana boo-boo!" she sing-songed.

Alex burst out laughing, almost choking on his pizza. It was so simple; sitting in his bed, in the middle of the night, with an amazingly sexy, naked woman, eating pizza and laughing with her unabashedly. It was good to let go of the structure and just *be*. "Don't get too cocky, Dr. Hemming." He leaned up against the headboard and watched her munch away.

"Are you gonna let me go home tomorrow? Even sex slaves need a reprieve and fresh clothes," she said with a grin.

"The jury is still out. I like having you here." The words were out before he thought about it, but it was the truth. "I'm really enjoying this."

Her face sobered as she handed him back the beer, which he set on the table by the expensive lamp his mother had brought back from Cairo. "Yeah. It's been fun, although your methods are unconventional. You could've just asked me to come over. Just sayin'."

"That was the plan, originally." He threw what was left of his pizza back in the box and moved it to the floor beside the bed.

"The housekeeper is gonna shit herself in the morning. Left over pizza, beer bottles, and used rubbers scattering the floor... classic," Angel quipped, crawling up next to Alex, and draping over him in a half-assed way. "Unless... she's used to it," she probed, looking up into his face, her chin in her clasped hands.

"Uh, I think I'll pick up the rubbers, and no, she's not used to it. She doesn't need to see that side of me."

"Believe me; every living thing with a *vagina* sees that side of you."

Alex let his breath out in a surprise and then chuckled. "Angel, that's crazy. She's sixty-something!"

"So?" Her voice was hesitant but a smile danced around her luscious mouth. "Does she have a vagina?"

He laughed again. "I don't know and it's not something I want to think about. Besides, she's like my mother. Only much more accommodating because she's on my payroll," he reasoned.

"Go ahead. Bury your head in the sand. Bet her vibrator and fantasies of you are best friends."

"Okay, that's gross!" His face contorted in agony. "Thanks for the visual."

They both laughed out loud, and he wondered if he'd ever be able to look at the woman again without hearing Angel's words in his head. *Ugh.*

"What's your mother like, Alex?" Angel asked and he balked. One of the few things he remembered from Bancroft's file was that her mother had left. His hand threaded through her hair again and again, which Angel found both erotic and soothing. She ran her fingers over the smooth skin and hard muscles on his stomach, concentrating her gaze on the fine trail that disappeared under the edge of the sheet.

He drew in his breath at her touch. "She's very elegant and proper, but a very good mother. She played with us a lot, but I think I was the one most like her; she expects more from me. Cole is reckless and carefree, and Allison is silly most of the time. She's relaxed her standards with them."

"Because she knows you expect as much from yourself," she said knowingly, and Alex was stunned by her perception. "I can see that about you—elegant and proper—but so passionate, too. Do you get that from your father?"

"I suppose. He's very driven; he knows what he wants and he takes it."

"Touché," she said softly, her words holding a heavier meaning. "I see that in you."

"Yes." His arms slid down to tighten around her, one hand resting on the curve of her hip.

"My father worked like a dog, and still we didn't have much. My mother left us when I was in second grade. I don't even know why, because Dad doesn't speak of it, but I can only assume he couldn't provide what she wanted."

Alex's eyes closed, painfully conjuring up the large brown eyes welling with tears in a younger Angel's face, beautiful, but very sad. "I'm sorry, Angel. Do you ever see her?"

"No." Her voice hardened, though she remained where she was, letting him stroke her hair and her body. "I used to cry when she missed birthdays and Christmases, but now, I have no desire to know anything about her. If you could see how my father suffered, you'd understand. She has to be a cold-hearted bitch to do that."

Alex's heart tightened at the pain in her voice. It hurt her more than she wanted him to know. "Do you visit your dad?" he asked softly.

"I rarely get down there, and he doesn't ever come to Chicago. He likes his friends and his life. He's content. I send him money, but I have to nag him to cash the checks. I just want to make his life easier. I miss him a lot."

"I'm sure he's very proud of you. How does he feel about the drama surrounding your job?"

Angel signed. "My job is mundane, boring, and sometimes heartbreaking. He doesn't know there are risks. I mean, he's probably thought about it, but we don't discuss it. He thinks the radio show is cool. He listens to the audio stream online sometimes."

"He's probably worried sick, in both cases."

She pushed back from him so she could look up into his face. "Alex, this is stupid. I've been doing this for two years and the current situation is no different, so relax. It'll blow over."

"Will it?" he growled. He realized he'd have to tell her. "The reason I brought you here is because I'm… Oh, *fuck*!" he exclaimed in disgust. "I want you here, Angel, but something happened last night that necessitates it. Someone vandalized my Audi in the garage and left a note. I can't believe that it's a coincidence, and this is the only way I can ensure your safety."

Angel frowned and sat up, clutching the sheet to her chest. A worried look settled on her face and she stilled. "What happened to the car? What did the note say?" Her voice wavered with apprehension and it only reinforced what Alex knew—that she was as worried as he was.

"If I knew what was good for me, I'd stay away from you." Alex's hand smoothed back her hair when her eyes widened and she gasped. "It wasn't that bad; the windshield was shattered, nothing more. It wasn't about destroying the car; it was about delivering the message."

She inhaled deeply and he could see the wheels turning behind her eyes. Alex reached for her and pulled her up to him gently until she rested on the pillow facing him. "So, you see why I worried that you were unprotected at the bar? Why I didn't want you at your condo tonight? Not until we find out who's behind this. Angel, tell me about your cases," he demanded.

She was preoccupied, her thoughts racing in her head until she finally met his gaze. "I can't tell you anymore than I have. Professional ethics—"

She felt him stiffen in her arms and his voice hardened. "We're talking about your safety, so, screw professional ethics!"

"No, we're talking about *your* safety. Maybe you should stay away from me for now, until this is over." She started to get up from the bed but he grabbed her arm.

Panic flooded Alex's body, his skin heated and it showed on his face. "Then what? The next case or the next?"

"This is only the second or third time it's happened, and the other times were nothing."

"Well, there's a first time for everything." Alex silently fumed, since he knew who it was, per Cole's intervention, and it pissed him off that she wouldn't trust him enough to tell him the truth.

Angel pulled her arm free with a warning look. He reached for her again, this time more gently, beseeching her to listen to his logic. "Damn it, Angel! This is dangerous. You don't know what you're dealing with." But he knew, exactly.

Angel's thoughts raced. It was his car that was damaged, not hers. She feared for his safety more than hers, and maybe this would be the last time she'd be able to be with him for a long time. God knew how long it would take to convict the bastard. Her heart sank into her stomach as she allowed Alex to gather her close and her own arms to stretch around his broad shoulders, her forehead resting in the crook of his neck as he soothed her by stroking her hair down her naked back. His nails raked softly, causing electric shivers to run over the surface of her skin.

"I have to re-administer some tests. See if I can get the subject to fail, then the D.A.'s office takes over and all I have to do is explain the findings in court."

Alex's heart seized. If Swanson was connected to the mob, she might be in more danger. He only hoped Swanson's contribution to their organization wasn't significant enough for them to come to his aid.

*Fuck! How can I keep you safe without telling you what I know?*

"I can see it in your eyes. I know you're scared." His nose nuzzled into the side of her face, hot breath mingling with her own, thinking that if she was in his arms, he knew she'd be safe.

"My job is part of who I am and that won't change. We've only just met, but you're acting like… well, unreasonably. Why does this matter? Can't this time together be ours?"

He knew what she meant. The world ceased to exist when they were together: nothing mattered but the insatiable need and the undisputed passion that flared between them like a tidal wave; each seeking and unabashedly taking what they needed from the other, but he was anxious and worried. But there was more. He was becoming more and more consumed with her when they were apart. She was in his head, not just igniting his passion.

"It matters," Alex growled against the curve of her neck, his lips seeking to taste her skin, his fingers greedily pushing the sheet from between them, and pulling her leg over his hip. "It matters, Angel. I don't want to lose... *this*."

\*\*\*\*\*

Angel couldn't help but arch into him, thrilled beyond recognition at the implications of his words—hoping he could be feeling a fraction of what she was, no matter how she tried to deny it.

They'd had sex three times in as many hours, and even though her body was aching and sore, her desire for him throbbed through her body. His cock was like silk and iron, hot and rigid, pulsing into her moist heat. He groaned, the sound hardening her nipples and making her moan his name in response. If she moved just an inch, he would slip inside. "Alex," she breathed, the ache in her voice went straight to his cock.

"Christ, I love it when you say my name like that. I could fuck you all night."

"Do it, then," she challenged, pushing away the thought that she should stay away from him. It was the last thing she wanted anyway. Her fingers wound in his hair, pulling his mouth down to hers, hovering. "Do it. Show me your strength. How many times can you come in one night?"

"You shouldn't challenge me. I'll win every time." His voice was low and throaty and she loved it.

"We'll see who wins," she whispered, her lips so close to his they were touching. "It's all in the point of view."

His tongue plunged into her mouth, teasing then plundering as he laid her back down and reached to the end table for another foil packet. "Ugh..." She moaned in protest as the air chilled her skin, instantly missing the heat of Alex's body next to hers.

"I hate these fucking things," he murmured, ripping the packet open with his teeth and quickly sheathing himself. He rolled onto his back, bringing her with him until she was straddling his hips. He wanted a clear vantage point of her expression and her body. His hands slowly ghosted over her curves, his thumbs reaching for her nipples as he paused to let his eyes drink her in.

Angel licked her lips and bit her lower one; the hungry look in his eyes, sparkling in the darkness, almost made her weep. "God, you are gorgeous. I've never seen a man as beautiful as you."

"Oh, Angel, so are you. I can't tear my eyes away. I want to watch you ride me. Take what you want from me. *Do it.*" He repeated her words as his hands slid to the gentle swell of her hips, and she grasped his length in both hands; his eyes roamed slowly over her face and the outline of her body in the moonlight, the dark hair tumbling down in tangled masses around her.

Her hands played over the muscles of his stomach, the ridges and valleys literally making her mouth water. His dick was at attention, long and thick, and she wanted nothing more than to feel him split her wide open.

"Why am I so out of control with you? Jesus, I hate it, but it feels so damn good," she asked in a breathy rush.

"Because it can't be controlled. I fight it, too, but I'm ready to let it happen. When we're together like this, all I want to do is *feel.* There is no other choice."

Angel was in the vortex of wanting to lose herself in him completely, but terrified of the consequences. She closed her eyes, letting the sensations of his body beneath and inside hers, and his hands on her flesh, sweep her away. The only thing she knew was that to exist right now, his touch was as necessary as breathing and her body responded, despite the internal battle she fought with herself.

She lost her breath when his fingers raked down the front of her body, leaving a trail of molten heat that ended in a throb when his thumb brushed her clit, so soft, so teasing. "Alex." His name left her lips in a rush as her eyes snapped open and her hands began a slow torture of their own, causing Alex to groan and push into her hands.

His green eyes blazed up into hers, becoming even more engorged under her ministrations. "God, Angel," he hissed as she finally joined her body with his, slowly, savoring inch by delicious inch. "Fuck!"

"That's the general idea," she murmured softly, loving the power she held over him, being able to watch how affected he was as she started to rock her hips into his, her hands now taking her weight as she leaned back on the solid muscles of his thighs.

Alex's hand continued to tease her tender flesh as he watched her face intently. "God, you are beautiful." His voice showed the strain of restraint as he let her take control. "Go slow, baby, please. I want this to last." His whispered words fell softly from his lips. She complied, slowing her pace, willing to give him anything he wanted. So much for control, but she didn't care. The lines were becoming blurred in the ecstasy of their passion.

The room was quiet, save for the gentle sounds of their pants and soft moans as they each brought pleasure to the other. Minutes passed, pleasure building until he could withstand it no more and he bolted upright, bringing him nose to nose with her as his arms wound around her undulating hips. Alex's mouth took hers hungrily, his tongue invading the soft, willing warmth of her mouth, sliding in and out in time to the thrusts of his body. The connection was incredible, he was buried so deep, the friction on her clit and G-spot pushing her toward one of the strongest climaxes of her life. Alex felt her start to tremble and clench around him. "I can feel you... I'm... coming... I can't stop, baby."

Her hands fisted in his hair as her mouth fastened onto his again, whimpering as she came around him, and he groaned her name into her mouth as he released inside her.

"Oh, Angel…"

Their bodies slowed, but still rocked together, breathing heavy as they rode it out together. Angel shuddered in his arms, overwhelmed by the magnitude of emotions she didn't want to face; her orgasm still causing her to jerk against him. His hands slid up her back and over her shoulders until he was cradling her face gently between his hands, his mouth still sucking softly on hers. Kiss after delicious kiss.

"Jesus Christ!" he moaned into her shoulder as he pushed into her one last time before he stilled and left a series of soft kisses from her temple to her jaw.

Angel breathed in, memorizing the salty muskiness of his skin as she collapsed in his arms, closing her eyes and trying very hard to remind herself that these moments, the incredible pull, and this astounding, amazing, man… were too good to be true.

# 13

## Never Tease a Weasel

ALEX ROLLED TOWARD the warmth radiating at his side, breathing in Angel's now familiar scent as he willed his eyes to open. He noted how soft the skin of her leg felt against the downy surface of his own. She was like silk; soft, warm and inviting.

"Mmmm." He nuzzled into the crook of her neck, pressing a kiss to the curve where her shoulder connected. She didn't stir, and he smiled against her skin. No doubt she'd be exhausted today. Even his own muscles complained as he stretched beside her. The whimpering of the dog begged for his attention as Alex lifted his head and cocked one eye open.

Max was lying next to Angel, his head resting lazily on her hip and eyes pleading with Alex. He whined again.

"Okay, Max." Alex groaned, rolled away, and pushed off the bed. "Come on."

He threw on his discarded jeans from last night without bothering with underwear and glanced back to the bed. Max hadn't moved, but Angel had rolled onto her back with one arm flung over her eyes; the sheet dipped low on one breast, hinting at the dusky nipple just under the surface. *I could get used to that,* he thought with a wistful smile and then shook his head at how Angel had changed his previous attitude about waking up with a woman.

Max's large brown eyes watched Alex as he gestured toward the door, but he refused to move from Angel's side. "Max, come!" Alex whispered urgently. "I thought you needed to go out. Come!"

The animal just groaned in response, his eyebrow slanting skyward in answer. Alex couldn't help chuckling at the dog's expression.

"Yeah, I know. What's not to like?" He padded softly out of the bedroom and into the hall, the plush carpet muffling his footsteps. Whistling softly, he was rewarded with the jingling of Max's collar and a thump as he bounded from the bed and followed.

After letting Max out the back door of the breakfast room, Alex pulled out his phone and dialed Darian, making a mental note of the time.

"Yeah?" his friend mumbled into the phone.

"Hey, D. Did I wake you?"

"Of course, but what's up? What time is it?"

"It's nine."

"Did you want to play squash or something later?"

"Not today. How extensive is the security at the radio station?"

Darian was a little taken aback by his friend's obvious intensity about something that shouldn't concern him. "Alex, it's standard. We have computer-controlled locks and keycard access on the outside doors and again on those that separate the studios and offices from the lobby. Why? Are you worried about me?" He laughed.

"Very funny," Alex returned in a dry tone. "No, but I think cameras should be installed in the parking lot and a guard in place after hours."

"Wait. What's going on?" He already knew where this was going and was surprised, but then again it *was* Angel.

"It's not safe for Angel to be—"

"*What?* Are you with her now?" Darian's laugh made Alex bristle. "That was fast, even for you."

Unwilling to analyze the relationship or his feelings, Alex pressed for an answer. "About the security—"

"She's only there one evening a week, Alex. You can't expect—"

"Look," Alex interrupted impatiently. "If it's about money, I'll pay for it. Just get it done. I can have the head of security at Avery call you and work it out."

Darian sighed. Alex was being irrational for the first time in his life.

"You know I'm not in a position to do it. I don't own the station, and security isn't part of my job."

"Well, whose damn job is it, then?" Alex asked shortly. "There were hoods around her car Friday night, D. It's the company's responsibility to protect its employees. I want it done before her next show."

"I'll talk to the general manager, but I can't promise anything will come of it. He'll think I've lost my marbles, like you apparently have. You can't just pay for the station's security. It's unreasonable and, frankly, it looks suspicious even if I explain that my best friend has the hots for one of our talent."

"Again, the comedian. I'm serious," Alex growled. "If the GM needs to talk to me about it, then give him my number. I can't just transfer funds from Avery to KISS for legal reasons, so work out some type of sponsorship of an event or something."

"Jesus, Alex. Did you lie awake all night thinking up this shit?"

"Hardly. Will you just do it?"

A flash of white in his peripheral vision made Alex turn to find Angel coming into the room wearing the white dress shirt he'd left hanging on the bathroom door. Her long legs were tanned and toned, and she was pushing her cascading hair off of her face with both hands. His body twitched at the sight before him. "I gotta go. Let me know."

"It won't be today. It's the weekend, relax."

"We'll see." It was his only answer before he shut off the phone and tossed it carelessly on the marble countertop.

Angel's eyes raked over the delicious picture he made, leaning up against the counter with his feet crossed in front of him. He was dressed only in dark designer jeans, the top button left open made her lick her lips as it hinted of the pleasure still fresh in her mind. Despite her resolve, it was impossible to resist his potent allure. He was strong and sexy, the muscles playing beneath the smooth skin of his chest and shoulders, the abs toned and defined. Remembering how her fingers had skimmed over his hard body the night before, she had to shake herself to keep from staring, biting her lip involuntarily.

"Good morning, Sleeping Beauty." He smirked, taking her in his arms when she was within reach. Her hands curled around his forearms, and her head tilted back so she could look into his eyes. Alex didn't miss the opportunity and soon his mouth was tasting and teasing hers. "How'd you sleep?" he whispered, as he ran soft kisses from her chin up to her cheekbone and then her temple.

Angel's eyes closed as his hot breath rushed over her skin. "When we finally slept, like a rock."

Alex laughed softly. "Mmmm, it felt so good."

"Yes. I didn't want to get up."

His fingers rubbed soft circles on the skin of her lower back through the fine cotton of his shirt, every touch reinforcing the strong connection that neither was ready to relinquish.

"I wanna get up…" he teased, pulling her against his body as her hands slid up his arms and over the smooth skin of his shoulders.

"You're good at it. The sex *is* incredible." Angel stiffened and pulled away, but Alex wasn't ready to let her go and pulled her back to him. "No denying your mad skills."

"Mmm, yes, it's indescribable, but I'm not just talking about that. I like you here. I find it unexpected." He coaxed another soft kiss or two from her mouth before releasing her and removing two coffee cups from the cupboard. He held one up and pointed to it with his index finger. "Coffee?"

"Yes, thank you, Alex." She loved the way his eyes caressed her body, their touch almost tangible in intensity, setting her skin on fire everywhere they touched, but she struggled against the ease of being here, in this unfamiliar house with an almost unfamiliar man. Despite the passionate hours they spent together, she knew she shouldn't let herself get closer emotionally. The problem was, physically, she was closer to Alex than any man she'd ever known, which she knew spelled trouble for her heart, if it wasn't already too late. "Um, sorry, I borrowed your shirt."

"It looks good on you." He stopped, his unwilling admission, though unspoken, left hanging between them. "But, my shoulders are cold." A half-smile settled on his handsome face as he tugged playfully at the front of it, his eyes dancing as emerald met chocolate. "Maybe you should give it back."

She pushed his hands away with a soft chuckle. "Not a chance. Suck it up, Avery."

Alex laughed out loud. "What'd you want to do today?" he asked casually, his green eyes daring her to resist spending the day with him.

Truthfully, it felt completely natural to let the events of the evening spill over into the day, but Angel knew she shouldn't let that happen... for a multitude of reasons.

"I promised Becca that I'd take Jillian for the afternoon and evening. She has a date and her parents are out of town. I thought I'd get some much needed work done after she's in bed."

Alex's brow creased as he pulled a chair out from the Indian marble table so that Angel could sit down, and then took the seat next to her. Everything about his home oozed luxury and expense; right down to the bone china coffee cups. He looked like a dark god surrounded by gleaming treasures that would mean so much to most anyone. Yet, to Alex, the sophistication and quiet elegance were inconsequential and expected.

"At your place?" he questioned, still frowning. The thought of Angel left alone with the little girl left him searching for a plausible reason to prevent it.

A little wrinkle appeared above her nose as her mouth twisted wryly. "Duh. Yes. I can't be your sex slave tonight, baby. Sorry." The corners of her rosy mouth lifted in a sly smile and Alex laughed out loud.

"Damn! Guess I'll just have to see what I have locked up downstairs. Maybe I'll have to come over there and be yours."

Angel admired the dimples, made deeper by his teasing grin. "Hmmph!" she snorted and rolled her eyes.

"I'd hoped to keep you in bed a little longer this morning, but Max wouldn't have it."

"Probably for the best. I'm surprised you can even walk today. I thought I drained you dry. It will be good to have a night free of me; regain your strength and catch up on sleep. We both have to work tomorrow." She peered coyly at him over the rim of her cup as she sipped her coffee, trying her hardest not to giggle.

Alex flashed a brilliant smile and reached for her hand, drawing her forward in her chair until his lips could graze the inside of her wrist. He felt her tremble beneath his mouth and met her eyes again, the intensity of his gaze was like fire licking along her nerves. "No, really; last night was reeeaaaally incredible."

"I—" she began as she struggled with the words, her heart beating at a frantic pace. "I'm..." *Scared. Terrified I'll get hurt. Terrified I'll fall in love. Terrified you'll break my heart.*

"Speechless?" he asked seriously.

Angel couldn't help but nod as she tore her eyes from his and glanced down toward her cup. "It would appear so."

They shared a moment of sober understanding before he finally dropped her hand and got up from the table. He bent and kissed her forehead gently, fingers tracing the back of her head. Angel flushed at his tenderness, marveling at the sharp contrast between the demanding and passionate lover and this gentle, tender man before her. Max barked at the door effectively breaking their bubble.

"Are you hungry? I'm absolutely famished," he said as the dog ran into the kitchen and landed the entire front half of his body on her lap, wagging his tail furiously as she hugged him to her.

"Good morning, Maxy Max! Such a beautiful boy!"

"Max, down!" Alex ordered sharply.

"Alex, it's okay. I adore him." Angel placed a kiss on the dog's head and hugged him tighter, enjoying the way her face sank into his silken fur. "Don't I? Yes, I love you!" Max proceeded to lap kisses on her chin and cheeks while she laughed in delight.

"Obviously, he adores you as well. But, nevertheless, his saliva does not belong on the table. Or your face, for that matter."

"Max, tell your daddy to relax and stop being so stodgy! Come on." She gently pushed the dog down and then sat on the floor against the dishwasher. The floor was the same expensive marble that decorated the rest of the kitchen and felt like ice on her bare thighs. She couldn't help but gasp.

Immediately, Max settled next to her with his head in her lap and one paw taking possession of her leg, his large brown eyes imploring up at Alex as her hand stroked his head repeatedly. "Satisfied?"

Alex's eyebrows shot up in amused astonishment as he removed eggs, bacon, and a bowl of oranges from the large stainless steel refrigerator. "Traitor," he retorted playfully.

"To whom are you speaking, Mr. Avery?" Angel laughed softly.

"Both of you."

*****

"You're kidding." Becca's voice was deadpan, but the amusement behind the words was unmistakable.

"What?" Angel smirked. "It's not a big deal."

"Bullshit! You're going to Lincoln Park Zoo with a gazillionaire-everybody-wants-him-playboy who probably doesn't know the ass end of a giraffe from a lion's. If that isn't shocking enough, it's obvious you like more about this guy than his dick."

Angel couldn't stop herself; laughter bubbled up and spilled over, causing Alex to glance her way. His hair had a deep sheen in the sunlight and his questioning look was met with a shrug and he shook his head. She couldn't see his eyes behind his expensive sunglasses, but his lopsided grin turned into a full smile.

"We'll discuss that later. Stop being so melodramatic," Angel mumbled into her phone, biting her lip to stop another bout of hysterical giggling. The wind was whipping her hair into her face and she struggled to push it back. It was a beautiful day, the temperature cooled by the breeze coming off of Lake Michigan. Alex's capable hands steered the sleek BMW convertible out of downtown after Angel had entered Becca's address into the GPS.

"Does this mean I have to find another sitter? Jillian will be heartbroken."

"Nope. We're on our way to pick up my little Jillybean. I've missed her and I may not give her back."

"Wha—*Alex* is going to babysit with you?"

"Don't hyperventilate. There are stranger things."

"I doubt that."

"We'll see you in about twenty minutes. Tell my baby I can't wait to see her!"

Alex reached for Angel's hand and pulled it to rest beneath his on his muscled thigh. "Everything okay? Does Becca think it's a bad idea that I'm going along?"

"No. It's fine. Although I wonder if it's your bag? Wouldn't you rather be with Darian or your brother?"

He glanced at her, his teeth flashing brightly in a wide smile. "What?" He scoffed. "Hairy, belligerent, alpha males versus soft, sexy, supple and irresistible. That's a tough choice. Maybe I should reconsider?"

Angel smiled as Alex's hand tightened around hers. He was so fucking sexy; she almost lost her breath looking at him, and scarier: she was starting to fall for the person wrapped inside all that masculinity. He could have any woman, and he usually did, so she was perplexed that he'd choose to spend time with someone as complicated as herself. There was no way this would end well, her mind argued. "Well, it will also be young, sticky, and giggly. Two-year olds are fun but sometimes a challenge."

"I'll take my chances. Do you think she'll like me?"

"She's a sweetie and she's female, so the chances are better than average."

"Stop. Your view of me is distorted. I've told you that I'm monogamous. Don't you believe me, Angel?"

"Sure." She shrugged and turned a little in her seat so she could study his profile, searching for some clue to what he was really feeling. If he was feeling anything other than lust. "But, I also know that you're not married and never get tied down, so I don't expect this to last. My eyes are open."

Alex was vested more than she was aware. He wasn't willing to admit it to her for fear she wouldn't believe him, or worse, retreat from him. He didn't stop to analyze the reasons. He enjoyed her company, both in bed and out of it, more than any woman he'd ever known and that was enough for now. "Close them, then. Do you enjoy being with me? Be honest, I can take it." He grinned.

"Your head's already big enough."

"Why, thank you. I was hoping you'd think so," he replied with a cheeky grin.

"Shut up!" Angel laughed.

"I'll let you shut me up, later." He smiled and pressed her hand further into his leg. Angel's fingers closed around the muscle beneath the dark denim, provocatively. "Yes, later."

When they pulled up outside Becca's apartment building, Alex came around and opened Angel's door, extending a hand to help her out.

*Always the perfect gentleman, yet so hot behind closed doors,* Angel mused. Her eyes took him in, casually dressed in dark jeans, Adidas, and a white T-shirt; he looked younger and more carefree than she usually saw him. His fingers closed around hers as they walked into the building.

"What?"

"Nothing. This will be fun."

He pulled off his sunglasses and bent to place a soft kiss on the tanned skin of her shoulder, left bare by the strapless coral sundress she was wearing. "I like this dress. Did you wear it to torture me?"

"Always."

He burst out laughing as Becca's door opened and Jillian toddled out ahead of her mother.

"Anga!" she squealed, and Angel scooped her up instantly, planting a big kiss on her cherub cheek.

"Jillybean! How's my girl? Hi, Becca."

"Hey. Hello, Alex." Becca stepped aside to allow them all to enter.

Chubby arms wrapped around Angel's neck, and Jillian's lower lip popped out in a pout and she frowned. She pointed at Alex.

"Who's dat?"

Angel smiled down into her face. "Jillian, this is Alexander. He's my friend, and he wanted to come with us to the zoo today. All right?"

She looked at Alex skeptically. "Are you nice?"

"Jillian!" Becca was horrified. "Sorry, Alex."

"No problem." Alex extended a hand toward the little girl, who took it hesitantly but pulled away quickly. "It's nice to meet you, Jillian. That's a very pretty bow you have in your hair."

Her little hand reached up to touch the bright pink ribbon as she nodded. "Yes. Do you yike ice ceam? We aways have ice ceam."

Alex laughed. "Yes! I love it! Chocolate is my favorite."

"Me, too!" Jillian's blonde curls bobbed as she nodded enthusiastically.

"Great! Maybe we'll get a bunch of it, okay?"

"Yay!" Jillian was now beaming at Alex, and Angel felt sure that it wouldn't be long before he'd have her in his arms. "Anga yikes ohnge."

"Orange ice cream?"

"Surboot."

"Oh! Orange sherbet. That's yummy, too."

"No. I yike choc-yut best."

"Okay. You and I will have chocolate. Deal?"

"Yep."

Becca rolled her eyes at Angel, both of them smiling.

"Another one bites the dust," Becca said under her breath with a small laugh.

"He's nice, Anga!"

"Oh, he's nice, all right." Angel flashed a bright smile, and
Alex winked at her, his dimples deepening in a pleased grin.

*****

Alex's time with Angel and Jillian had been magical and eye opening, showing another side of her that was unexpected. His gaze fell
on Angel and he'd studied her reactions with the toddler throughout the day as they meandered through the zoo's various exhibits.
He adored how she held Jillian, pointing out beautiful things, ex-
plaining and teaching about the animals and not just showing. Alex
found his heart pounding on several occasions where he had to
take a moment and regroup. She was so gentle and understanding,
it was no wonder that the little girl worshiped her. Angel became
more and more amazing the more time they spent together. The
more he learned about her as the days passed, the more enthralled
he became. It was exhilarating and, at the same time, daunting.

They'd come back to Angel's apartment at the end of the day
and Angel made dinner of chicken fingers, French fries and
applesauce. She apologized profusely to Alex for the unsophisti-
cated fare, but he laughed it off.

"Thank you, Angel. This is delicious, isn't it?" he asked as
Jillian, now fully ensconced on his lap, lifted one of her pieces of
chicken to share with him. He took a bite with relish, the two of
them happily munching away as Angel watched in amazement.

"You're wonderful with her." It occurred to her they'd never
talked about kids. Maybe he was a father. "Do you have children?"
She wondered if he had some hidden past that he didn't discuss.

"No." Alex smiled at her. He picked up his glass and took a
swallow of ice water.

"That's pretty incredible. It comes so natural to you; you must
have experience. Nieces or nephews?"

His expression was wry. "Allison has only been married a few months, and Cole, well, I'm praying he doesn't get some floozy knocked up. That's all we'd need. I've encouraged him to get clipped, but he refuses."

Angel knew he was teasing and she laughed, reaching out to stroke Jillian's silky head. The two days had been heaven, but it was Sunday night and reality loomed.

"Are you out of the country this week?"

"I'm supposed to go to Athens. Why?" His curiosity was piqued, and his heart quickened that she'd ask.

"Oh, no reason."

"Something's come up here that needs my attention, so I'm thinking of putting off the trip. Unless... Angel, do you want to come with me?" His voice was soft and seductive, and she started in surprise. Alex had finished but Jillian was still eating, licking the ketchup off the end of a fry, only to dip it in again. "It's only a book audit of one of our properties, so I should have a lot of free time. I can't think of a better way to enjoy the city than with you. There's so much history, and the Mediterranean is beautiful and really breathtaking at night."

"I have a lot of work to do. It sounds amazing, though." Her heart pounded in her chest. A whole weekend together, talks of trips, getting gooey over seeing him with Jillian; it was all overwhelming and unexpected. It completely contradicted her mental image, and he was scaring the shit out of her.

"Like I said, I can put it off. I'd love to take you with me." *And get you away from that bastard and his goons,* he thought.

"I'd love to go."

"Would you?" His eyes searched hers until Jillian lifted a ketchup-coated piece of meat and shoved it toward his face, completely missing his mouth and landing on his stubble-covered cheek. "Ugh," he said but laughter filled his green eyes.

Jillian was not put off and continued to make another jab at it, this time landing in Alex's mouth though, with his assistance. His face grimaced at the combination of the condiment and meat, but he chewed good-naturedly anyway. "Yum. Thank you, sweetheart."

Angel passed him a napkin and lifted Jillian off of his lap. "Come on, pumpkin! Time to get ready for bed."

"Let's make duh tent!"

"What? It's late, sweetie. We'll do it another time."

"Tent, Anga!" Jillian touched Angel's cheek with her little hand and her blue eyes looked up imploringly. "Wit Zanda!"

"Oh, honey…" Angel began.

Alex interrupted her as he stood to start removing the plates to the sink across the kitchen. "Is it a game?"

"When Jilly stays over, and Becca isn't here, we usually make a tent in the living room and sleep in there. At least, until she falls asleep." Her expression was full of apology. *Sorry*, she mouthed with a cringe.

Alex turned back toward the two girls and smiled, rubbing his hands together. "Sounds fun. Let's do it!"

"Yippee!" Jillian shrieked and wiggled in Angel's arms until she was set on her feet.

"Oh, no, miss. You're a mess." She was covered in remnants of the day. Cherry snow cone and chocolate ice cream stained the front of her flowered top and dripped down to the top of her yellow shorts and dirt had collected on the surface of it. Her face was filthy, despite Angel's repeated attempts to clean her up. "Into the bath with you first." Angel pointed down the hall and blonde curls bounced as she ran toward the bathroom.

"Kay," she said, disappearing around the corner.

"Alex, I'm sorry."

"I'm not. What should I do?"

"There are blankets and pillows in my closet, and I usually just push the two chairs closer to the couch and then drape the blankets between them. I'll get them for you, if you want to start?" At his nod, Angel continued. "She falls asleep fast, don't worry."

By the time Alex had constructed a makeshift tent and went around lighting a couple of the candles Angel had around her living room, his phone rang.

"Yeah?"

"Alex, one of Swanson's goons rented an empty apartment in Angel's building but doesn't move in until Wednesday. I just found out from Bancroft."

"*Oh, fuck!*" Alex's mind raced. How in the hell would he get her out of here? "Uh, did you get the specs that I requested on the building?"

"Yeah."

"Okay, are there any other vacant apartments?"

"Just one, but it's not on her floor."

"Come and see me at my office in the morning. If you get there before me, ask Mrs. Dane to give you what you need and then rent that apartment. And, Cole; good job."

"Too bad you can't tell Dad. Man, this chick must be something."

"Yes, she is." As he hung up the phone, Jillian came running out of Angel's room, all pink and freshly scrubbed.

Angel followed behind her, taking in the low lights and the soft glow of candlelight that shimmered all around the room. She cocked her head and sent Alex a questioning glance, but he only smiled in return. She'd changed from her dress into some grey sweatshorts and a white T-shirt, looking like she had just emerged from a bath as well. Her hair was piled in a knot atop her head, held in place by what looked like a white piece of fabric. She had on her Prada glasses, which were a dark green metal in a rectangular shape. Angel seemed younger without make-up, but still luminous. Alex stared until Jillian tugged at the leg of his jeans and he bent to lift her up. The little one smelled of baby powder and freshness. Alex inhaled deeply, enjoying her baby scent as she hugged his neck, her wet hair brushing against his chin.

"What are you looking at? It's a pajama party."

"I was just thinking that you look different every time I see you."

"Is that bad? I know, I look—"

"Amazing. That's how you look." His eyes perused her body, caressing her curves, and his perfect mouth lifted only slightly on one side. As always, it made her burn from head to toe. She could feel her skin physically flush. "Every time, no matter how you're dressed, make-up or no make-up; it doesn't matter."

Heat infused her face, the pleasure she felt at his words surprising her. "Thank you."

Alex had taken the comforter and extra blankets from Angel's bed and piled them on the floor inside the tent. Jillian scrambled in after Alex set her down and curled up on the pillows. Despite the heat of the Chicago summer, the apartment was cool, and she snuggled into the vast pile of down and fluff.

"Come on, Anga! Zanda!"

Angel and Alex laughed as he motioned for her to precede him. "You just wanna look at my ass," she whispered as she passed in front of him.

"So? You just wanna look at mine," Alex teased in return.

"I don't deny it," she said with a small shrug and a devilish smirk. Alex couldn't help the pleased chuckle that escaped him.

Angel settled Jillian in-between herself and Alex, tucking the covers around her. She turned onto her side facing both Jillian and Alex. His head was propped up against the edge of one of the sofas as he leaned on the pillows.

"Did you have a nice day, today, baby?"

Jillian smiled and nodded with a yawn.

"We should thank Alexander for coming along. It's been very nice to have him with us, hasn't it?"

Angel's wide brown eyes met his, the soft glow of candlelight filtering in through the blankets casting his features into half-shadow. His face softened and Angel had an almost undeniable urge to reach out and trace his strong jaw, the indelible cleft in his chin, to push the thick lock of hair back from his forehead. As if reading her mind, his hand reached up and pushed it away.

"Tank you, Zanda."

Angel bit her lip to stop the laughter that welled in her chest. *Zanda.*

"You're welcome, darling. I have a dog, named Max, who would love to meet you. Maybe we can take him to the park next time. Would you like to do that?"

She nodded and yawned again. Angel opened a tattered book and began to read as Alex looked on.

"Never tease a weasel," she began, reading the well-worn children's story lovingly to the little girl.

Alex couldn't take his eyes off of Angel as she read, mesmerized as usual by her voice and expression, his heart tightened at the tenderness she lavished on the baby.

"Why don't we tease, baby?" She touched the end of Jillian's nose with her index finger.

"Teasing isn't nice," Jillian quipped sleepily, her eyes half-closed. She blinked, trying to hold them open.

"No, it's not nice, is it?"

"I have a feeling you've read this to her before," Alex murmured, and Angel nodded as she continued to read, stopping only when Jillian was obviously out.

"Keep going. I want to hear the end."

"You're not serious."

"As a heart attack." Angel balked at him but he persisted. "Please?"

"Oh, Jesus." She rolled her eyes. "Okay." She reopened the book and found her place.

Angel's eyes flashed up to find Alex grinning at her, and he used his hand to motion for her to continue. "I'm gonna get you for this."

"Oh, I'm counting on it."

Angel giggled and continued until she'd finished the story despite feeling silly doing so.

Alex burst out laughing as she threw the book aside. "Shhhh… Satisfied, now?" she whispered urgently.

"Hardly. But you can remedy that shortly."

"Hmmmm," she said softly, as he reached for her hand and began rubbing soft circles over the top with his thumb. "Is the Beemer yours?"

"No, it's a rental. Why?"

"I just wondered." It wouldn't do to have another vehicle vandalized. "Thank you for today and being so nice to Jillybean. The whole weekend has been really nice."

"It's not over yet."

"Aren't you tired?"

"No more tired than you are, and I told you I'm not making the trip. What do you have going on tomorrow?"

"I'm meeting Becca for breakfast to deliver Jillian and then regular clients and case work. Nothing special."

"Will you put her to bed or do the two of you usually stay in the tent?"

"No, I put her in the crib I have in the spare room."

"She's incredible. Very sweet. I can see how much she loves you, Angel."

"I love her, too. It's almost like she's my own child."

"You're her godmother?" When her eyes widened, he explained. "Becca told me at the karaoke bar that first night."

"Yes."

"Becca did well in choosing you. Do you need help putting her down?"

"I got it." Angel was practiced in lifting the sleeping child without rousing her and Alex fell back onto the pillows when she crawled out with Jillian in her arms. It was surprisingly comfortable with all the layers of down and fabric underneath him; the pillows soft and scented like Angel. He closed his eyes against the flickering of candlelight on the roof of the tent, the walls composed of the furniture. Waiting for her return, he took out his phone to browse the messages and texts, two from his mother, one from Allison, and one from Whitney. He sighed, sorry that he'd hurt her, but not sorry he'd ended the relationship.

He didn't feel like answering any of them and placed the phone underneath one of the pillows after turning it off. He'd blown off the family brunch today, no doubt what his mother and sister were calling for. Cole hadn't mentioned it, so Alex assumed he'd skipped it also, but they never nagged his brother for missing it.

*Lesson? Fuck off and no one expects dick from you.*

However, Cole seemed to be taking his new responsibility seriously, which pleased Alex for two reasons: his brother was making progress, and his woman would be protected. *My woman.* He smiled at the thought, wondering if it were true.

"It sure as shit feels like it," Alex mumbled under his breath.

"What?" Angel was climbing back in the tent and pulling the covers up to her neck.

"Nothing. Are you cold, baby?"

Pleasure flooded through her once more, and she smiled before pulling the covers tighter.

"A little," she admitted. "I like it cool enough to have blankets, even in summer."

"Come over here then. I'll warm you up."

His arms reached for her under the blanket, and again, their legs tangled, their breaths mingled, and their bodies hummed in anticipation. Alex's fingers were warm against the down of her cheek, moving slowly along the bone before tangling in her hair. His mouth hovered and brushed softly over hers. She couldn't help it, her chin lifted, silently asking him to repeat it. He did, again and again.

"Are you hoping I'll tease your weasel, Zanda?" She laughed softly, mocking him in playful persiflage.

He growled in response, grasping her arms and pulling her closer. "I'll show you *my weasel*, Angel."

"Nah. That's okay. I've seen it."

They both burst out laughing, his fingers reaching for her ribs and anywhere he could tickle.

Angel screamed in delight, trying, unsuccessfully, to push his hands away.

"Shhhh! You'll wake Jillian." His touch turned from tickle to teasing, softly kneading the flesh of her back and up to her shoulder, down her arm. "Shhhh…"

His dick twitched and hardened as the laughter died and their eyes locked. He brushed her nose with his, his mouth seeking and finding hers, sucking her lower lip in and biting down softly with his teeth. "God, you taste so good, Angel. I've been dying for this all day."

He kissed her deeply and she responded, opening to him fully, her arms sliding up and around his back, tugging at the hair on the back of his head to bring his mouth deeper into hers. Her heart swelled, the scent of his cologne and his body fueling her desire. She let out a low moan and his movements increased in urgency. Soon they were dry humping and grasping at each other's clothes, Angel lifting his shirt until he pulled away and hunched his shoulders so she could remove it completely. He was hungry, his need for her never sated, his fingers found her supple breast under her shirt; cupping the tender flesh and pulling gently on the nipple until it elongated between his fingers. Heat rushed and pooled between her thighs, and she surged against him, seeking the hardness that would ease the ache. Her legs wrapped around his waist and he pulled them higher, pressing and grinding against her. They kissed and clawed, rolled, moaning and begging until finally they were both naked.

Alex pulled back and looked down at her, seeking to see the same struggle he was feeling in her face. He wanted to lose himself in her, but it went against everything he believed. She was so soft and sweet, so incredibly sexy—so beautiful. She took his breath away.

Settling his weight on her fully, he used both hands to cup her face, brushing his fingers along her temples and cheeks; emotions he never knew existed rushed over him in waves, his hips still grinding against hers, his dick slick in her wetness.

Angel stared into his face; the passion and something else she couldn't describe threatened to choke her. She turned her face away, squeezing her eyes shut as a single tear seeped from each one.

"Uhhhhh!" She sucked in her breath. "Fuck me, Alex. Don't be tender. I can't bear it. Just fuck me."

"This isn't just fucking and you know it." His nose traced the side of her face and then his mouth was trailing a series of soft, sucking kisses down the sensitive flesh of her neck to her shoulder and down to her breast. He laved first one nipple then the other, his hands moving lower, as his body lifted from hers. "It hasn't been. Not even the first time."

"I want it to be." Her voice broke and still she didn't look at him. He reached for his jeans, found his wallet and pulled out a condom. He'd wanted to taste her, every inch of her skin, as if making the sex last longer would keep their time together from ending. But, she said she wanted him to fuck her, and so he would give her what she wanted.

He sat back on his knees and rolled the condom over his length, slid his hands beneath her knees and leaned in until her knees were flung over his arms at the elbows. She was open and ready, wet... her chest heaving, yet she wouldn't look at him. He found purchase and slammed into her over and over. He knew what it was about and part of him wanted this as much as she did. Mindless fucking, amazing orgasms, and no strings, but it wasn't to be.

He let go of her knees and wrapped his arms around her. "No you don't, Angel. Look at me. Give me your mouth."

"Just come, Alex." She bucked beneath him and he sank into her again.

His heart pounded from the frantic fucking, but also in some unfathomable pain. "No. I won't come until you kiss me, goddamn it!"

She pulled away, scrambling back and flipped onto her stomach, hiking her ass in the air. "Please. I need you to come."

He was stunned by the picture she made: her perfect ass in the air, calling to him, her sweet flesh visible, the candlelight casting her in shadow, yet her wetness glistening. He couldn't resist and pushed into her again. "Sweet Christ!"

"Uh... yes, Alex. Harder."

He thrust into her again and again, bent over her body; he kissed her shoulders, hands moving over her arms and her breasts. His cock was so hard it ached, but he still couldn't come. "Angel, I can't."

He pulled out and fell back against the pillows.

She turned, her hair falling from the elastic and framing her face. Her mouth was swollen, open as she looked back at him. "Don't you want me?"

"Fuck. How can you ask me that? Yes, I want you. But I want all of you." His throat ached and his voice was tight.

Her eyes flashed and something that sounded like a sob burst from her chest as she scrambled around and straddled him. He moaned as her warmth engulfed him, his eyes never leaving her face as she sank down completely.

*This is determination, not desire.* This was not what he wanted.

She moved on him, her hands on his shoulders to steady herself, her inner walls squeezing and pulling on him as she worked him, trying to make his body betray him. Alex was motionless until he could take it no longer, her body milking a response from him, his release getting closer, but he didn't want to let it happen. It felt empty and wouldn't be enough. Not anymore.

"Ahhhh!" His hands gripped her hips and he lifted her off and away. "Stop! Not like this, Angel! What's gotten into you?"

Her eyes were wild, glazed with intensity. He wasn't sure if she even saw him, and her hands pushed him from her. "Not like what? Isn't this how you like your women, Alex? Isn't it all about sex?" Tears filled her eyes, until finally, two fat drops rolled down her cheeks. Her heart clenched; thinking about Alex with anyone else like this was gut-wrenching.

"No!" Instantly, Alex had her on her back, his hands gentle as he kissed the tears from her cheeks. She was shaking softly and then gasped as she pulled in a breath. "Not this way, babe. Not with you."

He hitched her leg over his hip, his hand gripping her firm thigh and slid into her slowly, deeply; each and every thrust with purpose. He wanted to show her this meant more to him than sex: He cared deeply for Angel, and the realization shook him. His mouth moved to her nipples, over her shoulders, sucking on her neck, his fingers gently coaxing her clit until she was helpless and unable to stop her body's response. He wrung it out of her, like only moments before she was trying to do to him—second by precious second—until she was finally clinging to him. Angel drew in a trembling breath, trying to hold back a sob that pushed against her chest. Letting it go would mean Alex would see how vulnerable she was and that would be the end of her. She turned her face into the curve of his neck and fought for control of her heart and body.

"Angel, shhh. Just kiss me. I need you to kiss me. Give in to this."

"Why do you want to break me? Make me lose control? Lose myself?" Tears rained from her eyes as his mouth ghosted over hers, and she trembled, her tongue finally coming out to lick his top lip, her fingers clawing at his back and ass to bring him deeper into her body. He groaned when he knew he'd won, his body tightening as her hips began to move with his in the slow rhythm that he demanded. Deeper and deeper their bodies dug into the other, Angel finally kissing him back with all the passion they both felt, until finally they pushed over the edge of control together. His heart broke at her sorrow, trying to understand her conflict, yet he couldn't stop.

"Alex! Uh… uh…" He felt her pulse around him, clenching around his length until he thought he'd die. It was ecstasy like he'd never known, and with three more strokes, he came hard, pouring his release deep inside her. They lay entwined, trembling, in the tent they'd built in her living room, the candlelight still flickering softly but waning in the darkness, unable and unwilling to separate.

"Oh, my God! Yes, Angel. That's it." He pushed her hair, wet with her tears, away from her face. "I don't want you to lose yourself, honey. I'm trying to find you. To keep you with me."

"I'm right here." Tears laced her voice.

His heart filled with the need to let her to know he was completely committed; that she didn't need to be afraid he'd leave her because he had no intention of desire to be apart from her. Alex pulled Angel closer and turned his head to kiss her temple softly, moving his mouth toward her ear. Alex's breath caught in his throat, as he realized he was about to make the biggest admission of his life. "Baby… I'm right here, too," he whispered. "I'm here, too."

Alex and Angel's story continues…
filled with intrigue, danger, secrets and

## Confessions After Dark

Coming, Spring 2014.

*Also by*
~Kahlen Aymes~

*The Remembrance Trilogy*
#1 ~ The Future of Our Past
#2 ~ Don't Forget to Remember Me
#3 ~ A Love Like This

~ When I Met You ~
Ryan & Julia's first meeting from *The Remembrance Trilogy*
in *Stories for Amanda*, a benefit anthology against bullying.

The Remembrance Trilogy is also publishing in FRANCE through City Editions, 2013–14

CPSIA information can be obtained at www.ICGtesting.com
Printed in the USA
LVOW13s2312270314

379273LV00001B/35/P